author of *Deathwish* and *Trick of the Light*

Praise for Diana Pharaoh Francis and her Horngate Witches novels featuring Max, "one of the top urban fantasy heroines." (Bitten by Books)

CRIMSON WIND

"[A] complex heroine, darkly twisted setting, and high sexual tension make this a series to remember."

—Fresh Fiction

"A fast paced thrill ride. . . . The novel [goes] from zero to sixty in a matter of pages. . . . Phenomenal world building, entrancing characters, and a thrilling plot make this a must read for urban fantasy and paranormal romance lovers alike!"

—Black Lagoon Reviews

"Max is back and lucky for readers, her life hasn't gotten any less complicated. Francis' magically enslaved heroine is a riveting mixture of guts, compassion, and furious anger as she struggles with a world coming apart at the seams. Readers should hang on tight, for this second Horngate Witches novel is filled with massive danger and gritty struggles for survival. You won't be able to put this one down!"

—*RT Book Reviews* (4 ½ stars)

"An exciting thriller. . . . With an incredible ending to an action-packed tale, readers will clamor for the third book in Francis's excellent epic saga."

—Alernative-worlds.com

"Once again, Max proves to be one of the top urban fantasy heroines. She's tough, actually cares about people, and is big enough to admit when she's made a mistake. I loved watching her grow in *Crimson Wind*, both as a leader and a woman."

—Bitten by Books

"Reading a Horngate Witches book is a bit like watching a big summer movie. Action! Explosions! Impossibly tough characters doing awesome things! It's a heck of a ride."

—FantasyLiterature.com

BITTER NIGHT

"This lush urban fantasy populated with witches, angels, Sunspears, and Shadowblades contains all the decadent delight of dark chocolate. One taste, and you'll devour this book."

—Ann Aguirre, national bestselling author of *Blue Diablo*

"High-energy, gritty . . . the tough, feel-good supernatural fights . . . will keep action fans coming back for book after book."

—*Publishers Weekly*

"Ms. Francis sends urban fantasy on its head in this fast-paced, dynamic story. Loved it, could not put it down. Unusual and terrific."

—#1 *New York Times* bestselling author Patricia Briggs

"Strongly crafted world-building, with exciting nonstop action and main and supporting characters that are vivid and varied."

—Sci Fi Guy

"A dark, unique, and electrifying world in the urban fantasy genre. . . . Max is a Shadowblade warrior to die for."

—Faith Hunter, author of *Skinwalker*

"Max is a volcano of seething anger and hatred. . . . Readers are sucked into this chilling world. Awesome!"

—*RT Book Reviews*

"A great start to a new series . . . blasts out of the gate and never stops running. Max is . . . bitter, proud, and lethal all rolled up into one stunning heroine."

—Fresh Fiction

All of the Horngate Witches novels are also available as eBooks

Also by Diana Pharaoh Francis from Pocket Books

Bitter Night
Crimson Wind

SHADOW CITY

A HORNGATE WITCHES BOOK

Diana Pharaoh Francis

Pocket Books
New York London Toronto Sydney New Delhi

Pocket Books
A Division of Simon & Schuster, Inc.
1230 Avenue of the Americas
New York, NY 10020

First Pocket Books paperback edition January 2012

POCKET and colophon are registered trademarks of Simon & Schuster, Inc.

For information about special discounts for bulk purchases, please contact Simon & Schuster Special Sales at 1-866-506-1949 or business@simonandschuster.com.

The Simon & Schuster Speakers Bureau can bring authors to your live event. For more information or to book an event contact the Simon & Schuster Speakers Bureau at 1-866-248-3049 or visit our website at www.simonspeakers.com.

Cover illustration by Shane Rebenschied

Manufactured in the United States of America

10 9 8 7 6 5 4 3 2 1

ISBN 978-1-4516-1385-8
ISBN 978-1-4516-1387-2 (ebook)

For Tony, Syd, and Q-ball, who make everything possible.

Acknowledgments

THANK YOU FOR EVERYTHING, JEN HEDDLE. I WILL MISS you. You've made my work so much better. Thanks also to Lucienne Diver, Christy Keyes, Melissa Sawmiller, Wendy Keebler, and Julia Fincher. Thanks also to all the people at Pocket who have worked behind the scenes to turn this into a book. There are no doubt others I should be thanking who helped me in the course of this book, and though I may have neglected to mention you here, know that you are very much appreciated.

My family has always been amazingly supportive and I could not do this without them. Thanks also to my friends online who keep me encouraged and cheer me on. You are the best.

Finally, thanks to my readers. You make everything worthwhile.

SHADOW CITY

I

ALEXANDER CROUCHED ON THE RIDGELINE. His head swiveled as he sniffed the crisp, still air. Uncanny and Divine magic washed across his tongue: bitter and sweet, caustic and cloying. His eyes narrowed as he tried to sort the scents of what belonged from what did not.

It was impossible. There was simply too much magic in the air. But at least one thing was clearly out of place. On a small flattish spot on the slope below him was a fairy circle made of deep-pocketed morel mushrooms. It was about seven feet in diameter, and the edges of the ring were thick and deep. There had to be at least a few hundred mushrooms. But that was not what caught Alexander's attention.

Inside the circle was a pile of skinned bodies. Alexander could see two wolves, five rabbits, three raccoons, a pair of ducks, three deer, and a small bear.

He reached for a rock. He found one the size of a hubcap and weighing a good fifty pounds. He tossed it one-handed. It thumped down heavily inside the circle. The ground heaved and funneled downward. The bodies and the rock plunged into the sudden maw. A second later, the grass rippled back into place. Alexander pursed his lips in a silent whistle. Something down there was hungry.

He frowned. A flicker of motion caught his attention, and he tilted a glance upward. An angel glided across the night sky, silent and deadly. Alexander's teeth bared as he watched Tutresiel circle. Suddenly, the angel's silver wings folded with a metallic hiss, and he dropped to the ground only a few feet from the fairy ring.

He landed in a crouch before straightening with tiger-like grace. He stared at Alexander with scarlet eyes. His face was pale marble, his body hard with muscle. His black hair hung to his shoulders in sharp contrast with his white skin. He wore black jeans, heavy biker boots, and a scarred leather vest laced loosely around the roots of his wings.

Alexander's nostrils flared, and his body went taut. He rose to his feet but held himself tightly leashed, despite the nearly uncontrollable urge to pummel Tutresiel's face into a pulp. Not that he could. But something about the angel triggered a primitive reaction in Alexander that had nothing to do with logic and reason and everything to do with animal instinct.

"What do you want?"

"Niko sent me to find you."

Alexander's lips flattened. "What for?" But he knew what for. Niko wanted him to become the Prime of Horngate's Shadowblades. He'd been after him about it since Scooter had taken Max. It was the last thing Max herself had asked for before she had been taken.

Fury, frustration, and unspeakable pain churned molten in his gut. It had been weeks, and there'd been no word, no sign. The beast inside him howled with loss, and he doubled over, bracing his hands on his knees as he fought to breathe. *She will return,* he told himself. *If she does not, I will go find her*.

He straightened, meeting Tutresiel's gaze, expecting mockery. But the angel only offered a short nod of understanding. Except he could not possibly understand. He was cold-blooded as hell and cared nothing for anyone. As his next words proved.

"When are you going to pull up your big girl panties and get over it?" he asked, folding his arms and cocking his head to the side. "If Max could see you now, she'd be puking up her guts with disgust. She needs a man, not a weakling child."

Alexander's anger hardened. His Prime bristled, and he went iron-cold as the beast took over. "What would you know about Max?" he asked softly as reason fled. He was going to kill the angel. Somehow. "You tried to destroy Horngate. The only reason you joined the covenstead was to get out of the Guardians' shackles. You are a coward."

A smile flickered over Tutresiel's lips and was gone. "Am I? Some would call me smart. Or lucky, even. You, on the other hand, they'd call stupid and suicidal, if you decide to attack me like you want to." His wings flared, each feather a shining blade, sharp and deadly. "I would flay you into hamburger before you put a hand on me. But maybe that's what you want. Better to lie down and die than act like a man, like the warrior you're supposed to be." His lip curled in a sneer.

Alexander did not move. Tutresiel's taunts were meant

to drive him into a frenzy so that he would attack stupidly. He was not going to succumb to the tactic. "And what would you have me do, oh great and wise angel?" he asked derisively.

"Do the job that Max wanted. Keep the covenstead safe until she comes back," was Tutresiel's cutting reply.

"I am keeping it safe. I do not have to take on Prime to do so," Alexander said.

Max was Horngate's Shadowblade Prime, or leader. Shadowblades were nighttime warriors created by witches. They had super strength, super healing, and many other varied abilities, according to the whims of the witch who created them. If they went into the sunlight, they'd burn up. Their daytime counterparts, the Sunspears, were poisoned by the night. Max was a good Prime. Better than good. The best Alexander had ever seen. But weeks ago, she'd been taken.

No, *taken* sounded like she had been kidnapped or like she had fought. The truth was, she had been *bartered* and had gone willingly, Alexander thought bitterly. Giselle, Horngate's territory witch, had bargained with the powerful creature Max irreverently called Scooter. An otherwise nameless being, he claimed to be the child of Onniont, the horned serpent, and Nihansan, Spider Woman, both of whom were legendary creatures, possibly gods. He had more magic in his elbow than most covens could command.

Giselle had traded Max to Scooter in exchange for a powerful warding spell to protect the coven. No one knew what Scooter wanted with Max, but once he had fulfilled his side of the bargain, he had come demanding his prize.

Now Horngate, already crippled by the attacks that had resulted in Tutresiel and the fire angel Xaphan's becoming part of the covenstead, and teeming with refugees from the Guardians' cataclysmic unleashing of wild magic on the world, was without a Shadowblade Prime. They wanted Alexander for the job. But if he took it, it would guarantee that Max would never come back. Not that he was going to tell Tutresiel about the prophecy Magpie had given him. It was none of the angel's damned business.

"The Shadowblades are sheep without a shepherd. They need you to step up," Tutresiel told him. He brushed invisible lint from the side seam of his leather pants. "Not that I care, of course. But they are so pathetic, it's getting hard to watch."

"No. Max is Prime. She is coming back. I will not steal her place." The words were hard as bullets.

Tutresiel laughed without humor. "Is that it? You think if you take Prime she won't come back?" He snorted. "As if anything you do or say could stop her. Count on it. The question is, what will be left when she gets here? You're not helping, going off to lick your balls while the rest of the covenstead struggles to pull itself together in time for winter. It's going to be ugly. There's not enough food, and we both know trouble is coming. Local humans are going to get hungry, and so are the Uncanny and the Divine. Horngate is going to look awfully tasty to a lot of creatures. We'll be fighting them off, if we can even harvest enough food to feed ourselves."

At his words, Alexander darted a glance at the fairy ring. Was it his imagination, or was the interior rising and falling as if something beneath was breathing?

The angel didn't notice. "Then again, maybe we'll feed you to them first. An appetizer. Getting rid of you and your bottomless Shadowblade hunger will leave more for everyone else."

"Someone really needs to kill you," Alexander said, feeling his anger drain as the truth of Tutresiel's words pulled him from the cauldron of his fury and pain.

"You've tried. More than once. Didn't do a very good job. Of course, I'm immortal."

Alexander snorted. "So am I. Until someone kills me. The only question is how to go about making you dead."

The angel smiled. "Good luck with that. There are only two in the world who know how to kill me permanently, and I'm one. I'll never tell."

"I guess I will just have to keep trying. I am bound to stumble on it one day. Just for giggles, want to step sideways into that circle and see what happens?"

The angel glanced down. "What is it?"

"Hungry, from what I can tell. Bet it would not object to an angel snack."

Tutresiel reached out into the air, and suddenly a sword was in his hand. Its seven-foot blade glowed with brilliant white witchlight. He paced around the outside edge of the ring. "I told you trouble was coming," he murmured.

"What is it?"

"A mouth."

"Thank you, Mister Obvious. I figured that out already."

Tutresiel continued, ignoring Alexander's comment. "The ring is to imprison it. The question is whether the fairies lured the mouth in to use it or if they're just pinning it down to protect themselves."

"I do not think they plan to kill it. It just sucked down more than a dozen animal carcasses. All skinned."

"Interesting," was Tutresiel's noncommittal reply.

"We cannot just leave it. How do you kill it?"

The angel gave an infuriating shrug. "Depends on what's inside."

"I thought you knew."

"Could be a lot of things. Fairies, demons, monsters. Possibly even Muppets."

Alexander scowled. Tutresiel was baiting him. He snarled, hating to ask, but having no choice. "What do you recommend?"

"Easiest way to figure out what's inside is to jump in."

"Sounds stupid."

"That too."

Alexander's Prime lunged to the fore. His human senses flattened, and the heightened instincts of the beast within took over. He rose and drew a combat knife from the sheath on his hip. "I guess Niko will have to wait," he said, and leaped down off his perch. He strode purposefully toward the circle of mushrooms, but Tutresiel's sword came down and barred the way. He glared at the angel. "Get out of my way."

"I wondered, but I didn't know for sure until now. You *are* as stupid as you look," Tutresiel said. "You'll die if you jump into that throat."

"I am not that easy to kill," Alexander said, shoving down on the sword with his knife. A jolt of electricity shot through him, and every hair on his body stood on end. His blood sizzled with the energy.

"Maybe. But as much as I don't care what happens to you, Max will, and she's just crazy enough to hunt down the one way to kill me if I let you die. So call this self-preservation." He paused for a moment and then frowned. "I shouldn't have to say this, but given the fact that most of you idiots at Horngate have a ridiculously overblown sense of responsibility . . . Stay put. I can handle this."

With that, he hopped into the circle. The moment his feet touched, the ground split open and the angel plunged inside. A moment later, the circle of emerald grass rippled flat and pristine.

Alexander could only stare in blank shock. Of all the things he might have expected from the angel, this was not one. Tutresiel was a selfish bastard. He looked after himself and no one else.

A few seconds passed, and a tremor shook the ground. Everything went quiet. Not even a bird chirped. A long minute passed. Then, suddenly, the grass inside the ring erupted. Blood, dirt, and gravel spewed in every direction. Tutresiel exploded upward in a shining whirlwind, his wings slashing and chopping.

He halted ten feet above the hole, his sword held high. Blood and gore clung to his wings and splattered his body. He grinned with vicious triumph, and the sword vanished. He extended his wings, and the blood ran off them as if expelled, leaving them silver-bright as usual. He floated down to stand beside the gaping hole he had made.

"Impressive," Alexander said, peering down inside. The walls had caved in and there was little enough to be seen. "What was it?"

"It was a nest of some kind and full of very hungry, very vicious young. I didn't see any adults. We'll have to keep watch. If they'd reached adulthood, they'd have infested the area like killer cockroaches."

"You should do a flyover," Alexander said. "Look for the parents. I will search on the ground."

"First, I'll go report to Niko. Unless, of course, you've decided to stop sniveling and do what you are made to do?"

Alexander gave a short jerk of his head.

Tutresiel shrugged. "Then I don't think I'm going to bother listening to you giving me orders."

With that, the angel launched into the air. Alexander watched him disappear. His teeth ground together. The problem was that Tutresiel did not understand. None of them did. He could not take on Prime. If he did, none of them would ever see Max again.

Pain boiled up inside him again, and he gasped, letting it flood through his body. He did not know how to survive it. But he had no choice.

HE PAUSED ON A PINNACLE OVERLOOKING A SMALL VALley. A small herd of elk grazed below. A mountain lion sprawled watchfully on a limb on the far end, waiting for the elk to wander closer. There was no sign of the adult creatures or the fairies who'd made the mushroom ring.

It was not long before Niko appeared. He was a blocky man with black hair. Muscles piled on muscles, moving like an oiled shadow over the ground. He was danger personified. But then, so was Alexander.

"Something on your mind, Niko?"

It pleased him to no end when the other man started. The thick smell of magic overwhelmed his own scent, and the power of his constantly aroused Prime was a thick cloud that spread over miles. Without a reliable scent trail, Niko had been forced to follow Alexander's tracks and Tutresiel's directions.

The other man stared up at him, his body tense. He was itching for a fight. Alexander's lip curled. Niko was good, but he was no match for Alexander.

"You need to come with me. There's something you need to see," he announced curtly.

Alexander turned away. "Get Tutresiel and Xaphan. Whatever the problem is, they can handle it."

"Fuck them. We want you."

"I just gave you my advice. There is nothing I can do that a pair of angels cannot. Besides, I am busy. We might have a fairy infestation, or did Tutresiel forget to tell you?"

Niko growled in frustration. "The fairies can wait. As for your advice, you can stick it up your ass. This is a lot more important."

That caught Alexander's attention. He gave Niko a long, hard look. The Blade looked worried, more than he had since Max's disappearance. "What do you want me to see?" he asked finally.

"You'd better come." Niko turned and leaped down into the gully and back up the other side. He glided almost soundlessly.

Alexander followed, feeling like a rhinoceros blundering through a china shop. He had spent the better part of a century in cities, and the quiet of the wilderness was hard to achieve.

The covenstead spread over miles of mountains west of Missoula, Montana. At its heart was the Keep carved inside a mountain. In the river valley outside were a dozen long greenhouses, and on the peaks around perched cabins where members of the covenstead lived. Or they had, before the Guardian attacks almost two months ago. Now many of those homes were deserted, their occupants dead.

Niko circled around to the other side of Horngate's necklace of perimeter wards. East of the covenstead, they came to a tightly rucked blanket of ridges. The trees were thick here. Boulders and loose rock littered the crevices between the steep hillsides.

They picked their way carefully over the broken landscape and down into a shadowy gorge. Alexander felt a surge of something the moment he set foot on the uneven bottom. The ground hummed with a low vibration that sent a dull ache up his legs. He glanced sharply at Niko. "What is this?"

Niko shook his head. "Up ahead. You'll see."

They wound through the piles of boulders and tangles of scrub juniper. The ground was dry, and the grass crackled beneath their feet. Above, the stars glittered like ice in the velvet night. The smell of Uncanny magic was suffocating, nearly drowning out the slighter scent of Divine magic.

They came through a notch between two granite blocks, each the size of a Greyhound bus. On one side was a clearing. On the far side was a power circle. The outer ring was grayish powder—a mix of salt, herbs, metals, and whatever else witches used to create binding circles. It was a good six inches wide. Inside was another ring. It glowed a sullen red. Within was a fat column of oily black smoke perhaps twenty-five feet tall. It curled and twisted with violent motion.

The hair on Alexander's entire body prickled. He forced himself to walk closer.

Tyler crouched on the hillside above, just outside Horngate's perimeter wards. He was a slight man, with a dancer's grace and an artist's skill with a blade. He'd recently shorn his hair to a short bristle cut, but his minstrel mustache and goatee remained. He spun a knife in his fingers. As Niko and Alexander approached, he leaped down the scree to land softly on the balls of his feet, sliding the knife into a sheath strapped behind his neck.

"What is this?" Alexander wondered aloud.

"We were hoping you could tell us. We've never seen anything like it," Tyler replied.

At the sound of their voices, the smoke whirled and bulged, pressing against the invisible walls of the containment circle.

"It lies in the path of the old perimeter wards," Niko said, pointing to a charred circle on the ground. It ran straight through the center of the ring. "That can't be coincidence."

"Have you told Giselle?"

"Not yet."

So they came to him first. His lips tightened. *Damn them*. He was not their Prime. Alexander turned away from the writhing smoke. "You should do that. She will want to know."

The other two men exchanged a glowering look. "You know, I'm about ready to kick your ass," Niko said.

Alexander smiled. It felt stiff and wooden. Inside, his Blade licked its lips, hungry for blood. "Try."

"What is your problem? You claim you want a place here, but all you do is throw it in our faces. This is what Max wanted. You know it."

"Time for you to step up, son," Tyler added in his laconic way, echoing Tutresiel's earlier statement. His tone did nothing to hide the tension coiling through him. Alexander was not the only one spoiling for a fight.

He barely held himself in check. Killing Tyler and Niko would not help get Max back. Besides, he liked them. Instead, he turned away and went to sit on an outcropping of rock. The others eyed him uncertainly. They had not expected him to just calmly sit.

Alexander rubbed a hand over his mouth as he considered telling them the truth. They might stop badgering him.

He reached under the collar of his shirt and hooked a woven leather strap with his fingers. He drew out a gold disk almost the size of his palm. On one side was a round black diamond the size of a peach pit. Small orange opals traced a glimmering line along the outer rim. Outward-pointing arrows were interspersed among the opals like the rays of a sun. Around the thick edge of the disk were written words in a language Alexander did not understand. They spiraled down over the back to the center to end in a small stylized Egyptian eye.

He pulled the strap over his head and gazed down at the disk. For years, he had craved it. It was worth a king's ransom. More. Now he wished he had never seen it. He turned it in his fingers, then came to a decision. Secrecy had done him no good so far.

He drew a knife from the sheath on his hip. It was a combat knife, both edges honed sharp. He cut deeply across the pad of his thumb and quickly smeared his blood across the amulet before his healing spells could close the wound. The cold, heavy stickiness of the invisibility spell closed over him.

"What the fuck?" Tyler exclaimed.

Niko just watched the place where Alexander was sitting, his brow furrowed.

Alexander wiped his knife on his jeans and sheathed it. "Did you know that Magpie has the gift of true prophecy?" he asked conversationally, the corner of his mouth lifting in a sardonic smile as Tyler started. Hearing the thin air talking took some getting used to.

"Prophecy?" Niko repeated.

Alexander turned the amulet in his fingers. "Apparently, whatever she sees always comes true. Or so she assures me. Giselle seems to be of the same opinion."

"Get to the point," Tyler said. His knife was back in his hand, and he was twirling it between his fingers. It would take barely a second for him to launch it, and even without seeing Alexander, he was sure to hit him.

"Magpie came to see me. The same day that Max's family was kidnapped."

He remembered it with preternatural clarity. He'd been in his apartment deep within Horngate's mountain fortress. Magpie had opened the door, pushing through the wards as if they were not there. At first, he had thought she must be Max, who was the only person he knew who could open any lock without trouble. It was one of the gifts Giselle had layered into her making.

Expectant hope had flooded through him and then died beneath a deluge of cold shock when Magpie entered. Foreboding grasped him in a hard hand. The witch's eyes were entirely white. She had fixed him with that unworldly gaze and had delivered the fateful prophecy in a guttural voice that was nothing like her own sharply cut tones.

The amulet is coming to you. It will give you your heart's desire. You will be Prime.

Later, she had assured him that her prophecies were always true, that he should ignore her words at his own peril. Alexander had long dreamed that the Amengohr amulet would be his. It lent him invisibility at night and allowed him to walk safely in the sunlight during the day. For a moment, he had been elated. He would have the amulet and his heart's desire—to be accepted at Horngate. But the cost was too high if it meant he would become Prime. He had known such a thing could only happen if Max was dead. Then the prophecy had started to come true. First, Niko and Tyler had begun to accept him as one of Horngate's Shadowblades, then Alexander had obtained the amulet, and finally, at the moment of her kidnapping, Max had ordered Giselle to make Alexander Horngate's Prime.

He would not do it. If he did, she would not have a reason to return. The universe would not have a reason to give her back. His face twisted. Maybe it was irrational, but he could not risk it. He could not chance that taking Prime would mean losing Max forever.

Alexander rubbed the blood away roughly, feeling the sticky cloak of invisibility fade. He stared down at the disk, his fingers clenching around it until the edge cut into his flesh. "I will not let it be true. I will not be Prime. Nor will I let anyone else take it. She will have to come back."

"Holy mother of fuck," Niko murmured.

Alexander glanced sharply at the other man. That was one of Max's favorite phrases. His jaw knotted as he fought down the ball of molten fury and pain at the reminder of her.

"Crap on a cracker," Tyler swore as he strode up and down in front of the column of black smoke. He did not seem to notice it. "So, all we have to do is kill you and it ends the prophecy. *Poof!* We get Max back."

"Not necessarily," Niko said slowly. "All it means is that Alexander won't be Prime. Doesn't mean Max will come back, even if we could kill him. Not likely if Magpie's prophecies really do always come true."

"Shit." Tyler's knife whirled in his fingers as he eyed Alexander. "Still, isn't it worth a shot? No offense, son, but I want Max back, and if it takes giving you a dirt nap, then I'm all for it."

Alexander smiled, cold and feral. "I do not disagree, though you understand that I would have to fight you all the same."

"I don't think it's going to come to that," Niko said thoughtfully, tapping his fingers on his thigh. "In fact . . . we want you to become Prime. Now more than ever."

"No!" The fury in Alexander erupted uncontrollably, and the Shadowblade took control. He moved in a blur. He lunged and snatched Niko by the throat, throwing him against the rock hillside with all his strength. Bones broke as Niko's body bounced like a crash-test dummy.

Alexander leaped to finish the kill, and Tyler knocked him out of the air. He landed on his side and flipped up onto his feet. He swept Tyler's legs out from underneath him and pounded a fist into the side of his head. Alexander moved fluidly, with all the sinuous grace of a cobra. Reason was gone. Only the need to kill remained.

Once Tyler lay sprawled and unmoving on the ground, Alexander spun to look for Niko. The other man stood dazed at the bottom of the slope. Blood ran down the side of his head and dampened his collar. He lifted his hands in a sign of surrender.

"C'mon, now. Settle down. Get ahold of your Blade. Just hear me out on this. You know I want Max back, and till just now, I would have said I wanted her as much or more than you. You know I wouldn't do anything to hurt her. You *know* that. So, listen."

He spoke carefully. Alexander shook himself, trying to ignore the words. He did not want logic or reason. He wanted action. He wanted Max. But she would hate him if he killed any of her Blades. She counted on him to look after Horngate. To look after her family, which included Niko and Tyler.

A tide of cold reality washed over Alexander, quenching the volcanic fury of his Blade. He forced the predator down until he was in control. It was a near thing. But finally, he grappled it into its cage.

"Explain," he ordered Niko through clenched teeth.

The other man sagged down onto a rock, wiping blood from his neck with his knuckles. "What if you've got the prophecy wrong?" he asked, then groaned and rubbed a hand against the back of his head. "Damn, that hurts."

When Alexander twitched like he was going to jump on him, Niko sighed. "Just think for a minute. You've been basing everything on the assumption that your heart's desire is to become a member of Horngate. But you're walking the thin edge of going rabid, and it's all because of Max. Because *she's* what you really want. Would you really be so eager to join Horngate if Max wasn't part of the package?" He didn't wait for Alexander's answer. "It sure as hell isn't because of the rest of us. You're bleeding to death without her.

"Don't you get it? If she really *is* your heart's desire, then only one part of the prophecy has actually come true. If you want her back, you have to make the rest happen. You take Prime, and then she'll *have* to come back, because the prophecy says you'll get your heart's desire."

Alexander stared as the words percolated through his skull. He closed his eyes and sucked in a harsh breath, hope knifing deep into his soul. *Could it be true?* It was possible. It even made sense. Niko was right. Since Max had disappeared, Alexander could think of nothing else but getting her back, of seeing her one more time. He opened his eyes. "I cannot risk it."

"The hell you can't," Tyler exclaimed as he struggled up. "Your reasoning sucks ass. You don't give a shit about Horngate. If you did, you'd have grabbed Prime with both hands. But you won't, because your dick's in a knot over Max. That should be proof enough for you."

Alexander said nothing. It made sense. But—

Doubt clamped him. He wanted desperately to believe it, but from the moment he had met Max, he had known that she would die before abandoning Horngate. The stone-cold certainty that if he took her place she would have to be dead would not let him go. He shook his head.

"Holy mother of fuck! What do we have to say to get you to pull your head out of your ass?" Tyler demanded.

Alexander tensed, his Blade peeling back the bars of its cage and lunging forth. Tyler fell back a step, but his own Blade was rising to the killing edge. He needed a Prime to keep him steady. Niko stepped between them.

"Enough," he said, his back to Tyler as he watched Alexander carefully. He dipped his gaze to seem less challenging. "Maybe you have a good reason to be so sure that stepping up to Prime will mean that Max won't come back. If so, I'd like to hear it. Nobody wants to push you if it means losing her forever."

Alexander opened his mouth. Words jumbled in his throat, but nothing made sense. He spun away, staring at the boiling column of smoke, trying to think. But all he could think of was this was something he could *do* to get Max back. And if Niko was right, he had no choice.

"All right. I will do it," he said a minute later. He would rather regret doing something than regret doing nothing. He swung back around. "But if you are wrong, I will make you hurt more than you ever dreamed you could, and then I will kill you."

"It's a deal," Niko said. He reached out a bloody hand, and Alexander shook it slowly. "Let's go tell Giselle about it." He glanced at the billowing column of oily, trapped smoke. "And that."

Tyler dusted himself off, his beast settling down. "She's going to love this. Not to mention Oz. He's going to have kittens."

"None of his concern, now, is it?" Niko said with a shrug. "His job is to look after the Sunspears. This is Shadowblade business. If he doesn't like it, he can bite my ass."

"Or kick it up to your ears," Tyler pointed out.

"Let him try," Alexander said softly. "No one fucks with my Blades without answering to me."

His two companions looked at each other, then at him. "You sound like Max," Tyler said. The muscles of his jaw jumped with suppressed emotion.

"Not as easy on the eyes, though," Niko said.

"I'll remember to tell her you said that," Tyler said. "When she comes back."

If she comes back, Alexander thought darkly. But hope continued to grow despite himself. *Damn her.* Where the hell was she?

2

MAX HIT THE GROUND AND FELT HER RIBS BREAK. Again. Her breath exploded, and she sucked in air, coughing as fire circled her ribs and sand filled her throat.

She rolled onto her back with a groan, spitting grit as she tried not to breathe. Her heart hammered in her chest, and she wanted nothing more than to crawl into bed. Instead, she made herself get up.

She put her hand down to help shove herself to her feet and fell onto her shoulder as her arm gave way. She sat up again, scowling down at it. No fucking wonder.

Splintered bone poked through the skin of her forearm, and two of her fingers were pointing in unnatural directions. The pain of her wounds was almost negligible. Which meant that either she was getting used to it, or her nerve receptors had gotten bored with the repeated torture she'd been inflicting on herself and had gone off to find something better to do. Like go to Jamaica, maybe.

She sighed and shook her hand to straighten things out, making a face as the ends of her bones ground together. *Disgusting.* It would only take a few minutes to heal back up—the perks of being a Shadowblade. Though maybe her body would get bored with that, too. Just at the moment, she wouldn't mind dying.

"Are you ready?"

"Mind if I take a second or two to heal up before you try to kill me again?"

Scooter did not answer for a whole ten seconds. "Now?"

Fuck. He was worse than a four-year-old. Add in the fact that he was at least part god, and she'd better get her shit together quick, because he was going to start in again whether she was ready or not.

"You do realize that the definition of insanity is repeating the same action over and over and expecting a different outcome, right?"

Max heaved herself up, staggering in the deep sand before facing him.

Scooter was sitting cross-legged on a flat tree stump. As if any tree had ever lived this far underground. But this was his house, and he got to decorate it the way he wanted, underground tree stumps and all. Maybe she should try to talk him into bringing in a load of feather beds for a softer landing. Of course, he'd probably say that would only encourage her to fail. The bastard.

He was beautiful in an austere, otherworldly way. He was also scary as hell. He could kill her without even twitching an eyebrow.

His skin was copper brown, and his black hair hung straight to his waist. His eyes were obsidian from corner to corner, except for flecks of drifting blue light. He rippled with muscle, his face square and blunt-featured.

He wore only a pair of buckskin pants. Magic thickened the air around him, making it hard to breathe.

"There is no other way," he said. "You will learn or die."

"Death is beginning to look better and better."

He didn't crack a smile. "Time is short."

Time is short for what? Max bit down on the question before it could get away. He hadn't answered it the first hundred times she'd asked, so why would he start now? Nor did she snidely point out that he was the one with the countdown watch; she had all the time in the world. Except she didn't. Not if she ever wanted to go home. Instead, she yawned widely and twisted to crack her spine. "Let's get on with it. I'm starting to miss all that tasty pain."

He made no motion, nothing to warn her. But suddenly, she jerked backward, propelled through the air like a rocket. Her body tensed, and she felt the magic from the angel feather embedded in her hand pull against the force of Scooter's magic. She slowed fractionally. Her mind whirled. She squeezed her eyes shut, trying to imagine a door. It was easier to do this time. Practice makes perfect. She reached out to open it. Before her mental fingers could close on the knob, she slammed against the rock wall. Bones snapped, and her lungs burst like overripe fruit. Her head cracked against the knobby stone, and she went blind.

The next thing she knew, she was falling. Her head spun, and she couldn't breathe. She felt herself slowing as the power of the angel feather embedded in her hand took hold. She clenched her fist around it, more from habit than intent. Her mind was fragmented, like loose pieces of a jigsaw puzzle. Coherence was impossible. Still, she tried to pull back on the feather's magic. She needed to fall.

According to Scooter, most people found the door to the abyss between worlds accidentally when they tripped over the threshold of life and death. He wanted Max to find the door so that they could travel together. She had no idea where or why or for how long. He wasn't saying. As for the door, she wasn't at all clear about why he just didn't open it for her. With all his power, he was perfectly capable. But he said she had to do it herself, and since she had no choice, she agreed. So, he was doing his best to bring her to the brink of death. A couple of times, she'd thought she'd gone over the edge, but he'd brought her back. It's good to be a god. If only he had a better way of showing her the path into the abyss. Apparently, he wasn't omnipotent. Too bad for her.

Suddenly, time seemed to stop. For a split second, Max could feel every artery, vein, and capillary in her body. Each cell seemed lined in diamond fire. She caught her breath—slow, so very slow—pain igniting as fiery needles pierced her healing lungs. She thrust it away impatiently. She needed to think.

Other pain gnawed at her. It caught her head in a steel bear trap. A searing ache wrapped her ribs, and her tongue throbbed where she'd bitten into it. She tasted the coppery flavor of her blood, and her stomach lurched. For once, she could neither ignore the hurt nor draw strength from it. Her mind wouldn't focus. Instead, she pulled away, retreating down into the depths of herself, into that cold place where she didn't have to feel anything at all. It was her fortress and armor. It gave her strength to do what she had to do when things got too hard.

She slipped inside, feeling everything else slide away. Her focus sharpened. She could still feel every cell of herself, her blood pulsing, her heart squeezing and releasing. She visualized a door again and reached for it. Her hand went through it, and the vision dissolved.

Fury flared inside her and then tugged away into the frigid chill of her inner fortress.

Into the frigid chill of her inner fortress.

Realization struck her at the same moment she bounced onto the ground. She lay there, the burst of agony a distant feeling. She concentrated on her newfound knowledge.

Ever since she'd been tricked into becoming a Shadowblade, Max had used her inner fortress as a haven, a way to survive the endless torture, the helpless fear, the hate, and the betrayal. In order to overcome Max's furious resistance, Giselle had tortured her until she could no longer fight the layering on of the Shadowblade spells. In order to keep herself sane as the years went on, Max had created the fortress. But now she knew it wasn't just a bulwark of emotional and mental protection; it was her door.

Scooter was right. He couldn't show her the entrance into the abyss. But she'd found it anyway.

She reached out to her body, still hyper-aware of every sinew and hair. She gathered herself and *yanked*. It was like dragging a house through the eye of a needle. She strained, refusing to give up. She might never find this clarity, this control over her body, again.

The world *wrenched*.

Max tumbled down into the dark cold of her stronghold. Everything went black.

She found herself hanging motionless in a starless night. In the distance, tangles of colored thread and thicker yarns spilled across the sea of ink. Flutters of rainbow caught her attention. Streaks and tatters, droplets, and bits of confetti. They swirled and drifted. Clouds of them formed and then dribbled away in streams or dove like flocks of starlings. They spun on invisible whirlwinds and fell like rain.

This was the abyss between worlds. The tangles of thread were pathways to other worlds. Scooter had told her that much. The dancing colors were bits of magic. All around her, she could feel movement, like ocean currents. They moved in all directions, pulling and pushing at her. She held herself still, with no idea how she did so. She wanted not to move, and so she didn't.

Now what?

She looked down at herself. She was naked. Bruises splotched her chest and stomach. No doubt, her back was a purple patchwork quilt. As she watched, the splotches started to turn green and then yellow as her healing spells kicked in. She drew a shallow breath. Her lungs and ribs ached, but she could breathe.

There was no sign of Scooter. She frowned. He didn't usually let her out of his sight. She was lucky to get privacy to go to the bathroom. So where was he? She caught her breath. Maybe he couldn't find her here.

She could escape.

She severed the thought. There wasn't any place she could go where he wouldn't find her, except maybe the abyss, and she sure as hell didn't want to hang here forever. Besides, she'd promised to help him, and that bound her in unbreakable chains.

Her mouth flattened as another possibility occurred to her. A wave of emotion crashed over her, and she doubled over. She could go home. Just for a few minutes. Long enough to—

To what? To say good-bye? To tell everyone what she should have told them long ago? To see Alexander?

She squeezed her eyes shut against the acid burn of tears and wrapped her arms tightly around herself. Guilt and loss spun through her, shredding her from the inside out. Her stomach churned. She had avoided thinking about him since Scooter had taken her. But now the dam broke, and she couldn't stop the flood. Guilt was the worst. Recrimination. Longing. Loss. Fear. Dread.

She forced herself to straighten. It was her fault. She'd had every chance to say something, and she'd balked. She'd let her fear take over. Fear of what?

Betrayal.

Even now she could barely admit it. After Giselle—her best friend then—had trapped her in the life of a Shadowblade, Max hadn't trusted anyone. She'd lived only for revenge. Then Alexander had come along. He'd proven himself to her over and over. Hell, he'd almost killed himself helping to save her family. The memory of his mangled body sent a tremor through her. She hadn't thought he could survive. And how had she repaid him? She squeezed her eyes shut on her tears. She didn't deserve to cry. Like an idiot, like a coward, she'd wasted their last moments together.

Fury and frustration rose in an inferno. Not just for Alexander but for Scooter and for herself. She screamed, deep and primal, her neck tenting with the force of it. Abruptly, she snapped her mouth shut, swallowing her emotions. She squared her shoulders and flexed her fingers. She was wasting time.

She looked around. Scooter had never talked about how to leave. The one time she'd been pulled inside, it had been a spell, and it had spat her back out again just as quickly as she'd arrived. So, now what?

She closed her eyes. She could still feel every particle of herself pulsing. Going out must look the same as going in, right? It seemed reasonable, anyhow. What was she worried about? She could only die once.

She pulled herself back down inside, half certain that the fortress would be gone. But it was there. Going back through was just as hard as before, and for a second, she didn't think she'd have the strength to drag herself through. But then she found herself sprawled on the warm sand.

Scooter knelt beside her as she panted. "You did it."

"Thanks for the news flash," she said, sitting up and reaching for her T-shirt. She pulled it over her head and shimmied into her underwear and pants. The hyperawareness of her body faded, but didn't vanish. She was pretty sure she'd be able to go back when she wanted. "What now?"

He stood, giving her a hand up. He wasn't much taller than she was, and he smelled musky and earthy, like the mountains after a rain. "You must eat. You need to refuel. Then we will go."

"Go?"

"To Chadaré."

She narrowed her eyes at him. "What's Chadaré? Where is it?"

"It is inside the abyss. It is the city of shadows."

Max nodded as if that made sense. "OK. What are we going to do there?"

"Exactly what you were made to do. We are going to Chadaré to hunt."

He smiled. The expression sent chills up Max's back, and the Shadowblade inside her leaped instantly to a killing edge. Her mind flattened, and her senses sharpened as the predator took over. Her teeth bared in an animal snarl as her body tensed, ready to kill.

3

ALEXANDER LEFT TYLER TO KEEP WATCH ON THE column of smoke, while he and Niko returned to the mountain fortress.

Much of the surface of the main mountain had been melted from Xaphan's battle fire and was frozen in a landscape of melted black ripples and bubbling pools. The trees were scorched for miles from the wildfires he had caused.

Four weeks ago, he and Tutresiel had been sent by the Guardians to attack Horngate. Giselle had refused to serve in their war to destroy most of humanity and return magic to the world. To punish her, the Guardians had sent a rogue witch and the two angels to wipe out the coven. But then Max had tricked them. Using a magical hailstone, she had wished for the Guardians to forget all about Horngate, then had offered the angels a chance to join the covenstead and be free of their Guardian masters. Both had agreed—being owned by a witch was better than being owned by the deathless Guardians. Alton, the rogue witch, was imprisoned in the bowels of the mountain, still awaiting Giselle's judgment.

Since the attacks, Xaphan had been a great help. Giselle had been drained nearly to death, and the fire angel's healing abilities had guaranteed her survival. Tutresiel, on the other hand . . . Alexander's lip curled. That bastard could rot in hell for all he cared. He did not trust him in the slightest.

"Whoa—what's going on?" Niko asked as the power of Alexander's Prime spiked and rolled off him in palpable waves.

Alexander shook himself and pulled his Prime back down, grimacing at his lack of control. He was walking the fine edge between sanity and going feral. It would not take much to push him over the edge. He looked at his companion, one eyebrow quirking. "Are you sure you want me for a Prime? I may be more dangerous than not."

Niko shrugged. "It's not like you're going anywhere, so we have to deal with you one way or another. Besides, even without Magpie's prophecy and Max wanting this, you suffer from the same terminal sense of responsibility she does. You'll keep it together, if only because that's your job. And oh, yeah, she'll kill you if you don't." He grinned at Alexander and slapped him on the shoulder. "We have faith in you."

"That is comforting," Alexander said dryly.

"Remind me to send you a bill for the therapy. I'm not cheap, you know."

"Funny. Word is that you are both cheap and easy." Alexander stiffened, his voice dropping. "Speaking of which . . ."

They had come to the main entrance of the mountain fortress. Below, a quick-flowing river snaked through the valley. Across it were rows of greenhouses where a great deal of work had been going on in the last eight weeks. The Guardians' war on humanity was turning the clock back to a fairy-tale time when magic ruled and there were no factories or tractors or grocery stores.

In an effort to restore magic and magical creatures to the world, the Guardians had unleashed a torrent of wild magic and not-so-natural disasters, from hurricanes and tornadoes to earthquakes, tsunamis, and volcanoes. The goal was to prune humanity back to nearly nothing so they could not crush out magic again. Already, most of California's central valley had been turned into an enchanted forest, and chances were, every human caught up within had been transformed into some kind of creature or had been eaten by one. Enchanted forests were not safe places for anyone, least of all ordinary humans.

There was little enough news about what had happened elsewhere in the world. But one thing was for sure—the grocery shelves were increasingly bare, and Horngate was going to have to produce all of its own food before winter hit. More, if they wanted to help the people in Missoula and the surrounding area. Giselle would want to. So would Max. All of that would not be so difficult if the coven were healthy and whole and if Shadowblades and Sunspears didn't need to eat a minimum of twenty or thirty thousand calories a day just to fuel the spells they were made of. As it was, the next six months were going to be rough.

Xaphan's fires had not destroyed the magically shielded greenhouses, but every plant inside had withered and died. Now every able body was tasked with coaxing seeds and cuttings to life. There was already a bite in the air that signaled early snows. There were few witches to help with the growing, although the recent additions of Max's father and brother had been welcome, not to mention the two Triangle-level witches Alexander and Max had rescued when their California covenstead had come under attack.

But those were not what caught Alexander's eye. A girl sat on a boulder just outside the entrance. She was slender and wore artfully torn jeans and a form-fitting blouse. Her hair was the color of ripe wheat and hung loose to her waist. Earbuds hung in her ears, and she tapped her fingers on her leg as she scanned the darkness. She had not yet seen Alexander and Niko approaching. But then, Shadowblades could see perfectly in cave darkness, and Tory was merely human. She was also Max's nineteen-year-old niece and a total pain in the ass.

Since Max's disappearance, Tory had started following Alexander around like a lovesick rattlesnake. She hated Horngate and hated that she had been dragged here against her will through the middle of a magical cataclysm. She hated that she was not allowed to go anywhere, that she had no friends, and that she had nothing to do except work. She was bitter and angry, and somewhere along the line, she had decided that Alexander was the cure for what ailed her. It did not hurt that her mother thought he was evil incarnate.

She did not care that he was not interested or that even though he looked like he was twenty-five, he was really more than a hundred years old. She wanted him, and with the supreme confidence of a beautiful young girl, she had decided she would have him.

Another time, her childish relentless pursuit should

have amused him, but now it only infuriated him. He had little patience for anything at the moment. But because she was Max's niece, he kept himself in check and avoided Tory as much as possible. She had taken to waiting outside for his dawn return, knowing that he could not survive the light of day. She followed him to the dining commons and to his apartment. She refused to accept even the most curt dismissals. Alexander was well aware that the other Blades found his predicament amusing, a fact that only ground his nerves more.

"Not again," he muttered. His patience was frayed to a thread.

"She's got a crush on you."

"She is a menace, and she is going to get hurt."

Niko's brows rose. "She's just a girl. Surely you can handle her."

"If she pushes much harder in the shape I am in, I could kill her. She drives me nuts. She is worse than a swarm of starving fleas. Just keep her away from me so I do not accidentally kill her. Consider it an order."

He strode away before Niko could answer. He was just ten feet away from Tory when at last she woke to his presence. She leaped down from her rock, yanking the earbuds from her ears.

"Alex! I've been waiting for you."

"You should be in bed," he said, not stopping.

"Hey, wait!"

She reached for his arm, but then Niko was there. He intercepted her hand and pulled her away. "Tory. You're up late. Can't you sleep?"

Alexander did not wait for the answer. He broke into a jog, swiftly leaving the other two behind.

Giselle's quarters were on the south side of the mountain. Outside was a hollowed-out area. It lacked a rug or any furnishings, those having been destroyed in the angels' battle. The double doors were firmly fixed, having been repaired twice—once just after the attacks and once when Giselle had lost control of her powers and nearly burned the mountain down again.

No one stood guard. Alexander glowered. That had to change. He banged a fist on the polished oak. The sound echoed. He waited a moment, then hammered again. It was another few minutes before Giselle opened the door. She was wrapped in a silk robe, her chestnut hair a shining cascade down her back. Her face was delicately formed, with high cheekbones and a pointed chin. Her blue eyes were relentless and cold.

"What's wrong?" she demanded.

"I am taking Prime," Alexander told her, shouldering inside.

She stared, her mouth flattening to a thin white line. "That's quite a change. What's your game?"

"The kind that brings Max back," he told her. His Prime had risen again. His emotions roiled. He looked away from Giselle, his teeth gritting. He wanted to kill her for trading Max to Scooter.

She folded her arms. "How do you figure?"

"You remember I told you that Magpie had given me a prophecy. That she said I would have my heart's desire and that I would be Prime."

"I do."

"You remember there was more to the prophecy that I did not tell you."

She nodded, her eyes narrowed. Magic gathered

around her. He grinned wolfishly. It looked like he was not the only one with control problems. The air in the chamber grew thick with it. "Get to the point."

"Part of the prophecy has already come true. All that is left is that I be made Prime and I will have my heart's desire. Since Max is everything I want, then I say we get on with it so we can get her back."

"You think it is that simple? Why should I just believe you?"

"You're blind if you don't," Niko said, coming in. "He's coming apart at the seams. I believe him. So does Tyler."

She turned a cold look on Niko, who stared back, not backing down in the slightest. Max's influence, no doubt. Alexander's mouth curved in a fleeting smile.

"I'm afraid *I* need more," Giselle said.

"Don't be stupid," Niko started, but his mouth snapped shut when threads of inky magic spun around her fingers and up her arms.

She made a frustrated sound and turned her back. She drew a breath and let it out slowly. Another. When she turned back around, her face was pale, but the magic had disappeared.

"Does that happen often?" Niko demanded as he pushed her into a chair.

"I'm fine," she said.

"Yeah, I can tell. How often do you lose it like that?"

Alexander went to a sideboard and filled a glass of water from a magically chilled pitcher. He brought it to her. She took it and sipped. Her fingers trembled.

Over her head, Alexander exchanged a glance with Niko. Giselle had been terribly weakened in the angel battle as she fought to protect the Keep from the worst of the damage. The rest of the coven had been killed when the rogue witch, Alton—who had also been an ally, or so they all thought—had somehow sabotaged the shields so that when the coven had tried to bolster them, every witch but Giselle and Magpie had been drained to death.

Giselle's recovery had been slow, aggravated by the need for her to rebuild the shield wards and get the greenhouses growing again.

"I'm just tired," she said, setting the glass aside and folding her hands together tightly. "It is, after all, the middle of the night, and I *was* sleeping. Couldn't this have waited until morning?"

"I don't think so," Niko said. "You'd better get dressed. There's something you need to see."

She went still, then stood and disappeared into her bedchamber without another word.

"You had better fetch Oz. Bring Tutresiel and Xaphan, too," Alexander told Niko. "We will meet you at the main entrance."

The other man gave a short nod and quickly left. Alexander stared after him. Whether or not Giselle actually bound him and made him Prime, Niko intended to act like she had. And if he did, so would the rest of the Blades. Giselle was in for quite a surprise.

She returned quickly, wearing jeans, hiking boots, and a fuzzy green pullover. Her hair was caught behind her head in a ponytail. She caught him examining her. "What?"

"It always surprises me how . . . natural you are."

"Natural? I bathe every day, and it's not like I let my armpit and leg hair grow wild," she said with a scowl.

"It was meant as a compliment."

"Oh. Where's Niko?"

"I sent him to find Oz and the angels."

"Did you, now? Making yourself at home as Prime?"

"I am at home, and I am Prime. You just have to decide if you want to bind me to service." His grin promised violence. "It will certainly make it harder for you if you do not."

Giselle came and stood close, looking up at him. Magic swirled in her eyes, and he felt it crackle through her body. He scowled. She was too much on edge and was losing control of her magic. She needed protecting from herself.

"You'll be Prime when and if *I* say you are and not before. Do you understand?"

He bent so that his nose nearly touched hers. "Try and stop me."

Her magic flared, and she drove a fist into his stomach. The impact was nothing, but magic lanced through him, and he staggered back a step. Without thinking, he knocked her arm up. Shards of rock blasted from the ceiling, and a black scorch mark curled in a short arc before she pulled the magic back.

Before she could react, he grabbed her and spun her around, holding her tightly against his chest. "Stop it before you hurt yourself. You are wasting your magic and your strength."

Magic sizzled across her skin and scorched his. He did not let go.

She drew a breath and held it, her hands clenching tight. Finally, the magic sank back down inside her. She slumped. Tears trickled down her cheeks and dripped onto his blistered forearms.

"You will never replace Max," she muttered.

Fury swept him, and he shoved her away before he snapped her neck. "You bitch. You weep for her now, but where was your concern when you sold her to Scooter? You have the power of foresight—where is she? Is she even alive?"

Her chin trembled as she lifted it defiantly. "I did what what I had to do for Horngate. If I hadn't, the covenstead would have been destroyed. You *will not* make me regret what I've done."

"Of course not. You do not have to pay the price. Max does. So why do you even bother with tears?" he demanded scathingly.

She went still. "I miss her more than you can imagine."

"Is she alive?" he asked, fear clutching his throat so the words barely escaped. "What have you foreseen?"

She shook her head. "Nothing. I see nothing of her. I don't know if it's all the magic the Guardians unleashed or if I no longer have the power to foresee. But she's alive. Her bindings are still intact."

His stomach lurched, and the bitter taste of bile flooded his mouth. Alexander swung around, not wanting the witch to see his reaction. *Not dead*. That still left a lot of room for her being hurt, but she was alive. He drew a painful breath, clawing at his Blade to settle. Finally, he faced her again and motioned for the door, his expression cool. "The others are waiting," he said. "We should go."

She eyed him and then nodded, going out ahead of him. It was a small gesture of trust, but enough. For now, they had a truce.

4

MAX ATE ALMOST MORE THAN SHE COULD STAND. Scooter had sped her healing and left her to her gluttony while he went off to prepare, whatever that meant. When she'd stuffed herself on potatoes, roast beef, ribs, eggs and bacon, fruit, and cheesecake, she went to clean up. Scooter had provided her with all the comforts of home, including a shower of sorts. Just beyond her bedroom was a small cavern filled with white sand and a deep pool. Thick steam rose from it and dripped from the walls. Hot spring water ran through an opening high overhead at the far end.

Practically waddling, Max stripped away the rags of her clothing and waded in. Steam closed around her so that she couldn't see. She swam to the end and sat on a natural stone bench beneath the cascade of water. It massaged the tight muscles of her shoulders and back as it pounded over her skin.

She sat mesmerized, feeling the thrumming pulse of the water on a level she never had before. She sank inside herself, giving herself over to all the sensations of her new awareness. There were *so many*. It was like her body was waking from a deep freeze. Sparks danced through her flesh and coursed through her blood. A different kind of heat sizzled along her bones like captured lightning. Magic limned every cell, and she could almost see the glow of it. The spells that tied her to Horngate and compelled her to protect and obey Giselle were green vines that snaked around her spine and wrapped her heart, lungs, liver, and kidneys in thick coils. She could feel them stretching away into the distance, where they anchored in Giselle's brilliant electric energy.

Deeper down, Max's inner fortress rose black and stark. She reached out spectral fingers to touch it. She felt the touch intimately, like she was brushing against her own soul. The cold was so intense it burned. She didn't pull away but let the sensation bleed through her until she could no longer feel the warmth of the water pouring over her. The chill soon turned to an ache and then grew into agony. Max let it go on, gathering the pain and pushing it back down into the fortress. When it became too much, she kept on. Her heart thundered and then slowed as she allowed the pain to consume her. Finally, she reached a point where it hurt so much she felt nothing. Her mind was clear, the edges sharp as shattered crystal.

It wasn't until then that she pulled away and rose out of her trance. The fortress was her protection. She hadn't been sure it would still hold her pain, now that she knew she had to pass through it to get to the abyss. She stretched, joints cracking, the memory of pain pulsing softly in her flesh. She reached for the soap and shampoo cached in a niche behind the curtain of water.

It was lightly scented with vanilla and oranges. She wrinkled her nose. The scent wasn't overwhelming to her Shadowblade senses, but she preferred things unscented. Too bad Scooter disagreed.

Once she was clean, she got out, dried herself, and dressed in a black short-sleeved T-shirt and black cargo pants. She wasn't sure how long she'd been in her trance, but she was positive that once Scooter was ready, he wasn't going to wait long for her.

She eyed the weapons on top of her dresser. There was a .45 ACP, a .9mm Glock, a couple of extra clips, and a silver witch chain. None of which were going to do her any good. She hadn't managed to pull her clothes into the abyss. She'd be lucky if she made it to this Chadaré city with a pair of socks, much less any weapons.

With a sigh, she flung herself onto her bed and closed her eyes. Hopefully she could catch a little sleep before Scooter came for her.

MAX SLEPT HARD BUT CAME INSTANTLY AWAKE THE MOMENT Scooter entered her room.

"It is time," he said. "We must go quickly."

She sat up and swung her legs over the bed. Scooter's face was taut, and she could hear his heart pounding. He wore only his buckskin pants and carried a gray bundle under one arm. Sweat glazed his skin, and a purplish blotch had appeared on the center of his forehead and another in the center of his chest. Each one was only the size of a plum, but the edges seemed to seep larger while Max watched.

"What happened to you?"

"I am dying," he said simply, like he was telling her the time.

Max gaped. "How?"

"Later. First, we must get to Chadaré before I lose my strength."

Lose his strength? The fucker was a god. Or a demi-god, Max wasn't certain. It was close enough. What could take him down?

She folded her arms. "I think we've got enough time for you to tell me just what the hell is going on. I'd like to know just how much trouble we're about to be in. Give me the quick and dirty version."

His mouth pinched together, and then he nodded. "Very well. You know I am the child of Onniont the Horned Serpent and Nihansan the Spider Woman. I was born with many of the powers of both my parents. Long ago, I was betrayed by those I thought were friends. They blinded me and stole my heart, my horn, and my silk." He touched the bruises on his forehead and chest. "They wanted all of me—every drop of my blood, my bones, my scales. I was able to escape Chadaré, and so I fled. They hunted me since and have grown impatient in recent years. They have begun to bleed my heart to force me back here. They know I will return and fight. I must have all three back, or I will die."

"Wait a minute," Max said, trying to take it all in. "You aren't blind."

"I have enough power to see using magic. Soon I will not."

Holy shit. "And what did you mean that they are bleeding your heart?"

"My blood still pumps through it, though it no longer

beats in my chest. Cut it, and I bleed to death. They must want me a great deal to risk destroying my heart and the rest of me."

She reached out and touched the bruise on his chest. His skin was raging hot. "How long do you have?"

"Not long. Returning to Chadaré will take all my strength. After that—days, maybe."

"Shit." She'd not realized how much her delay to fetch her family had cost him. Guilt wreathed through her stomach, and her body clenched. "This is what you wanted me for? To go with you and help you get your parts back?"

He nodded. "Those who have the ability to travel the abyss are few. But not only can you do it, you also are a strong warrior. I had hoped to find you much sooner. I would have had the power to fight at your side. No longer. If you cannot help me, I will die."

Max stared at him, chewing her lower lip. She owed him, and not just because Giselle had traded her to him. He had risked his own life to let her fetch her family, knowing she could die and leave him high and dry, and knowing he might not live long enough for her to return.

"Well, then, we'd better get on it," she said, standing up. "I guess this means you aren't going to be able to haul any weapons through for me."

He shook his head. "It will be all I can do to cross the abyss. Once we arrive in the city of shadows, I will be blind. I won't have any power at all. We'll need to find shelter quickly if we're going to survive."

"Great. No magic, no weapons, and you'll be helpless as a newborn. Can't wait."

"I won't be helpless. I'll have you."

"I *could* bounce right out and leave you there. You couldn't stop me or follow me."

He smiled, lines of pain bracketing his mouth. "You won't. I have your promise."

"What's to stop me from breaking it?" Aside from the fact that it would be physically impossible, of course. Promises meant something in the world of magic.

He cupped her cheek, his smile widening. He looked almost childlike. "I trust you. Enough of this. Let's go. I'll show you the way."

He held out his hand. Max took it, closing her fingers around his. He was right. Come hell or high water, she was going to do everything she could to save his life, promise or not. "Got any advice on holding on to my clothes when we go into the abyss? I'd rather not arrive in Chadaré naked."

His hand tightened on hers like a vise. "Don't leave them behind."

"Thanks. That's helpful."

"Anytime. On the count of three. One. Two. *Three*."

Max dove down inside herself, trying to focus on keeping hold of Scooter's hand while she pushed her awareness out through her body and beyond, to her clothes. They gave her little to hold on to except for the texture of the fabric against her skin. At least they were old, well-worn friends, retrieved from her quarters by an obliging Scooter. She knew the bottom hem of the T-shirt was unraveling, the edges curling. The pants had faded creases at the crotch and behind the knees. The bottoms were ragged where she walked on the heels. She hadn't thought to put on shoes, but she'd prefer to arrive in a strange and likely hostile city shoeless rather than stark naked.

Dragging herself through her fortress into the abyss hurt as much as before. Maybe worse. But when Max was through, her hand was still wrapped around Scooter's, and she was wearing clothes. Scooter, on the other hand, was not.

He gasped silently in the rainbow-ribboned night. Tendrils of purple spread beneath his skin from the bruises on his chest and forehead. He still looked mostly human, but his buckskin pants had disappeared, and he was now covered head to toe in a pattern of red-brown scales webbed through with thin filaments of gold. Threads of gold also gleamed in his raven hair. He was still sweating, and the flesh of his hand holding hers was scorching, enough to blister.

Max tugged, and he floated closer. The gray bundle bobbled loosely in his grasp. She pulled it away. Hopefully she could pull it through. By the looks of him, Scooter would be lucky just to drag his own ass to Chadaré.

He was still panting, and his blue-flecked obsidian eyes were dazed. Max tucked the bundle under her arm and grabbed his chin. When he didn't get the hint to give her his attention, she gave his cheek a sharp slap. That woke him up a little. He lifted his gaze to meet hers.

"Where now?" she mouthed slowly.

He did nothing for a long moment, and she lifted her hand to hit him again. This time with her fist. But before she could, he turned slowly away, closing his eyes and tipping his head. A moment later, he leaned forward, and they started flying through the night like Peter Pan through Neverland.

It didn't seem as if they were going that fast, but they crossed the vastness of the abyss in little more than a blink of an eye. Soon they were weaving in and out of colored streamers that curled and twisted together in a baffling maze. Scooter didn't slow down as the tangle grew more dense.

It came to the point where they could barely move without brushing through a ribbon. Scooter slowed to a stop. Ahead was a thick mass of colored strands wrapping around each other like a big yarn ball. Only not as organized as that. This ball had been attacked by a few thousand playful kittens, and the strings were a convoluted mess. Deep within, a heavy pulse of light brightened and dimmed in a slow beat. Max didn't have to ask to know that Chadaré lay hidden inside.

After a moment, Scooter tugged her downward. They slowly maneuvered through the jungle of glowing streamers. At last, Scooter found what he was looking for. It was a pale pink ribbon, finer than most of the rest and slightly translucent. They drifted closer to it, and suddenly it filled Max's entire field of vision, rising before them like an enormous wall.

They picked up speed. Max's teeth ground together, and she held tightly to Scooter and the bundle of gray fabric. When they hit, a shower of sparks burst around them. Silky warmth enveloped Max, and she smelled mold, ash, and burned sugar.

There was no warning that the path was ending. One moment they were rushing through the pink light, the next they were sprawled out on the ground. Max jumped up and spun around in a circle. They were in a narrow space between two tall buildings. High above, the sky was a dark gray. Max twitched. Even the slightest sunlight could kill her. But oddly, she didn't feel the usual urgency to duck into somewhere dark.

"No sun in Chadaré," Scooter mumbled as he sat up slowly. "You are safe." A grimace twisted his lips. "As far as the sun goes. We should move before we get caught. This path is a lesser-used one, but it hardly matters. Every entrance will be watched. They'll be sending someone to meet us very soon."

"I take it we don't want to be met," Max said.

"Only if you want to die."

Max pulled him to his feet and held him as he swayed drunkenly. The blue flecks had faded from his eyes, and the remaining black looked opaque, like scuffed marbles. The ugly bruising on his chest and forehead was shrinking as she watched. He straightened and pulled away. "Give me my robe."

She handed him the bundle, and he unrolled it. His fingers had long, curving black talons patterned with the gold that wove through his scales. His toenails were the same. Wicked hooks grew out of the sides of his forearms, and his muscles were all sharply defined beneath the taut covering of scales. His teeth were pointed, the canines long and curved. His cheekbones had sharpened, as had his jaw, and his brow bone had thickened and grown more protruded. His ears were upswept and pointed, and the cables of his neck had thickened and widened. It was as if a soft covering had been peeled away and what was left was not human. Which, of course, he wasn't. But then, Max wasn't, either. Despite his blindness and lack of magical power, he was still dangerous. A predator, like her.

"Help me put this on."

The robe was voluminous and fell over him in a multitude of gossamer layers. He pulled the deep hood over his head and reached out for Max. She put his hand in her right rear pocket and started down the alleyway.

"Where are we going?" she asked.

"I don't know. It has been centuries since I was in the city. Find somewhere for us to hide until you can scout and get our bearings."

Oh, goody. Instead of just impossibly hard, they were treading into the territory of definitely fatal. "How many people are looking for you?"

"Too many."

"Is this robe going to be enough of a disguise? Or can they track you other ways?"

"If they smell me, they will know me. Otherwise, the cloak will hide me well enough."

"Dressed like we are, how much are we going to stand out like sore thumbs when we go walking down the sidewalks?"

He shook his head, his fingers tightening on her pocket. "Chadaré is full of creatures from many places and times. Variety is expected."

"At least, it was the last time you were here," Max muttered as she pulled him along, staying close to the left wall. She glanced up. No one was coming for them from above, unless they were flying, which she wasn't about to rule out. Behind them, the alley led away into deeper shadows that she couldn't see through. That made her teeth itch. She could see in total darkness. These shadows should have been as clear as windows.

She started to ask about it, then stopped herself.

There'd be time to ask questions once they found a safe place to hole up.

The alley fed into a mostly deserted street. It was paved with cracked and potholed asphalt. The buildings were blocky and made out of dull concrete, and the windows and doors were protected with iron grilles. A motorcycle roared past as Max peered out of the alley. She was startled. She didn't know what to expect of this place, but a motorcycle wasn't on the list.

The air was full of both familiar and odd smells. Divine and Uncanny magics were thick, sliding through the air like heavy snakes. Nothing in either direction indicated which was better, so Max went left in the direction the motorcycle had come from. She walked swiftly and was glad when Scooter seemed to have no trouble keeping up, despite his blindness and the uneven road.

She turned right at the next corner and again at the next, weaving back and forth in a nonsensical path. If anyone was coming to find them, they wouldn't be able to reason out where they were going. Max sure as hell had no clue.

The city changed around her from one street to the next. She found herself walking through an area straight out of the *Arabian Nights,* with stone buildings and bulb-topped towers. Then they passed through a forest of soaring blue crystal buildings. Next was a block of squat igloo-shaped dwellings, behind that a collection of medieval castles. People—for lack of a better word—filled the sidewalks and roads indiscriminately.

Most of them were magical creatures of some sort. Many looked human, but only a few actually were, and many of those were branded on their cheeks. Max saw giants and a few centaurs, tall fairies—or maybe they were elves, she didn't know. There were beings that came only up to her knees and some with four arms. Skins were every color and texture. The smells made her want to wrinkle her nose. She'd thought American cities had strong smells, but they were nothing compared with this place.

"Why does everyone keep looking at me like I'm meat?" she asked Scooter as she began climbing up a steep hill.

"If you were human and unmarked, you would be fair game."

"Fair game for what?"

"For taking. Humans hold special interest for many who live here."

"Yeah? Why's that?" She glanced over her shoulder. A horn honked, and a stubby-looking car pushed through the crowd and turned off down a small street. The middle of her back prickled like they were being followed. No one in the shifting swirl of the street looked familiar. She hurried her steps.

"For games, for toys. Humans provide a great deal of entertainment in Chadaré."

Max glared at a pale, blocky man with red-slotted eyes who was scrutinizing her. When he caught her looking back, he opened his mouth to expose a red cave with short broken knobs of gray that looked more like rocks than teeth. His flat tongue lolled over his lips and licked up around where his eyebrows should have been. Strings of green saliva dripped down his broad chin.

Ew. Max wanted to stick her finger down her throat in the universal sign for "You make me want to puke," but she resisted. Instead, she kept moving.

At the top of the hill, the buildings gave way to a park. Or maybe a small country, Max wasn't entirely sure. It must have been at least twenty square miles. Bunches of towering trees dotted the landscape. Boulders like small mountains thrust up here and there, and a lacy pattern of rivers and ponds wove in between. Fruit trees and berry bushes of all kinds crowded into little copses. Rippling fields of grain ran up over a swell of hill, and animals grazed in lush pastures. It was Eden. And all around it as far as Max could see, the city rose, the impossible architecture defying the eye.

It was as if every period of architecture from all over the earth and far beyond had been imported into Chadaré, then a horde of bored witches, goblins, and whatever other beasties lived here had shaped and twisted and sculpted until they'd created a bizarre landscape of insane structures. Max could see spires that were so slender they were little more than spikes. Some buildings appeared to float. Others grew in zigzag shapes or leaned nearly parallel to the ground. The streets were a knotted mess, and people, cars, wagons, bikes, and mounts that Max couldn't identify swarmed through them like New York at rush hour.

"How did this place come to exist?" she wondered out loud.

"Your world was the root of it," Scooter said. "When magic began to drain away and so many were forced into hiding, some of us came here to create a haven. The city quickly grew, drawing more and more magical beings."

"Us? You were one of the founders?"

"I was."

He didn't seem inclined to say more, and the prickle was back between Max's shoulders. She looked back and was disconcerted to see that the street behind them had suddenly become deserted. The shadows hid far too much. An army could be massing, and she wouldn't know. One thing she was sure of: someone was watching them.

"We should go," she said, and urged him out into the park.

It wasn't the best place to hide. Their trail was too easy to follow. At least Scooter's robe faded into the gray light, making him nearly invisible. Smart bastard. He could have brought one for her.

Max guided them toward a thicket of trees overgrown with grapevines. On the other side, she peered out. Not far ahead was a pile of boulders with a creek running around one side of it. It wasn't perfect, but they'd have the high ground, and she'd be able to see anyone coming for a ways out. She dug around on the ground and found a couple of lengths of wood, one about three feet long, the other five. They were hardwood and wouldn't break when she started beating heads.

"We're going to crawl," she told Scooter. "It won't confuse anybody for long, but it will give us a little time."

She ducked down onto her stomach and pushed through the tall grass. She went slowly. Scooter was right behind.

At the creek, she got up in a crouch. She looked behind them. So far, she still saw no one, but every instinct told her they were there. "Across the creek now," she whispered.

Scooter grabbed her pocket again, and they crouched low as they waded across. The water was warmer than Max expected and came up to midthigh. Scooter's robe floated on top.

They were halfway across when something grabbed her ankle and bit her calf. Max kicked out viciously. Whatever it was let go, but a second later, another one chomped down. She gritted her teeth and started striding for the other side. Three more had fastened on before she stepped into the shallows. She swung the shorter club and knocked two away as she kicked off the other two. They looked a lot like scrawny little Muppets, with fuzzy green skin, bloated faces with doughy features, and yarnlike hair. Their mouths were full of teeth. They squalled and lunged at Max as her blood swirled away in the water, no doubt calling more of them to the feast.

She jumped up onto the bank and yanked Scooter up after her. They didn't seem interested in him. Either they didn't like the taste of his blood, or his scales were too tough to bite through. They grabbed the reeds growing on the edge of the creek and scrambled up after her. She punted one and then beat the others back into the water with satisfying crunches of bone.

"Hold these," she said, shoving the branches into Scooter's hands. He took them, and she hoisted him over her shoulder. Holding his legs with one hand, she clambered up onto the mound of boulders, her fingers and toes finding easy grips.

Near the top, she found a crevice and settled him down in it, taking the branches back. "Stay here."

She pulled herself up onto the granite dome, lying on her stomach. Below, she saw an unnatural ripple in the grass on the other side of the creek. Another. And another. Five in all. She watched the edge of the chuckling water, waiting for the trackers to emerge. One by one, they crept out of the grass. The first five were wolves with two thin horns curving from their heads. Down their backs, a multitude of spines pricked from their silvery fur. It took Max a second to identify them as she flipped through the pages of her memory. But with the horns and the spines, they could be nothing but Calopus. Deadly hunters and fierce fighters.

Behind them came the master of their hunt. He wore a studded leather vest over a blousy blue shirt. Voluminous brown genie pants were belted at his waist and laced tightly at his ankles above soft leather shoes. His hair was pulled up in a ponytail on top of his head and fell down to the middle of his back. It was woven with silver beads and orange feathers. He had a beautiful face, like most fairies. But there was a cruel twist to his mouth, and Max had no doubt that he was a stone-cold killer, and a good one at that. He carried two short swords on his hips and a wickedly hooked scythe in his left hand.

He crouched and ran the long, tanned fingers of his right hand over the sandy bank. He lifted a handful and smelled it, then let it drain through his fingers. He pointed to the opposite side of the creek, and the Calopus leaped over, never touching the water. Their master did the same. He strode forward, following Max and Scooter's trail unerringly to the base of the mounded boulders, the horned wolves weaving back and forth before him.

The master stopped and looked up. Max eased herself onto her feet and met the ice blue of his gaze.

"What are you waiting for?" she asked. "Come on up and get me."

5

Alexander followed Giselle through the Keep. It was nearly four in the morning, and most everyone was asleep. He hoped to hell that Niko had managed to send Tory off to bed.

Just inside the main entrance, they found Niko, Oz, and the two angels waiting. Oz eyed Alexander balefully and stepped between him and Giselle. Instantly, Alexander's hackles went up.

Niko made an annoyed sound and shepherded Giselle away. Tutresiel leaned one shoulder against the wall, his arms crossed, his silver wings folded. He watched Alexander from beneath hooded lids, his crimson eyes bleak and ruthless.

Xaphan stood on the other side of the entry. His wings were black and iridescent. Blue and orange flames licked the edges. Like Tutresiel, he was about six and a half feet tall, and his body and face looked like they were chiseled from the same block of marble. His eyes were just as bloody red. He wore a pair of faded, torn jeans that hung low on his hips, and his feet were bare, as was his chest. His hair was pale white. He nodded a greeting to Alexander.

"What's going on?" Oz demanded. He was tall, with dirty-blond hair that fell over his forehead and ears, broad shoulders, and a thick, powerful body. He reminded Alexander of a bull. He probably weighed one and a half times what Alexander did. He was also Sunspear Prime, which made him very dangerous.

"That is what we are hoping to figure out," Alexander said before Giselle could answer.

Oz scowled. "What does that mean?"

"Follow me." Outside, Alexander hesitated. Something tickled at the edges of his perceptions. It was a presence—vast and alien. It was different from what he had felt from the column of smoke, and it was close. He jerked around to the others. "Can you feel that?

"What is it?" Niko asked.

"It's powerful, like a Guardian," Xaphan said slowly, his eyes flattening.

"Guardians can't remember we exist," Giselle said. "Max made sure of that with the hailstone, and if it hadn't worked, you wouldn't be members of Horngate today. It has to be something else."

"What else is that strong?" Niko asked.

"I don't know," Oz answered. "But taking Giselle out of the Keep with something like that hanging around is too dangerous. She needs to stay inside." He reached for her arm and swung her around.

Oz was right, as far as it went, but the column of smoke was a threat they had to deal with now. Giselle had to deal with it. "I do not think this can wait." Alexander looked at Tutresiel, not caring whether Oz agreed or not. Nor did he ask for Giselle's opinion. "Carry the witch, and keep to the air until I tell you to land." To Xaphan. "Kill anything that attacks them. You other two, follow me."

He started off. Behind him, he heard Tutresiel and Xaphan launch into the air. Oz and Niko hurtled after Alexander. Oz came abreast of him, his Prime frothing with rage.

"If she gets hurt, I'll make sure you pay," he growled from between clenched teeth. "I may teach you a lesson or two anyhow."

"You can try," Alexander promised. "But I may do a little teaching of my own."

The feeling of the presence grew stronger as they approached the perimeter wards and the hidden ravine. Alexander looked up at the angels. They circled above and slightly behind, with Giselle cradled against Tutresiel's chest.

He led the way up to the top of the ridge above the ravine directly overlooking the column of smoke. Oz and Niko crouched on either side of him.

"Shit. What is that?" Oz asked, his attention riveting on the column, his anger turning into cold focus.

The smoke had grown more turbulent since they'd left. But Alexander's gaze went instantly to Tyler, who was lying unmoving on the hillside. Around him and on top of him sprawled enormous dogs. They must have weighed two hundred and fifty pounds apiece and stood three feet or more at the shoulder. They were blue-black, with thick ruffs of fur that ran around their necks and down their backs like a lion's mane. The rest of their heavy-boned bodies were covered in bearlike fur, and their heads were broad and square, with luminescent green eyes. Their long tails curled over their backs like feather plumes.

The entire pack turned in unison to look up the slope at the watching men.

"I count thirteen," Niko whispered.

"They are not alone," Alexander said, jerking his chin toward an outcropping on the other side of the ravine. A woman sat cross-legged on top, gazing at the column with rapt attention. Her short hair was vibrant red, her body comfortably curved. She was dressed in loose green pants and a matching tunic. Her feet were bare. She looked almost ordinary. But her eyes glowed the same green as the dogs', and there was no doubt that she was the powerful presence they had all been sensing. That made her anything but ordinary.

"Tyler's alive," Niko said tightly. "His chest is moving. I don't know for how much longer. We have to get him out of there."

Before Alexander could agree, the sound of wings whistling through the air close overhead made him spin around. Tutresiel settled on the ground with Giselle, and Xaphan dropped just beyond him.

"What the hell?" Oz's words were as sharp and hard as bullets. "Get Giselle out of here."

For once, Alexander agreed with Oz. He stalked forward and stopped in front of Tutresiel, seething. But the angel did not even look at him. His gaze was fixed on the scene beyond, and he looked . . . scared. There was no other word for it. That caught Alexander up short, his fury cooling instantly. Tutresiel was afraid of nothing.

"Explain," Alexander ordered, wasting no words.

Giselle started to push away so that she could get closer, and Oz slid an unyielding arm around her waist. "Hush," he said, hardly looking at her when she started to protest. Like Alexander, he fixed his attention on Tutresiel.

As if aware he had given away too much, an expressionless mask slid over the angel's features, but he could not tear his attention away from the woman and her dogs.

"Who are they?" Alexander prodded impatiently.

Tutresiel jerked his head side to side. "I don't know. No one knows exactly."

"Why don't you tell us what you *do* know?" Oz suggested.

The angel flicked a bloody look at the Sunspear and then back. "There are five of them. If you see one, it can be a blessing or a curse. If you see all five, it is conflagration."

"That is gibberish," Alexander snapped. "Speak plainly. What is she doing here? How do we neutralize her?"

Tutresiel snorted. "Neutralize? You can't. She's . . . Shit." He swallowed hard, and his body went rigid. His silver wings clashed together as they compressed tightly against his back.

Alexander whirled. Two of the dogs had wandered closer. The woman's attention had left the column of smoke and was now centered on their small group. The weight of her stare was like a mountain sitting on his shoulders. His legs shook and started to buckle. He firmed them, sweat springing up over his body. His skin heated, and in a moment, he was blistering hot. The sweat dried, and his skin felt dry and crisp. He stared back defiantly. When her eyes met his, the world shattered.

For a moment, he was spinning through darkness laced with streaks of light and dancing with colored confetti. He felt the entire world in his body. The touch of the sun in Australia, the dancing swirl of a school of fish off the coast of Chile, the pulsing swell of life in the Amazon, the arid sift of sand in the Sahara, the ancient solidity of ice and mountain in Siberia, the dark cold deep under the Arctic. Below it all was molten heat, searing . . . searing.

His body convulsed, and Alexander fell to his knees. Abruptly, the feeling peeled away, leaving him limp. He slowly pushed back to his feet. His bones were taffy. He took a breath, forcing air into his flattened lungs. The woman had returned her attention to the column. But the two dogs continued to watch their small group with avid interest.

Alexander looked at his companions. Each looked dazed. Tears dripped down Giselle's cheeks, and Niko was ashen. Oz trembled. Xaphan had crouched down, his wings closed tightly around his body, and Tutresiel twitched like he wanted to fling himself into the air and head for the South Pole.

"What is she?" Alexander asked softly.

Tutresiel started, and his wings flared wide with a soft chiming sound. "I don't know. No one really does, unless the Guardians do. All I do know is that there are five: the Harbinger, the Memory, the Seeker, the Illusion, and the Spirit. One or two tend to show up when there is serious trouble somewhere. Which means Horngate is in deep shit. With a magical war raging across the world, the fact that she is here says that something epic is about to go down."

Alexander scraped his fingers through his hair. "Which is this one? Is she going to attack?"

The angel's jaw knotted, and he shook his head again. "I don't know which one she is. They don't exactly wear name tags, and I prefer to be far from where they are if at all possible. She's here, no doubt, because of that—" He jerked his chin at the column of smoke. "Figure out what it is, and you might figure out why she's here. But my advice is to stay the fuck away from her."

"Tyler is down there," Alexander said. "I mean to get him back." He turned away and strode toward the dogs. He was startled when Niko joined him. "Stay back."

"Don't think so, boss."

Alexander slanted a look at the other man. "You are about to collapse. I do not need to pull two of you out of the fire."

"Worry about yourself. I'll be fine. Nice puppies," he said as they angled around the two watching black dogs.

"Those are Grims," Xaphan called in a quiet voice. "Spirit dogs. Soul dogs. Don't underestimate them."

"Of course they are," Niko said acidly. "Because every disaster needs soul stealers."

"What have you to worry about?" Alexander asked, easing down the slope toward Tyler and his new friends. So far, the dogs were content to watch them. "I thought you were a soulless man-whore."

Niko snickered. "I like to think I'm just generous with my attentions. After all, it would be selfish not to share myself widely. So many women and so little time, after all."

They were within thirty feet of Tyler now. One of the big black beasts was still lying over his legs. The others watched the two approaching Blades curiously. Three stood and wandered over. Alexander and Niko stopped abruptly.

"What do you want to do?" Niko murmured.

"Let them have a look and cross my fingers they do not feel hungry."

The big animals looked up at them with preternatural intelligence, then sniffed their legs and feet. One jumped up, its paws thumping heavily on Alexander's shoulders. He held himself still. The Grim sniffed his head and face. Its lips curled back in a snarl—or maybe it was a smile. Who knew? The beast smelled of Uncanny magic. It was a dense scent, as if the magic had been distilled to its most powerful essence.

The Grim dropped back to the ground. Alexander met its lambent gaze, waiting for the verdict. His fingers twitched toward the grip of the gun in his waistband, but he held himself still. He doubted even the steel-shot shells would have much impact on the beasts. He was not sure what would.

"You are stupid."

Tutresiel's voice made Alexander start. He had not heard the angel's approach. He twisted to look at him. "So you keep telling me. What are you doing here?"

Tutresiel's mouth twisted with bitter fury. "Helping."

"Out of the goodness of your heart?"

"No."

"Then why? You do not even like Tyler. Or any of the rest of us, for that matter."

For a moment, Tutresiel said nothing. Then, as if

against his will, "I like Max. She likes you. I don't have a choice."

Alexander grinned. "Welcome to my world," he said, and then they reached Tyler.

The Grim lying across his legs settled its head between its paws. It clearly had no intention of moving.

"Anytime you want to get me out of here, feel free," Tyler said, his lips barely moving. His eyes were open only a slit, and Alexander could hear his heart thundering in his chest.

"Looks like you have a new friend," Niko said, crouching down and settling a hand on Tyler's shoulder. "I hope it's house-trained." He looked up at Alexander and Tutresiel. "Any idea how to get the mutt to move?"

"We could try playing fetch," Alexander said. "Or maybe just asking nicely." He held out his hand. "Come on, boy. Let Tyler go now."

The Grim sniffed his hand, then opened its mouth and enveloped Alexander's hand. The beast's teeth punctured his skin. He did not move as a warm, wet tongue swept away the blood. A growl at Alexander's side made him jerk, and he looked down. Another Grim stood beside him, its lips wrinkled back in a vicious snarl. It growled again, and suddenly, the first Grim let go of his hand with a wet sneeze and heaved itself to its feet. It bent and swiped a tongue over Tyler's arm even as Niko helped hoist him off the ground.

"Damn, my legs are asleep," Tyler said, leaning against Niko. "Bastard must weigh a ton."

"At least it didn't eat you," Niko said.

"I don't know why."

"Let us get out of here, and you can figure it out later," Alexander advised. "Tutresiel can fly you out."

Tyler eyed the angel. "I don't think so. I'll walk."

"Suit yourself." Tutresiel launched into the sky and skimmed up to land between Xaphan and Oz.

"I hate him," Tyler muttered.

"I'm sure it's mutual," Niko said. "Can you walk?"

"Feeling's coming back."

"So is your new friend," Alexander said as he lifted Tyler's other arm over his shoulder and they started up the hill. Tyler's Grim followed.

"It's not the only one."

Tyler was right. Another Grim padded along beside Alexander, the beast's back coming up to Alexander's hip.

The three men said nothing more as they climbed back up to the ridgeline.

"New friends?" Oz asked, eyeing the big beasts narrowly.

"*You* tell them to go away," Niko said. "See if they tear your balls off or not. I'm not risking it. I like my balls just where they are."

"So how do we get rid of them?"

"More important," Giselle said, "what is in the ward circle that the woman finds so fascinating?"

Alexander had almost forgotten the witch was there. She had her arms crossed and was frowning at the boiling smoke.

"We could ask," he suggested softly.

She jerked her head to look at him and then Tutresiel. "Would she answer?"

He shrugged. "There is little known about them."

"I am willing to try," Alexander said. He looked at Giselle. "If you do not object."

She snorted. "Why let that bother you now? Go. I haven't a clue what this is"—she gestured at the black column—"and if she goes postal, I'd rather lose you than anyone else."

"Your concern is overwhelming," he said dryly.

"I'm sentimental like that."

"Like a rattlesnake," he murmured, and then turned and went back down the ridge. His Grim companion trotted at his side.

The woman did not watch him approach. He stopped at the bottom of the boulder where she sat and cleared his throat. Nothing. He grimaced, then leaped up to land on a slab just below. It put him at head height with her.

"I ask your indulgence," he said, bowing slightly. This close, he realized how flawless her skin was—almost radiant. If he did not know better, he would have thought her an angel straight out of a Michelangelo painting. Or a saint of some kind. She turned to look at him, and the world exploded.

His entire self shattered to bits. He could not think. He felt something moving around him, through him, swallowing him. It was beyond pain, beyond pleasure. At the center of everything was a hard kernel that refused to give. Something prodded it, then bit sharply into it. The kernel did not crack.

"Curious."

The word resonated, shivering through what was left of him. He gripped the kernel like an anchor and grappled to piece himself back together. It was like a jigsaw puzzle. Nothing seemed to fit as it should. He refused to give up.

"Impressive. You are strong."

The words pounded on him, and his rebuilt self collapsed inward like a crushed beer can, as if the entire weight of the world were pressing in on him. He held tight against it, refusing to crumble.

"Who are you?" He did not know if he spoke the words or just thought them.

Amusement. "What is the universe to a thing so small as you? Ah, yes . . . I see now. The Five." Her amusement quaked through him, and he sagged against her rocky perch. "That is what you little things call us." Apparently, Tutresiel was one of the little things. He was going to love that. "I am the one they call the Memory. It is apt enough, I suppose."

"And the column?" he gasped. He was smothering. Her attention was too much. Too heavy, too huge.

"It is an Erinye. Fury. A soul was betrayed here. She wants vengeance. Go now, little one. I should not like to see you die because of me, and I would remember. Keep Beyul well. He has chosen you."

With that, she withdrew, and Alexander crumpled like a marionette with cut strings. He tumbled from the boulder and landed on the flat below. He felt nothing. His mind was full of spinning lights. Something cold and wet nuzzled his cheek. It reminded him to breathe. He sucked in a long breath and turned on his side as he was racked with coughs.

At last, they faded, and he sat up. His companion Grim sat beside him, its warm breath puffing across Alexander's face. The beast leaned forward and snuffled him, and then swiped a wet tongue from his chin to his forehead.

"Thanks," Alexander said, and hoisted himself to his feet, wiping away the dog slobber with his forearm. He glanced up at the Memory. She ignored him, her attention fixed on the trapped smoke. He nodded to her and started back up the hill. When the Grim fell in beside him, he stopped.

"Beyul? That is your name?"

The beast nosed his hand and yawned. *He has chosen you.* What the hell did that mean? He would worry about it later. Right now, he needed to report what he had learned.

"She says she is the Memory," he told the others when he reached the top of the ridge. He was exhausted, and his legs shook. Beyul leaned against him, and he was grateful for the Grim's solid support. "She said it is an Erinye. Then something about a soul being betrayed here and that she wants vengeance. Oh, and she said *fury*."

"Erinye?" Giselle repeated, and went to look at the turbulent smoke. She closed her eyes and shook her head. "A Fury. Of course. Dammit. Sonofabitch." Abruptly, she swung around. "Xaphan, take me back to the Keep. Niko and Tyler, wake the coven. I want all my witches, Sunspears, and Shadowblades in the Great Hall in a half-hour. Oz and Alexander, meet me in my quarters right away." She hesitated. "Tutresiel, you'd better come, too."

Xaphan pulled her into the air, his fiery wings sending embers spinning across the ground. Alexander exchanged a look with the others. "Any idea what is going on?"

Tutresiel pinched his lower lip. "Erinyes are Furies.

They are born from the souls of women who have been brutally betrayed on a level that prevents their spirits from moving on."

"Sounds like ghosts," Niko said.

Tutresiel shook his head. "Ghosts are nothing compared to this. Women who become Furies somehow tap into something cosmic or elemental and are extraordinarily powerful and destructive. Think of the power of a volcano, a hurricane, a nuclear bomb, and a tidal wave all rolled into one, and you might be getting close. Their pain and betrayal are so deep and so massive because they embody the suffering of all women. Literally. It's an eternal reminder of what created them, as well as the source of their power. Their whole being is devoted to delivering justice and vengeance for the women who can't get it for themselves." He hesitated. "When they rise, they are—" He grimaced and shook his head. "It is going to be ugly."

"Define ugly," Oz said.

"She will burn Horngate to the ground and probably half of Montana with it."

"They do say payback's a bitch," Tyler muttered. "But just who the hell was she? What happened to her?"

"It wasn't anybody from Horngate. No one is unaccounted for," Niko said.

"Giselle suspects something," Alexander said. "We had better go find out what." He nodded to Oz, and the two started back to the Keep at a run. Beyul galloped soundlessly at Alexander's heels, almost as if he floated over the ground.

Oz's brows rose. "Friend of yours?"

"I hope so," Alexander said.

6

THE HUNTER SMILED AT MAX. HIS MOUTH WAS full of white teeth, the canines elongated, reminding Max of a whole lot of bad vampire movies. She hoped he wasn't into the whole blood-sucking thing.

He leaped lightly up onto the rocks. His pack of five Calopus followed as far as they could. Max was delighted to see that they couldn't make it all the way to the top. Nor could they reach Scooter.

As soon as the hunter outdistanced them, they started baying like banshees. Max winced. So much for taking care of this quietly. But apparently, the hunter didn't want an audience, either. He hissed something at the beasts, and the howls cut off instantly.

The hunter scrutinized Max from head to foot, pausing on the two branches in her hands before moving on. Finally, he returned to her face. His brows rose as if asking if she was ready. Fair play of sorts. Interesting. She gave a slight nod.

He dashed at her, swinging the scythe at her legs. She jumped out of the way, the magic of Tutresiel's feather embedded in her palm giving her more bounce than she was prepared for and nearly carrying her off the top of the battlefield. She scrabbled at the edge and spun just as he ran at her again.

This time, she vaulted over his head and smashed the shorter club into his back. He grunted, but he was smiling when he turned to face her again. Max found herself grinning back. He feinted. She flexed her knees and waited for him to commit.

He came at her straight on, the scythe whirling like a saw blade. Max took the longer branch and shoved it into the heart of the wheel. The blade chopped through it like butter, but it slowed the hunter's momentum enough. Max dropped and swept his legs out from under him. He tumbled onto his back, and she leaped on top of him. She wrenched the scythe away and tossed it. He punched her in the face. She head-butted him, and her vision spangled with stars for a moment. He was stunned longer. But then again, she'd been built to handle a beating, her bones and flesh reinforced with magic.

He bucked and rolled, and she was under him. He ground a forearm against her throat. His breath smelled of sour beer and sweet spices. He stabbed down at her eye with a dagger that came out of nowhere. She snatched his wrist and gripped hard. He winced and put more weight into his thrust. Max twisted, and bone broke. The dagger clattered onto the rock near her head. He yelped and slammed down against her throat. She pounded her fists into the side of his head until he slid drunkenly to the side. Max kicked him off her and snatched up his dagger. She grabbed him by the throat and pressed the dagger into his stomach until she felt it pierce flesh. It would be nothing to cut him open and spill his guts out on the ground. The question was, should she?

He watched her, blood trickling from his nose.

"What do you want? Who do you work for?"

He shook his head. "Can't say."

"Can't or won't?" The point of the dagger slid in further, and he gasped.

"Can't. Forbidden. Bound." His mouth snapped shut, his face reddening as if even that was too much.

It was too familiar. Max grimaced, her hand on his throat loosening slightly. She should kill him. He certainly wouldn't have hesitated to kill her. But then again, maybe she could use him to find out who was after Scooter.

She let go of his throat, grabbed his swords, and tossed them onto the rock. At least, she wasn't unarmed anymore. She pulled the knife out and wiped it on his pants.

"I'm going to let you go," she said softly. "I expect you to go straight back to your master. Don't pass Go, don't collect two hundred dollars. You go straight there. Got it? You owe me for not killing you. This is what I want in return. If you can't do that, then tell me now, and I'll gut you where you stand."

His eyes narrowed with understanding, and he nodded slowly. Binding spells were tricky things. They usually came with compulsions that said you couldn't betray your master or you'd die. But there were ways to think around those spells. Max had spent years perfecting the ability. She wasn't asking the hunter to hurt his master. All she was asking was that he go home and report. He was pretty sure she was going to follow—that was the price he had to pay for being allowed to live. But knowing it for certain and thinking it was likely left a world of gray area to exploit. If he wasn't certain, then he could tell himself—and his compulsion spells—that he wasn't being followed and that he wasn't committing any harm to his master.

"We will meet again," he warned. When they did, he would try to kill her again.

Her brows rose with grudging respect. It took honor to admit that. He risked her changing her mind and killing him. "I know. See you when I see you."

She pushed him away, and he paused to look at her once more before jumping down. He whistled to his wolves, and they started away through the grass. Next time, he'd be prepared for what she was. He'd expected someone softer, easier to take down. Now he knew better.

Max stuck the dagger in her waistband and grabbed the two swords. She went to the crevice where Scooter was still nestled. She squatted down. "You heard all that? I'm going to follow him. See who is holding his leash. You should be safe here."

He nodded. "Hurry. He will not be the only one looking for me."

"I can stay. Get you somewhere safe."

He grimaced and shook his head. "There is nowhere safe here. Better you find his master."

She glanced after the hunter and his pack of Calopus. They were fading quickly into the shadows. She had to hurry. She squeezed his hand. "I'll be back."

He lifted her fingers to his lips. "If I do not survive, make them pay."

Her grip tightened. "You can do it yourself. When we get your parts back."

His smile was pained. "So it is my hope."

A thought struck Max. "What if you get one of them back? Will that buy you more time?"

He shook his head. "It's too late. I must receive them all back at once in order to survive the ritual of return."

"Then that's what we'll do." She sounded more confident than she felt. "Watch yourself. I'll be back soon."

She put one of the swords in his hand and bounded down off the rock in pursuit of the hunter and his Calopus pack.

He had headed left, along the creek. Max ran through the grasses, letting her predatory senses take over. There were too many strange smells and sounds. Everything sounded like a threat. She sped up until the grasses whipped at her thighs, trusting that the hunter would keep his word and wouldn't be waiting to ambush her. She held the sword in one hand. There was no place to sheathe it.

She came to what appeared to be a massive vegetable garden, although she didn't recognize half of what was growing. Paths crisscrossed it, and she found the one that the hunter had taken. She slowed to a jog and followed him. There were workers in the field. Some sang softly, and every so often, Max thought she heard the crack of a whip.

Someone blundered across the path ahead of her. The hulking beast walked on all fours. It looked like a dinosaur with thick red skin and knobs protruding sharply all over its back. It smelled of Divine magic. Around one leg it wore a tarnished silver circlet carved with arcane symbols. The creature plodded on without noticing Max, pulling a two-wheeled cart in its wake.

She trotted past. She left dirt and grass, crossing onto a cobbled street. She stopped. It was like walking onto a movie set made to resemble ancient Persia. The buildings were massive and made of stone and tile. Minarets and bulb-topped towers mixed with tall arches and domed buildings. The windows were tall and pointed. Reflecting pools marched with battalions of ornate freestanding columns inside lush gardens. Stone grillework, elaborate carvings, and ornate tile mosaics covered every surface. She half expected to see Elizabeth Taylor and Richard Burton wandering around in flowy robes and eating peeled grapes.

The sounds of stringed instruments and drums percolated through the air, along with smells of roasting meat and vegetables. Max's stomach cramped. Traveling through the abyss had taken a lot out of her, and she needed to refuel. Later. First, she had to find the hunter and his master.

He'd turned to follow the broad avenue between the city and the park. Max went after him, ignoring the speculative looks she got. Her Prime was teetering on the killing edge, and power rolled off her in palpable waves. No one could mistake her for a weak human. Most gave way before her. Once she bumped into a gray-skinned man with pearl hair and eyes. He wore blousy maroon silk pants embroidered with ten or twelve bars of gold. Over them he wore a matching jacket. His chest was bare except for a gold chain and a heavy pendant. He looked at her, fury smoking in his eyes. Max could smell the Divine magic. It wrapped him in a choking blanket. She suppressed a groan. Just what she needed: a pissed-off wizard or sorcerer or whatever the hell he was.

"You have made a fatal mistake," he said, his eyelids dropping. On top, another set of eyes was painted or tattooed. They blinked at her as he opened his eyes again. The gray man smiled. His teeth were just as pearly as his eyes, and they were all pointed.

Max sighed. Before he could do anything, she drove a fist into the bottom of his jaw. He went flying through the air, landing twenty feet away. He bounced and lay still. Time to go. She started jogging again, and soon the scent trail turned in to the city.

She lost track of all the wonders she passed. It was like a piece of every place that had ever existed or been thought of had come to Chadaré and dropped roots. There seemed to be no rhyme or reason for anything. Magic was everywhere. In places, it was so dense it was like walking in quicksand.

Max stole a loaf of bread from a cart while the baker battled with a nearby competitor over who got to stand on that busy corner. It cut the edge of her appetite, but she needed a lot more.

She passed into an area that seemed impossibly more expensive than anywhere she'd been so far. There were high walls everywhere, and within, fantastic buildings rose. Spiraling towers of crystal soared. Massive trees grew together to form great castles in the air.

At last, she came to a wall at least twice as high as any

other. It was made of red and cream stone. There was a small door on one side, and the trail dead-ended there. Max stared up. She should be able to jump it, with the help of the feather Tutresiel had given her. But what was on the other side?

There was no way to tell. A mist hung over the interior like a jeweled cloud. Max ran her fingers lightly along the wall and yanked away, shaking her fingers as magic vined up her arm and down into her chest. It was sticky and searching. She wasn't going to be able to jump up on top and peek over. She grimaced.

There was no way to find out who lived inside without spending some time watching the entrance, and she didn't want to leave Scooter alone any longer. It had already been hours since she'd left him. She'd have to find them a bolt hole somewhere close and then start spying.

IT WAS ANOTHER THREE HOURS BEFORE SHE RETURNED. On the way, she managed to steal a spicy meat sandwich, a bag of roasted nuts, and three sweet rolls. She ate them all, needing the calories if she was going to help Scooter. She hadn't yet figured out what they did for money in Chadaré, but she was going to have to get her hands on some soon.

As she walked back into the park, she noticed a fire burning like a bright blossom not far up the avenue. Right near where she'd slugged the gray-skinned man. She winced. As much as she hoped he hadn't started it, something told her that he was perfectly capable of throwing just that kind of mean tantrum. She sighed and turned away. Nothing she could do about it. Hopefully he hadn't hurt anyone on her account.

Scooter sat up when she returned. Nothing seemed to have come sniffing around while she was gone.

"Well? What did you find?"

"A big house with a nasty ward system."

"That's all? You don't know who lives there?" He sounded both disappointed and accusing.

"Don't worry. I'll figure it out. But first, we need to find a place to hide, some money, and some food. Not necessarily in that order."

"I have gold and gems here. Hidden, for when I came back."

"Thank goodness. Anything else useful you've got stashed away?" she asked as she carried him back down to the grass and set him on his feet.

"Yes. Back then, there were factions of us squabbling over how to build the city and control it. I knew I could be attacked at any time. I just never thought my friends would be the ones to turn on me."

"I know all about how that goes," Max said, thinking of Giselle. She and the witch had been college roommates and friends long before Max knew that Giselle was a witch. On the night of Max's twenty-first birthday, Giselle had gotten Max drunk and started asking questions: What if you never had to grow old? What if you could be superstrong? What if you never got sick? So many questions, and all of them had seemed so stupid, so harmless. Max had agreed to all of them. The next thing she knew, it was a month later, and she'd woken up on Giselle's altar, no longer human.

For years, the betrayal had driven her half insane with

the need for revenge. But all that had changed when the Guardians had targeted Horngate. Then Max had discovered her priorities had shifted.

She pulled away from the memories, shaking herself. Old news. But she understood Scooter's bitterness. And if she could help him get his body parts back and get revenge, she would. No matter what it took.

"I don't suppose you have any good ideas for hiding spots?"

"I prepared to have to hide as well. If the wards have held all these years, then we will be safe enough."

"Tell me where we're going."

Getting there was not easy. There was no way to tell what was north or south or east or west, and many of the city's streets and landmarks had changed over the centuries since Scooter had last been there. When he started to veer away from the place where the hunter had led her, she pulled him to a stop.

"Got anything in this direction?" But there was no good way to show where she meant. "If six o'clock is where we came into the park originally, then we want to go toward ten o'clock."

He frowned and then nodded. "It is not in the . . . wisest . . . part of town. Too many eyes."

Max blew out a breath. "The trouble is, it takes forever to cross the city. The closer we are to where the body snatchers might be keeping your parts, the better. You said you have little time left. We can't waste it."

He nodded thoughtfully, then sighed. "Agreed. Take us toward twelve o'clock. We can hide in the Torchmarch. Be warned that they will probably be looking for me there especially."

"Why especially?"

His mouth tightened and his expression turned faintly roguish. "History," was all he said.

Again with the cryptic Max left it at that, since she had no choice.

She kept them in the park for as long as she could. Twice she had to fight off hungry little critters, but she didn't want to encounter the gray-skinned man or anybody like him. It was not long before her stomach began growling.

"I don't suppose you have a candy bar hidden in that robe of yours?" she asked.

Scooter shook his head. "I'm afraid not."

The area on the far end of the park was definitely cut from a different cloth than the rest of the city Max had seen. It looked industrial and postapocalyptic, along the lines of *Escape from New York*. A tall iron fence marched in both directions. Who did they want to keep out? Max wondered. Or maybe they wanted to keep someone in.

There were towers everywhere. It looked like a pincushion. Between them was strung a jungle of rope bridges and Tarzan vines. There were gondolas and other floating vehicles slipping between the spires above and below the network. A few of them looked like—No, they *were* animals. Dragons, gryphons, giant birds, and plenty more she couldn't identify.

"I haven't seen any flying vehicles until now," she said, describing what she saw to Scooter. "How come?"

"It was part of the struggle between factions. It is difficult to guard against attacks from the air, and complete privacy becomes next to impossible. So it was outlawed in the city."

"So why here?"

"This is the Torchmarch. Here, anything goes. From your description, it is much larger than it was. It didn't used to reach the park."

"How do we get in?"

The corner of his mouth lifted in a pained grimace. "The question isn't how to get in; the question is how to get out alive. This is no place for the helpless or the hunted."

"Beggars can't be choosers. And we don't have time to be picky."

"Indeed. Time is . . ." He let out a sigh and sagged against Max. She caught him around the waist.

"Scooter? Scooter!" His head tipped back over her arm, his hood falling away. Blood ran from his forehead down over his eyes and into his hair.

Max scooped him up. She had no idea where his hidey hole was, but she had to find someplace safe. Time was most definitely running out. Fast.

7

AN ALARM WAS SOUNDING IN THE MOUNTAIN KEEP when Oz, Tutresiel, Alexander, and his new Grim companion arrived. It was not loud, but the chime burned brilliantly in the air and vibrated deep into their bones. No one could ignore it.

"When did Giselle install this?" Alexander asked as they jogged through the corridors.

"While you were gone to California to get Max's family," Oz said.

"So she expected another attack. Anybody in particular?"

"We all see the writing on the wall. With the war, food will be getting short. That will bring all sorts of creatures down on us—human and not. Plus, there will be refugees and marauders. We have to be ready."

The none-too-subtle emphasis on *we* made it clear that Oz did not count Alexander among them. He grinned. Too damned bad for him.

Giselle's door was wide open when they arrived at her apartment, and they went in without knocking. Xaphan perched on the back of a chair. He nodded as they entered. Beyul ignored everyone and padded up onto a cream-colored couch and sprawled along its length, his black tongue hanging from his mouth as he panted.

"Make yourself at home, why don't you?" Oz said, eyeing the Grim.

Beyul bared his teeth and growled. It was enough to raise the hairs on Alexander's arms. "I do not think he likes you," he told Oz.

"The feeling is mutual."

Just then, Giselle pushed through a stone door on the left side of the room. It swung on a central pivot, and beyond was her workroom. She carried a book. As she came through, she snapped it shut and tossed it onto a chair.

"We're in trouble," she said. "I don't have anything that tells me how to stop a Fury. I'm open to ideas. Tutresiel? Xaphan? What do you know?"

"Only that Erinyes rise when a woman has been horribly betrayed, and they are capable of great destruction, especially on first rising," Tutresiel said.

"That much I found in my books," Giselle said. Magic smoked in her eyes, and threads of it crawled over her hands. Alexander frowned. She needed to take better care of herself.

"What about you, Xaphan?"

The fire angel shrugged, an elegant, liquid movement. "The kind of betrayal that creates a Fury is beyond imagining. There are few of them despite the evil that has been committed against women through millennia. Still, they aren't deathless, or there would be more of them."

"How many are there?"

Again the shrug. "No one knows for certain. Legends say there are only three at any given time. But legends lie."

Giselle nodded. "Yes, they do." She raised a brow at Alexander. "And you? Do you have anything to add?"

He shook his head. "No."

She grimaced. "Then it's time to go talk to Alton."

"Alton?" Oz repeated.

"Of course," Alexander said.

A former ally of Giselle's, Alton had allowed the Guardians to destroy his entire covenstead just to lure Giselle into a trap. She had not fallen for it, so when the Guardians had sent Tutresiel and Xaphan to attack Horngate, Alton had tampered with the shields, killing every one of Horngate's witches except for Magpie and Giselle, and the latter had nearly died. Giselle had had him drugged and put in one of her underground prison cells until she could decide what to do with him.

"He did something to the shields," Alexander said. "He bragged about it to me and Max. That spell circle is centered right on the old ward line." He frowned. "But waking him is dangerous. He is still bound to the Guardians, and they gave him a great deal of power."

"What choice do we have? I need to know if creating an Erinye was his intent and if he knows how to kill her."

Oz snorted. "He already killed her once."

Giselle glared at him. "The irony of asking the witch who betrayed this poor woman to tell me how to kill her again doesn't escape me. But it's our best hope at the moment. Unless you have a better idea?"

"No."

"Then let's get going. That spell circle isn't going to hold her long." She started for the door, then stopped, her gaze snagging on Beyul, who returned the look without blinking. "Is he watching us for her? The Memory?" she asked.

"She said he chose me," Alexander said. "Whatever that means."

Her mouth flattened, and then she spun around. "It means you can damned well keep him off my furniture," she called over her shoulder as she marched out.

Tutresiel and Oz followed. Beyul made a chuffing sound and stepped down. Xaphan fell in beside Alexander. The Grim nosed between them, completely unaffected by the flames brushing against him from Xaphan's wings.

"That's . . . unexpected," the angel said, his brow crimping. "I've never encountered anything my flames didn't burn."

"Remind me to hide behind him when you get pissed at me," Alexander said. He had a feeling that Beyul had a lot more surprises in store. He just hoped they were good ones.

Xaphan grinned. "Don't think a big dog will save you if I decide to barbecue your ass."

"I'll volunteer my sword for the skewer," Tutresiel said.

"I have heard your sword is too small for impaling anything bigger than an ant," Alexander said. "A very *dull* blade indeed."

Oz and Xaphan chuckled, and Tutresiel grinned. "Better a dull blade than none at all, as you should know all too well."

Suddenly, Giselle made an exasperated noise. "I

swear, men are such asses. Seriously, if you want, we can drop everything and send for a tape measure. You can all whip your dicks out, and we'll measure them. Or hell, go outside and have yourselves a good old-fashioned pissing contest. Whatever you do, get it the hell out of your systems, because personally, I'd like to stop messing around and figure out how to save Horngate before the Fury wipes us all off the map. In which case, how big your dicks are isn't going to make much difference to anyone."

She did not wait for a reply but turned and strode off, magic wreathing her in black tendrils.

"I guess we know whose is biggest," Xaphan murmured as they all followed after.

Alexander choked back a laugh, as did Oz and Tutresiel. Giselle glared back at them but said nothing.

They made their way to the western side of the underground fortress. The walls and floor were roughly carved, and there was no attempt at decoration. They entered a loop of barred cells. They were empty, their doors open. Beyond was a wide corridor etched with arcane symbols. Three cells broke off from the end. These were covered in grilles made of woven metals and wood impregnated with wards. Lise stood outside the one on the left.

Oz's second in command, Lise was five foot nine, with burnished brown hair that fell in waves around her gamine face. She was dressed in a tank top and a pair of loose-fitting jeans, with a Glock strapped to each hip. She paced in front of the door she guarded, her cell phone to her ear, whirling when their small company approached.

"What's going on?" she demanded. "What's the alarm about?" Her gaze skimmed them, stopping on Beyul. "What the fuck is that?"

"We need to talk to Alton," Giselle said, ignoring her questions. "Open up."

Lise's mouth dropped, then snapped shut. She glanced at Oz and Alexander as if to be sure that she should. Both nodded. She grabbed the door and yanked, her muscles bunching as the massively heavy grillework swung outward, the hinges squeaking.

Inside, the walls, floor, and dome ceilings were thickly inscribed with wards. Etched into the floor was an *anneau*—a triangle within a five-pointed star within a circle. The entire thing glowed with orange light. A thick pile of salt, herbs, and ground metals surrounded the circle, adding to its protections.

In the center of the triangle, the drugged Alton lay bound in witch chain made of silver and spells designed to suppress a witch's power.

"How do you want to do this?" Oz asked Giselle. "I don't want you going inside the *anneau* with him," he added quickly. "It's too dangerous. We don't know what he's capable of."

"Agreed," Alexander said.

"I've no intention of risking myself," Giselle said irritatedly. "I'll break the outer circle and release the *anneau*. You two can go inside, and once I've sealed the outer circle again, you can wake him up." She fished in her pocket and pulled out a small brown bottle with an eyedropper lid. "Put three drops on his tongue."

"And to put him back under?" Alexander asked. "Once you are through with him."

"I'm not going to. Not right away."

"You have no idea what powers the Guardians have given him. Will this cell even hold him if he wakes?" Oz demanded.

"It should."

"That answer doesn't exactly inspire a lot of confidence," Lise put in, her arms crossed. "I don't know what the hell is going on right now, but that bastard killed nineteen witches."

"I don't need to inspire confidence. I tell you what to do, and you do it. Right? So let's get on it."

Giselle bent, pulling a silver knife from her hip pocket. She drew it from its leather sheath and knelt outside the thick ring of salt, herbs, and metals. She murmured, and magic billowed around her. Snakes of black writhed along the outside of the circle. A burst of it detonated, and a sharp wind blew through the chamber as Giselle plunged her knife through it and scraped away a gap. Without pausing, she touched her fingers to the *anneau,* and magic flared and pulled up into her hand.

She stood. Her cheeks were flushed, and her entire body pulsed with power. "Go to it."

Oz and Alexander stepped over the ring. Beyul followed with a graceful leap. He went to snuffle at Alton's prone body. Giselle eyed him acidly. "Can't you control him at all?" she asked Alexander.

"Not that I have noticed," he said with a cheeky wink.

She made a frustrated sound and bent to rebuild the outer circle. Again, she murmured, and snakes writhed around the circle. The air inside hummed, and magic washed over Alexander's skin.

"OK. You're good. Wake him up."

Oz knelt beside the witch. He unstoppered the bottle while Alexander pried Alton's mouth open. The Sunspear squeezed three drops of the reddish liquid onto the witch's tongue. Alexander dropped his head. They waited.

It was nearly five minutes before Alton twitched and his eyes sprang open. Alexander recoiled. They were a golden yellow. Last time he had seen Alton, just before he had been locked up, they had been a dull blue.

"Where am I?" He lifted his head, taking in the cell, the witch chain, Alexander, Oz, and Lise. His eyes widened on the two angels. When he saw Giselle, his face flushed red. "You bitch," he seethed through clenched teeth.

"Welcome back to the land of the living, Alton."

He struggled, but his bindings held him. His face grew haughty. "How long have I been here? What's been happening?"

She smiled coldly. "Your plan failed."

"Don't count me out yet."

"Oh, I think you're done. But I'm here for answers. Whom did you sacrifice when you tampered with the shields?"

He settled back against the floor, no longer looking at her. "Why do you want to know?"

"Sit him up," she snapped at Oz.

He grabbed Alton's collar and yanked him up. The witch coughed raggedly and spat at him. Oz dodged easily and slapped the back of Alton's head. "Mind your manners."

"Whom did you sacrifice?" Giselle demanded again.

"Let me think . . ." He glowered defiantly at her. "Sorry. I can't remember."

Giselle shrugged. "Suit yourself. Perhaps you'll remember when you get hungry enough. Or thirsty. Come, Alexander and Oz. Let us leave him to his misery. We'll check him in a week or so and see how he's getting along."

She released the magic of the outer circle and waved them through, then engaged the circle again. Alton made furious noises as he strained against the witch chain, twisting from side to side and bumping over the floor. At last, he stopped.

"You can't hold me. I am far stronger than you think."

"You seem to be pretty stuck for the moment," Giselle said with an exaggerated yawn. "You'll excuse me. I think it's time for breakfast. I'm starving. I think I'll have bacon and an omelet. Maybe a cinnamon roll. Oh, and coffee. A whole pot of it with cream. Maybe there will be raspberries. What do you think, Oz?"

"No raspberries, I'm afraid," he said, his eyes gleaming. "But there are blackberries and a few huckleberries. They would be delicious on pancakes."

Alton made a low moaning sound that cut off abruptly. "You bitch. I will have you groveling at my feet yet."

Giselle whirled, her cheeks spotted red. "I'm a bitch? You ball-less coward. You were my *friend*. My ally. You let them slaughter your entire covenstead just so you could curry favor with the Guardians and steal Horngate from me. And what about Cora? Where is she now? The Guardians have unleashed hell on earth, and your daughter is—"

She broke off, her face going white as alabaster. She

pressed a hand to her mouth and sank boneless to the floor before anyone could catch her. Tears streamed down her cheeks. "Oh, damn. Damn you. Tell me you didn't. Tell me it wasn't your daughter in that charm circle."

Alexander felt the blood drain from his own face, his stomach twisting in revulsion. He turned woodenly to see Alton's reaction. The captive witch's face was utterly still. Slowly, life crept back into it. The animation was sickening, as if he had suddenly drunk from the fountain of youth. His eyes sparkled, and his lips seemed to grow red and full. He sat straight, one eyebrow rising in an expression of disdain.

"Yes. My daughter returned to me the life I loaned her. She served me well."

Giselle choked. "*Served* you? She was your *daughter*. You were supposed to protect her. You're a fucking monster!"

Her magic was spinning around her like a whirlwind of jagged black glass. The air turned thick, and it hurt to breathe. Alexander stood just beyond the thickening magic tornado. Was she losing control? If so, he had to shut her down. But how?

The chamber suddenly echoed with the sound of Alton's laughter. "Such a dramatic show, Giselle. But isn't that a bit like the pot calling the kettle black? You're a cold-blooded killer, no different from me. You are just as ruthless, just as brutal. You would have done the same, if you had the same rich payout promised to you."

Giselle flinched as if his words were physical blows. Alexander felt her gather herself, pulling her magic inward until only threads of it crawled like spider legs over her exposed flesh. It was disturbing to watch. She stood and straightened regally. "I am nothing like you," she told him. "I do what I do in order to serve my covenstead and protect my people. Whatever it takes, I will do it. For them, not me. But I never, *ever,* throw the innocent into the fire. Even if Cora wasn't your own flesh and blood, she was still a child. She couldn't defend herself. That was your job. You betrayed her in the worst possible way. And trust me, you *will* pay."

He snorted. "Do your best."

She bared her teeth in a smile of pure malice. "Oh, no. Not me. Your daughter is rising—a Fury. She will deal with you as only her kind can."

He drew back in consternation, then collected himself. He sneered, his lip curling. "I don't believe you."

Her smile widened. "You will." With that, she walked out.

Alexander and Oz followed, with Beyul, the angels, and Lise bringing up the rear. Lise shoved the door closed, and the wards flashed as they reactivated.

Giselle turned to the angels. "I want you two guarding Alton. If he makes the slightest move to escape, call me. You have your phones on you?"

Both nodded. While most cell service all over the world was down, witch phones continued to work, even deep inside a mountain. Magic had its virtues.

"Lise, come with me," Giselle said.

"Giving the Erinye her father won't satisfy her," Xaphan said quietly before Giselle could walk away. "Her fury and hunger will be insatiable."

The witch looked at him. "I know. But it's a start. If any of you have a bright idea, I'm all ears."

Alexander ran his fingers through his hair, hardly believing what he was about to say. "I know a mage. He is brilliant and powerful. It might be that he could offer some help."

Giselle eyed him narrowly. "What sort of price will he expect?"

"I do not know. We are not friends. He may not even be willing to come." But Holt would, Alexander knew. If only to see the birth of an Erinye. Holt would not be able to pass that up.

Giselle laughed, a brittle sound. "That's not exactly the most encouraging advertisement to sell me on him. Mages are trouble. One of them equals a whole covenstead of witches."

"Can we trust him?" Oz asked.

Alexander glanced at the Sunspear in surprise. He would have expected Oz to ferociously oppose the idea of allowing a strange mage into Horngate. "Holt—" He paused, searching for words. He and the mage had a long history and it was safe to say that mostly they wanted to kill one another. "Holt is arrogant, ruthless, and ambitious, like most of his kind. But he owes Max a favor."

Now it was Giselle's turn to look surprised. "He knows Max?"

Alexander nodded. He had not told Giselle or anyone all that had happened when he and Max had traveled to California to rescue her family. When Valery had delivered the amulet to Alexander, Holt—Valery's ex-husband—had attacked them. Alexander and Max had held him prisoner while Valery escaped. Max had befriended him, and when the Guardians let loose their magic on the world, she had rescued him from an enchantment. So he owed her.

"You've been keeping secrets," Giselle murmured speculatively, her brows rising as she clearly wondered what else he was hiding.

"I am not the only one." His chin jutted. He would not apologize.

After a moment, she nodded. "Call him. See if he will come."

Alexander watched her walk away, still stunned that he had volunteered to call Holt. He hated the bastard. But if anyone could help, it was the mage. Alexander rubbed a hand over his mouth and swore softly.

"What's wrong?" Oz asked.

"Holt may come help because of what he owes Max, but he will most certainly make *me* pay for it," Alexander said.

"Sounds like a mage after my own heart."

"Just wait until you meet him. You will want to strangle him before he says ten words."

"If he can keep this place from being destroyed, I'll kiss his ass."

Alexander grinned. "I will be sure to tell him so. He does like a good ass kissing."

THE SHADOWBLADES WERE HOUSED IN THE LOWER REgions of the Keep. The Sunspears' quarters were higher, where they could have windows to let the sunshine pour in. Blades lived deep underground, where darkness ruled.

At the bottom of a steep stairway, Alexander turned down the hall and keyed the wards of his room. He glanced down to the end of the corridor at the door leading into Max's apartment. His knuckles whitened on the handle of his door as a storm of emotions swept over him. He closed his eyes, leaning his forehead against the door, waiting for it to pass. How was it possible to miss anyone so much? The hurt was almost unbearable. When she got home, he was going to kill her for putting him through this.

Beyul nosed him curiously. Alexander started. Unworldly intelligence shone in the depths of the Grim's green eyes.

"Wait until you meet her," he told the black beast. "Then you will understand."

Beyul tipped his head as if asking a question. *Understand what?*

Alexander winced. He was most certainly going crazy, explaining himself to the Grim. "She is—"

No words came. She was so many things, and he felt like he was bleeding to death without her. It did not even seem possible. He had known her for less than two months. Hell, who was he fooling? He had been completely hypnotized by her within minutes of meeting her. She was different from any other Shadowblade—no, any other *woman*—he had ever met. Finding her was like finding a piece of himself he had not known was missing. And now she was gone. She might not be coming back.

He drew a harsh breath. *No*. He refused to even consider the possibility. She was strong and stubborn and very skilled. She would return. But whether or not she would be coming back to him, that he did not know.

He straightened, his body aching with pain that was

too great for him to contain. Beyul whined at him. Alexander grimaced and scratched the Grim's ears before wondering if the beast would snap his hand off for taking liberties. But Beyul leaned into his touch, his tail wagging twice.

"She agreed that we had something," he said. "I will not let her forget it. Whatever it takes."

He went inside, and Beyul immediately sprawled across his bed.

"Do not get used to it. I have no intention of sharing. Not with you, anyway," he told the Grim, who only pawed at the bed and rolled onto his back.

Alexander went to his dresser and pulled open the top drawer. Inside was a polished cherry-wood box. He lifted the lid and took out a folded piece of paper smudged with dried blood and dirt. He flattened it, reading the number written on it in bold black letters.

Holt had given Max the number after she had rescued him from certain death. He had been trapped inside a landscape of deadly magic. Holt had been wounded, and if Max and Alexander had not carried him out, he would have been eaten by a bunch of giant carnivorous plants. Enchanted forests were nothing but dangerous, and these plants had been very hungry. When he had given her the number, Holt had told her that if she ever needed anything, she should call him. He would not be pleased that it was Alexander on the other end of the line.

Alexander tapped his fingers on the top of the dresser, delaying the inevitable. Whatever he had told Giselle, the truth was, Holt would not come because of Max. Only she was going to be able to collect on what he owed her. But there was another way to get the mage here. Alexander sighed and punched a number in his speed dial.

It rang twice before Valery picked up, her voice rich and sensual. "Alexander. Is everything all right?"

As always, she did not waste time but cut right to the heart of things. He did the same. "No. We are in trouble, and we need Holt."

Silence. Then, "It must be really bad if you want him, of all people."

"It is. He will not come without something to make it worthwhile. There is only one thing he wants."

Another silence. "You know what you're asking?"

"I will make him promise to give you a head start when everything is done. All you have to do is be here while he is. He will not refuse the chance to be face-to-face with you."

"Dammit, Alexander!"

She said nothing more. Alexander waited. He considered her a sister. Both of them were Caramaras—gypsy folk who had fled from Egypt ages ago. He would do anything for her and she for him. But this was more than he had ever asked. She and Holt had been married, but a couple of years ago, she had left him and taken with her something he desperately wanted back. He had been chasing her ever since. Now Alexander was asking her to let herself be caught, if only for a while.

"I would not ask if—"

"I know. If there was any other way, you would try it. All right. I'll come."

"How long will it take? We have little time."

"Then I guess I'll have to ride the smoke. It won't take long. I'll home in on you."

"Should I go out beyond the shield ward?"

"Your shields won't stop me. See you soon."

She hung up. Alexander let out a slow breath. Now for Holt.

To his surprise, the mage picked up almost instantly. "This must be big if *you* are calling me," came the low baritone voice.

"I need your help." The words cut at Alexander's throat like broken glass.

"Do you? And why would I help you?"

"Because Valery has agreed to be here while you are. But you cannot try to take her by force, and you have to give her a full day's head start when it is over."

Holt laughed, a bitter, angry sound. "That's not much of an offer."

"You have not been able to corner her in the same room with you for two years. If you want to talk to her, this is your chance."

"All right. Suppose I do come. Why do you want me?"

"We have an Erinye rising. She will be born very soon, and we would like to keep her from wiping out the covenstead when she does."

Holt gave a low whistle. Then his surprise turned to anger. "You fucking ass. You called Valery into that mess? She could be killed."

"Then you had better get here quick. She is on her way."

Alexander snapped his phone shut, his blood pounding in his chest. Holt was right; he should not have asked Valery to come. But there was no other way if

Horngate was going to have a chance of survival. If the angels were right about what a newborn Fury could do, the coven was not strong enough to defend itself. He was Shadowblade Prime now, and that meant giving everything he had to protecting Horngate. Even if one of the things he gave was his sister.

If it came to it, she could escape on the smoke, he told himself as he headed for the door. But it was a cold comfort. If the shit hit the fan, there would be no time for her to catch the smoke. Besides, Valery would not abandon the fight if she thought she could help. Which meant that Holt damned well better have a few aces up his sleeve.

He yanked open the door, waiting as Beyul launched himself off the bed. He had better hurry. He wanted to be there when Giselle met Holt. It would be nothing if not interesting. Max was going to be pissed that she'd missed the fireworks.

8

MAX CARRIED SCOOTER OVER HER SHOULDER, leaving one arm free to hold her sword. The other, which he had dropped when he fainted, she held hilt down as she balanced his body.

There were no gates within sight. Inside the iron fence was a busy pulse of people—for lack of a better word. The shadows were thicker here, and torches burned everywhere. Hence the name of Torchmarch, she guessed. They put off a thick, greasy smoke that burned in her lungs.

Only a few people passed by on the boulevard, and most of them gave her a wide berth. She kept up a quick pace. She didn't want to give anybody time to get too nosy about her or Scooter. Especially Scooter.

She'd gone ten miles when she finally found a gate into the Torchmarch. It was tall and wide enough to drive two semi trucks through. An arch spanned the width of the road, decorated with ornate scrolling metalwork depicting haunted faces full of suffering and fear hiding in the branches of twisting trees and crawling vines. On either end were enormous torches shooting flames a good fifty feet in the air.

The gates were wide open and guarded by two hulking gargoyles. They looked roughly made, with hooked horns and massive paws. Their eyes bugged, and their noses covered half of their broad, squat faces. Their arms were longer than their powerful legs, and their backs bowed to accommodate the mismatched height. They had stubby wings that couldn't possibly have lifted a dead cat, much less the massive creatures they were attached to.

As Max turned to enter, they snorted loudly at her. One of them thudded forward, the ground shaking beneath its heavy stone steps. One swipe of a paw would crush her. Max stopped, waiting to see what it would do. Her fingers tightened on the hilt of the sword. It wasn't going to do much good. Gargoyles were made of animated rock. Nothing cut through them short of a jackhammer.

It lumbered closer, and its mouth fell open, revealing a set of short, triangular teeth. Streaks of rust smeared the cavern of its mouth and dribbled down over its chest. Gobbets of flesh were wedged between its teeth. It had eaten recently. A dark wet patch on the ground a few feet away told her that if she didn't pass whatever test was coming, she'd be dessert.

The gargoyle snuffled over her body, its eyes gleaming red in the torchlight. Its breath was hot and smelled of rotten meat. The beast shifted its attention to Scooter. It started grunting in excitement, or maybe anger. She shifted her burden away, putting as much of herself as possible between the rock beast and Scooter. Its grunting grew high-pitched, and it raked a claw at her. Fast. The damned thing sure didn't move like a statue. Max twisted aside before it could make contact.

It made a harsh barking sound and lunged. She leaped back, the angel feather embedded in her hand making her glide lightly up into the air. She landed on the top of the iron fence, balancing precariously. The gargoyle slammed against the fence, clutching the metal and shaking it fiercely. Max tilted sideways and leaped. She soared over a building and tangled in a net. She clutched it, hanging by one hand, the other grappling Scooter, who had begun to slip from her shoulder.

Both gargoyles began to bay with deep, bellowing noises that sounded like foghorns. Who were they summoning? She wasn't going to wait around to find out.

Below her, the top of the building was flat, with a variety of pots and benches arranged in a pretty garden setting. She let go of the net and landed in the middle of a raised bed of fragrant greenery. Instantly, she ran to the edge of the roof and peered over. Below, the street was teeming with people drawn to the noise. She pulled back out of sight. Across the way was a taller building anchored on four corners with needle-sharp minarets. In the middle was a glass dome. Between the towers ran a small stone ledge.

Without pausing to think about the stupidity of her plan, Max made a running jump and flung herself across the gap between the buildings. She crashed into one of the minarets and clung to it as she found footing on the narrow ledge. Scooter made a sighing sound and tried to push himself away from her.

"Hold still," she hissed, then eased around the spire

to the ledge on the other side. She trotted down to the next tower and jumped to the street below. She crossed to the other side and ducked into a recessed doorway before setting Scooter on his feet. He swayed, and she steadied him. The hood fell from his face. He looked bad. His scales had grayed, losing their luster.

Max brushed a lock of lank hair from his face, more worried than she cared to admit. When it came down to it, Scooter had treated her fairly, and that was saying a lot, given how desperate he was. She respected him. "What happened to you back there?"

He rubbed his chest. As he did, the robe fell open, and Max saw that the bruise had returned full force, staining a spot the size of a watermelon.

"They went after your heart again, didn't they?" she asked, her teeth grinding together with fury and disgust.

He nodded. "So it seems."

"All right. We have a shitty hand. So let's play it carefully. First things first: where can we go? If I can put you someplace safe, I can go hunt for your heart. They can't bleed it if they don't have it. It might buy enough time for me to find your horn and silk."

He put out his hand, fumbling for hers holding the sword. "You should know—if you go into the abyss, they can only follow you if you take one of the established roads. Very few can travel through the abyss without a road the way we can, and it's impossible to track anyone across it. Remember that if you have to run."

"Is there some reason I need to know that now, Scooter?" she asked, her voice sharpening dangerously.

"There is little hope now for me."

"Fuck that. You're alive, and that's all the hope we

need. Plus, I'm pretty good at this sort of business. So shut up and tell me where to go before our new gargoyle friends find us." The baying had grown closer, though it didn't sound like the beasts had found their trail yet.

Obediently, Scooter closed his eyes and tilted his head as if listening closely to a sound Max couldn't hear. He turned, searching. At last, he pointed. "There."

"Got any idea how far?"

"Not close."

"Then we should get moving."

She was about to step out when the flapping of wings made her duck back into the doorway. She glanced up. Mother of fuck. Approaching was a giant gondola, the passenger basket the size of a Greyhound bus. It was buoyed by a gold hard-sided balloon three times as big and pointed on both ends. All around it buzzed a horde of rainbow fireflies. The bottom was shallow, with swans rising on either end, their wings upswept and curving back along the sides of the carrier. Long streamers attached to the underside of the ship gave the impression of a long, feathery tail.

A merry spangle of music poured out, a combination of drums, flutes, and guitars. It in no way overwhelmed the loud laughter and voices of the passengers, most of whom were hanging over the edge and watching the street below. They were dressed elaborately in fine clothing and even armor. A few weren't dressed at all.

Surrounding them was a phalanx of flying creatures and smaller vessels, all joining in the rush to find out who had set off the alarms. They weren't the only ones. Suddenly, the streets were packed. It was like Mardi

Gras in New Orleans. There was little room to pass in the tide of oncoming people, and more were flooding in behind.

"Don't they have something better to do?" Max muttered. "Come on. Hold tight. I want my hands free."

She made sure that Scooter's hood covered his face before pulling his taloned hand through the crook of her arm. They eased out into the crowd, staying close to the wall. Max reined in hard on her Prime, trying not to call attention to herself. It was hard. She wanted to clear some walking space with the swords, but she kept them pointed downward and used her shoulder to wedge through the press of bodies.

At the corner, she turned, pulling Scooter with her. She pushed down another three blocks and then crossed, sifting through the wash of bodies, shielding Scooter, who was clutching her like a lifeline. On the other side, they ducked under a broad portico running around a squat building. It was held up by fat pillars carved in the shapes of rotund men and women, all displaying something malicious in their expressions.

Max stopped to look up. Far too many vehicles floated overhead. She had wanted to get back to the roofs so it would be easier to cover their trail, but it would make them too easy to spot from above. Suddenly, the baying of the gargoyles quickened and rose higher. They had found her trail. She had no choice now.

She pulled Scooter around the building, staying beneath the overhang. On the other side, she crossed into a narrow alleyway and found a stairway leading up. At the top was a plain door painted a dirty tan. There was no handle on the outside.

Without hesitation, she tossed Scooter over her shoulder and leaped up onto the roof. The building was topped by a series of dull metal juts surrounding a small garden. Max sprawled into a bed of prickly vines. She stood and set Scooter on his feet. "Are you OK?"

He coughed, holding a hand to his side, deeply grooved lines bracketing his mouth. "I may have broken something."

She dragged her fingers through her hair. "Dammit." He couldn't afford injuries. He was teetering on the edge, and she didn't need to push him off the cliff. "How bad?"

His lips curved without much humor. "Bad enough. You may be free to go back to Horngate soon."

She scowled. "I'll go when I'm good and ready. Now, sit for a minute. I'm going to scout." She eased him down onto a wood bench and went to look out over the Torchmarch. The thicket of ropes and bridges was thicker there. They'd be handy, but she couldn't risk dropping Scooter. Which left the ground and the rooftops.

The streets were still packed, and the sky was still crowded, though no one seemed to have noticed them yet. Maybe she could outrun the mob while they were distracted by the baying gargoyles.

She circled the garden. There were a couple of good buildings that offered a flat landing. She returned to Scooter. "Can you handle the rooftop route? I'll have to sling you over my shoulder again. If you can stand it, we can get a lot further faster."

He shook his head reluctantly. His breathing was short and shallow. "It's probably best if we stay on the ground."

Max touched his cheek. He skin was clammy, and he was starting to shake. "How can I help you?"

"Besides finding what they stole from me? Water would help. Food. A place that's warm. Sleep." His breathing sounded wet and thick.

"They have hotels with room service in the Torch-march?"

"Nowhere that's safe for us."

"Yeah, well, I'd risk a lot for an IHOP or a Denny's right about now," Max said.

He chuckled. "Chadaré has a wealth of good food, but I admit I wouldn't turn down a bucket of fried chicken."

"A deep-fried man? I wouldn't have guessed that. I'd have thought you'd be more into the kind of thing they serve at the Four Seasons."

"I wouldn't turn that down, either."

"You and me both, Scooter," Max said as she swung him up into her arms to carry him down the stairs. "You and me both."

"Why do you call me Scooter?" he asked, looking blindly up at her.

"It's a nickname. In place of the fact that you never told me your real name."

"What does it mean?"

"It means . . . You probably don't want to know."

"It's an insult, then," Scooter guessed.

She grinned. "Maybe a little."

"Only a little? You tend to be very focused in your anger, and you don't like me."

"I don't know. You've been growing on me."

"Like a bad rash."

She eased down the stairs, swiveling her head to

watch for attackers. "Now, Scooter, that sounds like something I would say."

"That doesn't make it any less true."

"You were the one bashing me against cliffs in order to get me to find the door into the abyss."

"That's also true."

She stepped off the last stair and set him back on his feet. "Do you have a point?"

"I know that you serve me here in Chadaré because of our bargain."

Max turned to look at him. "I am helping you because I *want* to."

He shook his head. "You didn't want to come here."

"True. But now that I have some idea of what's going on, there's no way in hell that I'm walking away. I'm not letting these assholes butcher you."

"Too late, I'm afraid. They hacked away the best parts of me long ago." He pulled up his hood and took a firm hold on her arm as she started to ease back onto the street.

"Not the best parts, and you're going to get them back."

"I have better parts? Do tell."

"Are you fishing for compliments?"

"Just curious about which you think are better."

"Must be your sparkling personality and the scales—I really go for scales on a man."

"Do tell," he said with a faint smile.

"On the other hand, I could be wrong. It's not like I've seen your horn, your heart, or your silk."

"That's not entirely accurate," he said. "Look up there." He waved upward at the tangled tapestry spreading across the Torchmarch.

"You made those?" Max asked incredulously.

"Not all. Not even most. It has, after all, been thousands of years since I held power in Chadaré. The city has grown a great deal since then."

"And they lasted all this time? Impressive."

Max *was* impressed. Awed, even. She'd known Scooter was powerful, but somehow knowing that he'd created so much of the web above the Torchmarch and that it had lasted so very long made what he was more tangible than anything else she'd seen him do. It was like seeing the ruins of the Parthenon or the Aztec pyramids.

"My silk is—"

He broke off, and Max could almost feel his agony over what he'd lost. She knew that pain. There was no relief. It hurt in a place that tainted everything. It was betrayal and bitterness and never being able to catch your breath. It was always as if there were a hand around your throat and a knife forever twisting in your gut.

"I'll make you whole again," she said softly, and despite the noise of the people around them, she knew he heard her. "I'll make you whole or die trying. I promise."

With her promise, a wash of magic poured out over her, running away on a rippling red tide. Suddenly, they became the center of attention as the surrounding crowd turned to look at them.

"We should hurry," Max said, and shouldered her way through the thicket of bodies.

"You promised," Scooter said, and he sounded shocked. "Why would you do that?"

"Some say I'm stupid. That's probably it." She knocked an outstretched arm aside and swept the legs from beneath a thin creature covered in bark. Its rootlike feet clung to the ground, and it swayed all the way to the side as Max shoved it over like a weak grass stem. Instantly, it bounced erect with a greedy smile. It reached for her with a mass of branchlike arms. With hardly a pause, she swiped the sword through the reaching limbs, and they sheared away, green ichor spraying from the stubbed ends.

She ducked away from the burning blood, yanking Scooter into a jog. The wounded plant creature screamed like metal tearing apart. The gargoyles would come running to find out what was up. There was no time for hanging out. Max reached down and slung Scooter over her shoulder. He gave a thin moan of pain and then fell silent, his body clenched and trembling.

Max broke into a flat-out run. She leaped over the crowds, up onto roofs, and back to the street. She held Scooter as tightly as she could, trying to absorb some of the shock of her escape.

In minutes, she'd put a couple of miles between them and the scene of her fight, but she didn't slow. She wanted a much larger margin of safety.

At last, she passed through a little plaza. There were few people here. She slowed and set Scooter on his feet. He straightened slowly, as if he'd aged two hundred years. There was no time to let him recover.

"How far to your safe house?" Max asked. "Are we going in the right direction?"

"I think . . ." He turned like a compass arrow searching for north.

Before he could say anything, something plummeted out of the sky. Golden wings arched wide. They were deeply pocketed, with hooked talons tipping each bony span. Within was a man. He wore a gold helm that covered his eyes. A sharply hooked beak curved down over his nose. Armor covered his shoulders and gauntlets circled up to his elbows. They bore razor talons that stuck out straight over his fingers. Over his hips was another layer of armor that circled his waist and ran in scales to disappear inside the greaves encasing his feet, shins, and knees. Like his gauntlets, these had sharp points that protruded from his toes.

Within the helm, his eyes were a tiger-eye brown. Where his skin was exposed, he was deeply tanned, his body ridged with powerful muscle. He had no body hair that Max could see or any weapons besides those on his armor and wings. They looked plenty deadly enough.

Even as she studied him, he was examining her and Scooter.

"Who are you? Why are you in my territory?" he demanded when he was at last finished. His voice was raspy and deep, like Johnny Cash after he'd put away a fifth of whiskey and smoked a carton of cigarettes.

"Who wants to know?" Max returned.

He'd started to let his wings fold, and now they flared wide again. The muscles in his biceps bulged. "As you are the intruders, I believe that *you* must answer *my* questions."

"All right. My name is Max, and this is Scooter, and we're passing through," she replied unhelpfully.

His cheeks flushed, and his mouth twisted with fury. "No, you're not. Not anymore. You're coming with me, or you will die."

"Or the third option, you let us go on our merry way, or you stop moving. Your choice." Max pulled away from

Scooter and stepped to the side to give herself room, both swords ready. "Let's get this over with. We don't have a lot of time to waste screwing around with you."

His eyes inside the mask narrowed. He faced her. Magic suddenly balled up between his palms. "Oh, it will be quick, I assure you."

Shit. He smelled of Divine magic, but she hadn't thought he was a witch. Max tensed, watching his chest. It would signal the launch of the magic torpedo. She'd need to jump instantly. She'd go over his head and slash his wings. She had only one good shot. If his magic struck her, he'd probably have enough time to close in and kill her. She had to hamstring him quickly, or she wouldn't have a chance.

He wasn't the sort to chat as he fought. Max found it both refreshing and unnerving. His chest muscles tensed, and he suddenly shoved the ball forward. It streaked at Max with lightning speed. But she was already in the air, her two blades wheeling as she slashed at his wings.

But he was faster than she imagined. One second he was there, and the next he wasn't. She landed as the ball exploded and the air shook. Debris flew through the air, cutting and pummeling. She spun around to find him. Already, another magic ball was heading for her. She dropped flat to the ground, and it flashed overhead. The heat of it scorched her skin, and flames erupted on her back. Behind her, another explosion and more debris. Stone, metal, and wood rained down. She rolled aside and leaped to her feet just in time to dance away from another one.

"Stop!"

Scooter's voice rang loudly in the now empty plaza. Anyone with sense had beaten a hasty retreat from the war raging inside it.

To Max's astonishment, the winged man paused, magic swirling around his hands.

"Are you ready to leash your servant and tell me who you are and what you want?" he demanded. He didn't look away from Max.

"Yes." Scooter pulled his hood back before Max could tell him not to, turning blind eyes toward the eagle witch. "You know me, Ilanion. You know what I want. I've come back to get what was stolen from me."

The magic faded from the winged man's hands. He took a step toward Scooter. Instantly, Max blocked him.

"Not so fast."

Ilanion looked at her, examining her again from head to toe. Then his gaze slipped past to Scooter. "I expected you a long time ago and at the head of a large army, old friend."

"I brought all that I needed. She is enough." He paused, his head tilting. "We *were* friends. Are we still? Or did you have a hand in what they did to me?" There was thick strain and exhaustion in his voice.

"I had no part of it."

"And now? What will you do?"

"Whatever I want. You're toothless, and your little wolf can't hurt me."

Scooter smiled, slow and sure. "You're wrong, Ilanion. She won't just hurt you, she will kill you."

Ilanion flicked a searching look at Max. "She's hardly shown any such prowess so far. I was about to char the flesh from her bones."

"You always had more pride than sense. If you like, you can finish your brawl. Though I'd hoped we could negotiate an alliance. Go ahead. But Max, do be quick. We should be getting on."

She grinned and pushed all of her emotions down into the cold fortress within. Her Shadowblade rose, overwhelming all her senses. Hyper-awareness swept her, just as it did before she went into the abyss. She felt every cell, every sinew, every pulse of blood. She could see that Ilanion registered the change in her. Before, she'd been holding on to herself, not letting the predator inside her free. But now she gave herself entirely over to it. She circled, and he turned to keep her before him.

"What is she?" Ilanion asked Scooter, respect coloring his voice.

"She is Max."

The answer frustrated the winged witch. "What is a Max?"

"She is . . . unique. And she is about to kill you."

9

DRAWN BY THE ALARM CHIME, MOST EVERYONE was already gathered in the Great Hall despite the late hour. The newcomers were especially frightened. They had come to Horngate to escape the magical upheaval sweeping through the country and the rest of the world, but they had no idea what they had really stepped into at Horngate. It was certainly safer than almost anywhere else—or had been until the Erinye started to rise—but it was never going to be a tame place to live. Nowhere in the world would be, now that magic had returned full force.

Giselle stood at the center of a large *anneau* floor talking to her small cadre of witches. Beside her was Judith, a newly recruited witch with long brown hair that she wore in a pair of braids. She was haggard and worn. She'd not yet recovered from the long, difficult healings she'd performed on Alexander and others a short time before.

Next to her stood Gregory, a tall, gaunt man with broad shoulders and narrow hips. Brown hair fell around his face in an unruly mop. He looked twitchy and nervous.

He was a Triangle-level witch, just like Judith, but his covenstead had been destroyed, and the two had barely escaped with their lives. It had crippled his ability to use his magic. No one knew if he would ever regain what he had lost.

Magpie came next. She was a Circle-level witch and head chef of Horngate. She had long black hair with two streaks of white on each temple, giving her her nickname. Alexander's gaze lingered on her. Although she was only a Circle-level witch, her gift for true prophecy made her unique and very special. She had given Alexander the prophecy about the amulet and becoming Prime but had refused to talk about it since. His jaw clenched, and the coil of hot frustration in his gut twisted tighter. His Prime clawed inside him.

Three others stood in the little group. Two men and a woman. Maggie hung back, looking terrified. She was a new witch, just awakening into her talent. A couple of weeks ago, she had not known that witches existed, and now she was one. If Alexander and Max had not rescued her in California when the Guardians attacked, she would have died. It might have been better for her. She was not sure how to handle her newly discovered powers, and neither was her husband, who could hardly stand to be anywhere near her, much less let her hold her own baby.

The two men crowded close to Giselle, both of their faces alight with eagerness and delight. Never mind that she was telling them that Horngate was in dire straits; they were like kids in a toy store. The younger one was Kyle. He was probably at least Star strength, but it was too soon to tell. He had never been in a coven before.

The older one was Peter. He was in his late sixties, with nearly white hair. Despite his age, he was hale and hearty. His magic was minor, lower than Circle, and he would not ordinarily have been invited into Horngate. But beggars could not be choosers, and more important, he was Max's father. Kyle was her younger brother.

Alexander could not help the disgust he felt for them both. Neither seemed to be bothered by the fact that Scooter had taken her. They were too excited about learning magic. *Bastards*.

Max's mother was off in a little cluster with Tris—Max's sister—and her two daughters, including Tory, who was dressed in a pair of sweats, a half-shirt, and the usual earbuds. When Alexander walked in, she stood and started toward him. Tris grabbed her hand and pulled her back and whispered something against her ear. Alexander grimaced. Tris did not like him at all and definitely wanted to keep her lovestruck daughter away from him. That suited him fine, but her dislike rankled. She hated anything smelling of magic, which made living at Horngate nearly unbearable for her, and the thought of one of its magical residents fooling around with her daughter set her off. Alexander snorted inwardly. As if he would have anything to do with that carnivorous little child. She was as appealing as a dead fish.

Tris made no effort to hide her repulsion for Horngate and everyone in it, and that is what stuck in Alexander's craw. Especially after everything he and Max had suffered to rescue her and her family from a pack of very hungry shape-shifters. Both of them had nearly died more than once, but all Tris cared about was her own petty prejudices. It was all right for him, but Max would be deeply hurt by her sister's antagonism, and that Alexander would not forgive.

The rest of the people in the hall included the few unmagical civilians who had survived the devastation wrought by the angels, and a handful of people Alexander and Max had rescued when they'd gone to California. All of the Sunspears were there, as was Niko, who saw Alexander and strode over to meet him.

"Well? Oz says you were calling in a mage to help. What's the story? Is he going to come?"

"He is coming. As is my sister."

Niko's brows rose high. "Sister? Seriously? Aren't you over a hundred years old?"

Alexander winced. "Valery is of my blood. We are Caramaras—a kind of gypsy to you," he explained when Niko looked confused. "But blood is enough. She *is* my sister in every way that counts."

Niko shrugged. "I'm not arguing. So who is this mage you're bringing in to help? Can we trust him?"

"His name is Holt. He is very powerful, and he says that he will help. He is an ass, and you will dislike him on sight. Far more than you hated me."

"I'm not sure I'm capable of that level of hate."

"You will find more. I am sure."

"I can hardly wait. But you didn't say we could trust him."

"No, I did not. I guess we will find out soon. Here comes Valery. Holt will not be far behind."

A lazy black smoke had filtered in through the rock, gathering high against the uneven ceiling. It sifted down, condensing into streamers that wound together into a shadowy figure. A moment later, the figure became a woman. Everyone had gone silent, and Alexander could feel Giselle gathering her power. He shoved through the assembly, thrusting himself between her and Valery, even as Niko, Oz, and the other Spears closed around Giselle in a protective wall.

"There is no threat."

Giselle stared at him, magic twisting around her like black pythons. Strange how much her magic resembled Valery's, and yet the reality was that they were entirely different. Giselle's magic was elemental, coming from stone and nature. Valery's came from somewhere else. Alexander had never understood it, but hers had little in common with the magic of coven witches.

"You said this mage, Holt, was a man."

"He is."

"Then who the fuck is this?"

"This is my sister."

"We're not having a family reunion, Slick."

Alexander's teeth gritted at the nickname. It was what Max called him and no one else. "Turns out I was wrong. Holt would not come for what he owed Max. So I played my ace. There is nothing Holt would not do to find Valery."

Giselle's eyes narrowed, magic still coiling around her body. "Explain."

"He's been hunting me for more than three years," said Valery, her voice deep and rich.

"Why is that?" Giselle's attention riveted on the woman behind Alexander.

"I'm that good in bed," came Valery's irreverent response.

Alexander grinned and held his hand blindly out to her, watching Giselle all the while.

Valery slid warm fingers into his and pressed a kiss to his cheek. "Sweetness, I'm glad to see you."

"Why don't you introduce us?" Giselle said quietly. The snakes of magic still roped menacingly around her. She waved at her bodyguards to step back. They did so reluctantly.

Alexander pulled Valery forward. She was as tall as he was, with golden, sun-kissed skin and black hair cut in a jagged fringe that swept across her forehead and sharply chiseled cheeks. She wore skin-tight black jeans with threadbare knees, a silky green blouse, and red high-topped tennis shoes covered in black skulls and cross-bones.

"This is my sister," he said. "Valery, this is Giselle, the witch who holds Horngate's *anneau*."

Giselle studied her for a moment. "You came quickly. We appreciate it," she said finally, her switch to courtesy shocking the hell out of Alexander.

"He called, I came," Valery said with a shrug. "I'd do anything for him. Even put up with Holt for a while."

Giselle glanced speculatively at Alexander. "Then I am glad he is on our side," she murmured. "Why is Holt trying to find you?"

Before Valery could answer, a light burst into brilliance above their heads. Flames licked around it, and colored sparks cascaded down like fireworks.

Valery rolled her eyes. "He has to make an entrance."

"I take it this is Holt?" Giselle asked, her wreathing magic intensifiying, even as Niko, Oz, and the wall of Sunspears closed around her again.

Valery grimaced. Her entire body was tense, and she looked as if she wanted to run, though whether toward or away from Holt, Alexander was not sure. "I'm afraid so."

His fingers tightened around hers. Despite whatever it was that had driven Valery to divorce Holt, she was still in love with him. Seeing him tore her heart out. He wished he had not had to ask it of her.

Giselle eyed the other woman shrewdly. "Will you be all right?"

"He has promised not to try to kidnap her, and he will give her a head start when she leaves," Alexander said. "He knows I will kill him if he tries anything."

"You can try, anyway," came Holt's liquid voice as the sparks dissolved and he appeared out of thin air.

Slightly taller than Alexander, he had a slim waist and brown shoulder-length hair that was caught behind his neck in a ponytail. He had thick, straight eyebrows and bloodshot green eyes, and he looked like he hadn't shaved in a few days. His arms were covered with blue hex marks that disappeared under his rolled-up sleeves.

"I will do better than try," Alexander said. He stepped protectively in front of Valery.

"He'll have some help," Niko said, and shockingly, Oz stepped up beside him. Menace rolled off them in palpable waves.

Beyul made a sudden growling sound and paced slowly forward until he stood in front of the mage. The Grim's lips wrinkled back from his teeth in a silent growl. Alexander stared. He had almost forgotten the beast.

"Friend of yours?" Holt asked, looking coldly down at Beyul and completely ignoring Niko and Oz.

"Something like that."

"Maybe you should put a leash on him. Wouldn't want to have to hurt him."

Alexander remembered how Xaphan's fire had not bothered Beyul. "I wonder if you can."

Holt narrowed his eyes at the Grim, his head tilting to the side, his thumbs hooked in his pockets. He was not an imposing man, and no one would imagine he was a mage with the power of ten or twenty witches rolled up in one. He looked more like a surf bum or a house painter. He continued to look at Beyul for another long moment, then back up at Alexander, one brow raised. "Interesting friend you have. What is he?"

"A Grim," Alexander replied unhelpfully.

Holt's hex marks glowed faintly. "What kind? Where did he come from?"

"I am sure this is very fascinating, but if you two don't mind, I'd just as soon you sorted this out after we deal with the Erinye," Giselle said, pushing out from among the Spears. She waved them away. Oz glowered at her.

Holt nodded, facing her. "Of course. You must be the territory witch here." He examined her from head to foot, taking in her diminutive size, her nearly emaciated state, the magic snakes still coiling around her, the unrelenting set of her jaw, and the flat, unwelcoming glare. "I understand you need my help."

"That depends. Can you contain a rising Erinye?"

He shrugged. "I have no idea. I haven't seen one rise before."

That irritated her. "Your confidence is underwhelming."

"Would you believe me if I told you I could handle it with no problems?"

She looked like she was chewing rusty nails. "No."

"Then why complain?"

"Maybe because my covenstead is about to be destroyed for the second time in two months. It would be nice to know you are worth betting on. Or should I be looking for someone else?"

Holt smiled arrogantly. "Oh, I doubt you can find anyone as good as I am. Even Alexander will admit that much, won't you?"

Alexander ground his teeth together. The worst part was, the bastard's arrogance was entirely justified. "You *are* a talented son of a whore," he grated.

"So, now that that is settled, why don't you take me to see the Fury?" Holt said, ignoring the insult. His gaze slipped to where Valery had knelt to pet Beyul. The beast responded just as any dog would, leaning into her scratching hand, his eyes drifting closed with obvious delight.

"First things first," Giselle said. "Do you accept that your payment is Valery's presence while you're here and that when it's over, she gets a day's head start?"

Holt's smile vanished, his eyes going cold. "Yes."

"Good." She turned to Valery. "What do you expect for payment?"

In the world of magic, you never said thank you, you never made promises you did not have to, you never said you owed someone, and you never accepted gifts without knowing what the cost was going to be. And there was always a cost.

Valery rose slowly, her fingers smoothing over Beyul's

wide head. "I'm here because Alexander asked me to come. I don't expect anything from you."

Giselle said nothing for a moment, then nodded shortly. "Good enough. I'll leave it between the two of you, then."

"That's where it belongs," Valery said.

Holt made a low sound in his throat, and Alexander grinned maliciously. Holt had always thought there was something going on between him and Valery, never accepting that they considered themselves family. The idea of anything romantic between them was both ridiculous and repulsive. Valery winked at Alexander and put her hand in his. She was not above putting the screws to her ex.

"So, Furies aren't born every day. Why now? Why here?" she asked.

"Her name was Cora," Giselle answered softly. "She was fourteen. A couple of months ago, her father made a blood sacrifice out of her in order to attack Horngate."

Valery stared, one hand rising to cover her mouth. "Oh, shit."

She was not alone in her horror. Clearly, Giselle had not informed anyone else of this. The news spread across the Great Hall in a whispering ripple, followed by a spike of crackling anger and, from many, fear.

Even Holt was affected. "Fucking bastard son of a bitch," he said, revulsion twisting his face, and for the first time since they had met, Alexander almost liked him. The mage collected himself, taking in the gathered people, his gaze lingering on the small group of witches. "This is all you have left?"

"Yes," Giselle admitted, though she clearly did not

like revealing Horngate's weaknesses. "Now, if you will come along, I'll show you the Erinye." She did not mention the Memory or Beyul's twelve brothers and sisters.

Alexander's mouth curved. Holt was in for a big surprise.

Oz and Niko fell in beside Giselle, and Holt followed. Alexander and Valery walked behind.

Valery glanced around, searching the gathering. "Where's your Max?"

The expression on his face must have said enough.

"Oh, no . . ." Her hand clenched on his. "Alexander—"

"She is not dead," he said, his throat knotting. Not yet, and never if he could help it. "She is not dead," he repeated.

He had not taken two steps when a scream ripped through the hall. He leaped forward, just in time to see Oz catch Giselle as she collapsed. Her face had gone white as glue, and she clenched into a fetal ball.

"What's wrong?" Oz demanded.

"What's happening?" Niko captured her face in his hands. "Giselle!"

Valery pushed in. "Let me."

Lise pushed the smoke witch out of the way. "Not so fast, bitch."

Holt whirled on Lise, his hex marks glowing lividly. "I'll kill you for touching her," he snarled.

Valery steadied herself and punched Holt in the arm with all her strength. "Shut up. I can take care of myself." She looked at Lise, Oz, and Niko. "I am a healer. I may be able to help her."

"Fuck that," Lise said. "I don't know you, and we have our own damned healer. Judith! Where are you?"

The witch wormed through the cluster surrounding Giselle. Oz lowered her to the floor, holding her against his chest as she convulsed.

Judith knelt and pressed one hand against Giselle's forehead, the other to her chest. Her hands glowed, and magic sank into Giselle, lighting her pallid skin with a golden glow. After a moment, Judith pulled her hands away and stood, her face grim.

"It's backlash. There's nothing I can do. All she can do is endure it and hope her heart doesn't stop."

"Who?" Lise demanded. "Who did we lose?

Backlash referred to a returning blast of magic when a Shadowblade or Sunspear was killed. It came from the severing of the binding that connected the witch with the warrior.

"Shit, shit, shit," Niko repeated without stopping, scraping his fingers through his hair and pacing back and forth. He dug in his pocket for his phone and hit the speed dial. Tyler answered. One by one, he called the rest of the Shadowblades. One by one, they all answered. There was only one he could not call.

"No," Alexander rasped. "No. It cannot be. The prophecy . . . It is not possible." But fear gripped his intestines in an iron grasp, and he wanted to throw up.

"She's gone. Oh, fucking Spirit, she's gone! I can't feel her. Max!" Giselle's wail echoed in the whispering silence of the hall.

Alexander could not breathe. He felt paralyzed, every single part of himself shattering. Suddenly, his Shadowblade Prime roared to life. His vision swam red, and his mind collapsed beneath the maddened frenzy of the feral beast inside.

He wanted to kill. The small scrap of Alexander that still clung to sanity told him to bolt. Run before he slaughtered everyone in the room.

He bulled through bodies blocking the door, beating at them when they tried to stop him. Flesh gave, and bone cracked. Heat seared his back like a brand straight out of the cauldron of the sun. He ignored it. A second later, he was through the door and running.

He burst out of the mountain into the night and kept going. Branches whipped his skin, and he felt a distant agony from the wound on his back. Up and down ridges, leaping and lunging, he sped like the wind itself, barely touching the ground.

He ran through the perimeter ward, feeling the tingle ripple across his skin. He had no idea where he was going. It did not matter. He wanted to hunt. To kill. To prowl. To slake his grief in the hot, thick blood of his prey as its heart beat its last.

Deep within, the last bit of Alexander clenched around unbearable pain. Max was gone. His mate was gone.

Death was the only explanation.

Alexander dissolved into a crucible of loss.

Vicious joy sang in the beast's blood, free at last from the chains of the man. He was pure brutality, pure animal. He howled, and he ran, smelling prey in the night.

10

MAX WAS NOT NEARLY AS CERTAIN AS SCOOTER was that she could kill Ilanion. Or even give him a stubbed toe. Battling him was like having a fight with the bastard child of Tutresiel and Giselle. She wasn't going to beat him in a head-to-head battle. She was going to have to finesse him. With his ego, that shouldn't be all that difficult, as long as she didn't die first.

She circled around him, a sword in each hand. He readied another ball of magic. Max tensed. This was so going to hurt.

The ball struck her in the chest, and she flew backward, landing flat on her back, the swords clattering from her hands. The breath exploded from her lungs.

Max's hands and arms twitched as the magic engulfed her in a fiery cocoon, its power searing through her flesh. She didn't bother to fight it, letting it pour through her. It sizzled along every nerve. She gasped, letting out a desperate moan. It wasn't such a stretch. She felt like she'd been dropped into a nuclear reactor. Then an idea struck her. Almost as if she had practiced it from birth, she opened the door into the abyss and let the magic drain away into it. It was no more difficult than putting away pain.

Her relief was instant. *Holy mother of night.* She'd have to remember that trick.

She drew sobbing breaths and made some whimpering kitten sounds that she hoped sounded like she was teetering on the brink of death. Ilanion paced nearer, his armor clanking softly.

"It appears your faith in your pet was misplaced," he said arrogantly to Scooter. "She's hardly worth bothering with."

"It's a possibility," came the noncommittal answer.

Max barely stopped her smile. Scooter wasn't fooled. He knew she didn't die that easy.

Ilanion leaned over her. She flicked a frightened glance at him, keeping her eyes wide and staring—the international sign for paralyzed with helplessness. He totally bought it. He smiled arrogantly and did a stupid thing. He assumed that Max was done for and looked away to Scooter. *Dumb shit.* No matter how powerful someone was, more often than not, his Achilles' heel was his vanity.

She didn't let him gloat. She wasn't the idiot in this equation. She snatched his throat. In one lunging move, she scissored his legs out from under him and shoved him onto his back. She landed on his chest, pinning his arms and outstretched wings with her knees. She dug her fingers into the flesh of his throat and clamped down to rip it out.

"Don't kill him," Scooter said. He sounded faded, like he could barely muster the strength to speak.

"Why not?"

"He can be useful."

"If I let him go, he'll barbecue us both."

"True."

Max heaved an annoyed sigh and pulled the dagger from her waistband. It had miraculously not fallen out in the scuffle. The metal was hot, no doubt cooked by Ilanion's magic. She shoved the point against his neck. He winced as blood flowed.

"I only have to shove another inch, and your carotid is cut through," she told him. "You'll not live long enough to kill me. So play nice."

With that, she loosened her grip on his throat. He coughed and dragged in a harsh breath. Both actions made the blade bite deeper.

"I wouldn't do that if I were you," she said helpfully.

His eyes narrowed at her, and he smiled, his teeth brilliant white against his tanned skin and the gold of his mask. "You're a jewel. What children we could have."

"Dream on, buddy," Max said, unable to resist grinning back at him. "You couldn't handle me."

"But it would be delicious to try," he said.

"Why is it men always have sex on the brain?" she asked. "You'd think you'd be worried about dying right now."

"Nayan doesn't want to kill me at the moment," he pointed out.

It took Max a second to understand that Nayan was Scooter. "Nayan? Is that your real name?" she asked him, never taking her eyes off Ilanion.

"It is one of my names. But then, so is Scooter."

Max grimaced. It was like talking to a used-car salesman. Nothing was ever the exact truth. "Fine. It doesn't matter. You'll always be Scooter to me. But can we get on with this? We don't have a lot of time, and you're about to fall over."

"You have a choice to make, Ilanion. Max can kill you, or you can help me take back what's mine."

"Help you? What do I gain?"

"Your life, for one," Max pointed out.

He ignored her. "Helping you will win me significant enemies. My life won't be worth much. Again, I ask, what do I gain?"

"I'll be your friend. Your ally."

"If you get your missing pieces back."

"Not if. When," Max corrected. "He's getting everything back that was stolen from him."

The point of her knife dug harder into Ilanion's neck. He looked at her. "You have no idea what you're up against. You have hidden depths, but I doubt it will be enough to beat the odds."

"With your help, we stand a better chance," Scooter said.

"True. But that still doesn't give me a reason to help you. If you don't succeed, I will lose a great deal. The Korvad will turn on me, and if I survive, I will have nothing."

"The Korvad?" Max repeated.

"The ones who took Nayan's heart, silk, and horn. The ones who own the city."

"They don't own it. No one owns it," Scooter said.

"Might makes right, and they have all the might they need," Ilanion said caustically. "Things have changed a lot since you left."

"Then it's time they changed back."

"Which still brings us back around to the question at hand. Why should I help you? What can you offer besides the threat of death? I have a snug territory inside the Torchmarch, and the Korvad leaves me mostly alone."

"You didn't strike me as the keep-your-head-down-to-save-your-ass kind of a guy," Max said. "I thought you had bigger balls than that."

"Spoken by one who's never met the Korvad or lived in Chadaré," Ilanion returned, his mouth twisting.

"I have little to offer," Scooter said. "Except the harvest of what's left of me, should I fail. That is worth a great deal."

"I am no butcher," Ilanion spat, earning him some respect from Max.

"Then our negotiations must be at an end. I have nothing else of value to offer," Scooter said in a voice devoid of any emotion.

"So I can kill him now?" Max asked.

Scooter let go a slow breath. "It would be safer for us," he said reluctantly.

"I can promise not to pursue you," Ilanion countered. "Or help your enemies. That much I can do."

"You think that's worth your skin?" Max asked.

"It means that if you kill me, you do so for no reason. I'm not a threat. Besides, time isn't your friend."

Just then, she became aware of the baying of the gargoyles. They sounded too damned close.

"I can turn them away from your trail," Ilanion said.

"They belong to you?"

"They listen to me."

"I don't think he wants to die today," Max said to Scooter.

"Neither do we. Make your promise, and we will be on our way," he told Ilanion.

"Let me up. I'll make my promise on my feet," the winged man demanded.

"Before or after you cook us?" But Max released him. She retrieved her two swords as he stood, his armor clanking.

He stared at her a moment. "Most would have kept the dagger in my throat until the promise was made."

She shrugged. He was right. But she had too much experience being compelled into something she didn't want. It went hard against the grain to wish that on someone else. "A forced promise isn't worth much in my book."

"Magically, it makes no difference. Coerced or not, I'd have had to stand by it. Now I could simply fly away or boil you in magic."

"You could. Will you?" Maybe she should have been worried, but she wasn't. He'd been too honest about where he stood with helping them.

The corner of his mouth lifted in a half-smile, and he shook his head. "No." He reached up and took off his helm. His hair was gold-streaked chestnut cropped close to his head. His cheeks were wide and sharply cut, his brown eyes almond-shaped, with long lashes and bold, expressive eyebrows. Max expected him to have a beak for a nose, but instead, it was large, straight, and blunt. More like the wedge of an ax. Blood continued to run from his neck wound. He seemed unconscious of it. He bowed to her, his wings flaring.

"My lady Max. It is a quite a pleasure to make your acquaintance."

Her brows rose as he straightened. *Seriously?* But he seemed completely genuine. "I'm sure having me poke you in the throat was seriously special, and you trying to cook me was just beyond all kinds of fun, but can we get on with this? Your pets are getting awfully close, and we need to be gone before anyone sees us." She glanced up as a flicker caught her eye. "Too late."

Something dark glided through the shadows. Max squinted but couldn't make out what it was. The thick shadows of the city were impenetrable, even to her Shadowblade eyes. Whatever it was, chances were, it wasn't friendly. They were out of time.

"We should get going," she said, reaching for Scooter. She swung him up in her arms. "Coming or staying?" she asked Ilanion.

He scowled, yellow sparks flickering in his eyes. Max's lip curled. He was too damned witchy for comfort. He jammed his helm onto his head and strode toward his two companions. "I am going to regret this," he grated, and then swept them into an iron grip. His wings beat the air with powerful sweeps that sent dust and debris scudding across the cobbles.

They rose off the ground and flew down the street like an arrow. Ilanion's speed and strength were stunning. Almost like Tutresiel or Xaphan. He turned on his wing at a right angle and then again. Scooter moaned as they jolted. Max firmed her grip, but there was no way to comfort him or make him feel better. It was all she could do to hold on to him and keep the two swords pointed down away from Ilanion. The points of his gauntlet talons cut into her flesh.

They swept more turns, staying low between buildings so they couldn't be seen across the rooftops. Max looked back. A shadowy shape followed them, a streak of charcoal sliding through the air behind them.

"We're being followed," she said to Ilanion.

"I am aware," he said, never slowing.

"What is it?"

"A minion of Kratos."

"Who's that?"

"A bad guy. One of the Korvad."

He dropped suddenly and skimmed close to the ground, gliding into a long tunnel that led beneath a sprawling compound of boxy gray stone buildings that looked like warehouses. Ilanion dropped to the ground inside the broad tunnel, releasing Max and Scooter. She set the latter on his feet, keeping her arm around him to steady him.

He leaned heavily against her, his body shaking beneath the sheltering layers of his robe. It was such a change from the all-powerful being she'd met just weeks ago and totally different from the bastard who'd tossed her against the cliff over and over just to make her learn how to get into the abyss. How much time did he have left? They'd been bleeding him for thousands of years. How long until he was dead? And why in the hell had he waited so long to come back and fight? Why had he waited all this time to find Max?

There was no time to ask or get the answers. From the looks of it, Scooter had maybe days, if not hours.

Max eyed their surroundings. It was as much a trap as it was a hiding place. The only visible ways in and out were the tunnel mouths, and those could be easily blocked. On the other hand, it was going to take a little while until anyone found out where they'd gone to ground. Except for that damned shadow creature. It had been following close. Even if it hadn't seen Ilanion drop into the tunnel, it would have a pretty decent idea where to narrow the search.

"I thought you weren't going to help us," she said.

"I was wrong," Ilanion said abruptly, and rubbed a hand across his mouth as he thought. "We haven't much time. Kratos will be coming."

"Got a plan?"

He shook his head. "I'm equal enough to Kratos, but the Korvad will destroy me. They want Nayan a great deal."

"Shouldn't *you* want him?" Max asked, an insane idea percolating in her mind. "I mean, he's valuable, if for nothing more than to sell to the Korvad. Am I right?"

Ilanion's wings flared as he thrust his shoulders back. His jaw jutted, his eyes turning to liquid gold. "I don't deal in butchery," he said in a cold, guttural voice. Magic flickered across his skin and wings as his entire body tightened.

Max waved away his protest. "Yeah, but you *might*, right? No one in their right mind would hesitate to take such a prize as Scooter. At least, my bet is that's what the Korvad thinks."

Beside her, the being in question nodded. "That's true." His voice was whispery and thin.

"I wouldn't!" Ilanion's anger was quickly firing into rage. His lip curled. "I should kill you where you stand."

"Oh, shut up," Max said, frowning. Everything hinged on her. On whether she could pull them all into the abyss and back out. Hell, she could hardly manage herself.

Now she wanted to take the golden boy and Scooter, too? She was insane. Not that she had any other choice. So she'd do it. She looked back at the bristling Ilanion.

"Hear me out. What I need is some time to retrieve Scooter's heart, silk, and horn. The only way I can do that is if he's somewhere safe and I can get around without someone crawling up my ass every minute. The best way is if you take us prisoner. You can set up some kind of auction or whatever. They'll see it as a play for power and money. That should give me time to do what I need to do. That is, if you really want to help us. You can walk away now, no harm, no foul."

"Except that the Korvad will shortly know I had my hands on you both, if they don't know already." Ilanion's eyes narrowed, and he folded his arms over his chest. "I can't walk away. They won't believe you escaped."

Max shrugged. "I can rough you up. I promise to make it look good. They'll never suspect a thing." She smiled wolfishly and rubbed her hands together.

He smiled unwillingly. "Thanks," he said dryly. "Suppose I agree? They won't let me take you back to my compound. They'll have it blockaded within the hour."

"Not a problem." She hoped. "All you have to do is agree or not."

He frowned, his attention moving to Scooter. "Nayan, what's going on?"

"I told you, Max is unique."

The answer clearly didn't make Ilanion happy. But he wasn't getting anything more.

"So? What's it going to be?" Max prodded.

He looked her up and down like he was hoping to develop X-ray vision. Finally, his mouth pursed as if he'd eaten a live scorpion, and he nodded. "Very well. What do you require from me?"

It took Max a second to understand what he meant. "Just don't actually try to take us prisoner when we get there," she said. "I don't want to have to kill you, but I will if you turn on us."

"You can try," he said. "I won't make the same mistake again. However, the issue won't come up. You have my word."

It wasn't binding, like a promise, but giving his word still had tangible power.

"Good. Then let's get out of here before we can't."

Max reluctantly dropped her swords on the ground. It was going to take everything she had to bring Scooter and Ilanion into the abyss. She didn't need extra baggage. She looked at the eagle man. "How attached are you to your armor?"

He frowned confusion. "What?"

She shook her head. "Never mind. But if we get there naked, it isn't because I want to see you in all your glory."

"How do I find a place to land?" she asked Scooter, realizing suddenly the flaw in her plan. She had no idea where she was going beyond Ilanion's compound, which sounded like a military installation.

"Just pick a place and want to go there. Try to narrow the choice," he told her weakly.

"That's all? So, like, just pick the kitchen, and that's where we'll end up?"

"Too many knives," he said with a ghost of a smile. "Pick a soft landing."

"Like a bed?"

Scooter nodded.

"What are you talking about?" Ilanion demanded.

"Saving our asses. Now, shut up."

She reached out and grabbed each man's hand. She snorted inwardly. *Men. As if.* Scooter was a god or a demigod, and Ilanion was no doubt the same. She wondered if they'd met at godlet preschool. Or maybe godlet Boy Scouts or Little League.

She pulled her mind away before she broke out into hysterical giggles and wove her fingers together with theirs.

She closed her eyes and sank into the awareness of every cell of her body. The wonder of it still amazed her. But it wasn't enough. She pushed out, trying to sense her two companions. It was different from her sense of her clothing. That was more simple. These were whole bodies, plus clothing. She wondered what would happen if she missed parts of them. What a jigsaw mess that would be. A liver missing here, a spleen there, a couple of arms and one eye, maybe a few toes and fingers . . .

Drawing a deep breath, Max concentrated. She pushed her awareness into the men. They were nothing like her. They felt entirely alien. Still, there was a cohesion to them, a sense of themselves. She traced the edges of their bodies and went deeper, finding where their blood pulsed. She paused as she found a twisting of putrid magic where Scooter's heart should have been. It felt swollen and hot, like a tangle of molten metal. She could feel its wrongness—it was rotten and festering, like a disease. She found the same on his head—a gaping hole filled with blinding heat and decay. It threaded through his body in a filigree of carrion and corruption. No wonder he was dying. He was rotting from the inside out.

Ilanion was different. He was filled with sunlight, and it did not burn. Gold ran through his veins and sheathed his wings. Internally, he had two hearts and a huge pair of lungs. The rest of him was enough like a human to make getting a sense of him easier. Max already felt tired. She chewed her lower lip, pushing once again to take in Ilanion's armor and Scooter's robe. She might as well go for broke.

She didn't give them any warning as she dropped down into her fortress. She plummeted, holding them tight in the net of her awareness.

She'd thought that going through the first time was bad. This was infinitely worse. Now, instead of pulling herself through the eye of a needle, she was pulling all three of them. And somehow both men seemed to have swelled up. They were the size of barns.

Max felt her hold on them slipping. Not in this lifetime. She set herself, planting herself solidly inside the fortress. She concentrated, holding on to them with all her might.

Strength flowed up her legs, accompanied by the searing chill of the abyss. She grasped it and hauled as hard as she knew how. Nothing happened. She gritted her teeth and dug deeper. Every muscle strained. Capillaries popped and healed. Bones snapped and knitted back together. Muscles tore, and tendons ripped. Max didn't let up. She'd get them through or die trying.

Stubbornness won the battle at last. The world split in half, and they plunged through her fortress into the blackness of the abyss.

She sighed with relief as pain ebbed. Scooter floated beside her in his robe. He looked terrible. Worse than the first time they'd come through the abyss. His blue-flecked obsidian eyes were dull, like scratched marbles. He was skeletal, his hair lank, the gold running through his scales and hair a tarnished gray. He nodded at her as if to say *well done*. She scowled.

On the other side of her, Ilanion didn't look any different, except that his armor and wings gleamed with an inner light, and his eyes had once again turned to liquid gold. He was staring at her in total shock.

She gave him a cocky grin, then dove back down into her fortress, all the while thinking of Ilanion's bed.

The first time, pulling them through had been like giving birth to a killer whale. The second time was much worse. It felt like she was being passed through a meat grinder. Or rather, like she was stuck inside it, getting chewed up over and over and over.

Still, Max held on to her companions tenaciously. If she let go, they'd be lost in the abyss.

She put all her strength into pushing back through her fortress. It seemed to take forever. Then, suddenly, they were falling. A moment later, they bounced onto a bed. Except that it was more like a cloud of feather pillows. Max sank face-first, swallowed up in a soft, cloying fist. The bed smelled of Ilanion, sex, perfume, and sweat.

She rolled onto her back and kicked her way out of the sprawling mass of comfort, bashing her head into one of Ilanion's wings as she did.

She slid off onto the floor. The bed was set on a broad, low platform in the middle of an enormous room with a coffered ceiling, deeply piled rugs, backless couches and chairs, a fireplace that could fit a moose inside, paneled walls with brightly colored paintings, and elegant decorations. Crystal chandeliers sent prisms of light dancing through the room.

It was about all Max managed to notice before exhaustion and pain swamped her. She swayed and felt herself melting to the floor in a liquid heap. Her head spun, and she couldn't focus on anything. Her body throbbed and flared with pain. She was broken, and she was out of fuel to heal herself.

"What's the matter with her?" Ilanion said.

"She is new to traveling the abyss. She used all her strength." Scooter sounded impossibly weary. "She needs healing and sustenance. Or she will die."

Max told herself to prove him wrong. *Move! Sit up and get on with the job!* But her body refused to answer. It felt like climbing up Mount Everest just to keep her heart beating and her blood flowing. It wasn't until that moment that she really believed she might be on the verge of dying. *Shit.*

A spurt of energy flooded her spirit. Not today. She *was not* dying today. She had too much to do, and she needed to get home and let Niko and Tyler berate her for vanishing and apologize to Alexander for being such a wimp about loving him. *Loving him? Crap.* But it was true. Apparently, imminent death had brought on a moment of clarity.

Her determination meant nothing to her body. She had used up everything. There was nothing left.

"She's bound somewhere," Ilanion said, and she felt one of his fingers glide across her forehead and down the bridge of her nose, as if it were following a trail of magic.

"To a witch."

"I thought she was yours."

"She was given to me."

"She can't be yours if she's bound to a witch."

Max could hear the disdainful curl of his lip when he said *witch*. Like he wasn't one. She wanted to point that out, but her mouth was frozen rubber.

Her heart slowed. She felt thin—wasted and transparent. She needed calories. A lot of them, all mainlined directly into an artery. If it wasn't too late.

She took a breath. Half a breath. Her lungs refused to expand. Her thoughts felt fuzzy, like someone was pulling apart the threads of her mind. Ilanion and Scooter sounded far away and blurry, as if they were under water. Or she was.

"Can you help her?" Scooter asked Ilanion.

"Possibly."

"You might want to hurry. She's fading."

Fading was the right word. Max didn't feel any pain anymore. She felt like a deflated balloon. The pain eased as she lost feeling. It was like she was evaporating.

A jolt of magic flashed through her. She felt herself flop and puddle back into herself. Blackness charred the edges of her mind.

Another jolt.

Fading.

The last thing Max felt was a distant snapping. Like fishbones and icicles. Then there was release and velvet blackness.

11

THEY CAME WITHOUT STEALTH, AND THAT SAVED their lives. Had they been hunting, he would have ripped their throats out.

He had exhausted himself. He sprawled on a shelf of stone above a small valley. Behind him, a cave wormed deep into the rock. He would have safety from the sun, if he wanted it. He could easily defend the entrance against a horde of enemies, or he could escape across the cliff face or leap to the valley floor. He would break bones, but he would heal. He had energy to burn.

He had killed things and eaten them. Blood smeared his chest, arms, and face. His shirt lay in bloody ribbons on the ground behind him. Fifty feet below, Beyul sat panting, his green eyes glowing softly as he watched him.

Alexander growled low from deep in his belly when the three Blades jogged over the opposite ridge and descended into the valley. Knowledge rose in his mind: Niko, Thor, Tyler. The names meant nothing to him, nor did the men. Before he could react to their appearance, a scent hooked his attention, and he looked up. The air whistled across metal wings. Tutresiel dropped out of the sky like an eagle.

Alexander sprang to a crouch, his body clenching tight. He bared his teeth and growled again. A warning.

The angel landed opposite. In his arms, he held a woman, dark-haired and slender. Valery. The silver wings curved forward around her, the feathers a shining fence of deadly knives. She started to pull out of his grip, but Tutresiel held her still.

"No," he said, his red gaze fixed on Alexander. "Stay here. See his eyes? He's gone totally feral. He's been teetering on the edge since Max was taken. His Prime is in total control, and the man is . . . far away. Just now, he's likely to kill you, no matter what you mean to him. I don't think you can bring him back to sanity."

"The hell with that," she said, struggling.

Alexander watched her shoving at Tutresiel's unrelenting arm, a snarling part of him wanting to leap to her aid, another part coldly curious.

She went still and focused on him. "Alexander," she said quietly. "You have to pull yourself together and come back."

He only stared at her, his lips curling back from his teeth in an expression of total contempt. *Never*.

"You'll have to do better than that," Tutresiel observed. "He's deep in the pit and still falling."

"Don't you think I know that?" Valery snapped. She elbowed the angel with no effect at all. "Alexander. This isn't you. Max wouldn't like you going all Cujo. She'd want you to come back to Horngate."

Words churned deep inside. They rose onto his tongue, ripping at his insides. They felt strange, as if he'd forgotten how to speak. "Max is dead." The words sent a jolt of shuddering pain through his body. He curled his fingers into claws as a red film clouded his vision.

"How do you know?" Tutresiel demanded. "She's broken witch bindings before. Have you no faith?" He shook his head, his eyes narrowing to slits. "You're a disgusting excuse for a Shadowblade. You don't deserve her."

Rage roared through Alexander, and he leaped at the angel. Tutresiel dodged aside, his wings pumping powerfully as he lifted himself and Valery into the air.

"Is it a fight you want? Then come get me."

Tutresiel dropped to the valley floor and shoved Valery toward Niko. He stood with his legs braced, his arms crossed, his wings spread as he looked up at Alexander.

Without thinking, Alexander launched himself off the stone shelf. He had hated the angel since their first meeting. He landed and lunged at Tutresiel. The angel folded his wings, a deadly smile spreading across his beautiful face. Alexander had fought Tutresiel twice before and knew what he was capable of. The angel could not be killed, but he could be made to hurt. Alexander meant to make him scream.

He charged like a bull. Tutresiel set himself, his smile turning arrogant. *Cocky bastard*. But Alexander was not stupid. Just before he would have crashed against the angel, he swerved. The angel stepped aside to dodge his rush, and Alexander drove his shoulder into his stomach. Tutresiel toppled back, caught in midstride.

Alexander's momentum made him sprawl past. Instantly, he was on his feet, but Tutresiel was, too. They circled each other.

"Alexander, stop this! You have to think!" Valery shouted. "He'll kill you. He's an *angel*."

He ignored her, his attention entirely focused on Tutresiel.

Thor's voice joined Valery's. "Son, you've got a Fury rising at Horngate. This ain't a time to let your brain go to mush." His slow drawl was tense.

"Max wouldn't want this," Tyler said, his voice thick with grief.

Suddenly, something struck Alexander from behind. He dropped to a knee as debilitating pain exploded in his gut. Niko kicked his leg out from under him and booted him in the chest—once, twice, three times. Bones cracked loudly. Alexander coughed, blood spraying from his lips.

Niko straddled Alexander, pinning the fallen man's arms under his knees, and jabbed a knife into his throat. A warm stream of blood ran down Alexander's neck. "Hold still, you motherfucker," Niko ordered between gritted teeth. "None of that telekinesis shit you use, either. I'll cut your head off before you can kill me. Be sure of it.

"Now, I want you to listen real good, because the sun is coming, and we don't have time to fuck around with you anymore. *Max. Isn't. Dead*. Got it?" The knife prodded deeper. "You've got that damned prophecy telling you she's not. But even if she was, we'd hunt her down in hell or wherever Scooter took her, and we'd drag her ass back. So you can stop with all this bullshit and get back to the work she left for you, which is being Prime of Horngate. Either that, or I'll let Tutresiel kill you. Trust me, he'll enjoy it."

Before Alexander could answer, a hulking shadow blocked his vision. Beyul snapped his jaws shut on Niko's knife hand. The Grim dragged him away as if he were wadded-up newspaper. Oddly, Niko didn't fight. He sagged, his face going gray. Beyul growled and shook his hand back and forth.

Niko toppled over onto his stomach, his eyes sprung wide. A gravelly gasp rattled slowly from his throat.

"Let him go," Alexander ordered. The words felt unfamiliar, and it was difficult to move his tongue and lips to form them. Beyul snarled at him around Niko's hand, the Grim's green eyes flaring brightly.

"He is *mine,*" Alexander said, leaping to his feet and baring his teeth back. "Let him go." His Prime had not receded, and his vision blurred as the predator clamped down on him. This time he did not give in.

Beyul eyed him for a long moment, then let go, dropping Niko's hand and sitting down, panting, looking like an ordinary dog.

Alexander reached down and turned Niko onto his back. The other Blade wasn't breathing. *No.*

"Val, can you help him?"

She dropped to her knees on the other side of Niko. She glared at Alexander, her expression taut, tears shining on her cheeks. "Don't go running out on me like that again. I couldn't take losing you."

The furious accusation in her voice made Alexander wince. "I will not," he said, his cheeks flushing as he dropped his gaze. Even so, he was still fighting for control with every bit of strength he had.

"Better not," she muttered, and then turned her attention to Niko. Her head tipped to the side, her eyes closing as she extended her hands flat above him. Silvery smoke wreathed around her arms and ribboned around his body. "Shit."

"What?"

"His soul has slipped out of his body."

"It what?"

"Whatever anchors his spirit to his flesh has been broken. He's going to die."

Alexander's body clenched, the feral part of him clawing up inside him. He fought it down. "Can you bring him back?"

"No, but you can. If he hasn't drifted off, he'll have to answer to your Prime."

"What do I do?"

"Cut him. You need blood contact. Then tell him to get his shit together and get back into his body."

Alexander reached for his knife, but it was gone. He had no idea when or where he had lost it.

"Here." Thor handed him one.

"Can we do anything?" Tyler asked, his voice emotionless. He had gone as cold as the black ocean depths.

"Pray, if you have gods that will listen," Valery said in a dreamy voice. The silvery smoke had taken on a tinge of green and brown. It curled around Niko's body and burrowed inside him.

Alexander grabbed the prone man's hand—the same one Beyul had been chewing on. The skin was doughy and white, with a dozen or more puncture wounds. They were bloodless, as if they'd been sucked dry. He glanced at the Grim. Beyul's tongue lolled from his mouth. It looked like he was grinning. "You could help," he told the Grim in a hard voice. Beyul closed his mouth, his green eyes flaring brightly, then he shook himself and lay down, propping his muzzle on his forelegs. *Bastard.*

Since he doubted that there was blood to be had in that arm, Alexander jammed the blade straight into the lower part of Niko's thigh, sawing back and forth until he found an artery. But instead of a bright red spray, the blood oozed out in a thick syrup. *Good enough.*

He had no idea what he was supposed to do, but Valery was too caught up in healing to answer questions. *So improvise.* He pushed his fingers into the wound, splaying them wide to keep the wound from healing before he got Niko back. Thick blood coated his hand. *Now what?*

"The dawn is coming, Niko. Time to get back into your body." He muttered the words, as if speaking to himself. Nothing happened. He looked up and then around at Tutresiel, Thor, Tyler, and Valery. His brow furrowed. "Get your ass back into your body, *now,* Niko!" The shouted words echoed from the valley walls.

He gouged his fingers deeper into the wound, as if he could force Niko's spirit to obey.

"Blood is all you need," Val whispered. "Be Prime."

Suddenly, Alexander understood. His hand clenched, and he pulled it free from Niko's flesh. His skin went cold. The risk was high. He'd almost lost himself entirely to his Prime when he'd heard about Max's death—

He sucked a harsh breath, and his mind veered away from thinking about the probability of it. He had to believe in her. If he let himself slide back over the line into feral madness, he would be lost forever. It was unheard of to come back even once; he would not bet on twice.

And yet—

To bring Niko back, Alexander had to give himself to the Prime inside him. He had to unleash the beast's power. He had no choice. It was his fault Beyul had attacked and it was his responsibility to keep Niko safe.

He looked at Tutresiel. The angel was the only one who could terminate him if he went rabid. He could not be allowed to roam free, killing. "You will do it if I go too far again?"

Tutresiel needed no explanation. He reached his hand out into the darkness, and a sword flashed into his hand. Its long length shone with brilliant white witchlight. "I'll be more than happy to help out," he said, flourishing the blade.

"I knew you would."

With that, Alexander let go of his humanity once again. It sloughed away like a shed skin. His Prime flexed, his senses spreading out. He searched the group around him. Not threats. No. His. *His to protect, his to punish*. His lips curled at the angel, his head dropping as he tensed. He growled softly.

"Remember Niko," Tyler urged hoarsely.

Alexander's head jerked around. The other Blade was rigid, his muscles twitching as he held himself still. He kept his eyes averted, unthreatening.

Niko's body was sheathed in a blanket of woven mist. A sheen of sweat gleamed on Valery's forehead. The caustic-sweet scent of Divine magic filled the air, along with his own sweat, blood, and the smells of the mountain.

There were no sounds except for their breathing. Every other creature had run or burrowed deep down where he could no longer hear their hearts beating or their wings flicking. He could feel the sun coming, like a fiery tide. It was only an hour away, if that.

"Hurry the fuck up before we lose him!" Tyler took a jerking step forward, his face twisting with unfamiliar fear. He had lost Max; he did not want to lose a brother.

Thor caught Tyler's arm and held him back as Alexander rose to his feet with a fluid, animal grace. He pushed outward, straining his senses, reaching out further than he ever had. Everything inside him bent toward retrieving Niko. The bastard was not going to get away that easily. Alexander was done losing.

He could feel Niko's spirit like a thickening in the air. There was a distinctive flavor to him: week-old coffee grounds, chocolate, and starshine.

"Niko, return to your body," Alexander ordered with all the power of his Prime. The spirit twitched and trembled, but nothing. He knew Niko was not unwilling, but the Blade needed something more. Alexander clenched his teeth, his jaw muscles knotting. He had to do more.

He had unleashed his Prime, but he had not given himself to the beast. It was not enough. He had to cut the last ties to his humanity. He might never come back. Even going feral, he had on some level remembered himself, his name, and who he was.

Now—

He did not think as he let go of the last of his humanity and fully embraced the Shadowblade.

The Prime glared around at those surrounding him.

Their bodies were ghostlike, overlaying cores of rainbow color. He sniffed, recognizing each one. His, his, his—

The angel was silver fire. No ghost, no rainbow. Heat rolled off him and around the Prime. He snarled, and the silver fire laughed low but said nothing. He held a long spike of power. It shone with fierce light, but inside was a core of black so hard and so cold that it felt like soulless death.

The Prime's attention shifted to the other one. A Grim. He could barely see it. Its color and shape were like clear water rushing in an ancient river. Despite the vast hum of the creature's power, he felt no threat from it. No threat from any of them.

A flicker caught his attention. His head jerked up. A cancerous gray blob boiled in the air. He wrinkled his nose, his lips pulling from his teeth. Rot. Sickness.

He growled deep in his belly and paced toward it. He was aware of everything. The brush of the wind, the smell of the rock and pines, the beating hearts of his companions, the billowing currents of power across a landscape of the spirit.

His attention honed in on the drifting spirit. It was being pulled away. The Prime felt it fight the dragging demand. Fury swelled inside him.

His.

He leaped. His body arced through the air, and he hooked clawed fingers in the gray. They caught. The spirit wrapped around him. Acid seared his flesh and bubbled his skin. He dropped to the ground, landing on his hands and somersaulting before coming to his feet.

Pain soaked through his flesh like water on parched sand. He snatched the gray spirit before it could flitter away. He balled it in his hands like moth-eaten silk, his skin blackening and dripping away in greasy blobs.

He clenched his hands, crushing the spirit. He felt its essence—anger, pain, fear, and, underneath all of that, a deep and unwilling trust.

The last shocked him and sent odd warmth down into his soul. Roots. He did not know why. The spirit was his. Of course, it would trust him. And yet . . . It felt remarkable. Strange and precious.

"Alexander!"

He wheeled around at the harsh shout. It came from the smoke witch on the ground. Divine magic poured out of her and wrapped a fading figure on the ground. She smelled of wind and freedom and the bones of the world. He had the urge to rub against her like a cat. She was safe.

"Put him back," she whispered.

He heard her heart pounding and smelled her sweat. It was sharp and bitter with adrenaline and exhaustion. He looked down at the gray spirit. His hands were entirely black now, and the gray had crept up over his forearms. He sensed its urgency and frustration.

He paced over to her and squatted down. Guided by knowledge he did not understand, he slammed the spirit ball down onto the mist-wreathed body. Pain exploded in his hands and jetted up his arms. He stayed that way, scowling down at the prone man. He was supposed to do more. He was certain. He had no idea what. He snarled silently.

"Tell him to stay," the smoke witch urged. She swayed back and forth with exhaustion, and he could smell copper-sweet blood. "You *have* to tell him to stay. He needs you to anchor him, or he's going to die. Hurry."

He reached for words. His mouth worked. Nothing came. It was as if he had never learned to speak. But he had once. He was sure.

"Hurry." The smoke witch gasped. Her voice had turned high and thin, like a trapped animal.

He hesitated. Urgency filled him with punishing force. He bent over. The gray spirit had unfurled and floated like a tattered sail above the body, pinned in place by the Prime's hands. The edges were curling like burned paper.

"Damn you! Fucking do something!" This from one whose colors swirled with fiery life. He was strong. Not a threat. Not now. Another wrestled him back. He was full of wild blue storm light.

The Prime turned back to the fallen one. Anger spiraled into a blistering tornado inside him. Impatiently, he grabbed the man's collar and pulled him up. He shook him. The man's head bobbled and flopped back and forth. The Prime sucked in a seething breath. Force would not do it. He had no words.

He felt his power ballooning with his frustrated fury. The fiery ghost and the storm-light ghost staggered back, both cowering to the ground. The angel stepped closer, raising his sword. The Prime snarled, and the Grim rose and went to sit between them. He stared up at the angel, who stopped dead in his tracks.

The Prime turned back to the spirit. He gripped the body behind the neck and began to shove the spirit into his slack mouth, even as the smoke witch fed more magic into the misty healing cocoon. It did not help. The spirit did not absorb into its home flesh.

The Prime wanted to howl. He gritted his teeth, refusing to be defeated. *His* to guard; *his* to punish; *his* to save. There was nothing more important. If he failed, he would not be forgiven. *She* would not forgive him.

In that moment, a shaft of pain thrust through him, marrying the Prime with the man. In that single moment, Alexander and the Prime knew each other. They burned in shared grief so deeply penetrating that for a moment, the world stopped turning, and there was nothing left but ash and despair. The pain was so vast it seemed as if they would shatter.

Alexander's head fell back, and his mouth opened in a silent howl that tore his throat with its brutal intensity.

And then time resumed, because one death does not end the world, not even Max's, and even in death, Alexander knew that there could be no escape from the hurt. All he could do was guard what was hers—what was now his.

"Niko," he said in a strangled voice. "Stay put." He put all the force of his Prime into those words. Power exploded from him, and Niko convulsed. His entire body shook and clenched. His hands and heels hammered the ground. His teeth clattered together, and his eyes rolled up into his head.

Alexander laid him down and stood. The ghostly sight had not vanished with the return of his sense of self. It continued to overlie the world. He blinked. It was going to take some getting used to. But as he watched, emerald color flowed into Niko.

The fallen man settled and stilled, except for deep, panting breaths. Valery withdrew her magic. Alexander helped her to her feet.

"Are you all right?" he asked.

"You could have been a little quicker," she said wearily as she dusted the dirt from her jeans. She glanced up at the sky. "Dawn's close." Her gaze settled back on him. She frowned. "You're different." She looked past him at Tutresiel, whose sword was still drawn. Beyul continued to watch him. "You can put that away."

The angel seemed to agree. The sword vanished like it had never been. It was enough for Beyul. The Grim made a wuffling sound and came over to sniff the supine man. He licked Niko's forehead with a broad swipe of his pink tongue. At the warm, wet touch, Niko's eyes flicked open.

"What happened?" he asked, sitting up. He pressed the palms of his hands to his head. "Feels like a freight train ran me over."

Thor and Tyler came forward, watching Alexander warily. Tyler reached out and helped Niko to his feet. The dark-haired man swayed and started to fall. His companions caught him.

"Shit. What's the matter with me?"

"Beyul decided I needed protecting," Alexander said. Words still felt strange in his mouth.

"You?" Niko said, spitting to clear his mouth of a bad taste. "Like you weren't going to kick my ass." His gaze narrowed. "You've changed."

Alexander snorted. That was an understatement. He stretched, feeling power roiling through him. He wondered what the change really meant.

"Your eyes," Thor said suddenly. "You've lost the feral look. But I can still feel the wildness inside you like a powder keg."

Alexander could hear the question the other man

didn't ask. All of them were wondering the same thing. Was he safe? Was he about to go off the deep end again? He wasn't. He and the Prime had become one in a way he had never imagined was possible. The wildness was harnessed.

"I will be fine," he said. He thought of Max and wondered if that would ever be true again.

"Yeah, right. Fine," Niko said. "I need a drink."

None of them could really get drunk. Their magically enhanced bodies processed the alcohol before it could have any effect. Still, it sounded like a good idea. "I would not turn one down," Alexander said.

"Then let's get back to Horngate before we fry," Tyler said.

Alexander looked at Tutresiel. "Can you take Niko and Valery?"

"I don't need the bastard to carry me," Niko protested.

"Maybe not, but he is going to, anyway," Alexander said. It was on the tip of his tongue to ask how far they had to travel back, but he caught himself. He closed his eyes, reaching out with his senses. The landscape rose around him like a ghostly terrain map. He felt the magic pulsing in the soil and stone, in the trees and foliage. He saw bright sparks of jeweled life and heard the deep thrum of ley magic deep underground.

He honed in on the weaving that was Horngate. It was beautifully wrought and strong, despite the attacks and losing the coven. Giselle truly was a powerful witch. His nostrils flared. He could almost smell the burning rage of the birthing Fury. Her magic boiled with hatred, betrayal, and rage. He could see the ward circle around her. It gleamed bright yellow, flickering beneath the onslaught of the magic it contained. It would collapse soon.

Alexander opened his eyes and shook himself. "We should hurry," he said. "We have a good fifty miles to run."

"Maybe you should stay the day in the cave you found," Valery suggested. "You have less than an hour."

"Then we should get started." Alexander flicked a look at Tyler and Thor. "You may stay if you are afraid."

With that, he broke into a ground-eating run. Soon he was flanked by the two men, and Beyul padded close behind. Alexander smiled as he lunged up a slope and leaped down the other side. It was a race against the dawn, but they would make it. And then—

No. He would not think about Max. He could not. He remembered Tutresiel's scathing words. *She's broken witch bindings before. Have you no faith?*

Faith was all he had left, and he clung to it with all his strength. He had no other choice.

12

Max was back in Ilanion's bed, and it didn't smell any better now than when she'd landed on it. She wrinkled her nose and sneezed, then fought her way out of the downy clutch of the pillows and thick comforters. She made it all the way to sitting up before being overtaken by an attack of coughing.

"Here." Ilanion held out a heavy purple goblet.

Max took it and gulped down the water. The coughing subsided. She sneezed again. The room stank of incense.

"You really need to open a window. This place reeks."

Ilanion chuckled, took the goblet, and set it on a table. "How do you feel?"

"Like I went through a wood chipper." She stretched and cracked her knuckles. Her hands were bony, and they shook. She fisted them. It wasn't until then that she realized she was wearing a silky nightgown that revealed more than it covered. She grimaced and pinched the fabric like it was a cockroach. "What's this?"

"Your clothing was in need of washing and mending.

You . . . reeked." He grinned maliciously at her, his eyes sparking yellow with laughter. "You were so filthy I took the liberty of bathing you." His grin widened, daring her to get angry.

"All by yourself? No maids? Wow. I didn't think someone like you could wipe your own ass without help," she said as she wriggled to the edge of the bed. "I hope you didn't break a nail or get dishpan hands or anything."

He laughed, a ringing sound that echoed in the enormous chamber. "I don't know what dishpan hands are, but it sounds dreadful. No, washing you was a pleasure, I assure you," he said with a smirk.

Max looked down at herself. She'd lost a lot of flesh in the last day or so. She looked a lot like a scarecrow on meth. "Then you have seriously bad taste, Goldilocks, because I look like roadkill."

She slid to her feet and staggered, grabbing for Ilanion when her legs started to give way. He caught her around the waist and helped her to a table where a variety of fruits, meats, cheeses, and breads waited for her. Max started bolting it down, shoving her mouth full with both hands. He sat opposite in a backless chair, his wings folded neatly as he watched her.

She cleared the platters and drank down a sweet, milky tea heavy with some spice she didn't recognize. It was slightly bitter and hot but tasty nonetheless. The food steadied her body, and she felt her healing spells kicking into high gear. She needed more. Ilanion read her look correctly. He went to the door and opened it and spoke to someone outside before returning.

"Supper will be sent in soon."

She nodded, and the hunger haze started clearing from her mind. "Where's Scooter?"

Ilanion sighed heavily. "He is resting. I've given him all the help I can, but I couldn't do much. He won't last much longer."

Max's face went cold, and her Prime jumped to the killing edge. Ilanion's wings flared in response. He'd removed his armor and was dressed in a pair of black pants that cuffed tightly around his ankles and was belted around his waist with a gold-embroidered belt. Over it he wore a soft blue shirt that hung open in the front and was laced in the back around his wings. His tanned chest and stomach were sprinkled with gold hair and rippled with muscle. He sat forward.

"It isn't just his health. I have sent word to the Korvad that I have him and will auction him to the highest bidder. I also made sure that other interested parties were notified. Maybe it will start a squabble and buy us some time. But the truth is that no one will risk opposing the Korvad. Their offer will come swiftly, and that will be that. After, there will be very little time before I must give him up or they attack. My defenses are strong, but they won't hold long against the strength of the united Korvad."

Max nodded, surprised that he would even suggest resisting. She figured he'd fold as soon as his ass was in the fire. "I should get his heart back first," she said. "That should buy him some time. Maybe give him some power back to help fight them off."

Ilanion shook his head, his mouth pulling flat. "No. He is very weak. He's quite likely to die if you return his parts piecemeal." He pounded a fist on the table, making the dishes jump. "In all honesty, there's an excellent chance he'll die if you return them all at once, but once they're fully reunited, he may have the magic to heal himself."

Max refused to consider the possibility that Scooter could die. He was just as stupidly stubborn as she was. And he had a lot of hate inside him for the bastards who'd looted his body parts. He wasn't going to give them the satisfaction. "You seem to care about him."

The eagle man tapped his fingers on the table. "We created the Torchmarch together. We have known each other a long time."

Not that they were friends, Max noted. She wondered just how much she could depend on Ilanion. Still, his anger at Scooter's condition seemed real enough. There wasn't much point in faking it. "How much time does he have?"

He shrugged. "If you get his heart back, that will at least keep them from bleeding him. But even so, he probably has a day or two at best."

Max cracked her knuckles and stood. "Then it's time to get to work. Where are my clothes?"

Ilanion eyed her from beneath sleepy lids. "Why are you helping him?"

"I made him a promise."

He shook his head. "There's more to it. You're too . . . passionate . . . for this to be just obligation." He leaned forward, his look shrewd. "Why?"

"Maybe I don't like bullies and slavers."

"Then you've come to the wrong place. And while I am sure that that is true, it is not the reason."

Max crossed her arms, staring back at him. "What if I told you it's none of your business?"

He smiled thinly. "I can wait. Nayan cannot."

She scowled and shook her head. "He's one of mine," she said reluctantly, knowing how completely stupid that sounded. Still, it was the truth. Scooter belonged to her as much as any of her Blades. She was responsible for him. At least, until he got his strength back, and even then—

Ilanion burst out laughing at her words and then quieted when she did not share his amusement.

"You're serious? But you're—Nayan is—" He threw up his hands in disbelief. "Are you lovers?" As if that were the only rational explanation.

Now she smiled. "No, Goldilocks. Not in this lifetime, anyhow." She sobered. "Time's wasting. Where are my clothes?"

"I'll send for them. But you must eat. You no longer have to worry about fueling the binding spells tying you to the witch, but even so, you were tremendously weakened. You'll never succeed in this condition."

Max stared at him. *No longer have to worry about fueling the binding spells tying you to the witch.* The words thundered in her mind. She searched for the invisible tie connecting her to Giselle and Horngate. It was gone.

Emotion broke over her in a torrent. Triumph. Relief. Horror. Desperation.

Loss.

A moan wormed its way up from her stomach and escaped before she could choke back the sound. She spun away from Ilanion and sucked in a deep breath.

"What's the matter? Surely you can't have *liked* being chained to a witch?" Ilanion asked.

"No, I hated it. I hated her." *And once upon a time, I*

loved her like a sister. Some of those feelings were still there. *Damn Giselle!*

"And yet you seem to be less than happy."

"It's complicated," Max grated, her throat swelled tight with tears she refused to let fall. "I've wanted to be free since the moment I was first bound."

"But?" he prodded when she stopped there.

Max shook her head, hunching her shoulders. "Horngate is my home. If I'm not Prime there, then what the fuck am I?"

Jagged laughter caught in her chest. For the first time, she really understood Alexander's situation. Giselle had never accepted him into Horngate, and he no longer belonged to his former witch, Selange. More than once, Max had told him to go out into the world and live his life. Now she had the same option. It sucked.

She turned to face Ilanion. "I appreciate you healing me and breaking the bindings. It's just . . . unexpected. I always thought I'd kill Giselle and free myself. Or die trying."

For the first time since she was made a Shadowblade, the thought of killing Giselle didn't invite the crushing pain of her compulsion spells. Now, *that* she could really get used to. She rolled her shoulders, loosening the tension in them. The corner of her mouth pulled up in a little smirk when she thought of the backlash that had to have hit Giselle. The witch-bitch had finally got a taste of her own pain. A moment later, Max's humor faded. She hoped it hadn't killed her.

Another thought struck her. Everyone would think she was dead. "Oh, crap," she said, sitting down on the edge of the bed and scraping her fingers across her scalp. "Son of a bitch."

"I take it something's wrong?"

"They're going to think I'm dead." What would Alexander do? Not to mention Tyler, Niko, and Oz. Giselle would soldier on. No question about that.

"You could leave—reassure them," Ilanion suggested.

She was more than a little tempted. She sighed and shook her head. "Traveling the abyss takes too much out of me. I need the strength I have left to help Scooter."

"Then come and sit," he said as someone knocked on the door and it opened. Servants brought in heavily laden trays and set them about. Max watched them in surprise. They looked like they were made of stone, and judging by the heavy thump of their hooves, feet, and claws, they probably were. They smelled of Uncanny magic, though with an underlying tang of something that Max didn't recognize. It was . . . electric and dark.

They looked at her and then away. Their eyes glowed like blue coals and were full of intelligence. They set their burdens down with surprising lightness before withdrawing. They all wore metal bands around wrists and ankles, the same kind she'd seen on many inhabitants of the city.

"Are they from Chadaré?" Max asked in a carefully neutral voice as she sat down.

"They were born here, though their people come from elsewhere."

"In captivity?"

"Yes."

"You keep slaves." Suddenly, Max was not at all hungry.

"Slaves?" He reached for a waxy yellow fruit and bit into it. "They are bound servants. I provide well for them, and they have freedom."

"Have freedom," Max repeated. "Like coming and going when they want? Like saying no when you tell them to do something?"

Ilanion finished the fruit and wiped his fingers on a napkin. "Of course not." He cocked his head, seeing her anger for the first time. "It is much like you were until I broke your binding. Clearly, you were not entirely unhappy serving your witch."

Since she'd just made a show of her very mixed feelings, Max didn't bother arguing the point. "It doesn't make it right."

"In Chadaré, might makes right. If you can't protect yourself or don't claim the protection of someone powerful, you are free for the taking. In this case, the Enay chose me. Centuries ago, they requested my protection. In exchange, they serve."

"Their whole lives."

"Some do. Some do not."

He didn't appear inclined to explain any more, and Max didn't push. Chadaré had its own rules, and she wasn't going to alienate Ilanion because she didn't happen to like them. She was going to save Scooter and then get the hell out.

She silently dug into the feast, bolting down the food without tasting it. A knock on the door signaled the arrival of her clothing, which another of the gargoyle servants brought in. She or he—Max couldn't tell—laid them on the bed and left.

Max shoved herself back from the table and started

pulling them on, not bothering to go hunting for privacy. It wasn't like he hadn't seen everything already.

"I need some weapons," she said when she was through. "I don't suppose you have a couple of forty-fives lying around?"

He shook his head. "Guns are not permitted in Chadaré."

"That doesn't usually keep them out. Smugglers are everywhere."

The corner of his mouth lifted. "You're right. But all the gateways are warded against them. Only those who can travel straight through the abyss can bring them in, and you and Nayan are a very rare breed."

Max digested that, then nodded. "What have you got?"

He stood. "Come. I'll show you my armory."

He led her through what was more a medieval palace than anything else. The walls and floors were white stone and broad enough for Ilanion to fly through. Here and there were joltingly modern touches, such as a CD player and speakers.

"Powered with magic," Ilanion said when he saw her surprise.

She wondered what his music tastes ran to but shrugged away the thought. It didn't matter. "Are there any more like you?" she asked, motioning toward his wings.

"I am one of a kind," he said with a slight smile that didn't really answer the question at all. He could just as easily have been saying that he was a special snowflake and no one in the world could ever compare with his wonderfulness. Or he might have been the only one of his race.

They came to a broad platform that overhung a vast cavern. It had to be a half-mile across, and it was full of shadows. She had no idea how deep it was.

Without warning, Ilanion pulled her against him, his chest warm against her back, his arms circling her waist. "Ready?" He didn't wait for the answer. His arms tightened, and he leaped out into space.

For long moments, they plunged downward. Then Ilanion spread his wings, and they jerked into a lazy spiral to the bottom, which had to be a good three miles down.

The cavern floor was covered in a layer of fine sand. The place was incredibly warm and smelled of rosemary and lavender. Gold witchlights flickered to life around them, illuminating the area in a dazzling glow.

Max stepped out of Ilanion's arms. "Nice place. Is this where you hatch your eggs?"

His eyes gleamed, and he smiled. "It is."

She had no idea if he was joking.

"Come on." He led her to a wall. He touched it, and wards flared brilliantly. The stone melted to reveal a short corridor on the other side. It led into the armory. The place was easily as big as an airplane hangar. The roof was about fifteen feet high. Racks lined the walls from floor to ceiling and also crowded the floor space. They were full of every weapon imaginable, and plenty of others that Max had never imagined. They were organized generally into categories: spears, swords, daggers, shields, clubs, armor, and then a bunch of miscellaneous stuff.

"Choose what you like," Ilanion told her.

It was like letting a kid loose in a toy store. But she

didn't have time to play. Instead, she strode through the ranks of weaponry. She needed to travel relatively lightly. At the same time, she had no idea what she was going up against, except that there were going to be witches on steroids.

She picked out a pair of plain swords with razor edges and a sword belt with two scabbards. She added two daggers to her waistband and a couple more to her pockets. She fingered a spear. The haft was six feet long, and it was topped with a slightly curved blade that was another two and a half feet. The thing was well balanced. She considered it a long moment, then reluctantly put it back. The swords were enough and she wanted to have her hands free when she wasn't fighting.

Next, she wandered into a collection that looked more like a fine jewelry store than a weapons locker. There were rings, necklaces, bracelets, arm bands, jeweled belts, headdresses, and crowns—you name it, it was there.

Max picked up a ring. It was a large emerald surrounded by a sunburst of yellow diamonds. Or something that looked like them. She turned it over to examine it.

"Careful," Ilanion said as he plucked it from her hand. He was once again dressed in his armor, his helm tucked under his arm. He held the ring carefully. "This one will drop you like a bag of rocks," he said, settling it back in its velvet case. "It's quite painful, and the effects are lasting. I spelled it myself."

She should have known. "Got a garrote hanging about in here?" she asked.

He nodded. "Of course. Right over here."

He led her to a case of necklaces. Some were crusted with jewels. Others were ornate twists of precious metals. A few on one end were plain. One looked like a torque. It was U-shaped gold with dragon heads on the ends. The gold was twisted to look like a cable. She picked it up, not seeing how to pull it apart. Usually, a wire was hidden inside. "How does it work?"

"Like this." Ilanion took it and pulled it wide. The metal stretched until it was easily long enough to put around a horse's neck to strangle it.

"Seems a little big," Max said doubtfully.

"It responds to your needs," he said. "You may trust it. I made it, and I tested it myself."

There was a grim look to his expression that said he'd tested it in an actual battle. Good enough for her. Max took it back and settled it around her neck. It was heavy and warm from Ilanion's hands.

"There is one other thing you might find useful," he said, drawing her after him into a section of armor. He pulled down a mail shirt. It was a silvery blue, and it shimmered in the light. It spilled over his hands like watered silk. "I'd like you to wear this."

Max took it from him and held it up. It was light and flexible. If she put it on, it would hang nearly to her knees and all the way to her wrists. It would totally hamper her movement. "I don't think it's my style," she said, and started to pass it back to him.

He shook his head. "Do you realize that that is the most powerful piece of armor I possess? Possibly the most powerful armor in Chadaré? It will protect you against bursts of magic—as long as they strike the armor. If you had been wearing it when we were fighting, you would not have been affected by my attacks. In some cases, it's possible to deflect attacks back onto the attacker."

"Impressive," Max said. "How is it against steel and claws?"

"Better than with magic."

"Why give it to me? Why aren't you wearing it?"

"If I wore it, the Korvad would take it as a sign that I am prepared to go to war with them."

"So what do you get out of all this? Helping me?" she asked suspiciously. There was no such thing as a free lunch in the world of magic. Favors meant payback. This armor counted as going above and beyond the call of duty. If she took it, she was going to owe him, and she wasn't sure she wanted to. She'd played that game once with Scooter. Not that she had a lot of choice at the moment. Not if she wanted to keep Scooter alive.

"I want Nayan to live," Ilanion said slowly. "And I want the Korvad broken. If you succeed, you rob them of considerable power—power they've used to control Chadaré for thousands of years. Without it, and with Nayan's help, Chadaré will become a free city again."

"Free? Or you want a chance at taking over and running the whole shebang yourself?"

"I have always been content with the Torchmarch," Ilanion said. "But there are others . . ." He drifted off, and for a moment, his gaze went cold and pitiless. Then he shook it off. "Others have suffered. It is time for change."

So he had a personal stake in this. That answered a lot about why he was helping at all. "If I take your help, then you don't expect payback?"

He shook his head. "If you save Nayan, then you break the Korvad. That's all I want. Your death would prevent that. So I want you to wear the armor. You can return it when you're done."

Max nodded. "All right." She removed her weapons and pulled the mail shirt over her clothing. It felt icy at first, then warmed. Suddenly, it shimmered and constricted, sinking under her clothing. It tightened around her arms and body like a second skin. It slid up over her neck and head and down over her legs until she was fully encased except for her hands and her face. "What the hell? How do I get this off?" She scraped her fingers over it, but it was impervious. She glared at Ilanion accusingly. "Is this your idea of a joke? Or is it a trap?"

"Neither. When you want to remove it, know its name, and tell it what to do. It will obey."

"Know its *name?*" Max repeated. "It has a name? Does that make it a living creature?" Somehow the idea sent chills slithering along her nerves.

"In its way," came the very unhelpful answer.

"Some people just need killing," she muttered under her breath, repeating Thor's favorite saying as she eyed Ilanion balefully. She felt like she was wearing a really bad comic-book-hero costume. Call her Peter Parker. Or Catwoman. She curled her toes, wishing she had a pair of boots. "OK, what's its name?"

He flushed. "It will tell you. It is different each time you put it on. That way, no one but the current wearer can control it. Blood is required to make contact."

"Of course it is. This keeps getting better and better," Max said dryly. No point in wasting time. She picked up one of the daggers she'd chosen and dug the point into her thumb. She smeared the blood on the armor sleeve of her other arm.

Instantly, the armor went hot. Prickles ran over her skin like bee stings, and then a ribbon of white spooled across her mindscape. It curled through her mind. It felt alien. Max flinched, and it halted, like a deer in the headlights. Max could feel shyness radiating from it. She frowned and reached out to it. The touch brought a flash of fierce joy and then a feeling like a cat rubbing up against her and purring. A big cat. Like a sabertooth tiger.

"What's your name?" she whispered.

The answer was not words but a kind of tune mixed with a dance of color and a faint flavor of salt. How the hell was she supposed to reproduce that? It repeated again and then again. Max could feel its impatience, as if it were waiting for her try. Her brow furrowed as she concentrated, and then she repeated the color and sound in her mind. She tried to imagine salt—sweat and ocean brine and blood.

There was a shiver like laughter and then a swirl of movement as if in celebration. Max repeated it again and then four more times, each time with a questioning lilt in her mind. *Is this right?*

By the last time, the armor creature seemed satisfied, and Max focused on what she wanted. *Pull down from head,* she thought, and instantly, the armor loosened and slid down to form a collar around her neck.

"Very good," Ilanion said with raised brows. "Impressive. It took me a bit longer than that to make the armor's acquaintance."

"Good thing I'm a fast learner," Max said acidly as she

strapped the sword belts on again and tucked the daggers back in. She put the torque around her neck.

"The armor is versatile. It can make pockets in itself and even become other forms of clothing, though I've never been successful in making it change color."

"I'm not looking to be going to any parties in it," Max said. "I just want to get going. And I know right where to start," she said, remembering the house where she'd followed the hunter and his pack of Calopus.

That surprised Ilanion. "Where?"

She described the place: the red and cream stone wall, the opalescent mist within, and the magic warding it.

He nodded. "Indeed. Asherah is a very powerful member of the Korvad and was my first thought, though getting inside her house will be difficult."

"Tell me something I don't know," Max said, starting back out of the armory.

Ilanion followed, the aisles too narrow to allow him to walk beside her. "Have you a plan?"

"Nope. But I am pissed off and armed." She stopped and turned around. "Just don't let Scooter die before I get back."

He frowned at her. "I'm coming with you."

"What? Why? This isn't your fight. If it doesn't work, the Korvad will come after you. I didn't think you wanted to risk that much."

He smiled, and it was cold and violent. Max remembered just how dangerous he really was. "After some thought, I've decided that I do. The worst they can do is make it impossible for me to live in Chadaré. There are other places to live."

"Have you seen Scooter? There's a lot worse they can do," she pointed out. "Like cut off your wings or pull out your heart."

"I won't let them."

"I bet that's what Scooter said, too," she muttered, then shrugged. "If you can live with it, then who am I to argue?"

He smiled again, this time with an arrogance and impudence that made her mouth go dry. She doubted that many women would be immune to it. If she didn't have her panties in a wad for Alexander, she'd be chomping on Ilanion like a crocodile on a wildebeest. "You can argue with me anytime," he said, brushing a strand of hair out of her face. One brow flicked up smugly. "I might even let you win on occasion."

Conceited bastard. Max reached up and caught his face between her palms, standing on tiptoe so her lips were a bare inch from his. He watched her, sparks spinning hot in his brown eyes.

"Here's the thing, Goldilocks. Right at this minute, I could twist your head off like the cap off a beer bottle, and there's nothing you could do it about it. Don't be dumber than you have to be, OK?" She patted his cheek and stepped back.

He grabbed her wrists and yanked her against him. His eyes were entirely gold now, and she could feel the magic thrumming along his skin. "There are a lot of worse ways to die. Besides, I usually get what—and *who*—I want."

She shoved him, breaking his hold easily and sending him staggering backward. "This is going to be one of those unusual times, then."

He grinned. "Can't blame me for trying. A woman like you doesn't come along often."

She rolled her eyes. "You just want someone to cart you through the abyss whenever you feel like it."

He didn't deny it.

"If you're done trying to flirt with me, could we get on with saving Scooter?" she asked. "I'd like him not to die."

He sobered. "Do you want to see him before we go? In case we don't return."

She shook her head. "I don't intend to lose today."

Ilanion motioned for her to go ahead of him. "Does anybody ever intend to lose?"

"No. But the difference is that I have a horrendous personality flaw: I'd rather die than lose. Most people can't say the same thing. If they do, they're lying."

"And you're not." It wasn't exactly a question.

Max answered anyway. "No."

"Does that mean you've never lost?"

She shook her head. "A few times."

"And yet you're still alive."

"My ass has been pulled out of the fire more than once. But the fact is that most often, I win. And I'm going to win today. Dying isn't an option."

13

LEAVING ILANION'S COMPOUND WAS TRICKY. THE place was under a giant microscope. No one was coming or going without the Korvad stopping them and grilling them over a crackling fire. Probably literally.

Ilanion wasn't unprepared. He led Max deeper underground through a series of rough-hewn tunnels. They were narrow, and more than once, the eagle man could barely fit his wings through.

"Going to have to have the Enay work on that," he said ruefully as Max pulled him through a particularly narrow spot. He had scrapes on his arms and legs where the armor didn't extend. His gold-scaled wings were too tough to be damaged.

They must have gone another mile underground before they entered a narrow cavern. Stalactites hung down like dragon teeth. Below, a river rushed past.

"You can swim, can't you?" Ilanion asked.

Max eyed the frothing water. "Haven't drowned yet."

"Let's hope you don't start today."

He grabbed her hand and jumped. The water was

frigid. Ilanion startled her by pulling her close against him. His wings folded around them both, and a moment later, the water drained from their cocoon, no doubt pushed by magic.

"Handy trick," Max said. "Or is this just your way of trying to get into my pants?"

He laughed. "If it were, you'd have to do all the work. I'm a bit busy at the moment. But I'm perfectly willing to let you try."

"Maybe next lifetime, Goldilocks."

The water carried them swiftly. They bobbed like a cork, spinning and bouncing off the banks. After a particularly hard hit, Ilanion gasped, his mouth clamping tightly together.

"Are you going to live?" she asked.

"Maybe. Maybe not," he rasped.

"Can I help? And don't tell me to spank your monkey, or I swear I'll kick your ass."

He laughed and choked. He rested his forehead on her shoulder until the coughing subsided. At last, he lifted his head. "Don't do that again, or we're going to drown."

"*You* might. I'll swim."

"Until you get eaten, maybe."

"Eaten?"

"Not everything we've run into has been rocks. We've been attacked seven times so far."

She scowled. "Are you OK?"

"How sweet. You're concerned for me. Or are you worried about your life raft?"

She just stared at him.

"I am well enough. I can heal myself, and my wings are largely impervious to their teeth."

"Largely? That sounds like mostly. From the way you've turned gray, you've been hurt. How bad?"

"Bad enough." His jaw clenched, and his eyes were yellow except for a pinpoint of black in the middle. "I've got a puncture that went through my wing into my back. There's poison in it."

"Can you heal it?"

He nodded jerkily. "It's going to take a few minutes. But we may have to leave the river before I can fly."

"You're not talking about climbing up onto the bank, are you?"

He shook his head. "There is a ward gate where we can drop away. No one knows of it, so we should be safe. As long as I can fly. Otherwise—"

He didn't need to finish the sentence for Max to get the picture. "I can pull us into the abyss. We won't die."

"Which will deplete you again and delay retrieving Nayan's belongings."

Max snorted. Belongings. As if his heart, silk, and horn were junk he'd left behind in an old apartment. "And if we don't leave the river through that gate?"

"Trouble."

"Then if you can't fix yourself, I'll take us into the abyss. I'd rather be tired than dead."

"Keep a tight grip. When we drop, I won't have the strength to hold on to you."

"Are you just trying to get me to feel you up?" Max said, putting her arms around his waist.

He chuckled but didn't reply. His eyes were squeezed shut. Magic flared around them and swelled thick inside the cocoon of his wings. It nearly choked her. Both of Ilanion's hearts thumped loudly in his chest, and his breathing was harsh against the wash of the river water. His muscles bulged as if he were struggling with a massive weight.

"Now," he whispered, his neck cording.

Suddenly, they were falling. Max's stomach lurched into her throat as they went into free fall. Just how the hell could they fall out of an underground river? The answer was obvious: she was trapped in an Escher painting. There was no other answer. She felt a rumble of laughter in her stomach and choked it back. Now wasn't the time to get hysterical. Or get a case of gallows humor. She held tightly to Ilanion.

"Can you fly?" she demanded.

He didn't answer.

She slapped his cheek with the flat of her hand. "Dammit! Do I take us into the abyss or not?"

She couldn't tell if he heard her. The air whistled loudly around them. How far did they have to fall before they splatted on something? Ilanion's wings still wrapped her tightly. She needed to make a decision.

"Ilanion!"

His eyes popped open. Golden light poured out of them. He stared, but she didn't think he saw her.

"Ilanion, if you don't start flying now, I'm pulling us into the abyss. Count of three. One. Two. Th—"

Before she could finish, his wings unfurled. There was a loud popping sound as they filled with air. He let out an agonized cry, his face twisting. The left wing wilted, and his arm hung limp. They started to drop again, spiraling like an autumn leaf on the wind.

"You can do better than that," Max called, clinging to

him. "Fight. It's just pain. Get us down to the ground, and you can rest."

She looked back over her shoulder to see just where the ground was. *Fuck*. It was coming up fast.

They were falling into a gray mass that might have been a lake or a parking lot. Either way, there wasn't going to be a whole lot left of either of them when they hit.

Ilanion went rigid. Max could feel him pouring his energy into his healing. His body flared with magic. Suddenly, his wings began to beat, and they steadied.

Magic continued to burn around the eagle mage, and Max was grateful that she was wearing the protective armor. Otherwise, she'd have been cooked extra crispy.

They sank lower, their progress growing more controlled as Ilanion healed himself. It was impressive. Self-healing took a huge toll, and to do it while flying pretty much confirmed that he was at least part god. Max blew out a slow breath. What had she got herself into? The Korvad controlled Chadaré and clearly made Ilanion nervous. They'd stripped Scooter of his power. How the hell was *she* going to fight them?

With style. She could almost hear Niko's voice. She grinned, despite herself. *Do try not to die, won't you?* That was Tyler. It would have been followed by a delicate yawn. And Oz: *Keep your head down and don't be stupid*. Lise: *Bitch, do not even think about leaving me alone with all this testosterone*. Giselle: *You can't win if you die, so suck it up*. Tutresiel: *Princess, you aren't even trying if you're dying*.

And Alexander: *Come home*.

Max closed her eyes, pain squeezing her hard. She

missed them all so much. Inside her mind, a ribbon floated through, questioning, distressed. Her armor. She laughed, nearly choking herself. Her armor was worried about her. She was going insane.

Swallowing hard, she stuffed her emotions down into her fortress where they belonged. She needed to keep her cool if she was going to survive.

She looked down again. The gray area below was neither a lake nor a parking lot. It was a pool of shadow. It rippled and swirled like smoke off a raging fire. Max couldn't see a damn thing through it.

"Hold tight," Ilanion said roughly. "Things are about to get interesting. Trust me. I'll get us through."

In other words, *Don't take us into the abyss*. Max nodded understanding. He gave her a pirate grin, and then his wings clamped tightly down, and they plummeted into the shadows.

Instantly, they were caught up in a maelstrom. Hurricane winds slammed them from every side, battering them with invisible fists. Had Ilanion's wings been unfurled, Max was pretty sure they'd have been ripped off.

She had no good sense of how long they remained inside the shadow storm. Nor could she tell if they were making any progress in any direction. They spun and whirled until she was dizzy and nauseated. Ilanion's magic continued to flare brightly, and his face was a mask of concentration.

Suddenly, the storm let them go. Ilanion tipped them sideways, and his wings flared. Max sucked in deep breaths, trying to steady her shaking muscles.

"What was that?"

"A shortcut. No one will track us through it. Only a

handful of people can navigate it all. Most who try get stranded inside and die."

"Nobody knows you can go through it, do they?" Max asked shrewdly.

He shook his head. "Only you."

"How's your wing and arm?"

"I'll live."

The aura of his magic was subsiding, and his skin was cooling. His eyes remained brilliant yellow, and he looked strong. His arm no longer hung limp, and his wings flapped powerfully as they flew high across the city.

Max stared down at the sprawling place in amazement. From above, Chadaré looked as if it went on forever. She could see the enormous open space where she and Scooter had taken refuge and she'd fought off the hunter. The Torchmarch was a sea of shadow pricked by flashes of firelight.

"How big is this place?" Max wondered.

"It's difficult to say. Chadaré is always changing. Parts of it sometimes simply disappear. Sometimes they return, sometimes they don't. At least, not yet. But I would guess there are at least eight or nine million beings inhabiting the city. The Torchmarch contains more than two million alone."

"That's a hell of a lot of sewage," Max murmured.

He laughed. "Magic has its perks. We're almost there. Are you ready?"

"Always. But do you suppose there's anything you can do to hide your shiny wings so they don't look quite so much like a lighthouse beacon?"

"Of course." He closed his eyes, and Max felt a layer

of magic fall over them like a blanket of soft snow. They were both covered in a sheath of what looked like ash. His eyes opened again and gleamed like liquid gold against the charcoal gray. "Good enough?"

"Show-off."

He smiled, and then he tipped forward, his wings closing tight against his body. Max yelped and wrapped her legs around his as they plunged headfirst into Chadaré. She felt laughter rumble through his chest. *Fucker*. He was enjoying this way too much. He was as bad as Tutresiel.

They dropped nearly a mile, and Max was pretty sure they weren't going to be able to pull out of the free fall when Ilanion flared his wings. The pockets of bone and leathery hide gave a loud popping sound. Max and Ilanion jerked upward like they'd been caught on a fish-hook. Instantly, he tipped into a shallower dive and flew them down to the ground, landing in a small courtyard in the corner of a spacious estate.

Max let go of him and staggered away on rubbery legs. She bent and put her hands on her knees, drawing in a couple of deep breaths before straightening. The ash spell still clung to her and Ilanion, making him look more demonic than not.

"Where are we?"

"About a half-mile away. Follow me."

He led her down several garden paths to the outer wall. There was a gate, but he didn't try to open it. Instead, he reached for Max, but she waved him away.

"I've got it."

He cocked an eyebrow at her and then at the thirty-foot wall but didn't argue. He gestured. "After you, then."

Max flexed her knees and jumped. The angel feather embedded in her palm made her soar well above the wall. She landed lightly on the far side of the street. Ilanion dropped down beside her.

"You continue to surprise me," he said quietly. There weren't any pedestrians close enough to overhear, but there was no point in taking chances.

Up the street, a carriage drawn by two beasts that weren't quite horses trundled toward them. In the other direction, a tinker driving a pedal wagon rolled along, his metal wares clanking loudly. Several robed figures hurried along carrying baskets and pushing hand carts

Max could feel the magic of Asherah's wards, and the opalescent mist billowed above the rooftops like a beacon. Together, she and Ilanion headed in that direction. In a few minutes, they stood outside the cream and red stone walls.

She started when the ash spell shrank away and disappeared.

"The less active magic we take inside, the better," Ilanion murmured with a glance back at the street to see if they'd been noticed. "Active spells can call attention to themselves."

"So, the old-fashioned way," Max said. She eyed the gate where she'd lost the hunter's trail that first day in Chadaré. The only way inside was through the gate or by taking a blind leap over the wall into the opalescent mist. Her locking spells would let her open the gate, which meant that she and Ilanion could walk in like they belonged there. Jumping over might trigger defense wards.

She grabbed the gate handle and twisted. Magic

reached out to her, sliding over her like sticky tentacles. But they couldn't find a grip on the armor or her skin. She was a walking key, and the lock couldn't hold. The ward magic curled away, and the bolt inside shot open. She caught Ilanion's startled look and winked. Another surprise. She pushed the gate open.

They stood in a kind of garden made of silver, gold, and jewels. Witchlights lit the place, making it glow with fairy-tale brilliance. The ground was paved with opals, the benches made from sapphires and rubies, all of it mortared with gold and silver.

It was hard to see through the dazzle, and Max's skin crawled with the feeling that they weren't alone. She felt exposed. There were no shadows at all to hide in.

She cast a questioning look at Ilanion. Did he have any idea where they were or where they were going? He shook his head. Time to explore, then. Motioning for him to follow, Max started away from the wall.

Despite the feeling of being watched, they encountered no one. Nor did they hear anything. The air was thick with silence. Even the jingle of their weapons and the rub of their clothing were muted. It felt as if they were walking into a trap, but Max didn't see any other choice. She definitely didn't want to leap up into the mist. She had a feeling that anything passing through it would set off very definite alarms, if they weren't killed outright.

The gemstone garden went on for what seemed like forever. Max stopped near a bridge that went over a frozen river of rubies and pearls. She bent close to Ilanion's ear.

"We should have got somewhere by now," she whispered. But even that small sound was caught by the trees and sent a vibration rippling through the garden. Leaves shivered, and a low crystal whine began to grow, slicing through the syrupy silence. "Shit," Max said through clenched teeth.

The sound around them increased. Max could feel vibrations resonating up through her feet and into her bones. Soon they'd shatter, like a wineglass when an opera singer hits just the right note. Ilanion had wrapped himself in a flickering sheath of protective magic. He might be able to hold out against the noise, but she couldn't.

She turned and started to run, holding on to her swords to keep them from jangling. Her feet were covered in the magic armor and made no sound. Ilanion was nearly as silent.

The noise echoed and reechoed again and again, growing louder as the vibrations of the leaves and flowers increased. It drilled down into Max's skull, sending darts of fire and darkness across her vision. It felt like her skull was cracking apart.

Frustation and fury roared inside, and she chopped at a tree with one of the swords. The trunk exploded in a hail of glass and metal. She turned away, letting her armor take the brunt of the burst. But it gave her an idea. If she didn't have a path, she'd damned-well blaze a trail out of the place.

She grabbed Ilanion and slung him over her shoulder and leaped into another tree. It was shaking like a wind was tearing at it. The mist swirled above her head and slid acidic tendrils across her cheek and neck. Her skin bubbled and blistered. Max ignored the pain and ducked to keep her eyes clear. She couldn't afford to go blind. She chopped at the branches of the tree, shattering its crown. Jagged chunks of glass and twisted metal crashed to the ground.

Max leaped to another and did the same, glad she wasn't on the ground where the glass shrapnel would have made her job impossible. She looked over her shoulder between every jump, making sure that she was going in a straight line. Sooner or later, she'd get somewhere, or she'd break every tree in the garden.

The vibrations were increasing. Every splintered tree seemed to double the level of cacophony. Ilanion's nose and ears were bleeding despite his protective spell. So were hers. Her vision blurred crimson as tears of blood overflowed her eyes. Although she could feel her healing spells kicking into overdrive, they weren't keeping up with the damage. She remembered her armor, and it slid up to cover her ears, lending her a little bit of relief.

She flung her head up. Smells. She launched herself headlong, following the scent trail. She leaped on a horizontal line, using all the spring of the angel feather to give her extra momentum. The resonance around them had grown into a shriek, and Ilanion's body had begun to twitch and convulse. He was about done.

Max flexed to land and jump again. Her feet passed right through the tree as if it weren't there. She and Ilanion sprawled on a metal surface in a pool of silence. Max rolled to her feet and swung around, blinking to clear her vision.

She stood on some kind of patio. It was circular and paved with gold. Tall, delicate columns made of solid amethyst ran around its edge, supporting an elegant cream-colored marble balcony. Behind it, broad arching doorways led away into the house. Or, rather, the palace.

It was huge. Like a half-dozen Walmarts big. Except that it looked like the bastard child of Disneyland, with shiny swaths of glitter-covered ribbons, sparkling fountains, and a stardust shine to every surface. Even the opal mist above sparkled. There ought to have been little talking animals holding a tea party, cotton-candy flowers on candy trees, and princesses singing on every corner. It was enough to make Max want to vomit.

"I told you I'd be waiting," came a masculine voice from behind. She spun around.

The hunter from earlier stood opposite, his five Calopus around his feet. His arms were crossed, and his eyes gleamed. He was aching for a rematch.

Max flicked a glance at Ilanion. He lay on his shoulder, his back to the hunter. He was watching her through his helm, his jaw taut with pain. She stepped over him, putting him behind her. She hoped he had the sense to escape while she kept the hunter busy. He could still get out alive.

"I hate to be late for a date," she said, cracking her knuckles. "Especially one so eager as you. Shall we start with dinner, or do you want to get right to the sex?"

He smiled, his long canine teeth gleaming. "Sex?" He shook his head regretfully. "It's tempting, but I think we won't get so far."

"Your loss," Max said. "Come on, then. Let's finish this."

His brows rose. "Do you want a moment to collect yourself? I wouldn't want to take advantage."

She eyed the spiked wolves at his feet. "What do you call those? They look like an advantage to me."

He followed her gaze and shrugged. "They are friends. And weapons."

"Not like taking advantage at all," she said.

"If you didn't like the odds, maybe you shouldn't have trespassed."

"You've got a point. All right, then, let's get on with it, Tarzan. I've got things to do."

He straightened, his arms falling to his side. Something flashed in his eyes. Anger, yes, but more than that. It was . . . broken pride. Not good. Tarzan had a point to prove about losing, and that meant he wasn't going to care about his own hide. Maybe Asherah had ripped him a new one and told him not to bother coming back if he failed again. Or maybe he just couldn't stand to lose. Either way, this fight was to the death.

Max drew the two swords as the five Calopus fanned out in a half-circle, lips peeling from their fangs as they snarled. She just hoped her new armor was as good as Ilanion claimed. A musical jab in her mind made her wince.

"Sorry," she said aloud. "Why don't you show me just how good you are?"

Tarzan thought she was talking to him. "I plan to," he said, drawing his own blades with a flourish.

Before he or his beasties could attack, Max took the fight to them, blades whirring. The clock was ticking, and Scooter was running out of time. Today, death had a deadline.

14

VALERY WAS WAITING FOR ALEXANDER WHEN HE, Thor, and Tyler returned to Horngate just a few minutes before dawn. His skin was turning scarlet with the burn of the predawn. That was new.

He stretched and shook himself. The sixty-mile run had been arduous but had burned up some of the raging emotion inside him. *Faith,* he told himself. *Faith*. Max *had* to be alive. Anything else was too awful to even contemplate.

"You're a son of a bitch," Valery told him, her hands on her hips. The air around her trembled like desert heat off the pavement.

"So I have heard." He reached out to hug her, and she shoved him away. He grinned and grappled her close.

After a moment, she hugged him back hard. "I thought I was going to lose you," she said against his shoulder.

He closed his eyes. Max meant so much to him, but she was not everything. She could not be. He had Valery and Horngate. He could not let himself be swallowed up. "It will not happen again."

"Better not." She pushed away, and this time he let

her go. "You need to eat. All of you." She looked at Thor and Tyler.

Their expressions were still pissed. He had some fences to mend. "We will meet you in the dining commons," he told Valery, and gave a slight jerk of his chin.

She hesitated, then nodded. When she was gone, Alexander turned to the two Blades. "You have something you want to say?"

Tyler exploded like a bursting dam. But if Valery had been hot, he was as cold as an Arctic winter. "You self-centered prick. Max left you in charge, and first you throw a temper tantrum and refuse to step up, and then you get a little bad news—" He broke off, his face contorting. He took a breath, his expression going flat as a snake. "And you run off like a pimple-faced teenager who gets pissed at his parents for grounding him. On top of that, you nearly get Niko killed."

Tyler flicked a bitter look at Beyul, who had dropped to his haunches beside Alexander and was watching the exchange, his pink tongue lolling from his mouth as he panted.

"It's time for you to suck it up. Do you want to belong to Horngate or not? Because if you do, you'd better stop acting like a pissy little baby and get with the program."

Alexander nodded and looked at Thor. "Anything you want to add?"

His friend grimaced. "Tyler about covered it, boss," he drawled. "'Cept to say that I expected more of you. You're old enough to know better."

Alexander winced. That hurt. Thor was his oldest friend in the world besides Valery, and he did not like disappointing either of them. "You are both right," he said, rubbing his hands over his face and then straightening. "I have learned my lesson. I will not fail you again." Or Max.

He stretched out a hand to Tyler. The other Blade looked at it and then gripped it solidly. "I'll hold you to it."

"Do that."

He put his hand out to Thor and found himself pulled into a bear hug. Thor pounded his back with his fist. "You mother-loving bastard. I swear, I'll kill you if you ever do that to me again."

Alexander grinned, but the grin faded as he looked again at Tyler and read the raw pain and loss in his eyes. "She is alive," he said. "I refuse to accept anything else."

Tyler stiffened and nodded.

"I had better go make sure Giselle and Holt have not killed each other. The two of you check on Niko and get some food. Make sure he eats, too."

Alexander's new senses told him exactly where Giselle and Holt were. If Tyler was a fiery spirit and Thor was a wild blue storm, Giselle was a tightly knotted mass of forest green. Holt was shining brown, like tiger-eye. There were others with them. Xaphan—he was a clear blue flame around a core of the same cold black as Tutresiel's sword.

His senses spread through the fortress. He could sense everyone, each with his or her own spirit signature color and blend, each with a spirit scent. He pressed out further. The Fury was pressing harder against the ward circle. The Memory was a splinter of green—heartbreakingly brilliant. The pack of Grims were like Beyul—the clear rushing water of an ancient river. But despite their sameness, he could sense differences among them. Eddies, currents, and ripples. They were as different from one another as snowflakes.

He split from Tyler and Thor and threaded his way down toward Giselle's apartments. He was not surprised when Valery stepped out of the shadows to meet him. He was not sure he would ever be surprised by anyone again.

"Are you really all right?" she asked. Her voice shook slightly, and she cleared her throat. "You've changed."

He nodded. "I have. My Prime and I—" How could he describe it? "It was like the Prime and I were separate and now we are united."

"What does that mean? Are you still you? Are you going to go rabid again?"

He shrugged. "I do not think so. I feel like me. I am just . . . more than I used to be."

"More?" She frowned.

"I have stronger senses. I have no idea what else."

She nodded, still scrutinizing him. Then she abruptly switched topics. "I'm sorry about Max."

The words knocked the breath out of him. The explosion of emotions inside him cut like shrapnel. He swallowed them down. *Faith*. He had to have faith.

"She will come back," he said.

Pity washed over Valery's face, but she only nodded. "She will." She clearly did not believe it.

"I have to see Giselle," Alexander said. He walked away, his body stiff and jerky.

He had collected himself by the time he came to Giselle's quarters. The door was ajar, and he went inside without knocking, Valery right behind.

Inside he found Giselle, Holt, Xaphan, Tutresiel, Oz, and the six witches who made up the rest of the coven. It was clearly a war council.

Giselle sat in a chair while the others ranged around her. She looked vibrant and healthy. Her face was flushed, and her body looked rounded and curved, as if she'd gained twenty pounds. She had more than survived the earlier backlash—she had flourished from the tide of returning magic.

Holt sprawled in a chair opposite. He looked sleepy-eyed, his fingers tenting together. Xaphan perched on the back of a chair in his typical eagle-like pose. Tutresiel leaned against the wall, and Oz stood beside Giselle with his arms folded. Despite his relatively calm exterior, Oz was enraged. The power of his Prime pulsed in the room. The witches sat in a small circle around Giselle, like children at story time. In the middle was a table with large sheets of paper covered in black pencil drawings.

Everyone looked up as Alexander and Valery entered. Holt gripped the arms of his chair, his gaze locked on his ex. He looked like he wanted to grab her and drag her off somewhere in chains. Which Alexander had no doubt was exactly what Holt wanted to do. Much as he disliked the mage, he could not really blame him. At the moment, he would like to do the same with Max. If only he knew where she was. If—

No. Faith.

"So, you're back," Giselle said, one eyebrow rising in delicate contempt. "Do I need to chain you up somewhere?"

Her voice was cold and hard. He recognized it. Max

did the same thing when she was hurting. She withdrew behind a wall of ice and did not let herself feel anything.

"I am fine," he said.

She examined him from head to foot, one finger tapping against her lips. At last, she nodded. "While you were out howling at the moon, the rest of us have been trying to figure out a plan to handle the Fury," she told him. "Holt has an idea. It might work."

She did not sound convinced. Alexander could almost hear Oz grinding his teeth, but the Sunspear Prime made no arguments as Giselle sat forward and outlined the plan.

The first step was to create a second ward circle around the one containing the Fury. Inside it would go Alton, the author of this mess. There was no one in the room who looked like they even remotely pitied his fate.

"We'll have to remove the witch chains," Giselle said. "They might get in the way of the Fury's vengeance, and we don't want to make her angrier than she already is." She studiously did not use the girl's real name—Cora. But her eyes were haunted when she spoke. "Taking off the chains means he's going to have a lot of power. Our circle has to be very, very strong." She looked at Holt.

"It'll be strong enough to hold the likes of him," he said arrogantly.

"You don't know *what* he is," Giselle pointed out. "The Guardians have gifted him with a great deal of magic."

"It will hold," he insisted. "You can rely on it."

"We have to," she said sourly before moving on. "We'll set up a secondary circle around our first one. This one will be made of three succeeding layers. On the inside, we'll have a salt and herb circle. The second will be stone and blood and a chain of hex marks. The third will be iron—a lot of it. None of them will likely hold her. But together they'll hopefully slow her down and drain her enough so that she can be reasoned with. When we're all ready, we'll break the circle Alton made to hold her and let her at him."

"Furies by nature are not reasonable," Alexander said with a frown. "They are female rage, betrayal, and vengeance embodied."

"We'll have fed her justice in the shape of Alton. That may calm her. And possibly, she won't have entirely forgotten who she once was. I may be able to talk to her."

He shook his head. "It is too risky. There is no reason to think she will not be insane. You cannot go near her."

"Exactly," Oz chimed in. "It's suicidal."

Giselle's jaw tightened, and she took a slow breath and blew it out. "We don't have a choice. She knows me. Yeah, I know she knows you, too, Oz, but no man is going to be able to talk to her. That would set her off as sure as pulling the pin on a grenade. If you have a better idea, I'm all ears."

"How do you plan to protect yourself?" Alexander asked. He was not going to argue about it until he heard the full plan.

"She isn't," Oz said flatly. "She wants all of the Blades and Spears to hang back, especially the men. She doesn't even want Holt close by. Or the angels. Just Magpie and Judith."

Now Alexander knew why Oz was so angry and why his Prime was on the killing edge. He held his own down hard but felt the protective fury leaking through his grip. Giselle was the heart of Horngate. Oz was driven by his compulsion spells to keep her safe. The pain had to be excruciating. Alexander was not bound in the same manner, but he knew what Max would want, and the drive to fulfill her wishes spurred him as hard as any compulsion spell Giselle could have inflicted on him.

The group of witches sank into themselves beneath the onslaught of the Prime power—all except Magpie and Giselle, who simply looked irritated. Maggie, new to her power and scared of it, made a whimpering sound and leaned against Max's brother, Kyle. He started in surprise and put his arm around her.

"No," Alexander said. "We should evacuate. Tutresiel and Xaphan can fly Giselle and the other witches far enough away for safety. Everyone else can drive. Start now."

"And leave every soul within hundreds of miles to die?" Giselle shook her head adamantly. "Forget it. I chose this territory. Whether or not the people here know what this covenstead stands for, I won't let them suffer if I can stop this. What's the point of Horngate if all we do is run away from danger?"

Which is exactly what Max would say. And Alexander would point out that Horngate had been nearly decimated and was not strong enough to handle a Fury. And then she would say, "So what?" And that would be the end of it. Because Max never would let the innocent suffer when she could help. Or die trying.

Alexander exchanged a look with Oz. He was thinking the same thing. The Sunspear's mouth twisted, and he gave a tiny nod.

"If you are going to do this, then you have to have

protection," he declared flatly. "Otherwise, I will haul you out of here myself."

"Think you can, Slick?"

"Try to stop me," he said, teeth grating together as she used Max's nickname for him.

"Push me, and I will."

"Then you might have a problem."

"How so?"

He smiled. "Even though I would tell her to stay out of it, Valery would not take kindly to anything you might do to me. She would challenge you. You might not win. But even if you could beat her, you would never get the chance. Holt hates my guts, but he is obsessed with my sister, and so you would have to face not just me and her but him, too. I do not think you could beat the three of us."

That made her think. Giselle glanced at Valery and then at Holt, and what she read on their faces convinced her. Her sour expression almost made up for her calling him "Slick."

She folded her arms. "What do you have in mind?"

"Use us. Put the angels, Blades, and Spears in another protection circle. We can withstand a lot. We certainly will add to her exhaustion. Then make your stand with Holt and the rest of the coven."

"You want to be cannon fodder? The Fury will slaughter you." There was something in the way she emphasized the last word that told him she was thinking of Max, of keeping him safe for her. Bleak humor almost made him smile. Giselle was holding on to her faith in Max, too.

"Then we die. This is what we were made for."

"You aren't even bound to Horngate."

He went so still that it felt like his heart stopped pumping. Oz tensed behind Giselle as violence filled the room. "Fuck. You."

He wanted to leave, to turn his back on her and go hit something. Destroy something. Shred metal with his bare hands. But he stood there, his jaw thrust out, refusing to back down. He belonged here, and he did not give a fuck if she disagreed.

Her lip curled, and she taunted him. "Maybe you won't even get to come to the party, Slick. Maybe we'll do this in full sunlight. *My* party, remember?"

Magic swirled in her eyes like black whirlpools, and her hair drifted on an invisible current. The room crackled with power. Holt watched her, fascinated.

"No," Alexander said, stepping forward. When Oz started to intercept him, Alexander pinned him in place with a single look. The circle of witches scooted apart, and he stopped in front of her. "This is not just your party. You may hold Horngate's *anneau,* but *we* hold you. This is our home, and you are *our* witch. If you are going to do this, you will do it at sundown. The Spears will suffer from the night, but that is the price they pay. Better that than any of us sitting on the sidelines while you go to battle."

Giselle stared a moment, then gave in. "And if she breaks her containment barrier before sundown?"

"Make sure she does not."

"I can do that," Valery said. "And I can help with the rest."

"No," Holt said, rising to his feet. "You're going to get the hell out of here. It's too dangerous. And before you go protesting, know this: I won't help as long as you're here. They need me more than you, so you can get your ass on the road."

Valery stiffened and glared at her ex-husband. But he held all the cards. Finally, she nodded. "I'll leave. But first, I'll set up a strengthening spell around the containment circle. It won't take me long, and none of you needs to waste your strength on it."

Reluctantly, Holt nodded. "If anything happens, if she starts to break out before you finish, I want you to ride the smoke out of here. Promise me."

"Forget it. I don't make promises," she said. "Not to you."

His face twisted, and his fingers curled like he wanted to strangle her. Alexander grinned. He knew that feeling. He had felt it often enough with Max and sometimes with Valery, too. But there was nothing Holt could do.

The mage glared at him. "Let's get it over with, then." He started for the door.

Valery put her hand on Alexander's arm. "I'll be back to say good-bye." Then she followed Holt out.

Alexander watched her go. He could not argue with Holt over her leaving. He was almost glad that Max was not here for this. But he had a feeling that she would be safer at Horngate with a Fury than wherever she was with Scooter.

He thrust the thought away and turned to the diagrams on the table. "All right. Let us figure this thing out so that everyone is still standing when it is over."

15

THE ARMOR WAS EVERYTHING THAT MAX COULD have hoped for. The teeth of the Calopus couldn't cut through it, and Tarzan's blades bounced off. That didn't mean she didn't get hurt. The mouths of the spiked wolves were powerful enough to break bone, as were Tarzan's heavy blows, and the armor could only do so much.

She slashed at the Calopus, chopping at their legs and necks, but they seemed to heal as fast as she did. They snapped and growled, leaping onto her and trying to drag her down. If any one of them grabbed her throat, they'd crush it for sure. Meanwhile, Tarzan circled behind them, leaping in to strike whenever she wasn't paying attention. Which was a whole lot more often than she would have liked. He had picked up on the fact that her armor didn't keep her from blunt-force damage and had resorted to smashing at her with his swords like they were clubs.

He was nearly as fast as she was, and he had definitely learned from their first fight. He was being patient, letting the wolves wear her down. There was no time to rest. They kept coming and coming with relentless violence.

Killing them seemed impossible. She couldn't seem to find their hearts, and no matter how hard she chopped at their necks, she couldn't seem to cut through.

Tarzan taunted her. "They were bred for survival. You won't kill them easily."

No shit. Like she hadn't noticed. She glanced at the balcony above. She needed height if she was going to keep the beasts from dragging her down and killing her. A couple of seconds to heal up wouldn't hurt, either. But a Calopus was fastened onto her ankle, another on her left bicep. The other three darted in. Max kicked out and punched the one on her arm at the same time. It dropped away.

She shoved the three into one another, ignoring the pain and weakness of her broken bones. She slammed a sword across the head of the one on her leg, and it let go with a screech. She whirled her swords at the others and leaped up to the balcony. Her leg failed. She didn't have the height.

Max let go of one of her blades and clung to the railing, her legs swinging just above the snapping jaws of the Calopus. She pulled herself up, clambering over the balustrade and sprawling onto the marble floor of the balcony. Tarzan yelled commands, and she heard the scrape of toenails as the Calopus rushed to obey.

She pushed herself up and looked down into the courtyard. Tarzan had vanished, as had the wolves. She could hear them baying. It sounded hollow, as if they were in a stairwell. Ilanion was nowhere to be seen. *Good*. He'd gotten away.

She drew a breath. Her ribs hurt, but she could feel her splintered bones knitting back together and her bruised muscles strengthening again.

The balcony opened into a lavishly decorated room. Max pushed the glass doors open and limped inside. It was a room for entertaining, with a grand table, glittering chandeliers, plush couches and chairs, and an open space for dancing or whatever other entertainments people enjoyed in Chadaré.

The baying of the Calopus was louder. There wasn't much here to use to her advantage. Still—

Max went to the massive dining table and shoved it up against the wall, putting broad gouges in the shining parquet floor. Oops. She leaped on top just as Tarzan thrust open the double doors at the far end of the room. His pets galloped past him, falling silent as they fixed on their prey.

The first one leaped. Max met it with a kick and flipped it onto its back on the table. She chopped down at its throat and through until her blade met its unyielding spine. But it was enough. The animal didn't move. She shoved it away. The next few minutes were a blur of pain. She skidded on blood and dropped heavily to her hands and knees.

Max rolled off the table and vaulted over a couch, spinning in time to knock a beast from the air. She rolled it onto its side and chopped at its ribs. They cracked loudly, and the beast yelped in pain. The sound cut off as she severed its throat and neck to the spine.

One by one, she brought them down, dodging and running and singling them out. Tarzan yelled commands all the while. The beasts were in a bloodlust and ignored him. Max didn't give them a chance to calm down. She kept at them, letting her Prime take control of the fight. Tarzan tried to wade into the fray, but he couldn't keep up with her running attack.

Finally, she was down to just one Calopus. She was stunned when Tarzan stepped between her and the slavering beast.

"Enough. It's between you and me," he said, and she could see sorrow mixed with hate in his eyes. He called out something to the beast, which hesitated but didn't move. He said something else, and it slunk away, lying down near the massive fireplace at the end of the room.

Max wiped a trickle of blood from her eyes with the back of her hand. "We don't have to do this, you know," she said. "I just came to get what was stolen from a friend. All you have to do is step aside."

"I can't."

This was a conversation they'd had before. "Can't or won't?"

"Both. I'm bound to obey my orders, and even if I wasn't, you and I must finish this."

"That's too bad," Max said, and moved to the open dance-floor area. She shoved aside a Calopus carcass. "I was beginning to like you."

He followed. He rolled his head on his shoulders to loosen his muscles. Like Max, blood smeared his clothing and covered his hands. He had a good share of bruises and cuts but was in pretty good shape compared with her. She wasn't worried. Now that the Calopus were out of the picture, he didn't have a snowball's chance in hell. He had supernatural strength and speed but nothing like hers.

They launched at each other at the same moment, as if in unspoken agreement. Their swords clashed together. Back and forth they danced, tapping, feinting, testing, evaluating. He wanted to know how good she was, which was pretty damned good. Max had trained with every weapon under the sun. She kept in good practice with swords, because they were always a good bet against most Uncanny and Divine creatures. The iron content alone meant that they did a lot of damage. Add in the sharp edge, and they were the weapon of choice for close combat.

She ducked under a broad swing and spun from the jab of the other sword. Not a good time to let her mind wander.

Tarzan continued to harass her, but he stayed out of reach. She lunged, and he danced out of the way. It was like he wanted to prolong the fight.

Maybe he did. Maybe he was hoping for backup to arrive.

The moment the thought struck her, Max was certain it was true. She switched into overdrive, smashing at him over and over, driving him into a corner. It wasn't long before he figured out her tactic and tried to escape. She gave him no room. His face was set in an expression of grim determination. He knew he was out of options. Between her skill and her armor, she was unbeatable.

But he wasn't without tricks of his own. Max drove forward, only to have him toss a handful of something at her. She was in the middle of taking a breath and sucked it into her lungs. It burned like acid. Her eyes burned and swelled almost instantly, and she couldn't see or breathe.

Instinct swallowed her. She dove, curling into a ball and knocking Tarzan's feet out from under him. He sprawled over her. She grabbed one arm and pulled herself on top of him, not letting him have the leverage to swing his swords. He squirmed and bucked, driving a knee into her thigh. He knocked her sideways and got an arm free. He hammered at her head. Despite her armor, the blows felt like mule kicks to her skull. She grabbed his neck and got hold of his chin. She gave a sharp twist. His spine cracked, and his body went limp, his final breath bleeding out of him in a quiet exhalation.

She rolled off him and staggered to her feet. She bumped into the wall and leaned against it weakly. Her lungs felt like rotten watermelons. She tried to breathe but couldn't manage to get any air. She coughed. Chunks of clotted flesh came up. She spat them out. She desperately wanted to breathe, but even though she drew more air in, she couldn't feel it. She coughed again.

Her eyes were running, tears flowing down her cheeks in a flood. She touched her eyes gently. The skin was raw and ulcerated. Her lungs were probably the same.

Her head spun, and her knees gave out. She was strong, but even she couldn't do without air. *Hurry the fuck up and heal before you die!* she screamed at herself. She pushed at her healing spells, but they were working overtime, and she'd expended a lot of energy getting through the crystal garden and fighting the Calopus. *Damn damn damn*. She didn't want to die this way. She didn't want to die at all.

She forced herself to stay calm and tried to draw a shallow breath. Across the room, she heard the scrabble of nails and the padding of feet. The last Calopus. Holy mother of fuck. She was screwed.

She dug for one of her daggers. The one in her waistband was long gone, but another in her cargo pocket was still there. She drew it. Her hand shook.

The beast stopped a few feet away. It sniffed, then whined. Max heard the scrape of a claw across clothing as it pawed at Tarzan. A moment later, its nails clicked again, drawing closer. Max tightened her hand on the dagger, but her fingers felt rubbery. She tried to firm her grip, but the knife slid to the floor with a clatter. Her heart was pounding so hard it felt as if it were going to rip out of her chest.

A whuffling puff of wind cooled her cheek. Max put up her hand to shove the Calopus away, but it was more of a pet than not. Her hand fell to her side. She panted, trying to get air. Blackness closed around her mind, and her muscles seized, and her body went limp. Her head dipped forward, and she passed out.

MAX WOKE SLOWLY. SHE BLINKED. HER EYES STILL FELT swollen, but she could see at least blurry shapes. She took a careful breath. Her chest hurt and sounded wet, but she wasn't dead.

She pushed herself upright. Tarzan's body lay a few feet away. The last Calopus stood beside her, its milky eyes fixed on her. Its fur was matted with blood, but whatever wounds it had were closed now. Max fought the urge to pat its head and call it a good doggie. It would probably bite her hand off.

She fumbled for the dagger she'd dropped and eased herself up the wall until she was standing. The Calopus just watched her. It looked like it was expecting something.

"Sorry. I'm fresh out of biscuits, Lassie," Max said. Her voice scraped low and raspy.

The Calopus wagged once and went still again, its tongue sliding along its lips.

Since it didn't look like the beast was about to jump her, Max bent and picked up her sword and one of Tarzan's. She wiped them both off on the back of a couch and sheathed hers. His was lighter and slightly curved. It wasn't going to fit into either of her scabbards.

She started for the door, keeping one eye on the horned wolf. She had no idea how long she'd been out and was just glad she hadn't been found and the Calopus hadn't eaten her while she was napping. She went to the double doors where Tarzan had entered and looked out into the hallway. Her luck was holding; it was deserted.

She eased out and started to shut the door behind her but found it blocked by the Calopus, which had followed her.

"What are you doing?" she whispered. "Stay."

The beast looked up at her and wriggled its way out into the corridor. Max sighed. *Crap*. She didn't need this. But the animal wasn't going to be left behind. And killing it would take more out of her than she had to give at the moment.

"Fine. Keep it quiet, and if you so much as think about biting me, I will kick you all the way to the moon. Got it?"

The beast gave a little whine as if it did understand. Max scowled at it. The beasts had understood Tarzan's commands, but he'd spoken in a strange language. Maybe it was telepathic on some level. Or maybe it was a coincidence. Whatever. It didn't matter. She had to find whatever of Scooter's that was hidden there. If it was. But Ilanion had seemed to think it likely.

There were a lot more servants than Max expected to find. And a lot of guards. She overheard some talking and found out that Tarzan had ordered them to keep away from the fight. She thought back to the way he'd given her the chance to get ready in both of their battles. He had a sense of fair play and a code of honor.

Maybe he figured that if she defeated him, she deserved a chance to get what she'd come for. He might have meant to give her a head start. Or maybe he hated being bound as much as she did, and this was his way of getting revenge. He couldn't just let her go without a hard battle, but he could set it up so she could explore for a while without alarms. If he had even the slightest idea what she'd come looking for, he would know that stealing it could topple his mistress's power.

She made her way through the mansion as fast as she could. She knew what she was looking for. A stronghold somewhere inside that could be guarded from both friends and enemies. It would have to be someplace where this Asherah would be able to perform magic and keep secrets. It would be a place where she would feel safe enough to sleep and relax.

Max quickly left the public rooms behind, along with the guest and servant quarters. Asherah would want privacy. A lot of it.

She avoided being seen relatively easily. There were a lot of places to hide, and no one seemed to notice the

Calopus. It was like the beast was camouflaged, even though Max could see it without any trouble. She wondered why.

Once, she startled a pair of guards and quickly and quietly slit their throats and dumped them in a closet. Time was running out. She couldn't count on them not being missed. She hurried.

As Max pressed deeper into the mansion, there started to be more locked doors and fewer guards and servants. Good thing she was a walking key. At first, the locks were ordinary key locks. Then they became simple wards, then complex wards. She had to be getting close.

The palace rooms were also becoming more sumptuous, if that was even possible. Everything was perfumed with a heavy, syrupy scent that coated Max's tongue and made her want to spit. It made it impossible to smell anything else. The floors were covered in thick woven rugs, delicate silks, and other fabrics that Max didn't recognize. Everything was gilded. It was like being inside Donald Trump's bathroom. The walls, the furniture, the ceilings—everything was gold. Jewels crusted much of it. It was all lit by candlelight, and the air danced with fairy sparkles.

"Let me take you to Funkytown," Max muttered.

There were fewer and fewer exits. She was being funneled down to the main entrance. She'd expected as much. Give people only one or two ways to get in and out, and you had them trapped if they were breaking in. Plus, it allowed for killing fields along the way and limited how many defenders you'd need to keep out intruders.

She went carefully along a narrow gallery. It echoed.

Above was a long balcony. Shooters could make a crossfire and fill her full of arrows if they wanted. But there was no one. It didn't feel right. She didn't trip alarms when she unlocked doors, but she hadn't expected the place to be so empty. Unless—

She could have kicked herself. *Of course*. Asherah and her minions were off laying siege to Ilanion's compound. She wouldn't want any of the other Korvad to get the bright idea that they could just steal Scooter out from under her nose, so she'd gone in force. Which meant security was right now at its weakest.

Max broke into a jog. Her lungs had mostly stopped hurting, and her eyes were pretty much back to normal. The Calopus trotted at her heels. At the end of the chamber was a narrow door. It had no handle, and its gray surface seemed to absorb the light. The wall was made of the same material, she realized, stepping back to get a look. The rest of the chamber was made of some translucent pink stone that was crisscrossed inside with darker pinks and whites. The balcony was made of carved wood inlaid with more of the pink stone.

She returned her attention to the door. This was the stronghold. A completely separate building, if she had to guess, and probably made entirely of the strange gray stone. It pulsed with power the way a fire gave off heat.

Max brushed her fingers over the wall. Magic glowed white where she touched, and sharp jabs of power skewered her hand and arm. She pulled back. This was going to hurt. She didn't waste any time but splayed her hands on the door and shoved with all her might.

She was instantly coiled in brambles of magic, the thorns cutting deep inside her. Max ignored it. It wasn't half of what she'd felt when she'd gone into the abyss the first time. She pressed harder, and then the door gave. It folded downward and lengthened impossibly to become a bridge over what looked like a moat of shadows. They rose on either side and made it impossible to see the other side. A gale wind scoured the new bridge. Max hunched and walked out into it.

Her feet slid as the wind caught her. She bent and clawed her fingers around the edge of the bridge as she inched across. The wind pounded her, and more than once, it felt like she was going to go flying into oblivion. She dropped to her knees and shoved the sword through her belt, holding on with both hands as she went further and the gusts blew harder.

She lost track of time. The wind echoed in her skull and tore the breath from her throat. Inch by inch, she crawled. Her arms ached and had begun to shake, when suddenly, hands grabbed her and pulled her up. Ilanion shoved her into a deep-set doorway. Both watched as the bridge rose and disappeared. Beside them, the Calopus growled low.

Ilanion looked down at it. "Friend of yours?" he shouted above the howl of the wind.

Max grimaced. She wanted to ask him what he was doing there. Or hell, *how* he had gotten there, but first, she wanted to get inside. She pushed Ilanion away and turned to the handle-less door.

Opening it hurt just about as much as the first one and took longer. But Max wasn't going to be denied. She kicked it open and thrust inside, Ilanion following close behind. The door swung shut, and blessed silence descended.

Max braced her hands on her knees and panted. She felt like she'd been put through a meat grinder. But no rest for the wicked. She straightened.

"What the hell are you doing here?" she asked Ilanion.

"Looking for what we came for." He sounded surprised that she would ask.

"Why?"

He scowled beneath his helm, fury kindling in his eyes. They were molten gold, without a trace of his original brown. "I told you, I'm in this to the end." His lip curled, and the air around him crackled with magic.

"Don't get your panties in a wad," Max said. "You know this is a borderline suicide mission at best. I wouldn't blame you for cutting your losses. As far as the Korvad knows, you aren't involved. You can still get out of this without any real damage."

He stepped close, leaning in so that the eagle beak of his helm brushed her nose. "I'll say this once more. I am in this fight. I want to break the Korvad's back. If you doubt me again, we're going to have a problem."

Max put a hand on his chest and pushed him back a step. "If you wanted to hurt me, you shouldn't have let me wear the armor. You don't have the skills to take me down at the moment. If you ever did."

He stared and then shook his head wryly. "Where did Nayan find you?" he wondered aloud.

"In the ass end of nowhere," she said. "How did you get here through that tornado outside?"

"Once we were inside the protective barriers, I was safe to fly. I found the tower. It was just a matter of riding the wind until I found the entrance. And you."

"Riding the wind?" She looked him over. His armor

was scraped and dented, and blood smeared his exposed skin. Bruises splotched him like spots on a giraffe. "Looks like the ride was rough."

He shrugged. "No worse than your journey, I'm sure. Now, we should get on with this. Asherah is certainly sitting siege at my compound, but she might return at any moment."

They were in a broad, round room. The walls and floor were made of the gray stone, and there were no decorations or furnishings to soften the bleak space. In the middle, a broad stair corkscrewed through the floor.

"I guess we go down," Max said.

They proceeded down the stairs, with Max leading the way and the Calopus on her heels. Ilanion brought up the rear. He eyed the spiked wolf. "How did this happen?"

"Hell if I know. It's not trying to rip out my throat. That's a plus."

They'd gone down fifty steps or so when the way was suddenly blocked by a barrier of red magic that stretched to the walls, rolling and rippling like a red lake.

Upon seeing it, Ilanion sucked his teeth. "Lords of air," he muttered, squatting down to look at it. He was careful not to touch.

"I take it this is bad."

"I might be able to break through it, but it will take me some time."

"Then I guess I go alone."

He jerked his head to look at her. "This will kill you. It's an extremely powerful shield, designed to hold back far more powerful creatures than yourself. You'll never survive."

"You might be surprised, Goldilocks," she said.

"Wouldn't be the first time," he said.

The barrier reminded Max of the one separating Horngate from Scooter's den. Lair. Whatever it was. All it was was a door on steroids, and doors couldn't hold her.

"Wait here for me. I'll be back."

She started down. Magic swallowed her step by step, creeping up her legs, over her hips and chest, and then over her head. Her armor squirmed, and she could feel it straining against the bite of the magic. But for Max, it was no worse than walking through a pool of bleach. It stung enough to clear the sinuses but was easily bearable. The wards on the two outer doors had been worse.

When she got to the other side, it was like stepping into a genie's house. There wasn't a single surface that wasn't covered with a pillow in some shade of pink. It was revolting. Maybe the genie lived in a Pepto-Bismol bottle.

She looked around for something to key off the barrier and nearly tripped over the Calopus. She frowned. "How did you do that?" The beast just stared back with milky eyes. Not a wag, not a blink. Max shook her head. She'd worry about it later.

She circled the room, searching for the barrier switch, finding nothing but pink froth. She returned to the foot of the stairs, and there it was. A small pink spray of gemstone flowers inlaid in the riser of the bottom step. She bent and brushed her fingers over the surface. A jolt ran through her hand, and the barrier fell like a rain of rose petals. A moment later, Ilanion joined her.

"Neat trick," he said. "I'm beginning to understand what Nayan sees in you."

"Gee, thanks," Max said. "I'm so flattered."

"We should hurry. Shutting down the ward barrier might have sent a warning to Asherah, if her servants haven't sent for her already. You don't want to meet her in her stronghold."

Max couldn't have agreed more. They ran down the steps, passing through several levels. They were mostly living quarters. But both she and Ilanion were in agreement that they needed Asherah's magical workroom.

It was on the bottom level, thirteen floors down from where they'd started. A nice magical number, Max thought. The floor space of each level had been steadily increasing as they descended, and this was the largest by far. Max stopped on the bottom step to survey the room.

On the left was an open space that was clearly used for working spells. To the right were long rows of work tables littered with plants, rocks, wood, cages, herbs, bones, feathers, jars, boxes, and many things Max couldn't identify. Lining the walls all the way around the chamber were shelves full of more supplies and thousands of books and scrolls.

It was clearly the place where Asherah practiced her magic, but nothing jumped out as belonging to Scooter.

"What now?" Max asked. Her Prime was beginning to feel itchy, like trouble was about to come crashing down on their heads. "We don't have much time."

Ilanion strode toward the tables on the right. "Look for something strongly warded. She might have a vault here."

Max looked down at the Calopus. "I don't suppose you can sniff it out, can you?" Again, that completely unreadable look.

She started on the left. The open floor wasn't all that likely a place to keep valuables, but she might as well rule it out and meet Ilanion on the other side.

Magic filled the room with such intensity that it was impossible to sort out stronger spells from the minor ones. But—

She was looking for something that belonged to Scooter, and she knew his smell almost as well as she knew her own. Nothing could hide it from her. She stood still, closing her eyes and pushing her predatory senses outward. Now that she was looking for it, she couldn't believe she'd missed it. It was just a thread of scent, but it was strong as steel.

It led her back to the open floor space. She'd walked right past it and never saw it. Why should she? It was small—only about eight inches wide. But size wasn't what disguised it. It sat on a shelf in the back on the end in the shadows and was warded to be invisible. If Max hadn't had Scooter's scent, she'd never have found it.

She lifted it down. The moment she touched it, the invisibility spell evaporated. It was a box made of ebony wood wrapped in layer upon layer of silver, gold, and copper wires woven in spell patterns. It was closed with a simple hook catch.

"I found it," Max called to Ilanion. He joined her.

"It's in your hands?" he asked, following her gaze.

"Can't you see it?"

He shook his head. Max described it. He chewed his lower lip. "It's possible that opening it without the proper incantation will destroy whatever's inside. Even your ability to pass through locking spells might not be enough."

She rubbed a hand over her mouth. Should she risk it? It meant Scooter's life. But getting Asherah to open the box wasn't going to happen. "Can you figure it out?" she asked Ilanion.

"Given time. But Nayan doesn't have it."

"I know."

"You could wait."

"For what? We have to know what we have and what we're still looking for." Holding her breath, Max flipped open the catch and slowly lifted the lid. Magic jolted through her like a lightning strike. Her hair crackled and stood on end, and she smelled it burning. Even her armor couldn't absorb the entire blast.

Inside, a massive diamond filled the confines of the box. It was roughly shaped and unfaceted. Max lifted it out and hissed. "Shit." Within the diamond was Scooter's heart. A crystal straw had been thrust through the top of the stone to disappear into the slowly clutching pink muscle. A thin line of crimson filled the tiny straw.

"Good," Ilanion said. "Blood was drawn off, but Ash hasn't had time to use it yet. She's probably hoping to get her hands on Nayan first. Even that small amount will help strengthen him when we return his heart to him."

"I'm going to kill that bitch," Max said through clenched teeth, carefully settling the diamond back into the box.

"Not today. We need to get out of here before she comes back."

They dashed up the stairs, taking four at a time. The sense of danger was growing stronger. Asherah was on her way. Max knew it without a doubt. She also knew that Ilanion was right—today wasn't the day to face her. Not without first getting Scooter's horn and silk back.

When they reached the gray room where they'd entered, Max thrust open the outer door, wincing as the wards lashed at her. The paranoid bitch had locked the door from the inside and out.

"Can you fly out of here?" she asked Ilanion over the roar of the wind.

He nodded. "Of course."

Max snorted but didn't challenge him. "Get back to Scooter. I'll meet you there."

"How—" He broke off. How she was traveling was obvious. "You're going to hide his heart?"

She nodded. "Somewhere the Korvad will never find it."

He gripped her shoulder. "Stay safe." With that, he launched himself out into the wind. It grabbed him, and in an instant, he was gone.

Max shut the door and looked at the Calopus. "This is where we part ways," she said. But she made no move to leap into the abyss. Not yet. Instead, she waited.

The minutes ticked past. At last, the air thickened, and Max felt Asherah approaching. The smell was familiar. It saturated every corner of the tower and the outer palace. Sensual, sweet, and nauseating.

Pink light filtered in from the shadows above. It twisted and slithered, gathering together into a woman. Of sorts. She had long black hair that shone like the back of a beetle. Her face was oval, with black eyes, greenish-white skin, and pink lips. Her body was curved and luscious. She had four arms, each delicate and graceful. Her fingernails were curving talons painted pink. She was clearly as deadly as she was beautiful.

Instantly, Asherah fixed her gaze on Max, her expression frigid with fury. Her mouth was full of sharp white teeth. She pointed with one of her left hands. "Who are you?" Her words were oddly slurred and breathy.

"I'm the one who's going to kill you," Max said. "Don't forget it."

With that, she dove down into her fortress and escaped into the abyss.

16

THIS TIME, GOING INTO THE ABYSS SEEMED ALMOST easy. Maybe practice made perfect, Max thought. She hung in the blackness for a long moment, gathering herself for what had to come next. Finally, she dove back through her fortress, all the while picturing Scooter's lair.

She dropped onto the sand beside the stump. It was cold. The sand looked dull. It was the safest place she could think of. No one but she and Scooter even knew how to get here. She set the box on the stump and opened it again. Her stomach turned, and she closed the lid.

For a moment, she pressed her forehead against her knees. Her stomach ached from hunger, and the rest of her felt like a wrung-out rag. She needed rest. Not that there was any time for it. She needed food, too. There was some of that in her apartment. It would be nothing just to step through the abyss and be there.

She looked at herself and wrinkled her nose. She stank of blood and sweat, and her clothes were shredded. What she wouldn't do for a shower! And her guns.

She could bring her guns through to Chadaré. Her mouth curved. *Yes*.

Slowly, she stood, not letting herself think of the real reason she wanted to go home.

Alexander.

She wanted him to know that she was still alive. She wanted all of them to know. But there wasn't going to be time for any of that. She would eat, clean up, get her guns, and leave. That's all.

Having left the box on the stump, Max returned to the abyss. Her heart pounded, and her stomach fluttered nervously. *Stupid*. She *wasn't* going to see him.

She pictured her quarters, imagining her bed. A soft landing. But when she dove into her fortress, the image in her mind shifted to somewhere else.

Max bounced down in Alexander's quarters, sprawling across *his* bed. He wasn't in it. He should have been. It was daytime. Disappointment jerked sharply inside her.

She couldn't wait for him. Her stomach clenched, and her eyes burned. She didn't let the tears escape. Instead, she searched his room for a pen and paper. She'd let him know she was alive, at least, if her scent didn't tell him that already. She held her Prime tamped down. She didn't want any of her Blades sensing her presence. They'd come running, and she didn't have time for that.

The point of the pen hovered over the paper. What should she say? *Dear Alexander,* she wrote. She clenched her fingers on the pen and forced herself to loosen her grip before it snapped. *Dear Alexander?* It sounded so cold and formal. She was anything but. She felt wild and explosive. But she couldn't think of anything else, so she left it.

She tapped her fingers on the table top. What else could she say? *I was here. You weren't. See you next time.* Brilliant. She had to do better than that.

She was concentrating so hard that she neither heard nor smelled him coming.

The door thrust open. It slammed against the wall and bounced shut with a bang. Alexander charged through like a hunting lion, his body taut with emotion.

He said nothing. He grabbed her, crushing her against him. She held on just as tightly. His mouth came down on hers with the violence of desperate need. His tongue thrust inside her lips—devouring, demanding, owning. She clutched him, her kiss equally hard. Everything she felt poured out of her into that scorching caress.

He made a sound deep inside, raw and urgent. His hands slid over her as if trying to make sure she was really there. He picked her up, and she wrapped her arms around his waist, grinding herself against him.

Cloth ripped as he tore away her shirt and flung it to the floor.

She was barely coherent enough to tell her armor to get lost before grabbing the back of Alexander's shirt and shredding it. The armor slid away, leaving her fevered skin feeling cool. Alexander hooked his hands into her waistband and encountered the sword belts. That caught him up.

He set her on her feet and stood back, his hands tight on her hips, his eyes so hot that Max thought she might burn up. She made a noise and pressed against him. He was too far away. She wanted to feel his skin on hers; she wanted his tongue in her mouth and his body hard against her. She wanted to be so close to him that she couldn't tell where she left off and he began.

"I thought you were dead," he said, his voice rumbling through his chest. "I thought you were not coming back."

"I know. I came back to let you know. But it's not over. Scooter still needs me."

He snarled, jerking her against him. "Needs you? What for? You belong here. With me. You are *mine*."

"Yes," she agreed simply. That much she'd figured out. "But I made him a promise. He's dying. They're *torturing* him."

That caught him. "Who? What is going on?"

There was so much to tell and no time. No time at all. "I want to tell you," she said. "But it doesn't matter. Not now. Just—"

She unbuckled the sword belts. They fell to the floor with a thud. Before she could unbutton her pants, he was there, pulling them open and shoving them down. His own swiftly followed. He didn't wait. Couldn't, no more than she could. The need between them exploded.

He lifted her again, turning her to brace her against the wall. His cock pressed against her, and she wriggled, hissing with pleasure as she sought to impale herself on him. He groaned and clutched her tighter, stopping her movement. Max kissed his shoulders and neck, touching him frantically. His skin was satin and tasted purely of him. It was enough to send her reeling, her mind lost in a haze of want. Her body throbbed. She couldn't contain her moans as he licked and caressed her throat and shoulders, all the while teasing her, keeping her from driving herself down onto him.

He bent and sucked her nipple into his mouth. She went rigid, throwing her head back with a mewling sound of pure delight. He growled satisfaction, and drew harder. The feeling pulled tight down to her crotch and sent whorls of exquisite pleasure dancing through her body. If she'd been standing, she probably would have melted to the floor. He bit gently and then switched to the other breast. Max could hardly contain herself. She wanted to return the caresses, but her mind had spun out of control, and all she could do was feel. Her hips ground against him.

"Please, Alexander," she whispered.

Her world exploded. He slid inside her with one thrust. Her body pulsed around him. She clutched his shoulders as her body spasmed. He groaned and bucked against her helplessly, driving hard. Now it was her turn to laugh with the power that came with knowing his need. She rocked herself against him, and he clenched his hands on her ass.

His mouth closed on hers again. Their tongues thrust together, sweeping, devouring, adoring. Another spasm shook Max, and her mind broke apart. She cried out, not knowing what she said. He whispered against her ear, but she couldn't hear it. She couldn't hear anything. All she could do was feel, and it was nothing like she'd ever felt before. As if she was full of fireworks and a delight so intense there were no words for it.

He thrust harder and then stiffened, his head buried against her shoulder as he came. His raw, rasping moan brought her to the edge of bliss one more time, and she tightened her legs as her body quaked with his.

They stood panting for a long minute before Alexander lifted his head, brushing the damp hair from her forehead. His eyes were molten, his expression faintly awestruck. Max knew how he felt. It was like the universe had cracked open and they'd swum in a primordial ocean of light and fire.

"That was—" Alexander shuddered and then kissed her long and slow. He made love to her mouth, teasing and licking, delving with deft sureness. He slid his hands around her neck and around the back of her head, deepening the kiss until Max felt as if she were drowning in desire.

But there wasn't time. She gently pushed against his chest and reluctantly let her feet slide to the floor. He groaned protest and kissed her harder, but she twisted away. "I can't stay."

He went utterly still, his face turning savage, his hands tightening on her. "No. Do not leave."

"Scooter's waiting for me," she said. "I'll come back." But she couldn't promise, and he knew it. "I need some food, weapons, and clothes. Then I have to go."

His face contorted, and he shoved himself away. He pulled on a pair of pants and took out a shirt. He pulled it over his head. His hands linked behind his head, and he folded his elbows forward, staring sightlessly at the wall. "This is impossible," he muttered, so low Max wasn't sure she was supposed to hear.

The words kicked her in the stomach. "What is?"

He turned slowly, as if he'd forgotten she was there. His expression had smoothed and was now austerely chiseled, like the sharp peak of a wind-scoured mountain.

"What's impossible?" she asked again, her stomach

crawling up into her throat. She already knew the answer. She'd expected—no, demanded—so much from him and given little back. She was still making demands. Who could blame him for throwing in the towel? He wasn't bound to Horngate. He could walk away and never look back. At the thought, Max felt herself drawing up inside, curling up around a hurt that was too raw, too deep to bear. She could lose him.

"Nothing," he said in a clipped voice that did nothing to assuage the pain.

She couldn't leave it at that. "C'mon, Slick. Spit it out. What crawled up your ass and died?"

His body jerked forward, and he caught himself. The power of his Prime filled the room like a thunderstorm as his emotions rose. It was dense and turbulent. Her own rose eagerly to meet it. She tamped it back. If the others realized she was there, they'd come running. As it was, she wasn't sure how Alexander had figured it out. But that wasn't the important question now.

"What's your problem?" she asked.

His jaw knotted, and he folded his arms, his biceps bulging like he was fighting not to strangle her. Probably he was. It was a fabulous ending to their first time together.

His lips thinned as his mouth pulled tight. "I am sick of you walking out on me," he said finally.

"It's not by choice. You know that."

He snorted disbelief.

Max had the grace to flush. It was true that she'd been dodging and running from Alexander for weeks before Scooter took her. She hadn't known how to cope with the tidal wave of feeling she felt for him. She still didn't, but she was done running. She was willing to drown in them, but first, she had to help Scooter. She'd promised.

"It's different this time, Slick," she said, knowing how lame that sounded.

"Of course it is," he said. Then his gaze ran over her. She fought the urge to cover herself. Desire burned in his eyes, and his nostrils flared. He stepped back. "Do not let me keep you. Scooter is waiting, and I need some sleep," he said coldly.

"That's it?"

"What else is there?"

The question hung between them. Max had no answers for him. The pain inside her swelled, becoming so massive she could barely make herself move. "Right," she said, her lips like wood. "I'll get going, then." She bent slowly and gathered up her armor and weapons, leaving her filthy clothing. Tears burned in her eyes, and she could barely see. She turned and stumbled toward the door. Her hand was on the handle when he snatched her close.

Alexander spun her around, his arms like iron bands as he held her against him. He pressed his forehead against hers. There was agony in his eyes. "What have you done to me?" he said, his voice rough as uncut diamonds. "I have done things for you that I would never have done for anyone else. I called on that bastard Holt for help. I persuaded Valery to come and be the reward for him."

Max stared. He'd called Holt? He hated the mage bitterly. And he'd used Valery as bait to get Holt's help? The knowledge stunned her to the core. Only she knew how deep a sacrifice it was. She had seen for herself how much Alexander hated Holt and how much he loved his sister. It was humbling. It made her emotional cowardice all the worse. She'd made him chase her when she only wanted him to catch her and hold on forever.

Ever since Giselle had betrayed her and turned her into a Shadowblade, Max had wrapped herself in emotional Kevlar. She didn't risk her feelings. And even when they escaped and anchored themselves in her friends, in Alexander, she'd made herself believe that she could cut those ties and survive. That she couldn't really be hurt. To make that happen, she'd kept them all at arm's length. But now—

She couldn't escape them. She didn't *want* to. Not if it meant losing him.

"Do you hurt as bad as I do?" she wondered suddenly, the words escaping before she could even consider what she was saying.

"*Do* you hurt?" He loosened his grip and tipped her chin up. It felt like he was looking all the way through her. Nothing could be hidden from that dark intensity. A finger brushed gently below her eye. "Tears?" He sounded startled.

Her mouth bent in a tense smile. "It happens. I'm not a statue." The heat from his body was curling through her, but it did nothing to cut through the ice in her belly. She didn't know how to talk to him, to fix what was broken between them. Her mouth opened and then closed like a dying fish. *Stupid*.

"No, you are not." His fingers ran down her cheek and curled behind her head. She leaned into his touch.

"I—will you wait for me?" she asked in a rush. Time seemed to stop as she waited for his answer.

He gave a soft laugh, devoid of humor. "Do I have a choice?"

"Yes."

He bent and brushed his lips against hers, feather-soft and all too fleeting. "No," he whispered. "I do not. I have never had a choice when it comes to you."

Max closed her eyes, relief and desire cascading through her. She shuddered with the force of it. Mother of night, how she wanted to stay! But Scooter was dying.

She opened her eyes. "I have to go."

He hestitated, his jaw tightening. Then he nodded and let her go. Pushing her aside, he reached for the door. He checked the hallway and motioned her out. She stopped dead. Lying on the floor was an enormous dog with black shaggy hair and luminescent green eyes. It sat up and looked at her with preternatural intelligence. Max didn't need to be told that the animal wasn't just a dog. It was a Grim. Magic was layered thick around him.

"Friend of yours?" she asked, raising her brows at Alexander.

"Something like that. His name is Beyul."

"OK." She stepped carefully around the big animal and ran down the hall to her apartment, sliding inside with Alexander and Beyul close behind. "Makes himself at home, doesn't he?" she said as the beast climbed up onto the U-shaped black leather couch and sprawled along it. "I hope he doesn't have fleas."

She dropped her gear on the bed and went into her closet. She grabbed a couple of liter bottles of Mountain Dew and a canister of peanut butter pretzels. She ate several handfuls and guzzled down the soda before heading for the bathroom. Alexander followed her.

"Do not even think about helping me wash," she said, pointing a warning finger at him. "I know how that will end up, and I have to get back."

The last words were thick with meaning. Alexander nodded soberly, watching her as she went around the steaming natural tub carved out of the bedrock in the middle of the room. She went to the shower and turned on the spray. He leaned against the wall outside, watching her. It was incredibly erotic and all Max could do not to drag him inside the shower with her and have her way with him again.

"Tell me what is going on," he said.

"The short version is that Scooter is dying. Some people have stolen some of his body parts, and he needs them back if he's going to survive. I got back his heart, and now I have to get his silk and his horn. I've got some help, though. Ilanion is an old friend of Scooter's."

"You can trust him?"

"As much as I can trust any stranger who has his own agenda. He's powerful. Like Scooter. But with wings."

She rinsed the shampoo out of her hair and rubbed in some conditioner, then took a loofah and started scrubbing away at herself, carefully not looking at Alexander watching her.

"Wings?"

"Yep. But he's not an angel. Though it would be fun to see him take on Tutresiel. I'd pay to watch that. Speaking of angels, what's going on here?"

He hesitated. "Trouble." The word was flat, toneless.

She stiffened. "Is it bad?"

"Looks like it."

"How bad?" Her voice had gone hoarse. She was trapped. Scooter needed her, and she'd promised to help him. But if Horngate was in trouble, she couldn't just walk away. Everything that meant anything to her was there.

Alexander gestured dismissively. "That is why I sent for Holt. We will handle it. Focus on helping Scooter. And staying alive."

She drew a deep breath and let it out. He was right. And it wasn't like she had a choice. But still. "Is everybody OK?"

He nodded, his gaze following her motions with intense concentration as she resumed washing. She could almost feel the heat on her skin. "Niko had an episode, but he is upstairs eating now and recovering well."

Max looked at him, her Prime rising despite her effort at control. "Episode? What the hell does that mean?"

"It means it is over, and he is fine. You do not have to worry. Giselle also survived the backlash of your broken bindings. In fact, it has given her a lot of strength." He chewed his bottom lip. "How did you break them without dying?"

She turned off the water and stepped out of the shower, grabbing a towel and drying off. "I had an *episode,* and the next thing I knew, I woke up without my bindings."

Alexander stalked toward her. "What episode?"

"Oh, don't worry," she said. "It's all over, and I'm fine." She flashed him a taunting smile and scooted past him to get dressed. She pulled on underwear, a sports bra, and socks and then slid the armor over herself. Once again, it lengthened to cover her and tightened into a skintight suit.

"What is that?" Alexander asked, and his voice was dangerous, his Prime fully roused.

"Armor. Ilanion lent it to me. It deflects magic, and blades don't cut through it. It's already saved my ass."

"Another episode?" he asked, the muscles of his jaw working. His eyes were almost white.

Max froze in the middle of pulling on her pants. "Are you going feral?" But there was no mistaking those eyes. Fear and desperation clawed inside her. No, she couldn't lose him this way! But how could she stop it? Then she frowned. Despite the feral change to his eyes, he didn't seem to be out of control.

The corner of his mouth curved up. "I have. I am. I have . . . changed since you have been gone. Call it an *episode*." His brows rose on the last, taunting her.

Point to him. She finished pulling on her pants. "So you're OK? How is that possible? Your eyes—"

"I am fine. As I can be," he added. "Let us just say my Prime and I have grown much closer than we used to be. The beast is closer to the surface now."

She chewed her lip, taking it in. He didn't seem about to go off the deep end. "What happened to cause all this?"

His mouth hardened. "You died."

"Shit. I'm sorry. I wanted to tell you I was OK, but there was no way."

He nodded, his arms folded over his chest. "I know. How did you get here?"

"It turns out that one of the reasons Scooter was so

eager to get his paws on me was that I can travel through the abyss between worlds. I can go anywhere I want, whenever I want. I can even take passengers with me."

He said nothing as she finished dressing and went to the big walk-in closet to dig out her favorite throwing knives. They were thin and well balanced. She buckled the sheaths around her forearms, then pulled on a shoulder holster with her .45. Her Glock nine-mil went into an ankle holster on her right leg. She filled the big cargo pockets of her pants with full magazines for both guns.

Next, she wrapped a witch chain around her waist. She didn't know how much good it would do against the kind of trouble she was walking into, but it wouldn't hurt to have it. The garrote Ilanion had given her remained around her neck. She buckled on the swords and strapped a pair of combat knives to her thighs.

Finally, she turned to face Alexander, her stomach knotting painfully. It was time to leave him again. She had no idea how she was going to make herself do it.

His face was remote as he leaned in the doorway, trapping her inside.

"I have to go." She could have left right then through the abyss. He couldn't stop her. Judging from his expression, he knew it and sure as hell didn't like it.

His cheek twitched with hard-held emotion. "I want you to do something for me," he said finally.

"What's that?" she asked cautiously.

"If you get in trouble, if you need help, you come get me. Through the abyss."

Max stared. The idea had never occurred to her. Not in her wildest dreams. Her gut reaction was to say no.

Hell, no. She didn't want him anywhere near Chadaré and the Korvad. It was too dangerous, and she'd be damned if she'd risk him for Scooter.

It was on the tip of her tongue to say so, but she bit back the words. He wasn't offering for Scooter; he was offering for her. No, she corrected herself. It wasn't an *offer* at all. It was a demand. She licked her lips. His eyes riveted on the motion, and an electric shiver swept across her skin. He saw it, and his eyes flared with hunger.

"Stop that," she said, stepping back. "I can't think when you do that."

"Who wants you to think? It only gets us into trouble." He straightened and came to stand in front of her. He didn't touch her. "If you get into trouble . . . Come. Get. Me."

"What about Horngate?"

He made a sound of frustration, stepping back and slamming a fist into the wall. She heard his bones crack. He didn't seem to notice. "This is not about Horngate. This is about you and me and the fact that nothing matters if you die. So let me help."

His blunt words pounded her like fists and made her flush. Why was it so hard to take what he was giving? What was she waiting for?

"I'll come."

He closed his eyes and let out a long breath. "Good."

She stepped forward and gripped his face, pressing her lips hard against his. The kiss was fast and thorough, and it left her heart thundering like a jackhammer. She pulled away. "See you when I see you, Slick."

He jerked her back again and brushed his lips over

hers with heartbreaking softness. "Watch yourself." With that, he let go.

Max couldn't wait any longer. She had to get back to Ilanion's compound. But first, she had a couple of errands to run. She dropped into her fortress, and Alexander vanished from sight.

17

MAX DISAPPEARED. ONE MOMENT SHE WAS standing before him, the next it was empty air. All that remained was her scent and the taste of her on his lips.

Alexander closed his eyes, savoring the memory of her, of having her in his arms, of being inside her, of her need and her frantic taking. It had happened so fast that he could hardly believe it was true.

He had been on his way to the dining commons to check on Niko when Max's presence had lit up his heightened senses like a beacon. Her spirit color was a rich mix of orange and blue hues, reminding him of fire. He had come running like a starving man for food. Even so, he had not been sure whether it could be true, whether Max was really back. Then he had thrown the door open, and any hope of control had gone out the window. All he knew was he had to touch her and make her his. Thank the spirits she had felt the same way.

He opened his eyes and turned, feeling dazed. He had gone from the depths of despair to the height of joy, and now she was gone again. But not dead. His hands clenched. Not dead. And once she was done with this Scooter business, he would not be separated from her again. Not if he had anything to say about it.

He turned and went to the door, stopping with his hand on the handle. Should he tell anybody else of Max's return? But he knew the answer before he finished thinking the question. *Of course*. At the very least, Niko, Tyler, Oz, and Lise deserved to know. Even Giselle.

Beyul trotted out into the hallway behind him. The beast wagged his tail, and Alexander could not help the broad smile that broke across his face. Unrepentant joy bubbled through him. "She is alive," he told the Grim unnecessarily.

Niko was still in the dining commons with Tyler and Thor. Magpie was in the kitchen banging pots and pans. A few other people were also eating, but the place was otherwise deserted.

Alexander slid into the open chair beside Thor. He waited. He was covered in Max's scent. It would not take the others long to catch a whiff of it.

Niko was first. His hand tightened on his fork, and the stainless steel crumpled like tin foil. He carefully set it down and turned a tight look on Alexander. He said nothing, but his expression was one of terrified hope.

Alexander nodded. "She was here."

Niko slumped, scraping his fingers through his short black hair. "Thank the spirits."

By now, the others had figured it out.

"Where is she now?" Tyler demanded, his chair flipping over as he leaped to his feet.

Thor just folded his arms and rocked in his chair, a wide grin splitting his lips.

"She left. She was not done with Scooter's business," Alexander said, and all three of the other Blades wilted. "She has promised to come to me for help if she needs it."

Tyler sat back down as Alexander explained what little Max had told him of her ability to pass through the abyss and how she was helping Scooter retrieve his body parts.

"Someone stole his heart? What did she mean, silk and horn?" Tyler asked.

"No doubt, exactly what it sounds like," Niko said. "The bastard didn't show any of us his real self. Likely he's a web-making rhino or something."

The others laughed at the prospect and then slowly sobered. "She's alive. That's something. Have you told Giselle?" Niko asked.

Alexander shook his head. "Not yet. I thought you should be the first."

"Thanks, boss," Niko said, sipping coffee. "You know Giselle isn't going to like that Max went to you and not her."

"Too bad."

"If Max isn't bound," Thor started to say slowly, and then stopped as the other three men looked at him.

"What?" Tyler demanded, his Blade rising dangerously. He spun his fork in his fingers. At any moment, he could drive it into Thor's eye, and the other man would never get out of the way in time.

"If she isn't bound to Giselle and Horngate, will she come back to stay or will she leave?"

It was theoretically a possibility, and the fact that Niko

and Tyler clearly feared it was almost laughable. Alexander looked at them in disbelief. "You actually think she *could* ever leave any of you? Do you know her at all?"

Niko looked away, playing with his food. "She's always wanted out of here. She hates Giselle."

"And she loves you," Alexander said. "Not to mention her family and everybody else here. The only way she is leaving here is dead." He shook his head. "You are the ones who were so sure she could not have died. You would have faith in her return but not in her staying?"

Tyler had the grace to flush. He stabbed the point of the fork into the table top. It stuck straight up, the tines planted deep in the wood. "Did you tell her about the Fury?" he asked.

"No. She could not stay to help, and I did not want her to be distracted. We will handle it." Alexander hoped to hell he was right. He stood. "I will go let Giselle know. How do you feel?" he asked Niko.

The other Blade stretched, his joints cracking. "Like I had a bad case of the flu. Made me feel almost human again," he said with a dark look at Beyul, who was sitting beside Alexander, his broad, shaggy head well above the level of the table. "Thanks for that, you stupid dog."

The Grim tipped his head and then nosed Alexander's arm. He scratched behind the big animal's ears, caught by the bizarre contradictions of the beast. Beyul was an incredibly powerful being, with abilities Alexander could not imagine. Yet it was hard to remember that when he acted so much like an ordinary dog. It seemed almost insulting to pet him, and yet the Grim leaned heavily against his hand, making a moaning whine of pleasure.

The other three Blades watched the interaction in disbelief. "What *is* that thing?" Thor asked finally. "He acts like a chicken in the feed when you're petting him, then he nearly kills Niko."

"Killed," Alexander corrected. "Niko was dead."

There was a moment of silence. "Niko does seem to have a buzzard's luck, don't he?" Thor said after a moment.

Tyler slanted a look at him. "What the hell does that mean?"

Thor look startled, then grinned. "Means he's been diggin' up more snakes than he can kill."

Tyler looked at Alexander. "Is he even speaking English?"

"Niko has bad luck," Alexander translated.

Tyler looked at Thor. "You couldn't just say that?"

"I did, son, but you just can't seem to spot a goat in a flock of sheep."

Tyler scowled. "I'm pretty sure that was an insult."

"Only because it was," Niko said.

"How the hell am I supposed to get all self-righteous and pissed if I can't understand what the idiot is saying?" He glared at Thor. "I know that down-home Texas crap isn't natural. You don't talk like that all the time."

Alexander chuckled dryly. "It comes naturally, though he has learned to tone it down here and there."

"Anyhow, back to the dog. What are you going to do with him?" Niko asked.

"Do with him? I do not think I have any choice in the matter. He will do what he likes. He has made that clear enough." He frowned at Tyler, memory stirring. "I thought one followed after you, too."

Tyler lifted his shoulder. "I got lucky. It must have

changed its mind. At any rate, it stayed back with the others."

"Take it a bone," Thor suggested.

"Now, why would I do that?

"Figure you might want someone warm to sleep with." Thor's lips curved in a grin. "I noticed you haven't been finding any lady company lately."

"That's because I'm not a tasteless whore like Niko. I have standards."

"Your standards knock boots with what most people call hard up. You're so dry your ducks don't know how to swim."

"I've heard about enough," Magpie said, pushing in from the kitchen with a couple of quiches. She set one in front of Alexander and the other in the middle of the table. "You need to quit flapping your lips and start eating. Tyler, take your fork out of my table."

He hurried to comply, looking guilty and more than a little worried. Upsetting Magpie meant oversalted and burned food for however long she was annoyed.

"You going to tell her?" Niko asked Alexander.

Magpie stopped, hands on her hips. "Tell me what?"

"Max was here," Alexander told her.

The stripe-haired witch froze, then her eyes closed. "Thank the elements." Her eyes sprang open, her black eyes drilling through him. "Was?"

"She left."

Magpie's lip curled, and Alexander knew he was in danger of eating garbage for the next year. He relented. There was no point. It was his anticipation of what was to come later, trying to contain the Fury, that was driving him to act like an ass.

"She said she was not done with Scooter's business. She came to let us know that she was still alive."

"Have you told Giselle?" Then she waved her hand. "Never mind. Of course not. She's preparing herself to battle the Fury. And I am supposed to make sure all of you calorie-load so you're at full strength. So eat." She cast one last dark look at Alexander before retreating to the kitchen.

He dug into the quiche, while the others ate obediently. Magpie bustled in and out of the kitchen with an array of high-calorie and high-protein foods. Ordinarily, Shadowblades and Sunspears needed around twenty thousand calories a day to keep themselves running. The various spells that went into their creation drew a lot of energy. If there were not enough calories to supply them, the spells would eat flesh and bone, eventually killing the Blade or Spear. Battles and healing drove the calorie requirements up exponentially.

Alexander kept eating long past the point where he was stuffed. So did the others, despite groans of pain.

"Think she'd notice if we just ran for our lives?" Tyler whispered, staring balefully at a steaming plate of sausages and eggs.

"I think she'll make you pay dearly if you do," said Niko as he took a bite of bacon from the several dozen strips on his plate. "I used to love bacon. After today, I may never eat it again."

"Yes, you will," Magpie said as she swept Thor's plate away and put another in its place. He stared at the three-decker hamburger with a look of horror. "You'll eat it, and you'll like it. Understand?"

Niko wilted. "I've never had such good bacon before,"

he said, and stuffed it into his mouth with false eagerness. He made sounds of delight and gave Magpie a sickly smile.

She grinned and patted his shoulder. "Very good." She bustled back to the kitchen.

Niko put his head in his hands and moaned. "I hate it when we know shit is going to come down and I have to go into battle feeling like a Thanksgiving turkey."

With a fatalistic sigh, Thor picked up the hamburger. "I never thought I had a mouth *this* big," he said before biting into it.

Alexander was doing his best to eat the rest of the steak and the Everest-sized mound of mashed potatoes and gravy on his plate. He was almost happy to see Holt stride into the dining commons.

"Come look at this," the mage demanded, stabbing a finger at Alexander. He was carrying a sheaf of papers, which he laid out on an empty dining table.

All four Shadowblades crowded around to see.

"This isn't going to work," Holt said, looking down at the plans they had made earlier.

Foreboding clenched Alexander in a tight grip. "Why not?"

"The first problem is the outer iron circle. There's not enough room to get the iron in there. I'd thought we'd use cars and such, but now that I've seen it, it can't work. We won't have time to tear them down to fit them into the space we have."

"There's a railroad that runs close," Niko said. "We could pry up the rails. They'd fit. Plus, pull off what we can of the cars and such. Might do the trick."

"It's going to take a lot of iron to even get her attention," Holt said. "She's a primal being. And she's going to be a newborn, which means she's not going to be in control of her power, even if she wants to be. If only we could have found a way to bleed some of that power away before . . ." He shook his head, glaring down at the papers. "Getting the rails is a start. We need to do more. This isn't going to be enough. Her power is just too big."

"What are you suggesting?" Alexander asked as Niko turned away to call Oz and get the Spears started on the train rails.

"I don't know."

"You're a mage," Tyler said quietly. "You've got to have *some* idea what we can do."

"Come on, Holt. You are telling me you have no ideas at all? That must really hurt your pride," Alexander goaded.

The mage scowled and bit his lower lip, making it bleed. The look he leveled at Alexander was murderous. "Someone could try to reason with her like Giselle planned," he said finally. "Let her have her revenge on her father, and then, while she is sated, step in and talk to her. If you're lucky, you can break through her mad lust for revenge and persuade her to control herself. Here's what you're up against: she'll be driven by a desperate compulsion to bring justice and vengeance. There's a lot of betrayal in the world, and because she was a child when she was killed and because her father is the one who did it, I'm guessing she's going to hear all the horrors not only of women but of children, too. The clamor from all over the world is going to hit her like a dozen freight trains mowing down a mouse. It probably already is. It's going to drive her insane. To reason with her, you're going to have to break through her madness. The thing is, nothing in any legend I've heard of says that a Fury is anything more than a mindless drive for revenge. There's not the smallest suggestion that they have any capacity for reason.

"But suppose you *could* talk to her—and as a man, I'm not thinking *you* actually could—the next problem is that just the fact of her birth is going to release a burst of power that is going to be on the level of a small nuclear bomb. I'm not convinced she has the power to stop that. So even if you could convince her not to kill everything in sight, it still might make not a difference."

"There has to be something we can do," Alexander said, unwilling to admit defeat.

"If we had more time and resources, maybe we could funnel the power somewhere," Holt said, tapping his fingers on the table as he scowled at the papers. "If we could create some sort of trap for the power to absorb it . . ."

"We could," Valery said.

She was leaning in the doorway. Alexander had not even noticed her arrival. It was obvious by his start that Holt had not, either. He turned jerkily around.

"You're supposed to be gone."

"I hadn't said good-bye to Alexander yet," she said as she walked in. "Besides, it sounds like you could use my help."

"No. We'll figure it out without you." Holt thrust out his jaw, his legs splayed. Blue magic made the exposed hex marks on his hands and arms glow.

"From the sounds of it, you need all the help you can get," she said. "You didn't think I'd just leave Alexander here to die if there was any chance I could stop that, did you?"

"I told you, leave, or I will," Holt said, his face darkening with fury.

"I don't think so," she said. "You aren't thinking real clearly, are you? I know the real reason you want me gone. I'm the only one who knows where I stashed those tablets you want back so badly. If I stay, you risk losing all that precious information. So you have to stay if I do, if only to keep that information alive." Her smile was taunting.

Holt stepped close to her, his body rigid with what Alexander suspected was the effort to keep himself from putting his hands around her throat. Or kissing her. Either was just as likely. "Right now, I don't give a shit about those tablets. I. Want. You. Safe," he said slowly.

"Then you'd better work with me. I'm not leaving," she said, not backing down in the slightest.

Holt knew he was over a barrel. He looked sick, and Alexander could almost feel sorry for him. Whatever was going on between the two of them, Holt and Valery still had a deep emotional connection. Hell, Alexander knew for a fact that Valery was still in love with her ex. He was beginning to doubt that the only reason Holt wanted her back was to retrieve the tablets she'd stolen. Alexander could smell the rage and desperate fear on the mage.

"If I work with you?" he spat out at last. "If I we build some sort of trap for the magic, you'll go to safety when she breaks out? You'll promise me?"

She gave him a long, steady look, then slowly shook her head. "I can't. You know that. I'm not abandoning my brother." She flicked a hard glance at Alexander. "And don't you start in on me, either. Just shut up and accept it." Her gaze returned to Holt. "I don't belong to you anymore. I get to make my own choices."

His hand flashed out, and he grabbed her bicep, pulling her against him. "You will always belong to me. I don't care if you took back the marriage marks. You'll be mine until you die."

She jerked away. "You can't hold smoke. Haven't you learned that yet? Anyhow, we both know you're more interested in those tablets than you ever were in me. Now, can we quit arguing and get to work? We don't have a lot of time."

His nostrils flared white, and his eyes closed to slits. "We are not done with this conversation. Not by a long shot."

Valery shrugged. "I am. There's nothing left to say."

"What do you have in mind to contain the Fury's power?" Alexander asked as Holt opened his mouth to snap back at her. He scowled at Alexander, then subsided.

"We need to trap it and sink it into something. Mages infuse objects with magic all the time to store it for later or to fuel a spell," Valery said.

"True, but never this much. We use trickles of power over time, not an ocean-full all at once," Holt returned peevishly.

"Doesn't mean it can't be done," she said.

"Don't you think mages would do it that way if they could?" he demanded, his eyes sparking with anger.

She shrugged. "Probably not. You all are so stuck on your traditions that you probably still use an abacus instead of a calculator. You forget to think outside the box," she said. "We *will* fail if you keep thinking like that. So grow a pair, already, and start acting like the cocky bastard we all know you are."

He went still, and then a slow grin spread across his lips. He turned away to look at the papers. "What are you thinking?" he growled.

"The problem with the break of power is that it will be explosive and fast, right?" she asked. "So what if we make something to trap it and slow it down and feed that force into a well of some kind?"

Holt did not answer for a long moment. He drummed his fingers on his thigh, staring sightlessly as he thought. Finally, he wiped a hand over his jaw and nodded. "It could work. But it will require a lot of magic, and we don't have much time." He glanced at his watch. "Maybe eight hours. We're going to need a lot of supplies we don't have here."

"We'll fetch what we need. As long as you don't try to use it as a way to get rid of me."

"We all do what we have to," he said with a taunting look.

"I will never forgive you if anything happens to Alexander because you sabotaged what we're doing," Valery said in a low, intense voice. "That much I am willing to promise you."

"No," Alexander interrupted. He knew that witches needed to give one another total trust when working this kind of spell, or they endangered themselves and everyone around them. Starting out with ultimatums only increased the chances that this would not work. "Holt will be a good boy. He will not risk you, Valery, and since you plan to be here when the Fury is let loose, he will do all he can to make sure this works. Right?" he asked Holt.

The mage gave an unwilling nod. "You shouldn't be letting her do this," he said to Alexander. "You should be trying to get her out of here to safety."

"I am her brother, not her keeper. She is a powerful smoke witch. If she wants to risk herself, that is her choice. You will notice she is not trying to stop me from risking myself. Can I do any less for her?"

"Maybe I love her better than you do," Holt said.

Valery snorted. "You love those tablets," she said.

Before Holt could argue, Alexander jumped in. "What do you need from us?"

Holt turned reluctantly away from Valery and pulled up a chair. He grabbed a pen and started a list. "Let's see what you have here at Horngate," he said, writing quickly. "Then we'll fetch the rest."

"What are you going to use to collect the magic?" Valery asked, leaning over his shoulder to read. "It has to be able to hold it."

He paused. "I was thinking a stone. Or possibly a metal. Gold and silver would work. Titanium is too brittle."

She straightened. "Those might not be able to withstand the pressure of the magic . . . Wait. What if we made a seed instead? We could use a stone at the center and wrap the magic around it like fruit around a pit. We could use quartz. Smokey or rose quartz are calming and healing. Infused with power, they might help us calm the Fury enough to talk to her."

"That's a long shot," Holt said.

"We take what we can get," Alexander said.

Holt looked at Valery. "We'd have to channel the power into some kind of matrix and then hold it until it filled with magic. It could end up being a hell of a big piece of fruit. I don't know what we'll do with it then."

"Let's worry about that when it's a problem," she said. "The spell will be difficult. You can't shut me out, or it won't work," she added.

He nodded. "We'll do it together. Partners again." He smiled with arrogant triumph and undisguised pleasure at the prospect. He handed Alexander his list. "See what you have. Valery and I will stay here and work out our spell and then go set it up when everything is ready."

Alexander took the paper and passed it to Niko, who knew far more about Horngate's resources than he did. "Is there anything else you need?"

Holt's mouth twisted. "I need to stop answering the phone when you're on the other end."

The corner of Alexander's mouth quirked. "They do say that curiosity killed the cat. Maybe it will kill the mage, too. But not until tomorrow, I hope." With that, he left to go shower and get himself ready for the night to come. He hoped that Horngate would still be standing when Max came back for good.

18

THE SHADOWBLADES GATHERED INSIDE THE MAIN entrance before sundown. Giselle, the small cadre of coven witches, Holt, Valery, and the Sunspears were already down in the ravine getting ready. The angels were with Alton, waiting for Alexander.

He scanned the small group, Beyul leaning heavily against his leg as Alexander absently scratched his ears. It was a motley bunch, and most of them he knew well enough to know that they would not hesitate to lay down their lives for one another and for Horngate.

Tyler and Niko stood with the four Alexander knew least. Jody was a tall, athletic-looking black woman with short-cropped hair and toffee-colored skin. Noah looked like a redheaded lumberjack, with broad shoulders, enormous hands, and shoulders like an ox. Simon reminded Alexander of a mink, with delicate features, a small frame, and quick, darting movements. The last one, Nami, was part Japanese and part Mexican. She was about five-foot-six, with voluptuous curves and exotic dark eyes. Her skin was caramel-colored. All four were relatively young, having been made into Shadowblades within the last few years. The fact that Max had trained them meant they were tough.

Another group of four clustered patiently on the other side of the passage: Oak, Ivy, and the twins Steel and Flint. They were new to Horngate. Alexander and Max had helped save them from a trio of ice witches—or something like that. The witches had been beyond deadly and had almost entirely destroyed a covenstead—sterilizing it so that nothing could ever live there again. The witches Judith and Gregory had come from there, as had these four Blades and three Sunspears.

Their coven had been peaceful, which meant that they knew precious little about fighting. Since their arrival, Alexander, Thor, Tyler, and Niko had been drilling them steadily. The fact that they'd already been through hell meant that none of them broke easily. Alexander trusted them.

That left Tyler and Thor. Tyler was pacing up and down, pinwheeling his knives in each hand. Thor slouched with one shoulder against the door, one booted foot crossed over the other, his battered straw cowboy hat pulled low over his eyes. His stance did not fool Alexander. He was tense, ready, and deadly as a panther.

There were only a few more minutes before the sun vanished and they could go outside. Alexander cleared his throat loudly to get their attention. They all turned to face him. Thor pushed his hat back with one finger.

"First, for those of you who have not yet heard, Max was here for a short time today. She left to continue her business with Scooter, but she is not dead. She plans to return to us shortly." There were looks of shock and relief. Max anchored them all in profound ways. "I would really like her to have a home to come back to. The odds are against us; I will not lie. But we do have a plan, and it is just possible that it could work.

"Your job is to protect the witches and, most of all, Giselle. We are going to be the front line between the Fury and the coven. Hopefully she will be stopped before she comes through us, but if not, then we fight so that she uses up her energy. We will try to weaken her so that when she gets to the witches, they have a chance to stop her. Any questions?"

"Yeah," Oak said. "Do we get hazard pay?"

"Only you if you don't die," Tyler said. "And I'm thinking of killing you myself."

"Aw, now you've hurt my feelings," Oak said with a puppy-dog expression.

"I'll hurt more than that," Tyler said. "But don't worry. If you die, we'll throw you a grand funeral with lots of whiskey and a couple of strippers. We'll hardly miss you."

The group of Blades chuckled, and it broke the tension.

The sun slipped down to the point where the Blades could be safely outside. The feeling rippled through Alexander. "Get going," he said. "Niko, make sure everyone is set up. Tyler and Thor, let's go get Alton."

Lise, Tutresiel, and Xaphan were waiting outside Alton's prison when the three Blades arrived.

"Keep him wrapped in the witch chain," Alexander warned as Lise opened the cell.

Alexander broke the containment circle with the knife Giselle had given him for that purpose. Magic roared up in a sheet of fire and then curled away to nothing.

Within, Alton lay on the floor, watching his captors with cold golden eyes. He reminded Alexander of a cobra.

"What do you want?" he asked.

"It isn't so much what *we* want," Lise said. "It's what Cora wants. You remember her. Your daughter? A pretty little girl, only fourteen years old? Her hair was the color of honey. She was smart and funny and brave, and you killed her so you could have more power. Well, guess what? She's back, and she wants to see you. Personally, I can't fucking wait for the reunion."

The Sunspear yanked Alton to his feet. He spat at her, and she slapped the side of his head. Alton fell to the ground like a tree and lay gasping. "You bitch. I will make you pay for that."

Lise jerked him up again, holding him by his collar. "Bring it on, you dickless wonder."

She dragged him out of the cell and passed him to Thor and Niko, who gripped him under the arms. Xaphan and Tutresiel took up positions behind. Tutresiel's sword gleamed like a small star.

"Did you eat?" Alexander asked Lise, falling in beside her as they led the way back to the main entrance. Beyul nosed between them.

She nodded. "Magpie sent me enough to feed the entire coven for a week," she said.

"Good. You are going to need all your strength to try to talk Cora down."

She stopped and stared. "I'm going to what?"

He motioned her to keep going and explained their plan to her. "We want you to be the one to try to reach her, since you knew her pretty well. You will be in a circle just outside of the one containing Alton. That alone will be dangerous, since the power she expends could burn right through it and you both. But if it does not, then you will try to remind her of who she was and who we are. Help her find herself. She will be insane with rage and betrayal, with the change and with all the voices she will be hearing. Not just voices—she will feel their pain, too. She will need to stop it; it is her nature. But we hope you can get her to see us and to control her destruction."

"Oh, goody, a suicide mission." Lise scraped her fingers through her burnished hair, her brow pinched as she thought. "What if she doesn't listen to me? What if I can't do it?"

"Then she tries to break out of the next circles, and the rest of us try to weaken her enough to keep the damage to Horngate at a minimum."

"This is a crappy plan," she pointed out.

"Yes, it is," Alexander agreed. "But it is the best one we could come up with. Feel free to suggest improvements."

"Don't die?"

"I will take it under advisement. Feel free not to die yourself." He glanced over his shoulder. "That goes for the rest of you, too. Except, of course, for the child killer. He can die painfully."

The angels flew Alton and Lise to the ravine where everyone waited. The three Blades made their way on foot.

When they got there, they stopped on the ridge. The Memory still perched on her stone vantage point, the pack of Beyul's enormous black cousins wandering through the gathered witches and Spears, snuffling and nosing. They crossed the spell circles as if the spells were not there.

In the center of it all was Alton's original circle containing the rising Fury. Thick black smoke boiled inside, and the air sizzled with magic. Alexander's hair prickled over his body, and his Prime surged. His new ghostly vision strengthened suddenly, and the world changed into an odd combination of hard reality and shimmering spirit.

The Memory was like a sliver of jade, and it hurt to look at her. Like Beyul, the other Grims evoked an ancient flow of water. Giselle's green and Holt's tiger-eye brown glittered with power. Valery was a shifting palette of green and black. He had not noticed that before. Mostly, he remembered her smell: ancient, solid, and free. Even now, the smell teased from the skein of the others and hooked into his heart.

She and Holt were off to the side, working together. Neither looked damaged, so their day had gone politely, at least. Alexander hoped it had also gone productively.

They had built a reinforcing circle around Alton's original and another one made of salt, herbs, crushed stones, and metals surrounded that one, with about ten feet in between. That's where Alton would go. The next circle was made of the same materials. Lise would go there, along with the angels. The last circle was actually three layers. The inner one was pure sulfur. Written in the yellow powder was a chain of hex marks. Next was a complex mix of nettle, knot grass, nightshade, thistle, wolfsbane, myrrh, cedar shavings, and wormwood.

Behind it was a wall of metal. It was made of train rails, bits of barbed wire, car and truck doors and hoods, and whatever spare bits of metal anybody could collect, from tools to tire rims, a watering trough, horseshoes, some rusted chains, and some fenceposts that looked like they'd been newly pulled out of the ground. Fairy creatures hated cold iron, and steel was made of mostly iron. Over the centuries since humanity had spread across the earth, their sensitivity had gone down, but it still hurt them. Whether it would hurt a Fury or not was debatable. But it was worth a try.

The Sunspears and Shadowblades had gathered behind that line, with the witches behind them. If the Fury broke through, the Spears and Blades would do everything in their power to slow her down and give the witches a chance to deploy a defense. Alexander was hoping it would not come to that. Holt and Valery would be among them, which boosted the witches' power considerably. But even if that was enough, a lot of people were going to die.

He drew a breath and let it out before looking at Thor and Tyler. "Are you ready?"

"It's a good day to die," Tyler said, and then smiled at Alexander's scowl. "Something Crazy Horse was supposed to have said."

"Right before he died?" Thor asked.

Tyler shrugged. "He won a lot before that happened. Just like we will today."

He reached out and shook Thor's hand and then Alexander's. "See you on the other side." With that, he descended into the ravine.

Thor adjusted his hat and spat on the ground, then

also shook Alexander's hand. "Been a pleasure," he said.

"It is not over yet."

"This ain't my first rodeo," Thor said admonishingly. "Brother, the one thing we didn't talk about was who is going to break that circle to release the Fury. Ain't one of us who don't know you're fixin' to do it, which puts you dead in the crosshairs. It's a suicide mission." His Texas drawl had broadened, revealing his tension more than anything else.

"I do not plan to die," Alexander said, knowing his friend was right.

"Do any of us?" Thor asked with a rakish grin. He touched the brim of his hat in a two-fingered salute. "See you on the other side," he said, and followed Tyler.

Alexander looked over the valley once more. There was nothing more to be done except to get on with it. He looked up at the night sky. The moon was down, and the stars sparkled, almost close enough to touch. For a fleeting moment, he thought of Max. He had not left her a note. If she came back for help, there was a good chance he was not going to be there to give it. His stomach twisted, and he looked away, his body going taut. He pushed away all thought of her and started down the hill. Time was wasting, and every second the Sunspears were exposed to the night, they weakened.

He went to Holt and Valery first. "How did it go?"

The mage was practically giddy with excitement. "It went perfectly. I don't know if it's strong enough to hold that much power, but if anything can, this is it."

Valery nodded. She looked as happy as Holt did, but there was a shadow of sadness in her eyes. She was already looking toward the end of this mess, when she would leave him. This working together had been bittersweet.

Alexander reached out and squeezed her hand in silent sympathy. Holt scowled at their affection. "Come on. We've set it in place over here."

It was much bigger than Alexander had anticipated. He had imagined something the size of a peach or even a grapefruit. The matte-black marble was the size of a small car. It sat on a ring of silver within the circle where Alton was but on the opposite side of the column of smoke.

"You are putting it inside with Alton?" Alexander asked doubtfully. "If he breaks his bindings, will he be able to tap into that magic?"

"It's a risk," Valery admitted. "But we're betting that the Fury isn't going to give him the chance. This way, we can drain away some of her power while she's distracted with him. It will continue to draw as long as any binding circles remain in place. The longer it draws, the weaker she gets, and the better the chance of everyone staying alive."

"What if she breaks it?"

Holt smiled. "That's the beauty of it. It looks and feels like polished obsidian, but it's not. It's a spell matrix. The combination of our magics lets us create something extremely durable. As soon as the last circle breaks, it stops drawing, so it won't sap power from any of our witches."

"It won't weaken the spell circles?"

"No. We took care of that."

Alexander put his arm around Valery and pulled her tight. "You did well. Thank you." He looked at the sour-faced Holt. "You, too."

The mage kept his gaze locked on Valery. "Keep your thanks. I didn't do it for you."

Valery stiffened, looking back at Holt. "Don't," she said. "We got along for the day. Don't ruin it."

"Then don't run away again. Dammit, as soon as this is over, you'll be gone. Doesn't today show you how good we are together?"

She pulled away from Alexander and crossed her arms. "Sure. We make great magic together. That was the whole point from the beginning, wasn't it? You wanted someone who'd increase your power, and you didn't care who it was."

Holt went white. "I loved you. I still love you," he said, the words like bullets.

"Maybe. As much as you know how to love. But I want more. I want a man who loves me more than anything else in this world or the next. And that isn't you. I'm lucky if I come in a distant second after your ambition. At least I loved you enough to take those stupid tablets so you could stop trying to kill yourself with them. If I hadn't, you'd be nothing more than a memory right now."

Her words were equally furious as her hurt and anger poured out of her. Alexander ached for her. He even sympathized with Holt, who had a desperate look on his face that Alexander found all too familiar. It was the expression of a man who was about to lose the thing he held most precious in all the world, and there was nothing he could do to stop it.

"You're wrong," Holt rasped. "I want those tablets back because they make you a target. I can't protect you if you have them. Valery—I'm telling you the truth."

She stepped back, her face shuttering. "Trouble is, your version of the truth isn't always accurate. Most of the time, it isn't even close. But that's old news, and this is water under the bridge. Let's get this done before the Fury breaks free."

Holt stared, his jaw knotting. Then his head jerked in a nod. "We're not done with this," he said to her back as she turned away. "We'll never be done."

She stopped, then walked on.

Alexander went around to check on Alton. The witch had been staked out spread-eagle. The witch chain lay across his legs, but he was helpless to kick it away. He stared in terror at the column of smoke.

Alexander crouched beside him. "Do you believe your daughter has come back now?" he asked.

"You can't do this to me. I can help you. I'm powerful. You should use me. I swear, I'll be loyal. I'll swear whatever you want. You can bind me however you want."

"I don't want a bastard like you," Giselle said, coming up to stand beside Alexander. "Besides, Cora deserves a chance to talk to you about what you did to her. Don't you think?"

She put a hand on Alexander's shoulder and drew him away with her. "Is it true? Max was here?"

He nodded. She had been deep in meditation until near sundown, and he had not had a chance to tell her.

She pressed her palms over her eyes. A moment later, she dropped them. "What did she say?"

"I will tell you when this is over," he said. "We should get on with it before the Fury breaks free."

"Right." She looked out over the ravine. "Take your places. We'll start closing the circles in a moment."

Alexander looked at her and then slid the sheath containing her silver knife from her belt.

She glared at him, trying to snatch it as he backed away. "What are you doing?"

"Taking up my position," he said as he headed to the inner circle.

"No. That's not your job," she said.

"Somebody has to do it. Who else is there?"

She opened her mouth, then clamped it shut. There was no one else, and both of them knew it.

He could see that she was thinking of Max. He was, too. But it made no difference. As soon as he had realized that someone had to go in and break the circle and that there would be no escape, he had known he had to do it.

"Maybe now you will believe that I am committed to this covenstead," he said. "Just like Max and all the rest of the Spears and Blades. They serve because they want to, not out of compulsion. That is why Max will come back to you. You should remember that."

She said nothing else as she closed the circle. Valery watched Alexander inside, eyes wide. "What are you doing?" she demanded.

His mouth twisted in a semblance of a smile. "Try to stay out of trouble. I love you."

She started forward, and Holt grabbed her. "Let me go," she hissed, struggling violently. "Alexander, get out of there. No! You can't do this!"

Alexander shook his head. "There is no one else." He watched as her chest began to jerk with wrenching grief. Holt pulled her close, pressing his lips to her hair and murmuring. Alexander turned away, his own chest tight.

Giselle took a knife from Niko and sliced her hand, dribbling blood around the circle and chanting. When she returned to where she started, the circle flared white. The light was so dense that Alexander could not see through it.

He waited as the other circles were closed. A few feet away, Alton wept and begged for release. Alexander's lip curled.

"Did your daughter beg when you cut into her?" he asked softly. "Stop your sniveling. You made the poison, now you can eat it."

"She wanted it," Alton argued. "She said she wanted to do whatever I needed. She said she was proud to help me!"

Alexander could not help himself. He strode over and planted his foot on Alton's chest, bending down so he was only inches from the other man's face.

"She did not want to die, you bastard. She wanted you to love her and protect her. She wanted a father, and she got a sadistic killer. Now it is time to pay. Take it like a man, if you can. I do not mind saying that I am damned well going to enjoy watching it."

He straightened and took up his position again. Beyul was waiting for him. Alexander looked down at him, then shook his head. The beast could walk through live spell circles, and Xaphan's fire had no effect on him. Chances were he was safer than anyone else at the party.

By the time everything was ready, Alton had begun to cry, and there was a smell of urine. A damp patch spread across the front of his pants.

"Start anytime," Giselle called.

Alexander slid the sheath off the knife and dropped it. The silver blade was nearly two feet long, and Giselle had painted symbols thick on both sides of it. He crouched. Alton's binding circle was a thick gray powder with glints of red, green, black, and silver. A dribble of brown splatters went down the center. Blood. Running along outside it was a glowing band of hex marks. It was elegant, and the marks were crisp and powerful. Holt's work. Alexander was going to have to cut through both to free the Fury.

He straightened and approached the black spell ball. With any luck, the ball would absorb the explosion of magic and let him survive. His mouth twisted. It would take a hell of a lot of luck.

Bracing himself, he bent and slashed through the two circles. He drove the blade deep into the rocky soil and pulled it across the two of them.

The magic burst free. Alexander went flying high in the air. He smashed against the wall of the next binding circle. Bones snapped. The air went out of his lungs, and he dropped to the ground in a heap.

He could not move. He was utterly paralyzed. Sound roared in the air like an avalanche. The reverberation grew louder, and magic pounded at him. Then he heard something else. Felt it. It was a scream. It was full of madness, rage. It churned through the ground, which rose and fell as if it were a storm-driven wave. Wind, smoke, gravel, and dust spun through the air in a stinging hurricane. It tore the breath from him.

The sense of a presence rolled near, and fear grasped Alexander deep in his intestines. Horror washed through his mind, and if he could have moved, he would have screamed. He would not have been able to stop.

The presence came closer. A primitive voice in Alexander's head shrieked at him, *Danger! Run!* But he was powerless to twitch so much as a muscle. His lungs moved only with great effort, and his heart stuttered unsteadily.

Then he heard a growl. It cut through the sound and seemed to come from the core of the earth itself. The presence stopped and answered with a screech that ruptured Alexander's eardrums. Pain spiked through his skull, and sound went hollow and spongy except for a ringing that pounded at the inside of his skull like a fire alarm. Nausea washed through him, and his head spun drunkenly.

The wind increased, and the scream went on. Alexander convulsed and seized, the sound tearing him apart. Then, suddenly, a weight sprawled across him. Beyul. The beast growled again, and it vibrated down through Alexander. Instantly, his body stilled, and the scream was dimmed. He felt the presence lunge, and Beyul snapped his teeth. A wave of power exploded from the Grim, and the Fury's scream cut off suddenly. She retreated across the circle.

Beyul licked Alexander's cheek wetly and nuzzled his ear. Very doglike. Except that no ordinary dog could have chased a Fury away.

Feeling began to return to his body as his healing spells kicked into high gear. Slowly, he sat up, pushing Beyul off him. The Grim was not having it. Beyul snuggled close, onto Alexander's lap. He scratched the beast's ears and then pushed him away. He staggered to his feet, squinting through the blinding whirl of smoke, dust, and debris.

All at once, the wind stopped. The sudden lack of sound was almost painful. Alexander stumbled as the thrust of the wind vanished. The dust and smoke slowly settled.

As it thinned, he could see across the circle to where Alton was staked to the ground. He could hear the witch sniveling. Beside him was the Fury. It was hard to see what she looked like. Smoke coiled around her, and shapes shifted within. He caught a glimpse of shining white claws, curved teeth, and black wings.

"Cora," Lise was saying. She stood on the edge of the circle, with Xaphan and Tutresiel flanking her. "Please listen. Please remember who you are." She was crying, and her voice was choked.

"Please!" Alton echoed. "I told you. You said you wanted to help me. You wanted it!"

"Wanted?" the Fury repeated. Her voice was metallic and unworldly, a weaving of a thousand or a million voices into one. Then she laughed, and it echoed across the ravine and up into the mountain peaks. The sound wrapped around Alexander's intestines and sent fear burrowing down into the deepest recesses of his soul. It was all he could do not to let his bladder go.

The laughter cut off.

"Does a daughter *want* her father to cut her apart and bleed her? Does a daughter *want* her father to listen to her beg for her life with deaf ears? Does a daughter *want* her father to reach into her body and drench his hands in her blood so that he can write his spells on her flesh?" Her voice was almost emotionless, except for the thread of rage that underlined each word.

She reached out with a smoky, spectral arm and

flipped away the witch chain. Instantly, Alton burned through his bonds and rolled away. He leaped to his feet. He balled magic between his hands and sent it rushing at her. It disappeared inside the whirling gossamer smoke that clothed her. She laughed again, and Alexander sank to his knees beside Beyul. He needed to make himself smaller, to keep her from noticing him.

Not giving up, Alton hit her again and again. Nothing had any effect.

Except . . .

The Fury's rage thickened until it was nearly choking. Alexander wanted nothing more than to dig a hole and bury himself until she passed.

At last, she had enough. She swept forward with preternatural speed and grasped Alton by the throat. She lifted him into the air, and then, with delicate grace, she cut into his chest with a single claw. It was thin and razor-sharp. She started at the sternum and drew her finger slowly downward.

Alton shrieked and kicked as she held him. Blood gushed down his body, drenching his clothes and dripping to the ground. When she'd cut to the middle of his stomach, she veered left and then right, until she'd cut an upside-down Y, allowing his guts to spill out.

No longer able to scream past the Fury's grip on his throat, Alton keened like an animal caught in a metal trap. Alexander could not find any pity for him. He had made his bed, and now it was going to kill him.

The Fury continued to cut him, though nowhere fatal. She wanted him to bleed and suffer. Her hold on his throat allowed him to breathe and to feel all that she was doing.

Soon ribbons of blood were pouring off him. His clothes hung in shreds. He was growing weaker and weaker. He would be dead soon. Then the Fury did something unexpected. She pulled him close and kissed him. It was a chaste kiss, the kind a daughter presses upon her father. Alton spasmed, his body twitching violently. Then he went limp. The Fury held him out from her, examining him, and then dropped his body to the ground like a broken doll.

Alexander's stomach clenched. Now they would find out if their preparations had meant anything. He glanced at the matrix ball. It pulsed with power. But had it leached away enough? The Fury did not seem crippled in any way.

She was still for a long moment, and then she began to walk the edges of the binding circle. Or, rather, she floated a foot or more off the ground. She gave wide berth to Alexander and Beyul and paused at the spell matrix ball. A moment later, she returned to Alton. Then Lise caught her attention.

"Cora. Do you remember me? I'm Lise. We were friends. Do you remember? We used to go fishing together. And remember the time I took you shopping for clothes? Your father hated me that day."

The Fury drifted closer and reached out to Lise. The circle blocked her. She pushed against it. It did not give. Once again, the air inside thickened with rage. Alexander felt a *drawing,* as if she were pulling power in from the earth and the air. She drove at the barrier again, hammering it with blows that shook the ground. Flames rolled around her, rippling like wildfire.

"Cora! Calm down! We just want to talk to you. We need you to calm down before you kill innocent people!" Lise was shouting.

The Fury stopped. "There are no innocent people," she said in a cold, cruel voice. And then she renewed her attack.

Against such elemental power, the circle could not hold.

It burst, and Lise and the two angels were thrown backward to bounce against the invisible wall of the next circle. The force battered at Alexander. Once again, his eardrums burst, and blood ran from his ears and nose. He jumped to his feet and lumbered forward. The Fury was in a killing mood. He had to stop her before she broke through and slaughtered the coven and everyone else within a couple of hundred miles; there had to be a way.

He reached Lise before the Fury did, but only because the creature had turned her attention on the two angels. She seemed confused by them.

Both stood still as she approached. It was as if they had rehearsed the moment. Tutresiel did not have his sword. Neither looked worried. Alexander hoped they did not need to be.

The Fury reached out to touch Xaphan's chest, and he batted her hand away. She made a low screeching sound and thrust her hand out again. This time, he caught her arm and shoved her back. Alexander pushed Lise down beside Beyul and stepped in front of her. What was Xaphan doing? He had to know he was only making her angrier.

The Fury screamed and came at the fire angel with

both hands outstretched. She trailed an unearthly dress of smoke and flame. She slashed at Xaphan, who dodged and shoved at her, sending her careening into Tutresiel, who caught her in his arms, his wings closing tightly around her. She struggled and screamed as Xaphan wrapped himself around the other two, until the Fury was sandwiched between their bodies and wrapped in a cocoon of metal and fire.

Magic built inside the circle. It pulsed and pounded as if an ocean were pouring down on top of them. The spell matrix could not hope to gather it all.

A low sound built deep in the ground. No, it was more than sound.

A shiver of fear spiraled down Alexander's spine as a knife of ice slid along his nerves. Pain fractured him as the pitch grew higher. Rocks exploded. Sharp-edged gravel hailed down. Alexander could hardly get a breath. The air had congealed. The pressure clamped his body and organs, and he felt his insides rupturing. His head was being squeezed in a vise, and the coppery taste of blood filled his mouth.

Lise lay on the ground. Blood ran from her eyes, nose, mouth, and ears. Her chest jerked with desperate gasps, and her lips were blue. Beyul sat beside her. He appeared unaffected by the noise or the pressure. Alexander reached down to help Lise, although he had no idea what he could do.

He never touched her.

The world exploded in fire. It rushed outward with what felt like the force of a nuclear bomb. The ground burned. Alexander burned. He fell on Lise to protect her. The outer three-layered circle burst, one layer at a time. The stench of burning sulfur filled the air. They were in hell.

He heard screams, and a wave of powerful magic smashed back through the flames. The world bucked and heaved. Alexander went blind, then deaf. Then he felt nothing at all.

19

Once Max stepped into the abyss, she cleared her mind, considering what to do next. She'd told Ilanion that she'd meet him back at the compound, but she meant to run an errand or two first. Specifically, since she could go right where she wanted to out of the abyss, she was going to try to find Scooter's silk and horn.

Which to go for first? Not that it mattered. He needed both, or he was going to die. She decided on the horn for no better reason than that it reminded her of the Calopus that had been following her.

She had no idea what it would look like or how big it would be, but she focused her attention on going to Scooter's horn as she dove into her fortress and pulled herself through to the other side.

Max dropped into a lightless room. Her night vision easily penetrated it. She could see in cave darkness. It was only Chadaré's weird shadows that gave her problems. Did that mean she wasn't in the city? Not that it mattered.

The room was empty of any furniture or decoration.

The walls, ceiling, and floor were covered with symbols painted with—

She sniffed.

Blood. It was Divine blood. Every square inch of the place was covered with tiny overlapping symbols except for a round pedestal in the middle. It was made of petrified wood. On top was the horn. It was about three feet long and twisted in a thick, whorled spiral, about six inches across at the base and ending in a dull point. It had been crusted with gold and jewels and was gaudy as hell. It sat on a green cushion. Where it sat was surrounded by a dark stain, as if blood had leaked there. Or still did. The fabric looked wet and smelled distinctly of Scooter.

Max's lip curled with anger, but she reined it in. Now wasn't the time. She glanced around again. There were no windows or doors. What was this place?

She twisted to look behind her, not moving her feet. Something was wrong. It felt like a trap. But how did she spring it? Or had she already done so?

She waited. Nothing happened. Minutes went by. Five. Ten. Fifteen. Still, she remained immobile as she tried to figure out just how much trouble she was in. Finally, she sighed. Every minute she waited was another Scooter didn't have. She had to move. She could jump the ten feet to the pedestal. Hell, she could grab it in the air and drop into the abyss before she ever hit the ground.

It sounded good. Possible, even. She didn't have a lot of other choices. She drew a breath and flexed her fingers. She tensed and then sprang. In that moment, the writing in the room flashed brilliant crimson.

Max found herself frozen helplessly in the air, stuck like a bug in amber. She tried to kick herself forward and swim through the air. It was futile. She couldn't even swear out loud at her own stupidity.

Inwardly, she fumed. *What a stupid, fucking idiot.* Well, she sure as hell wasn't going to stick around until someone came and got her. She had the abyss. Max dropped into her fortress, but as hard as she yanked, she couldn't pry herself loose. She was really and truly trapped.

Minutes ticked past as she waited for someone to come for her. No one did.

Hours creaked by. A whole day. Still no one came.

What were they waiting for? Were they trying to torture her? She was hungry, and she was going to explode if she didn't pee soon.

Max wasn't sure how much more time had passed when another presence entered the chamber. Her muscles clenched against her prison to no avail. Then a scent reached her. The Calopus? How was it possible? How had it found her, and why?

The spiked wolf padded across the floor, completely oblivious to the trap. Maybe once sprung, it had no effect on anyone else. But how did it get there in the first place?

It stood up on its hind legs, bracing its forelegs on her shoulders as it looked into her face. It licked her, its tongue rough as a cat's, before dropping to the floor with a whining sound.

It was an intelligent creature, but Max didn't know the language Tarzan had used to order the critters about, and even if she did, it wasn't like she could say anything. Frustration burned in her stomach. *Fuck fuck fuck. Drag me out of here!* she wanted to yell, but the words dissolved on her paralyzed tongue.

It seemed that the Calopus heard her, or at least had ideas of its own. It stood on its hind legs again and closed her forearm in its teeth. Hope clutched in Max's chest. The beast dropped back to the floor, dragging her down. Max dropped to the height of the beast's head. *Good,* she thought. *Now, get me the hell out of here.*

Again, the Calopus answered her unspoken command. Still gripping her arm, it backed toward the wall. And then through it like it wasn't even there.

Max closed her eyes when her head was about to smash into the symbol-inscribed paneling. But instead, she passed through as if through ice water. On the other side, she fell to the floor with a thud. The Calopus let go of her arm and nosed her urgently. *Get up. It's not time to rest. Dangerous.*

Max couldn't hear the words, but she understood the message well enough. But instead of getting up, she reached out and grabbed a handful of fur just below the Calopus's spikes. Then she dove into her fortress. Just before she did, she felt a whir of wind and a streak of pain just over heart. Then she and the Calopus were in the abyss.

The spiked wolf trembled and clawed closer to Max, who put her arms around the beast. Thank goodness for the armor, or the spikes would have turned her into a sprinkler.

A second later, she was going back through her fortress to Ilanion's compound. There wasn't any point in going after the silk. It was probably booby-trapped, too. She had to figure out another way to get them back.

Once again, she landed on Ilanion's bed. The Calopus yelped and scrambled frantically out of the smothering nest of blankets. Max followed.

Her shoulder ached where she'd been hit before her escape. She looked down at herself. A black patch the size of a grapefruit stained the armor. There was actually a hole in it about the size of Max's middle finger, and it looked as if an arrow point had started to go through her shoulder. Her skin was about as black as the armor, but her healing spells were fighting off whatever poison had been on the tip. The armor wasn't so lucky.

She called the ribbon of notes in her mind and was answered with a spatter of painful sounds that had no harmony. She looked down at the damage to the armor again. The black patch was growing. What the hell could poison it?

Quickly, she told it to loosen so she could pull it off. She didn't know if it would help, but returning to its natural shape couldn't hurt. It took a long moment for the armor to respond, and when it didn't fully release, Max had to struggle out of its grip.

"We need help," she told the Calopus as she cradled the armor gently in her hands. The beast whined in what sounded like agreement.

"But first, I have to go to the bathroom."

She left the armor on the table and went through a door on the opposite side of the bedroom. It was disguised by some gauzy *Arabian Nights* drapery and made to look exactly like the wall except for the handle sticking out of it. Inside was an enormous closet the size of her apartment and full of all sorts of clothing. It smelled of Ilanion and musk and clove sweetness. She went through into a huge bathroom. It was all carved from rock. There was a bathtub big enough to hold eight people and deep enough to dive into. She supposed that bathing with wings required a lot of space.

Past it was a kind of shower. The top was a rotunda, sort of like the top of the White House. It was nacreous, like the inside of an oyster shell, with nothing that resembled a shower head. There were no spigots to turn on water and no walls to contain it, but there was a series of gold-colored drains. Or, knowing Ilanion, they were probably real gold. Max couldn't resist waving her arm under it. Instantly, a rain of steaming water cascaded down. Outside it was a light sprinkling, and in the middle it came down like a waterfall. She pulled back her wet arm. Tutresiel and Xaphan would totally love this.

The toilet was in its own small room, with *small* being relative. It was twelve feet across. The toilet itself looked a lot like a throne. It was set in the center of the room, and it had steps leading up to it, no doubt to also accommodate Ilanion's wings. It had no tank at all and no obvious way to flush. It was also made of gold, and the seat was padded. The bowl swirled with white mist. Max wrinkled her nose but was too desperate to look for someplace else.

She climbed up and did her business with a groan of relief. There was no sound of water, and the mist in the bowl was warm. When she was done, she looked around for toilet paper. Nothing. Then she became aware that the mist had gone from wet to drying and realized that there was a built-in cleaning system. She sat frozen for a long moment, wondering when she should stand up. Finally, she got impatient and pulled up her pants and hopped down off the pedestal. She eyed the toilet, half expecting a loud flush, but there was nothing. She turned on her heel and went looking for a sink.

Once she'd washed up, she returned to the bedroom and picked up the armor. She opened the outer door. This time, no one was waiting outside. Where was Ilanion? She didn't want to have to waste time searching this mausoleum. She sucked in a breath and yelled, "Hey! Anybody there?"

The words echoed up and down the halls. She hollered again, then went back inside Ilanion's room to look for some kind of bell pull. She had about given up and was returning to the hallway to go hunting when one of the gargoyle servants appeared. It looked at her impassively. Pretty much the way a statue would. It was annoying.

"Where's Ilanion?" she demanded.

"He comes. You are to wait here," came the gravelly voice.

Max's chin jutted. "Bite me. I'm going to the kitchen. You can show me the way, or I'll find it myself." A scent of something incredibly mouthwatering clung to the gargoyle and brought home to Max just how hungry she was. Her stomach cramped painfully. She needed to calorie-load, anyway.

The gargoyle watched her with electric blue eyes. The seconds ticked past, and still it didn't move.

"Well?" Max said finally, and when it didn't answer, she shrugged and started to shove around it.

It grabbed her arm in its surprisingly hot stone grip. She froze.

"Are we about to have a problem?" she asked. Knocking the stuffing out of a hunk of stone wasn't going to be easy, but she was willing to try.

Instead, it tugged her in the other direction before dropping its hand. "This way."

Slightly mollified, she fell into step beside it with the Calopus at her heels. From time to time, it nosed her leg as if to remind her it was there. She shook her head. *Another fucking stray*. She reached down and scratched its ears, wondering if it would snap at her hand. It didn't.

She eyed her escort. There was nothing to indicate if it was male or female. No obvious breasts or penis. Its clothing, such as it was, was utilitarian. It wore a vest with leather pants. No shoes. A short sword was belted to its waist, along with a dagger. Dangling from a strap on its left side was a small crossbow. There was a thick quiver of bolts on its back and, of course, the band of servitude around its wrist.

"Has there been trouble?" she asked, wondering if the compound had been attacked.

The gargoyle shook its head. "Not yet. Soon."

How did it know? She'd have to ask Ilanion. The gargoyle didn't seem to want to chat. But Max couldn't resist the urge to poke at him and make him talk.

"Where is Ilanion?"

The gargoyle slanted an annoyed look at her. "He is on his way."

"Do you get good punch on that crossbow?" she asked, gesturing at the weapon.

That warmed him up some. "It pierces most armor. The bolts are tipped in magic."

She frowned, thinking of the armor. "What about poison?"

The creature nodded. "Usually. We all use different varieties."

"You don't know what would do this, do you?" She stopped and held out the armor with its growing black rot and then showed him her shoulder. The wound hadn't closed yet. Her healing spells were having to work overtime.

It examined both closely, careful not to touch any of the infected area. "It is similar to some that I've seen before. Quite deadly."

It looked at her again, and Max thought maybe she saw dawning respect. Or not. Who could tell what a statue thought? But it meant that Master Goldilocks had better show up soon, or the armor was going to be in trouble.

The kitchens were down two flights of stairs and just below Ilanion's chambers, if she was judging things right. It was a big place, with a high ceiling crisscrossed with heavy beams carved in intricate tracery and painted with bright gingerbread patterns. It felt a little like being in Hansel and Gretel's kitchen. Bunches of herbs and cured meats hung down from them. There was a wall of ovens, each radiating heat. There was also a wall of stovetops entirely covered with bubbling pots and sizzling pans.

Another long wall held a set of sinks and what could have been a magical dishwasher. Lined up in rows in the middle were five long marble-topped tables. Three doors led away, one clearly into a pantry containing foodstuffs, another into a dish room, and another probably into some sort of dining room.

The place bustled with activity. Gargoyles in aprons dominated, but there were a few different creatures, too. One was tall enough to pluck whatever he wanted from the ceiling stores. He was stick-thin and looked like an oversized grasshopper with a narrow hatchet face, a Pinocchio nose, and square yellow horse teeth. He also had four arms and a brown, hairless tail that he kept wrapped around one leg to keep it out of the way.

There were some brawny dwarf types, hulking, with broad shoulders, shaved heads, humped backs, and hairy feet. They were kneading bread while singing something that sounded a lot like rocks rolling down a mountain.

A few of the kitchen's denizens glanced curiously at Max and her gargoyle but otherwise ignored them. Her escort motioned for her to go through the dining-room door. It held long rows of trestle tables polished by years of use. The floor was slate, and the walls were hung with tapestries. High above, the ceiling was coffered wood. Witchlight gleamed down, and thick white candles flickered along each table.

A handful of gargoyles were eating and talking in low voices. She saw that they were armed and ready for battle.

Max sat where the gargoyle pointed, and the Calopus leaped up onto the bench beside her and sat down, curling its tail neatly around its feet. Max smiled. So it was hungry, too. She had an urge to peek and see if she could tell if it was a male or a female, but she resisted. It wasn't polite, and she had a feeling the Calopus would tell her so.

"I will have someone bring you food," the gargoyle said.

"I appreciate that. Will you tell me a name to call you?" she asked before it could walk away.

For a second, she thought it would refuse, but then it relented. "Drida." It walked away.

A few minutes later, one of the dwarves brought her a steaming platter of meat, bread, vegetables, and some sort of grain pudding. It also set a bowl of chunked raw meat in front of the Calopus. It ignored Max's thanks, retreated, and returned with a bowl of water and what appeared to be an entire pitcher of beer. Good beer, as it turned out. It tasted of honey and orange and went down smoothly.

The food was delicious, even though she had no real idea what she was eating. As soon as she was done, her plate was refilled, along with her glass. The Calopus had seconds, too. Ilanion joined them when Max was half done with her fourth serving. With her intake of calories to boost her healing spells, her wound had finally closed, although it was still puckered and red.

She didn't bother greeting him. She shoved the armor across the table. "Can you fix that?"

He picked it up and examined it, turning it in his hands. He was already looking grim, and his expression didn't improve. "I can't afford the power right now," he said, and sat down. "You were gone longer than I expected."

"What's going on?" Max asked, ignoring the accusation in his voice. She wasn't ready to explain that she'd spent twenty-four hours hanging in the air like a side of beef.

"I have received an offer from the Korvad. Or an ultimatum, depending on your point of view. They have declared what they will pay for Nayan and demand that I turn him over within the hour."

"How is he?" Max asked, swallowing down her sudden nausea.

"Fading," Ilanion said tightly. "He has very little time. Perhaps as long as a day, though I doubt it."

"I tried to get the horn," Max said, and told Ilanion of the trap. "I have no idea how to get to it without traveling through the abyss, and that clearly isn't going to work. I don't suppose you've got any ideas about where it actually is or where the silk is?"

"There are only four other members of the Korvad beside Asherah. The horn and the silk will be with two of them."

"That'll take too much time."

He nodded. "They'll attack here long before you could snatch them. If you could. The trap you've described sounds more than formidable. In addition, whoever has the horn and the silk will have boosted their defenses as soon as you stole Nayan's heart."

Max's lips tightened. "You're saying it's hopeless."

He looked away.

"There is a way, isn't there?" she said, studying him. Judging from his expression, it wasn't going to be easy. "What is it?"

He didn't speak for a long moment, as if he weren't sure he wanted to say anything at all. Max tapped her fingers on the table impatiently. Finally, he blew out a breath.

"There's a tradition in Chadaré. You may challenge someone, and if they accept, then there's a battle in the coliseum. Whoever wins takes the previously agreed-upon prize, and the loser becomes a bond servant to the victor, along with anyone who might fight alongside him."

"So I can challenge the Korvad, and if I win, I get the horn and the silk?"

"*If* they agree to the challenge."

She sat forward. "What's the catch?"

"Isn't it enough that if you lose, you'll become a bond servant and they would have both Nayan and his heart? You would have to pledge both if you want them to put up the silk and the horn."

"I don't intend to lose."

"That's because you don't know what you're up against."

She shrugged. "It's not like I have a choice, now, do I?"

He looked like he was trying to swallow a rotten egg. Max glowered. "Come on. Whatever you're trying not to tell me, spit it out."

"As the challenger, you have no choice in the nature of the battle. If the Korvad accept—and they will—then they decide how many fighters will be allowed in the arena. For this prize, they might even step into the ring themselves. Word is Asherah has declared she won't rest until she kills you."

"So they can say they'll bring fifty fighters to the party and I'll have to do the same?"

"Of course not. You may have up to fifty, but you can use as few as you like."

Max shook her head. "Dammit." She had no army and no way to get one. But she also had no choice. "I have to do it, no matter what they throw at me."

"Shouldn't you consult Nayan? It's his life and body you're risking." Ilanion flicked an eyebrow up at her.

"And mine. Besides, if I ask, he might say no, and then he'll die, and I break my promise to save him or die trying. Better to ask forgiveness than permission. Just do me a favor. If I lose this, incinerate him with your magic."

Ilanion stared at her. "If I survive. But I plan to die before I become slave to the Korvad."

"This isn't your party," Max said, surprised. "No one expects you to hit the piñata with me."

His handsome face went hard, his lips pulling down. Gold swirled in his eyes, and curls of magic spun across his skin. "I will take part as I see fit," he said loftily.

"What happens to your . . ." Max waved in the direction of the seated gargoyles and company. "Your . . . bond servants . . . if you are taken by the Korvad?"

"As you said, I don't intend to lose."

"So you'd risk them, too?" She shook her head, her stomach churning. How had she managed to hold so many lives in her hands? "You can't do that. It's selfish. This is my problem. I'll deal with it."

"It's not just your problem. I choose to fight, and that is the end of it."

"If they want more than a one-on-one duel."

"They will. They will want to draw out your co-conspirators, and they will want to crush us. No one is permitted to challenge the Korvad and walk away."

"All the more reason for you to stay out of it."

"It's my choice, and I've made it." He stood abruptly. "I'll go send the challenge. They'll answer quickly. You'll have to fetch the heart. All of the artifacts will need to be present."

"Artifacts? Scooter isn't an artifact."

"To them, he is. Are you going to tell him your plan?"

She shook her head. "Let's wait until it's done."

"He's having trouble staying conscious. If you wait much longer, you won't be able to speak with him."

Max sighed. "Lucky him. He'll wake up either free or dead."

He stared at her in surprise and then gave an unwilling chuckle. "Together, we might pull this off," he said.

She eyed the puddle of poisoned armor. "Too bad it's broken. It would have been a nice help." She looked back at him. "What are we likely to be up against?"

He folded his arms, scraping his bottom teeth over his upper lip thoughtfully. "Asherah will certainly take to the ring herself. The others—it's difficult to say if they'll be willing to risk themselves, though whoever does participate in the battle will certainly earn a bigger piece of the winnings, and that's a strong motivation. After that . . . They have many servants. My Enay, however, are fierce fighters and nearly impossible to kill."

Max scowled. She hadn't thought about who would be going to battle for Ilanion. She didn't like the idea of dragging the gargoyle critters into this. They didn't get the choice of saying no. But who else was there?

If you get into trouble, if you need help, you come get me.

Max's stomach churned. *No*. She wouldn't bring Alexander into this. But . . . He wouldn't forgive her if she didn't. And his help could make the difference.

She drew a shaky breath. "I'm going to get help," she told Ilanion. "How long are we likely to have before this showdown begins?"

"Hours. Four or possibly five. Long enough to establish terms and send word through the city."

"I'll be back as soon as I can." She unbuckled her swords and laid her guns and knives on the table top. Now she had the attention of the other diners. She grimaced. Apparently, a strip show got you attention whether you were on earth or not.

"What are you doing?"

"May as well leave these here. I'll be bringing more guns."

"They are not legal here."

"Because the Korvad says so, and it's better for them if nobody is shooting at them. I don't plan to listen. You said it yourself: in Chadaré, might makes right. I'm planning to have more might. If you have a problem with that, you don't have to use them."

"The only problem I have is that none of my people knows how to shoot."

"Shooting an Uzi is simple," Max said. "It's point and spray and kill whatever's in front of you."

He snorted. "Somehow I doubt it's that easy."

"For this, it's going to be."

She scratched the ears of the Calopus. "I'll be back," she told it. It licked her hand.

Ilanion shook his head. "How did you end up together?"

"I have a bad habit of picking up strays," Max said.

"It tried to kill you. Can you trust it?"

"I was trying to kill it. Can *it* trust *me*?" Max asked with a shrug. "It got me out of that trap. That's all I need to know."

Ilanion narrowed his eyes at her. "You are very unexpected, do you know that?"

"Is that your way of calling me stupid?" she asked wryly.

"If the glove fits," he said.

"It fits all too well sometimes," she said. "I'll be back." With that, she dropped into her fortress and stepped out into the abyss.

20

ALEXANDER WOKE ON THE FLOOR. HE *HURT*. Layer after layer of pain cocooned him. He blinked at the rock ceiling above, unable to make himself move.

He heard the muttering of voices and the wheeze and whistle of tortured breathing. There were whimpers. He smelled charred flesh and death.

He closed his eyes, trying to remember what had happened. The Fury had killed Alton and then broken through the next circle. After that—

The angels had wrapped themselves around her, and the world had burst into flame.

He opened his eyes, foreboding digging into his entrails. He pushed himself up on his elbows, biting back a moan of pain. He looked down at himself. A blanket covered him from the waist down. Above that, he was naked. Some of his skin was runneled and twisted like melted wax. Patches of it were pink and shiny as if they were new. Others were black. IVs were hooked to both arms. Beyul lay against him and lifted his head as Alexander struggled to sit upright. He pulled the tubes in his arms free.

The beast sat up, and his tongue swiped over Alexander's cheek and eye. He winced. "Good to see you, too," he rasped. He could barely hear himself. His throat was swollen and throbbing. He looked across the room. Other bodies lay on the floor like a row of logs.

A hand clenched in his chest. Who was hurt? Who was dead?

Alexander struggled to his feet, the blanket puddling to the floor. He looked down at himself and nearly puked. His cock and balls were shriveled and black, and his skin matched the patchwork of his chest.

"Here," a voice said, and he jerked around to find Max's sister, Tris, holding his blanket out to him.

She was gray-faced and drawn, her lips trembling.

"Thank you," he said in a harsh whisper, and wrapped it around his waist. His legs shook, but he ignored them and the agony stabbing up through his bones and burrowing through his flesh.

"Here, drink this," she said, and gave him a cup of something.

Alexander drank it and gasped as his gut exploded. "What is that?"

"Medicine. The witch—Valery—made it. It's supposed to get you better a lot faster. It's got magic in it." She said *magic* as if she were being force-fed cockroaches.

It was working. He felt strength flowing through his veins, and his pain was fading. His skin was smoothing. He did not dare check his genitals while Tris was watching, but he could feel them healing, too.

Suddenly, someone hit him in the shoulder. He turned, and Valery pulled him into a tight hug. "You bastard," she said softly, tears running down her face. "Don't ever do that to me again. I thought I lost you."

"I couldn't get that lucky," came Holt's annoyed voice. He stood behind Valery, his arms folded and his lip curling as he watched their embrace. He was haggard and thin, like he had lost twenty pounds.

Alexander bared his teeth at the mage in something like a smile. "I guess today is not your day to play the lottery, is it?"

Valery pushed away and looked him over from head to foot. She, too, had lost weight, and her face was pale. She had a cut on her cheek and a hash of them on her forearms. Alexander touched the wound on her cheek. "What happened?"

"All the rocks exploded, and suddenly we were inside a blender," Holt answered for her. "Valery is lucky she didn't die." His voice was hot with accusation. His hex marks glowed blue. "No thanks to you."

She cast an annoyed look at her ex and then returned her attention to Alexander. "I'm fine. I shielded myself."

"Not fucking well fast enough," came Holt's furious response.

"What business is it of yours?" she asked. "I'm a grown woman and perfectly capable of taking care of myself."

"You're an idiot, and if you took care of other people the way you supposedly take care of yourself, you'd be arrested for neglect."

Valery grinned up at Alexander, her eyes snapping with humor. She was riding an adrenaline high. The same kind she got when she was stealing. He was sure that Holt knew it and that was what was driving the other man insane. Valery took risks for the fun of it. "No harm, no foul," she said with a shrug,. "Time for you to get over your big bad self."

Holt was beside himself. He grabbed her arm and pulled her around. Alexander started to interfere, then checked himself. Valery did not need a hero, and Holt deserved a chance to make an ass of himself. After suffering Max's rejection for so long, Alexander could not help feeling sympathetic to Holt. He hated the mage, but the man was clearly desperate.

"What the hell is wrong with you?" the mage demanded through gritted teeth. He gave Valery a shake. "You could have died."

There was a wealth of horror in the words, and his cold expression cracked. Suddenly, he pulled her into his arms, wrapping her tightly and pressing his lips against her hair, his eyes closing. She hesitated, then hugged him back.

"You have to stop scaring me like this," he said, his voice unsteady.

Alexander decided that he did not need to eavesdrop on the rest of what they might have to say to each other and walked down along the row of bodies, Beyul at his side. Tris followed.

He came to Lise first. Bile flooded his mouth. She was in bad shape. If he hadn't recognized her scent, he would not have know it was her. Absently, he reached down to pet Beyul, wanting the touch of someone warm and alive.

"Is she going to make it?" he asked Tris.

"They say so."

"Who are *they*?"

"Those two." She hooked a thumb back in the direction of Holt and Valery. "And Giselle. She's been through a few times since—"

Tris broke off, and her face twisted. "I've seen a lot in my life," she said quietly. "I thought the worst of it was when those shape-shifters attacked our orchard and you came out of it like hamburger. But this . . . Is it going to be like this always?"

Alexander nodded. "The Fury rising—no one could have predicted that. But the Guardians unleashed a flood of magic into the world. A lot of people were displaced, and a lot of magical creatures have returned from wherever they went. Everyone is looking for a home. I expect that for a while, we will be living in the old west, where there are no laws and everybody is fighting to establish their territories."

"How long is a while?"

Alexander shook his head. "Maybe longer than you will live. Maybe longer than your grandchildren will live."

Her mouth pinched, and she nodded. Then said, "Thank you. For keeping us safe."

He looked at her in surpise. "It is our job. But you are welcome."

"I heard you saw Max. That she was here for a little bit. Is she OK?"

It was easier to look at Lise than to see the pleading look in Tris's eyes. She missed her sister more than he had thought. "She was. But that could have changed by now."

"But she's strong, right? Stronger than most?"

He nodded. "She has a lot of reasons to come home safe, too."

"I hope so," Tris said. "We—things weren't good between us when she left. Mom spends half the day crying and the other half yelling at my dad. I'd like to have a chance to know her again."

"You will get it."

"You sound sure."

He smiled without humor. "I have to be. Otherwise, I would shoot myself in the head." He changed the subject, not wanting to think about Max. "How long has it been since the Fury rose?"

"Fourteen or fifteen hours."

A long time for him to be out. He must have been hurt badly. Thank goodness for Valery and Holt.

He turned away and went down the rest of the line. Oak and Steel were there, and so were Nami and Simon. Steel's brother, Flint, was sitting beside him. There were also three Sunspears, and Judith and Gregory were huddled under two mounds of blankets at the end. They were shivering, and two Sunspears, Maple and Ivy, sat with them, talking softly.

"What is wrong with them?" he asked.

"I'm not sure. Something to do with the magic that was unleashed. Holt and Valery worked on them, but now it's just wait and see."

Alexander frowned, looking around the space again. "Where is Xaphan? He can heal."

Tris opened her mouth and then closed it, shaking her head. She pointed through another doorway.

He went through it slowly, feeling numb. The smell of

death assaulted his nose. Blood and charred flesh. His stomach lurched again, and he swallowed it down, his body clamping tight.

Out in the broad antechamber was a makeshift morgue. There were five tables holding sheet-covered bodies. Two of the sheets were folded back to reveal Xaphan and Tutresiel. The other three—

Alexander refused to acknowledge what his nose told him about their identities.

Tyler was standing at the foot of the tables holding the angels. Xaphan's fire was out, and Tutresiel's wings were a tarnished gray. Their skin was white marble, and their faces were slack, their crimson eyes closed.

"I did not think they could be killed this way," Alexander said, standing beside Tyler. Sadness filled him. He had liked Xaphan. As for Tutresiel, the cocky bastard had been a thorn in his side, but he had been good for Horngate.

"They saved us," Tyler said in a blank voice. "They wrapped themselves around the Fury. She used a lot of power breaking free. Because of it, the witches were able to deflect the worst of her leftover attacks. The Grims helped, too. They wandered out among us and somehow boosted the shields. I've got one now."

Alexander became aware of the big Grim lying a few feet away and watching Tyler like he was dinner. It was an intense, possessive look.

"Fire caused the worst of the damage for you and Lise. For everybody else, it was the force of the blast and the rocks. The whole ravine exploded, and it was like a war zone. Missiles were flying everywhere." He finally looked at Alexander, and there was a feral ring growing around the outer edge of his eye. "Niko's gone."

Alexander closed his eyes and let his head fall back, a knot growing in his throat. "Damn." Grief filled his chest. He had counted Niko a friend. But to Tyler, he was a brother. And Max. He drew a breath and blew it out. This was going to cut her in ways he could not begin to think about. She was going to hate herself for not being there to protect him; she was going to hate Alexander for failing to keep him safe.

With stiff steps, Alexander went to the next body and peeled back the sheet. Niko lay there, his body charred, the left side of his head a pulpy mess. Gently, he pulled the sheet back up. "Mother of night, guard his soul," he murmured.

The second body was Derek, a Sunspear. He was burned much the same as Niko, but there was a startled look on his face and no obvious wounds.

"He took a rock to the back," Tyler said from the foot of the table. "Destroyed his spine. He was dead before he hit the ground."

Next was Noah. He was dark-haired and quiet. One of the newer Shadowblades, less than two years old. He was burned, and his chest was caved in as if a boulder had landed on him. Alexander covered him again and turned away.

"What about everyone else? Thor? Oz? Tris said Giselle was all right."

"All the civilians inside the mountain were protected. Thor and Oz are fine. Thor's helping Giselle, and Oz and his Spears are out on cleanup."

"What happened to the Fury?"

Tyler shook his head. "She's gone. Just vanished. Giselle thinks she used up all her power and has to recharge. Or maybe she wasn't ready to be born yet. She could come back, but Holt says she'll probably start answering the voices of betrayal that she hears. She won't be able to stop herself. Chances are, we'll never see her again now that Alton's dead. The Memory left, too. One minute she was there, and the next she was gone. The Grims stayed, though. The whole pack."

That caught Alexander up short. "The whole pack? Why?"

"Guess they took a shine to the place."

Tyler looked back at Niko's shrouded body, his face contorting with emotion. His hands clenched. "Wasn't supposed to happen to him," he said, loss and pain leaching into his voice.

Alexander put a gentle hand on Tyler's shoulder. He knew how he felt. There were no words that could make it better. Still, Tyler was teetering on the edge of going feral, and Alexander had no intention of letting him go over the edge. "Women everywhere will be weeping," he said.

Tyler's shoulders jerked with his sudden bark of laughter. "Won't they? Damn, but they went after him like flies."

"And why not? He was a legend in his own mind."

"What'll we do without him?" Tyler asked quietly.

Alexander squeezed his shoulder. "We go on. Like he would want us to." He paused. "And possibly throw a parade. Maybe build a monument on the side of a mountain."

Another laugh. Alexander could feel the other man's Blade settling, pulling back from the edge of going feral.

"He deserved—" Tyler broke off, his mouth working, tears rolling down his cheeks. *Good*. Tears were good. "He was killed by a goddamned rock! There's nothing to fight and nothing to do about it. He's dead, and there's not a damned thing we can do."

"You can get on with the next job."

Tyler spun around faster than Alexander at the sound of Max's voice. She had come in from another corridor. Her face was ashen as she stared at the tables. Slowly, she stepped forward. She touched Tutresiel's hair and brushed her knuckles over Xaphan's cheek.

"What happened?" she asked in a strangled voice.

"Birth of a Fury," Tyler said.

She stared at the table holding Niko, and silent sobs shook her frame. She gently drew the sheet back away from his face. "No, oh, Spirits, no," she whispered. Tears rolled down her cheeks. Alexander wanted to comfort her, but there was nothing he could do. He and Tyler could only watch helplessly.

She pressed a kiss to Niko's lips. "Damn you," she said. "You weren't supposed to *ever* die on me. You promised me I'd get to go first."

She rested her head on his chest, and now the sobs escaped, loud and wrenching. Tris appeared in the far doorway, as did Holt and Valery and Flint, Maple, and Ivy. No one came any further. No one wanted to intrude.

Finally, it was Tyler who pulled her gently away, cradling her in his arms as she wept on his shoulder. He talked to her, words tumbling out of him. Alexander covered the body while Max gathered herself. It was what

Tyler needed, too. The more he spoke to her, the more his Blade calmed.

Slowly, Max's grief subsided, until Alexander could no longer contain himself. He took her from Tyler and pulled her close. She hugged him tightly for a long minute, then extracted herself and drew a long, steadying breath. Her eyes and nose were red, and her face was blotchy. He watched her visibly push her grief down and retreat into that cold place that allowed her to function when she was hurting terribly.

When she had herself under control, she looked at him. "I came for you. I need help."

Fierce triumph and pride surged through him. "Of course."

"Not so fast." Giselle strode in. She was hashed with cuts, and there was a purple bruise spreading across her jaw. Her hair was pulled back from her face in a tight braid that hung down her back.

Max looked at her in shock. Alexander suppressed a smile. The last time Max had seen her witch, Giselle had been weak and emaciated. The backlash of power from Max's broken bindings had boosted her health as nothing else could have. She was back to full strength.

Giselle came to a stop opposite Max. "That's it? You run in and out when you feel like it and never stop in and mention you're here?"

Max's brows rose in mock surprise. "You gave me away. Why would you care if I was here or not? Besides, I'm not bound to *you* anymore."

"If you aren't bound to me, then you aren't bound to Horngate, and you don't belong here."

"I belong here as much as you do. I just don't happen

to belong to *you,*" Max said. "Don't forget it. Now we really are partners. You don't get to *make* me obey you."

Giselle snorted. "As if I ever could."

Max's smile was smug. "You tried real hard. Succeeded a lot, too."

It was Giselle's turned to shrug. "I did what I had to do."

Neither sounded particularly angry, and Alexander did not get the impression that Giselle was intent on binding Max again. There was an edge to her voice, as if she was worried and even hurt.

"What are you doing here?" the witch asked.

"I came to get Alexander. I need some help."

"Oh? Do tell."

Max considered a moment, then glanced at Tyler, who was intent on the exchange. "There's a group in Chadaré—that's this weird city in the middle of the abyss—"

Giselle nodded. "I know of it."

Max looked surprised a moment and then continued. "This group called the Korvad runs the city. Apparently, Scooter and them were founders of the place, and at some point they stole his heart, his silk, and his horn. Now he's on the verge of dying. He's blind and powerless, and I promised I'd help him get his parts back."

That earned a gasp from Giselle and a rueful shake of the head from Tyler. Alexander was unsurprised. It would have been far more shocking if she had not promised to help. When she decided to commit to a friend, she did not go halfway.

"I got his heart back," she continued, "but the only

way to get the horn and the silk before he dies is to issue a challenge. My new buddy, Ilanion, is doing that now. He's something like a mage. Or a god. Maybe a demi-god." She waved her hand dismissively. "Hell if I know. Anyway, I'm putting up Scooter and his heart against the horn and the silk. Winner takes all, including the opposing fighters. If I lose, I'm heading into an all-new slavery." She slid a look at Alexander. "So are you, Slick. Be sure you want to help."

"I am coming with you," he said, and his voice left no room for argument.

She nodded as if expecting nothing else. His chest swelled at her trust. "You might want to put something on besides the blanket, though." She turned back to Giselle. "I have no idea what I'll be up against. Ilanion is going to let me use some of his people, but the Korvad gets to name the nature of the challenge and how many can fight on each side. We're pretty sure that at least one mage-type will be in it."

The witch said nothing. She walked away and stopped, staring at the far wall. Finally, she turned around. "I'm coming with you."

Max's jaw hit the floor. "What? No fucking way. Why?"

"I need you back. I don't want you to die. And I got you into this mess. I owe you." Giselle ticked the reasons off on her fingers. "You stand a better chance of winning with me than without me."

"And leave Horngate without a witch if we fail?"

"We won't fail. You don't know how," Giselle said with cool determination.

"I'm going with you, too," Tyler said. He glared at Giselle, but she said nothing.

"I guess that means I'm going, too," Oz said, entering from the doorway. Max started to object, but the look he turned on her was deadly cold. "My witch. I'm going with her."

Max made an exasperated sound and tossed up her hands. "Anybody else want to come? You know I have to drag your asses through the abyss, and it isn't exactly easy."

"You're strong," Giselle murmured with the kind of smile that said she was spoiling for a fight and could not wait to get started.

All of them were. They needed to relieve their grief and fury from losing five lives. Alexander was no different.

"I'll buy a ticket to the circus if there's room for me," Thor said, slouching into the room with those long, liquid strides of his.

"That's enough," Max said before anyone else could volunteer. "I can't take everyone, and someone has to watch over Horngate until we get back."

"You're leaving again? What about us?"

Max flinched at the sound of Tris's tart voice and looked across the room at her sister, who had her hands on her hips and a look on her face that reminded Alexander of Max in a stubborn, angry mood.

"I'll be back."

"Will you?" There was doubt and pain threading through the cutting accusation in her words. "You come back from the dead and drag us to this godforsaken place just to abandon us. You said it would be safe. Do you have any idea what happened? It was—" Her mouth pinched shut, and she swallowed. "Now you're running off again," she said finally, her voice softening with unshed tears.

Max faced Tris, the muscles in her jaw knotting. "Scooter needs me. He has no one else."

Tris wrapped her arms around her stomach. "You said you could die."

"I could. But I don't plan to," Max said. "I haven't yet."

Her sister thrust her chin out, her lips quivering. "See that you don't. I've lived with that once. I don't need to do it again. None of us do." Tris spun on her heel and marched back into the Great Hall. Alexander could hear the sound of her crying.

Max swore under her breath, then shook herself. "Everybody get prepped. Then hit the dining commons and calorie-load." She hesitated. "And thanks."

Oz pulled her into a hug. "We're family. Don't forget it. We've lost too many today. We're not about to lose you, too." He stomped away without another word. The others followed until it was only Giselle, Max, and Alexander.

Giselle followed Max's gaze to the five bodies. "I couldn't protect them. I wasn't fast enough." Her words were bleak and harsh.

Max exchanged a look with her, and the two women nodded slowly at each other, then Giselle left.

"What was that about?" Alexander asked curiously.

"No one gets taken alive," Max said softly. "We come home or die trying." She looked at him. "Still want to come?"

"I sure as hell am not getting left behind," he said.

He hooked his arm around her neck and pulled her to him, kissing her hard. He lifted his head. She smiled, and there was a darkness in her eyes. It would not soon go away. She had a lot of grieving to do.

She touched his face gently. "Thanks for not dying. I wouldn't—" She swallowed hard. "I wouldn't have liked that much. But now, it's time to finish this for Scooter and come home for good. I'm going to get Scooter's heart. See you in the dining commons."

And with that, she melted away into nothing.

21

IT WAS A SOMBER GROUP THAT GATHERED IN THE DINing commons. Max stood in the doorway, watching them for several moments before coming to sit between Alexander and Tyler. She caught Oz's glance. They exchanged a look of understanding and shared sorrow.

Tears burned in her eyes as she thought of Niko broken, bruised, and burned. *I'll never hear him tease me again. I'll never hear him laugh or make fun of his clothes or the way he chases women.*

She was glad she'd already eaten. She wouldn't have been able to force anything down at this point. It was taking all she had to keep from throwing up.

He wasn't the only one. Noah and Derek were gone, too. She hadn't had to pick up the sheets to smell who was under them. She could hardly believe that Tutresiel and Xaphan were dead.

She'd liked Xaphan from the first moment she'd met him. He'd been a messenger for the enemy and a slave. He was noble, though—full of honor and a clear sense of right and wrong. Maybe she didn't always agree with it, but he had lines he didn't cross. Tutresiel, on the other hand, was a total rogue and mostly an ass. But he was honest far past the point of rudeness—if it suited him, and it frequently did. Somehow, Max liked him. Maybe because he hated the chains of binding as much as she did. Maybe because he made her laugh. Maybe because he wasn't always the ass he pretended to be.

She was never going to see any of them again.

Pain shafted through her, and she got up and walked blindly across the room. She felt eyes on her, but no one followed. No one, that is, except for the witch-bitch herself.

"I'm sorry about Niko," Giselle said.

Max jerked her head in a nod. It took her a moment before she could speak. "Why are you doing this? Everything you've done for most of your life has been to build this place, and now you want to leave it pretty much unprotected while we go off to fight an enemy we don't know anything about. What's in it for you?"

Giselle didn't answer for a long moment. Then, quietly, "I always thought Horngate was about a strong witch and a strong coven and everyone playing their proper parts. I was supposed to run things the way I saw fit. I always thought that was the ticket to maintaining our strength. I was wrong. It's about sacrifice, family, and love. Your bindings were never why you gave your heart and soul to this place. It was always the people. Same for everyone else."

"Wow. You are quick on the uptake. Only took you decades to figure that one out," Max said mockingly, though in truth, she was shocked to hear Giselle's confession.

"I always like to be fashionably late to the party," Giselle said wryly. "Anyhow, I've realized that I'm not part of the family. I've never let myself belong to my own covenstead. Even Alexander, Xaphan, and Tutresiel belong more than I did. That changes today. I'm done standing on the outside looking in. I traded you to Scooter for Horngate's safety, and that was the choice that needed to be made at the time. But now what needs to be done is for me to fight by your side. Horngate isn't about *where* we are, or the *anneau*; it's about *who* we are."

She turned to look at Max, and magic circled smoky black in her eyes. "We are a team. That is Horngate's real strength. That's why Tutresiel and Xaphan are dead. They gave their lives because they felt something for us." She shook her head. "For you. You infected them with this idea that Horngate was worth it; that this *family* was worth it. I can't believe they did it—" She looked away, her face tightening with resolve. "I won't do less. Not anymore. I'm not going to be like—" She broke off, her mouth clamping shut, then continued before Max could ask questions. "I've got your back as much as you have mine, and I plan to put my money where my mouth is."

Max reeled from the speech and the change it implied in Giselle. But before she could marshal her thoughts into any semblance of a reaction, Giselle changed the subject.

"Tell me about this Ilanion. Can we trust him?"

"I do," Max said simply.

That brought a frown to the witch's face. "He plans to fight?"

"He does. I didn't ask him to."

"What's in it for him?"

"Helping Scooter. Plus breaking the backbone of the Korvad. He gains a lot if they are out of power."

Giselle nodded thoughtfully. Then she did something unexpected. She reached out her hand. Max eyed it like it was a coiled rattlesnake. What was the witch up to?

"This is our new start. Phoenix from the ashes. Let's do better this time," Giselle said huskily. Her face was graven with emotion. She caught herself, shaking her head. "No, that's wrong. *I'll* do better this time. Like I should have from the start. I always knew this place was supposed to be different, but I followed the old rules anyhow. But I want you to know this: you can trust me."

Max's mouth twisted. She couldn't help her snort of disbelief. Giselle had always lied to her. Even when she told the truth, it was wrapped up in secrets and distortion. "Yeah, right," she said, not taking the proffered hand.

"You'll trust this Ilanion—a total stranger—more than you will me?"

"Can you blame me?"

The witch hesitated and then shook her head with a sigh, her hand falling to her side in resignation. "No. I hoped you could, even though I knew it wasn't reasonable. But I'm telling you, I *will* prove myself to you, Max. Don't give up on me yet."

Max gave a bitter laugh. "Don't you think I would have if I could? I'm as dumb as a box of rocks when it comes to you. I'd love to be wrong this time."

She turned back to look at the group at the table.

They had heard the entire exchange. It was impossible for them not to. Still, they focused on their food as if they were doing open-heart surgery. "All right. I hope you're all full. Let's get a move on. I don't know how much time we have left."

Magpie came out of the kitchen and stood near the door, watching, her face still as stone. Whatever she was thinking, she wasn't sharing.

The three Blades and Oz rose, gathering their packs. Max left hers on the table. She was going to do this in several trips.

She motioned toward Oz and Tyler. "You two first."

They stepped over, and with them came Tyler's Grim. She didn't know how, but even though it looked exactly like the one following Alexander around, they were as different as apples and oranges. It wasn't a smell or anything about the way they looked. It was something more subtle than that. But she had no problem telling them apart.

It stopped a few feet away from Tyler, as if it wasn't all that sure it wanted to be closer, and yet it didn't want to be left behind, either.

"Forget it, dog," Max told it. "You can just stay put."

"How does this work?" Oz asked uneasily.

"I take you first into the abyss and then into Chadaré."

"What do we have to do?" Tyler asked.

"Hold on tight."

Max took their hands and plunged down into her fortress. Going into the abyss was getting easier and even slightly less painful each time. Or maybe she was just getting used to it.

A moment later, they hung in the abyss. Both of her

companions looked wonderstruck as they gazed about themselves. Max found herself staring in shock at Tyler's Grim. The beast drifted a few feet away. It shook itself and padded forward through the air to nudge up against Tyler, who started, then stroked a tentative hand over the beast's broad black head.

Gathering herself, Max pulled the men out of the abyss into Ilanion's compound. She chose to bring them into the dining room.

They dropped down about five feet and crash-landed on a table. Max was more ready than Tyler and Oz and stayed on her feet. The other two windmilled and leaped to the floor, and the Grim settled gently on the table top. All around them, gargoyle creatures jumped to their feet, drawing swords and leveling crossbows at the intruders.

Max held up her hands. "It's OK," she said loudly, hoping no one would start shooting before she could convince them that they were friends. But she was in luck.

"Quite an entrance," Ilanion said.

He stood up from his seat at the far end of the room. He was surrounded by a group of gargoyles and a couple of other creatures that were sort of pinkly gray and soft-looking, like earthworms. They had elongated faces, three round eyes each, lipless holes for mouths and ears, and tall, thin bodies. Their bodies were thick with sword and knife belts, an array of throwing stars, and what looked like darts. Long tubes strapped to their backs suggested that they were blow darts.

Max looked at Ilanion. "Did you get a reply to the challenge yet?"

He nodded. "We've got about two hours. At that time, they'll ring the city bells, and we'll have one hour to show up or forfeit." He glanced at Tyler, Oz, and the Grim. "Is this the help you went to get?"

"Some of it. I've got another trip or two to make," she said. "This is Tyler and Oz, and that—" She gestured at the Grim and shook her head. "That I'm not sure about. This is Ilanion," she told Tyler and Oz. "I'll be back."

Back in Horngate, she found the others waiting in tense silence.

"That was fast," Giselle said.

"Are you ready? You and Thor are next."

They stepped forward, and she took their hands. A few minutes later, they dropped into the dining hall in Ilanion's compound. The tables had been cleared to provide a safer landing area. Max and Thor kept their feet easily, while Giselle sprawled heavily across the floor. She got quickly to her feet, examining her surroundings with a cool eye.

She and Ilanion exchanged a sharp look. "You're Ilanion, I take it," she said, not waiting for an introduction.

"I am. And you are?"

"Giselle."

"A witch." He glanced at Max. "The one you were bound to?"

"That's her," Max said, and stretched. She was starting to feel hungry. When she got back again, she was going to need to eat, regardless of her grief. She was just about to leave when the Calopus appeared and whined. It pawed at her leg.

She was ridiculously happy to see the spiked wolf.

"Not you, too," Oz said. "What's with all the pets all of a sudden?"

"Friend of yours?" Tyler asked with a smirk at Oz.

She glanced at his hand, which was scratching his Grim's back. "Seems to be going around."

"Love is in the air," Oz said sardonically. "Pretty soon, Horngate will be overrun with puppies."

"You're just jealous," Tyler said. "No one picked you."

"Remember that when you're cleaning up dog crap and I'm not," Oz said.

Max smiled and then felt an ice pick drive through her heart. Niko would never join in their banter again. "I'll be back in a second," she said abruptly, and headed back into the abyss. It took her a few minutes there to gather herself and return to Horngate.

Alexander was pacing when she returned. He held the box with Scooter's heart and had Max's gear slung over his shoulder. His Prime was high. But then, it had been since the last time she'd seen him.

"I am ready," he said, and laced his fingers with hers. Beyul pushed between them. He looked down at the beast. "You have to stay here."

"I don't think he does, actually," Max said. "But you do have to get there by yourself," she told the Grim.

A few minutes later, they were back in Ilanion's compound. Max was exhausted. The last trip was a lot to handle. If she had to pull them all into the abyss at one time . . . She wouldn't be able to. Which meant there weren't going to be any backdoor escapes from this challenge. She wasn't leaving anybody behind.

She sagged down at a table. The Calopus and the two Grims were exchanging stiff-legged sniffs.

"Are you all right?" Ilanion asked.

"I should eat," she said.

He sent a gargoyle for food. She noticed that Drida, the gargoyle who'd guided her to the kitchens, was among those he'd been meeting with.

"Tell me about the terms of the challenge," she said. "They agreed to the winner takes everything? They won't cheat or hold back on their side of it?"

He shook his head, leaning back on the table behind him, raising his wings out of the way. Tyler, Alexander, Oz, and Giselle stared at him, grim-faced. One by one, they looked away, but she knew it was going to be a lot harder than that to forget Xaphan and Tutresiel. Or to stop missing them. She smiled inwardly. Tutresiel would be irritated to find out he'd actually be missed. He'd worked so hard to make sure that never happened.

"The coliseum has rigid rules, and even the Korvad can't circumvent them. Upon entering, both sides declare the nature of the challenge and the prize for the winner and the cost for the loser. The judge then oversees the contest. If anyone tries to cheat, they are killed."

"Just like that? The judge has that power?"

"Challengers give her that power as part of the contract."

"OK. How big a fight is it going to be?"

"You can have up to twenty fighters. The playing field will be a section of the city."

"Wait. I thought this took place in some kind of an arena," Max said, frowning.

"The coliseum exists anywhere in Chadaré. As the ones who were challenged, the Korvad chose the location. It is being established there now."

"Established?" Giselle asked.

She had propped herself on a table between Tyler and Oz. Just one of the team. Max eyed her narrowly. Was she for real?

"The coliseum is a boundary. Inside it, the judge rules. When it is established on the chosen ground, it begins no bigger than a pinprick and expands outward until it is the desired size. Anybody in its way is pushed outward. Only combatants are allowed inside. Anybody may watch, however. The events within are transmitted throughout the city. There will be a festival today while everybody watches."

"How's Scooter?"

"He wants to see you."

Just then, a couple of dwarves set food in front of Max. While she dug in, Ilanion looked at her companions, taking in Thor's battered hat, holey jeans, and tattered boots; Tyler's lethal silence and ubiquitous twirling knife; Oz's clean-cut brutality; Giselle's quiet volcanic power; and Alexander's wild savagery. His gaze slipped to the Grims, and he did a double take.

"What?" Max asked around a mouthful of potato or something like it.

"Your shaggy friends. I—" He cleared his throat. "They're unexpected."

"Why?"

His surprise was evident. "Don't you know what they are?"

"Sure. They're Grims. Spirit dogs."

He stared at her and then broke into roaring laughter. Max quickly grew annoyed.

"What's so funny?"

His laughter subsided slowly, and he shook his head. "Calling them Grims is like calling Chadaré a village. These beasts are . . . legendary. And independent. How did you convince them to help you?"

"Convince them?" Max snorted. "They came all on their own, and I'm not at all sure they plan to actually help. What do the legends say about them? And how do you know what they are?"

"I can *see* what they are. And I suggest you be polite. As for what the legends say? Just that they go anywhere they want and nothing can keep them out, magic has very little effect on them, and they have mysterious powers."

"Mysterious?" Giselle prodded. "That's vague."

"They often appear when there are cataclysmic events."

"Like what?" Giselle asked.

Ilanion shrugged. "Destruction of cities and worlds, the draining of oceans, and the genocide of entire peoples. Some stories claim the . . . Grims . . . are responsible."

"Sounds like fairy tales to me," Oz said skeptically.

"Might be," Ilanion said, watching Beyul thoughtfully as he sipped his ale. "Might not."

"Still, this one saved my ass," Tyler said, scratching the Grim's head. "When the Fury blew. That was pretty cataclysmic."

"I never thought to see even one in my lifetime, and yet you have *two,*" Ilanion mused. Then he blinked. "A Fury?"

"Yeah," Tyler said in a tone that warned Ilanion not to press further on the subject.

Silence fell. Then, "Actually we have an infestation of the furry bastards," Oz said, breaking the tension.

"It's called a pack," Thor corrected.

"A pack," Ilanion repeated, dumbfounded. "Of these . . . Grims? How?"

"They moved in. They didn't ask," Oz said darkly. "Like termites."

"What have you got against dogs?" Tyler demanded.

Oz rolled his eyes and didn't answer. He turned to Ilanion. "Will this coliseum protect us from the sun and the dark?"

Ilanion frowned in confusion.

Max answered for him. "Didn't I tell you? You can be outside around the clock without any trouble. The place is made of shadows."

That startled Oz. She was aware that Alexander had remained quiet during all of this exchange, and now he spoke up. "There are seven of us, plus the two Grims. Who else do we have fighting on our side?"

"The Calopus is coming," Max said, having no doubt that it was true. "So make it an even ten." She eyed Beyul and the other Grim. "I hope you two plan to be more than just window decoration. We expect you to pitch in if you're going to take up space. You, too, Spike," she said to the Calopus. She looked at Ilanion. "That leaves ten spots to fill."

"I'll take a squad of seven Enay and the two Zo'ons."

He pointed at the gargoyle and earthworm creatures. "They are solid fighters."

"We should talk about the layout of the area and make a plan of attack," Max said.

"We've already begun." Ilanion pulled a map over.

Instantly, it grew into a three-dimensional layout, with the fighting area marked by a bright pink square. It looked like it covered about a square mile. It was an industrial area, with blocky buildings in gray brick and rusty metal and not a whole lot else. Nothing green, no water. Some of the buildings were tumbled down, and others looked as if they ought to be condemned. Except for the lack of graffiti and cars, it could have been a run-down part of Chicago or Detroit.

The others moved closer and started to discuss plans. Max ate, not paying much attention. Her mind wandered to Niko, Tutresiel, and Xaphan, and she found herself sinking into a mire of sadness.

She started when a cold nose pushed against her neck. She turned. The Calopus had jumped up onto the seat again and was staring at her with those shimmering silver eyes. There was intelligence there and something that looked like concern.

"I'm all right, Spike," she told the beast, stroking its head carefully to avoid its spines. The beast huffed and lay down, settling its head on her thigh. She looked down at it, her lips curving in a smile.

When she'd eaten all she could, she stood and motioned to Drida. How she could tell him apart from the other gargoyles, she didn't know. Just like with the Grims, now that she knew him, she didn't have any trouble telling him apart.

"Can you take me to Scooter? Um, Nayan, that is."

Drida nodded, and she followed him out with Spike at her heels. Alexander caught her hand as she passed and gave her a questioning look.

"Scooter," she whispered, and he nodded and let her go.

Drida took her out through another door, avoiding the kitchen. "This way," he said, and started back toward Ilanion's rooms. Before he got there, he stopped and touched a blank wall. Wards flashed, and part of the wall dissolved. Beyond was a small vestibule leading to a pair of broad red-lacquered doors. Six gargoyle guards stood watch outside.

Drida opened the doors for her and motioned her inside. He shut them, leaving her alone with Spike and Scooter.

The chamber had a high ceiling, thick carpets, heavy furnishings, and beautiful art. It was clearly designed for VIP guests. Inside was warm, with a smell of cinnamon and vanilla permeating the air. It didn't cover the rotting stench emanating from the bedchamber.

Max went across the sitting room. A bed at least the size of four king-size beds dominated the room. What sort of guests did Ilanion get? she wondered. Giants?

Scooter was lying on the near side and covered in a light sheet. His hair was dull black straw. Bandages covered his forehead and chest. He drew shallow, jerky breaths, and sweat covered his skin. His eyes were closed, but as Max came to stand beside him, they opened, staring blindly as he turned his head.

"You're here," he said, his voice nothing more than a thready whisper. He lifted his hand, clutching at the air.

She put her hand in his, and his grip was surprisingly strong. "Take . . . me back. Don't . . . want to die . . . here."

"I'm not taking you back. I've got your heart," Max told him. "I've got a plan to get your horn and your silk."

"Too . . . late."

"Fuck that. You're not dead yet."

"Won't let them . . . have me. Take . . . me . . . back."

Fury flared hot inside her. "I promised you that I would get you whole or die trying, and that's what I'm going to do." She caught her breath, pain exploding in her chest. "People *died*, do you understand? They died because I wasn't at Horngate. I wasn't there. I'm not going to let those deaths be for nothing, you got that?"

Her hand clenched into a fist, and it was all she could do not to hit him.

He struggled to breathe. Then, "Who? Who . . . died?"

"Niko. Both angels."

"Both . . . angels?" He sounded incredulous.

"Yeah. And Niko. You remember him, right? He was my best friend and my brother, and he's dead because a Fury rose at Horngate, and I was here with you. So you're going to make sure that their lives weren't wasted. I've challenged the Korvad. We're meeting in the coliseum shortly. They're putting up the silk and the horn, and I'm putting up you and your heart."

She waited for him to respond. He said nothing.

"I brought some help from Horngate, and Ilanion is joining the fight. We aren't going to lose. Do you understand? We aren't going to lose."

He wheezed. "I . . . understand."

His mouth worked as he tried to say more, but then

he collapsed in on himself. For a moment, Max thought he was dead. A few seconds later, he drew a rattling breath, and relief flooded through her.

Slowly, she smoothed the sheet over his chest and then took his hand in hers. "We're going to win," she told him. "You're going to be OK. We're all going to be OK."

She just wished she was sure of that.

22

IT MADE ALEXANDER ITCHY WHEN MAX LEFT THE DINing room, and he did not settle until she returned with the spiked wolf right beside her. The animal clearly was as attached to her as Beyul was to him. He wondered how that had happened. He would ask later when they were alone.

He felt his face tightening into an animal mask. For that, for the chance to have her in his bed and at his side for the rest of his life, he would not lose this battle.

She came to stand beside him.

"Everything all right?" he asked, seeing the hollow look in her eyes.

"If we don't hurry, there's going to be no point." She looked around the table. Everyone had fallen silent. "This fight has to be quick. Figure out how to kill and fast. No mercy. Don't leave anybody behind who can come back to stab you in the back. Scooter is close to death. The only way to save him is to get this over with fast. I count him as mine," she added, her gaze lingering on Giselle, who had remained silent.

The others looked slightly startled and then nodded

as if it made perfect sense for her to adopt the creature who had kidnapped her. But then, for Max, it did.

She looked at Alexander, Tyler, and Oz. "What do you think?"

It was Oz who answered. "The place makes for urban warfare. There's no open spaces to have a standing fight unless we make one."

"Which we could do," Ilanion said. "We could level everything if you want."

He was deferring to her. Alexander wondered at that. It was smart, in its way. She knew exactly what her people were capable of, and clearly, she had learned a lot about Ilanion and his people, enough to use their strengths to the best advantage. Plus, her life revolved around fighting. It was what she was made for. Still, this was Ilanion's home turf, and he was at least a mage. Giving leadership over to Max was not what Alexander had expected. He reorganized his impression of Ilanion.

"If we could trap them in the rubble, that would be fine, but razing the coliseum would only create unstable footing. That hurts us, too. Plus, it'll clog the air with dust. Kills our ability to see and smell," Oz said. "We're better off picking them off one by one or herding them into smaller areas where we can ambush them. Or knock a building down on them."

"What are they likely to do?" Max asked Ilanion and Drida.

"Brute force is Asherah's style," Ilanion said. "She'll hit hard. Keeping buildings standing might not be our choice."

"We have one of two options: attack or defend," Max said. "If we defend, we bring them to us. That way, we can set our own traps. Trouble with that is, they can take their time to find us. If we go on the hunt, we can keep them too busy to set any traps. So I say we hunt."

"You know me. I'd rather chase than sit on my ass and wait," Tyler said, and Thor and Oz nodded agreement. Alexander was of the same mind.

"We'll break up. Each of us"—she pointed to the four Blades—"will follow someone. My bet is that they won't divide their forces that much. A max of four teams, most likely, but I bet they'll only split into two. They'll want plenty of protection for their mages."

"OK, we follow them. What next? We need a way to coordinate," Oz said, frowning at the map.

"I can do it," Giselle said. "I can walk in astral form. If it doesn't take too long. I'll be able to find all of you through your bindings. Even unbound, Max isn't going to be any trouble, since I made her. If Alexander gives me a little blood, I should be able to connect to him, too, and guide you all."

"Will you be able to speak? Or is this all silent?"

"Not out loud. But I can write a few words on the ether. You will be able to read them."

"OK. Good," Max said, drumming her fingers thoughtfully. "We can work with that."

"Can these mages shield against physical attack?" Oz asked Ilanion. "Witches on earth usually can't."

Ilanion nodded. "How long or how well those shields will hold when they are distracted and under attack, I can't say."

"Ilanion's people can sniper them with arrows," Alexander said, with a glance at Drida, who nodded. "That will keep them off balance."

"What about the mages? They aren't going to let you just harass them. They'll come back at you hard," Giselle said sharply.

"This isn't a garden party," Max said, rolling her eyes. "Of course they will."

Thor started to laugh and turned it into a cough.

"We've got witch chain," Alexander said.

Max showed hers to Ilanion, who turned it in his fingers. Finally, he let go. "It won't hold any one of us for more than a few seconds."

"That's all we need, if we time it right," Tyler said. His knife was twirling in his fingers again. "All we have to do is get it around one of them and then put a bullet through their heads."

"How do we get close enough?" Oz asked.

"We'd have to set up a trap. Push them somewhere where someone could step out and do it. The Zo'on dig in the dirt like fish swim in water. They can come up out of the ground and wrap a foot," Drida said.

"That could work," Alexander mused, examining the layout of the city. "Ilanion could distract them to keep them from realizing that they are being herded."

"Or he could be bait," Thor suggested. "If he got hurt or if they thought they could catch him easily, they might get so eager that they won't think too hard about what they might be running into."

"I like it," Oz said.

"It's a good plan," Max said. She looked at the winged mage. "If you're up for it."

He nodded. "That could work for one or possibly two, but three? There are five members of the Korvad, though I can't imagine all will participate."

"Murphy's Law says they'll all want in on the action," Tyler said, and Thor and Oz nodded.

"All right. Then we'll expect everybody and be happy if we get fewer," Max said. "Doesn't change the plan any. We take them in stages. First stage, we harrass them and take out a few of their minions. As many as we can get. Then we melt back. For the second stage, we'll let them think they are leading us into an ambush. We'd just better make sure we spring ours first. We need to get one or more into a building and drop it on top of them. Let's hope we catch more than one in the trap. That means Ilanion and Giselle will need to get out in front of us and lure them in. If they shield against the collapse, they'll have to blast themselves out. My bet is that they'll drop their guard in order do it. We'll be waiting."

"What's the third stage?" Tyler asked.

"Set the witch-chain trap," Alexander said. "They will be disoriented and will want to regroup. We will just push them where we want them. After that, if there are any more of them . . ."

"Then it's up to me and Ilanion to distract them so you can kill them," Giselle said quietly. "By that time, they'll have used up enough energy to make our attacks more than just annoying. If they're angry or frightened, that will only make it harder on them."

"I don't like risking you," Oz growled.

"Worse, it's going to hurt like hell," Max said cheerfully. "With your compulsion spells nagging at you to protect her, that is."

"And if I don't do it, then we may lose and be taken as slaves. Your compulsion spells will hate that more," Giselle said quietly.

There was a dark undercurrent to her words that made Alexander wonder what she was thinking. Max caught it, too, and gave the witch a long look.

Before anyone could say anything else, a series of bell sounds resonated through the compound. The floors and ceilings shook, the lamps swayed, and the tables rattled. The sound rode through like a wave and disappeared, leaving behind a profound silence.

"That's it," Ilanion said at last, straightening up and putting on his helm. "Ready or not, it's time to go."

"Gear up," Max said, and Oz and her Blades moved swiftly to gather their weapons.

Alexander had little to do but slide on a combat vest. It held dozens of magazines for his .45s in the loops covering the front of it. The guns were already belted around his waist. He also fished out a bottle of single-malt scotch. When everyone was ready, he opened the lid and held it up. Silence fell again.

"To absent friends. May they be proud of our work today."

He drew a deep drink and passed the bottle to Tyler. One by one, they drank. Tears slid down Max's cheeks as she took a swig and handed the bottle to Giselle. The witch gasped as she swallowed, the color rising in her cheeks. Then the bottle traveled to Ilanion and the rest of the room.

When they were through, Max took the empty bottle and set it gently on the table.

"How are we getting there?" she asked Ilanion.

"Air barge. Drida, bring Nayan up to the balcony."

"No," Max said. "I'll do it."

Alexander took her hand. "No. Let them."

She shot him a blistering look. "Ordering me around, Slick?"

"Yes. Torturing yourself right now will not help us."

She snorted. "What makes you think I'm torturing myself?"

"Oh, I don't know. Maybe because he's known you for more than five minutes?" Tyler said. "If you had a whip, you'd probably be beating yourself with it."

"If I had a whip, I'd be beating *you,*" she said, but she did not pull out of Alexander's grip.

Ilanion led them up a spiral stairway that opened up on top of his compound. They stepped out on the flat summit of a tall mountain. It was covered with greenery, and waterfalls cascaded down its sides, sending up a veil of mist that swallowed the base of the mountain entirely. Shadows thickened and hid much of the rest of the view, but Max could tell they were still in the Torchmarch from the twining ropes and bridges and the flames that flickered like stars all around them.

The top of the mountain was smooth as glass. Sitting in the middle was the air barge. It looked like an origami blimp made from black paper. It was all sharp edges and angles. On either side, steps led up to a door in the gondola.

Ilanion led everyone onboard, all except for the members of Horngate. Max would not board without Scooter, and Giselle would not board without her. Which meant that none of them left.

Finally, Drida appeared. He pushed Scooter in a stretcher-like basket that hovered several feet off the ground. Alexander was shocked by the demigod's appearance. He smelled of sickness, and his red and brown scaled skin was slack and loose. Bandages covered his forehead and chest, and his long black hair was dull and crisp. He was barely breathing.

He felt Max stiffen beside him, her teeth grinding together. Then, without a word, she followed Drida and Scooter into the belly of the air barge. Giselle followed, and then went the Blades, Oz and Alexander, the spiked wolf, and the two Grims.

The interior was comfortable, if not luxurious. It had several decks connected by stairs, each much the same. Couches lined the angular walls in odd zig-zag patterns. They were upholstered in soft black leather and polished gold buttons. There were no windows or tables or any other passengers.

"The judge provides transportation," Ilanion told them as they settled themselves. "It will get us there in time."

They lifted off, the gondola swinging drunkenly at first and then steadying into a gentle sway. It was impossible to tell how fast they were going. No one spoke except Giselle and Ilanion. They were talking about magic and what to expect of the super-witches.

Max paced uneasily, the spiked wolf watching her. Beyul had sniffed Scooter all over and now sprawled along a couch with his head on his forelegs. Tyler's Grim was off by itself, watching Tyler with unblinking eyes. Oz and Thor went up the stairs to explore and returned a few minutes later. Oz checked his gear and then sat back to wait. Thor lay down on a couch and pulled his hat down over his eyes. A moment later, he was snoring. Alexander smiled thinly. A handy talent, that.

The trip seemed to take the blink of an eye. Soon he

felt them descending. A wave of magic crackled through them, bringing nearly everyone to stiff attention.

"That's just us passing through the coliseum ceiling," Ilanion said. "There's no going back."

"That's all right, friend," Thor said in his slow Texan drawl. "We all came to play."

A minute or two later, they settled onto the ground. The doors opened, and they descended, stepping out onto a small paved plaza. As soon as they stepped off, the air barge collapsed flat.

Max stood beside Scooter. Alexander joined her, as did Giselle. Thor, Tyler, and Oz arranged themselves to block any attacks on the witch. The two Grims and the Calopus sniffed around in front of them. Beside them, Ilanion stood surrounded by his people. On the opposite side of the plaza, their enemies waited.

"Is that a *dragon*?" Tyler asked.

"It is Kucedre. She is one of the Korvad. Careful of her breath—it will drown you, but not before it melts the skin and flesh from your bones. She has another form, a beautiful woman. She's very powerful, but she must have time to write her spells out. I'm sure that someone is carrying a bagful of prepared spells for her. Magic has little effect on her in this form, and ordinary arrows cannot penetrate her hide."

"Ordinary arrows?" Alexander asked quickly.

"My people carry arrows that will pierce her."

"One thing's for sure. If we're going to make our building plan work, we'd better find a hell of a big one to drop on her," Tyler said.

"I didn't really expect her to be here. She likes to hang back and let others do the dirty work for her. Asherah must have made a strong impression on her, or she has too much to lose if she doesn't help. She'll take to the air," Ilanion said. "Unless we damage her wings." He looked at Drida, who nodded and began talking to several of the other gargoyles.

"Tell us about the others," Max said.

"The good news is that only three showed up. You've seen Asherah. Aside from her magic, she's fast, and her claws will rip through just about anything. She likes to use them, too. They're naturally poisonous, so stay away from them."

"Which one is she?" Alexander asked.

"The four-armed woman," Max said. "Who else?" she asked Ilanion.

"Pradaku. He's the black panther."

"Panther? He's bigger than my truck," Oz said.

"You have to watch him. He emits a fragrance that steals your will, and you won't be able to resist. He will enslave you and turn you against your companions. As with the others, he is capable of powerful magic. He can also change form, though he retains his black skin no matter what he looks like."

"And the rest of them?" Alexander asked.

Ilanion eyed the Korvad's collection of minions. "The cat heads are pretty obvious. Half jungle cat, half human, all deadly. They are fierce but nothing you can't handle. The tall, thin ones on the end wearing hoods are what you might call ghouls. They are devourers of flesh and spirit. They are fast and difficult to see when they choose not to be seen, and their bites paralyze. They might give you a little more trouble."

"How do you kill them?" Thor asked.

"None of these creatures likes iron. An arrow in the eye or the heart will drop them. Or a bullet."

"That just leaves those four ape-looking things," Max said.

"I've never seem them before," Ilanion said, frowning at them.

The creatures in question were thick-shouldered and hunched, with arms that hung to the ground. They walked on all fours like apes, although their faces and bodies were human enough. They carried wide, curved swords and wore chain mail and hobnail boots.

Before they could speculate any more about the creatures, a column of white light rose out of the ground between the two groups of challengers. It was a good fifteen feet tall. A figure shimmered into being atop it.

The judge, Alexander guessed. Her head was covered with a white and gray feathered headdress, and her face was hidden behind a white mask that had no eye, nose, or mouth holes. Her flowing robe wrapped her entire body and gave no clue to what she might look like underneath. The only reason Alexander knew she was female was because Ilanion had said so.

"Challengers, step forward," she said in an ethereal voice that sounded neither male nor female—nor human, for that matter.

Ilanion started to move, and Max pinned him in place with a look. "This is my challenge," she said. "Stay here," she told her Blades. She gripped Scooter's stretcher and pulled him with her as she walked away. The box with his heart was tucked between his feet. As always, the Calopus went with her.

She stopped at the base of the column, just across from

Asherah. The creature was dressed in silver-studded leather, her four arms naked except for silver gauntlets that ended at the elbow. Her clawed feet were bare. Her entire presence radiated magic and menace. It was all Alexander could do not to join Max. Beside him, he felt the beasts inside Thor, Tyler, and Oz roaring to the fore. They were no more happy about this than he was.

"You have agreed to the terms," the judge intoned. "You shall place the prizes in the light. At that time, the first bell will sounds, and you may go prepare as you see fit. When the second bell sounds, the challenge begins. It ends when one side forfeits or dies."

The judge fell silent, and Max hesitated a moment, then guided the stretcher toward the pillar of light. She stopped and bent down, whispering something against Scooter's ear. Then she pushed him through. At the same time, Asherah shoved in a twisted horn about three feet long. It glittered with gold and jewels. Next went in a small box, no bigger than Alexander's fist.

As soon as all four of the prizes were inside, the pillar flashed and hardened. At the same time, a bell sounded, like the one that had summoned them all to the coliseum. It resonated through Alexander's bones, and the ground trembled beneath him. Max spun around and trotted back to join them.

"We don't have much time," she said. "Remember. Hit them fast and hard, and don't leave anyone alive." She glanced at Alexander, Thor, Oz, Tyler, and Giselle. "Try not to get dead," she said softly. "See you when I see you."

They dispersed. The game was on.

23

MAX UNLEASHED HER PRIME, LETTING HER human senses deaden. Hate filled her. The focus was Asherah. For Scooter's pain and suffering. For Tutresiel and Xaphan. For Niko.

It didn't matter that Asherah had never met Niko or the angels. Max still held her responsible. If not for the four-armed bitch, Scooter would never have needed Max, and she would have been there to help when the Fury rose. For that, Asherah would pay. All of them would pay.

She, Oz, Tyler, Thor, and Alexander fanned out in a wide arc across several streets to trail their opponents. Behind came Drida and four of his gargoyles. Ilanion had taken Giselle somewhere where she could be safe while following everyone's progress astrally until they could figure out a place to lay the building trap. The earthworm critters and two remaining gargoyles went with them.

Unexpectedly, team Korvad did not split up but stayed together, heading east. Max wondered if it was just stupidity or arrogance that made them bunch up into a big fat target.

It was seven minutes before the second bell sounded. When it did, the dragon arrowed up into the air, her blue wings pumping powerfully. She gained height and looped around, flying back toward the starting point. She'd probably spiral out from there, searching for someone to kill.

That gave them only a few minutes' window to attack her friends before she and her bad breath got back. Max ran forward. She stopped at the corner of a building and scanned the street ahead. She saw no movement. She was about to start out again when Giselle appeared, her body mostly transparent.

Max didn't wait for her to speak. "Go back to Drida. Have him and the earthworms set up an ambush for the dragon on top of those buildings just ahead." She pointed. "We'll go bait the ambush and bring her in. Hurry."

Giselle vanished. Max waited. A couple of minutes later, the witch reappeared and gave Max a nod. Drida and the earthworms were on their way.

"Go tell everyone else what's up. Team Korvad's about four blocks ahead. We'll harass them a little, and that should bring the dragon quick."

Giselle disappeared again, and Max jogged forward. She encountered some kind of a magical land mine in the middle of the street but easily went around it. The work was fast and sloppy, and she wondered if it was done that way on purpose to make pursuers think they didn't need to watch too hard for trouble.

She sharpened her watch. The next trap was just as sloppy and obvious, but the third was subtle. She knew it was there more by the slight tingle in the air than anything else. It stretched across the entire road.

Unwilling to test it, Max jumped up to a ledge on the third floor of the squat building beside her. From there, she climbed onto the roof and ran to the edge in front. From her vantage point, she could see team Korvad. They were loosely strung out over a two-block length. She saw Alexander one street over, and then Thor trotted up behind him. She didn't see Oz or Tyler, but if they weren't in place, they soon would be.

She leaped to the next building and ran across the roof, then jumped one more time. Asherah's team wasn't watching the rooftops. They trusted the dragon to protect them from the air.

Max looked over her shoulder. She couldn't see the dragon. Although the air seemed clear, Chadaré's weird shadow atmosphere prevented any long-distance vision. She smiled. *Good*. That would help keep the dragon's search pattern to small spirals. Drida would have time to get his ambush set up.

She leaped to the next building and then another. She was ahead of team Korvad now. She went to the far side of her building and climbed down, easing around the corner to glance up the street. Asherah and the panther were walking in the middle of the street, with the four ape guys boxing them in. The ghouls and the cat heads were evenly dispersed around them.

Max readied herself. A flicker of movement across the road caught her attention. Thor moved up on the opposite side. He winked at her and grinned. She returned the smile. She nodded, and they both swung around the corner and opened fire.

Oz and Alexander joined in on the other end of the block at almost the same moment. The cat heads died quickest. The Shadowblades fired with deadly precision, and team Korvad wasn't expecting guns. Astonishment held them still for deadly seconds. Then they started shooting arrows. The ghouls flickered across the ground like skeletal shadows, moving so fast that Max could barely track them.

Poison-tipped arrows clattered around her. She pulled back and popped the clip free of her gun and clicked in another. She glanced around the corner again.

Asherah was facing Oz and Alexander at the other end of the block. The panther was heading for Max and Thor. She frowned, remembering Ilanion's warning. Pradaku the panther emitted an odor that would turn his enemies into slaves. She pinched her nose shut, calling out a warning to Thor. He looked at her and followed suit.

They both emptied their guns at the enormous black beast. The bullets tinkled to the ground without ever hitting him. *Damn. Shit. Fuck.*

Suddenly, three ghouls came out of nowhere and darted at Max. She twisted away. The move brought her too close to the panther, and she was forced to let go of her nose as she lunged away. She sprawled on her stomach, then rolled to the side and flipped to her feet.

The ghouls were only a few feet away, the panther hanging back to let them work. They were a patchwork quilt of skin, as if they'd been sewn together from the discards in Dr. Frankenstein's workshop. And whoever had quilted them together hadn't been neat about it. Bone and dirty gray flesh were exposed here and there. All three were pocked with bullet holes that dribbled black blood. Their mouths were round and lipless, with snapping piranha teeth.

One of them flickered sideways around to her left. She jerked her head to watch him, and another skimmed closer, reaching out with long, skeletal fingers. Max flinched away, but then ice knifed through her side as the third ghoul plunged its fingers through her skin and under her ribs. Blood ran down her side. She gritted her teeth against the pain and the cold and yanked herself away. The other two ghouls rushed at her, making an excited humming sound at the smell of her blood.

But then Spike was there. The wolf snarled and launched itself at the ghouls.

"No!" Max shouted. She dropped her gun and whipped out a sword.

Before she could swing, Spike exploded like a porcupine. Spines drilled through the ghouls, and they staggered back, keening. Then they dropped to the ground like wet rags. Spike shook and nosed one with a growl before wagging once at Max.

Before she could move, the panther prowled forward. His eyes were a sunset orange, and he stood a good eight feet at the shoulder. He sat down just beyond Spike and tilted his head at Max as if waiting. Her lip curled. That's exactly what he was doing. He expected her to fall at his feet and grovel.

She held her breath. But that wasn't going to work for long. Spike bared its teeth at the panther. Max reached out and grabbed Spike by the ruff and pulled the animal back. Several spines went through her hand, and it burned with poison, but she didn't let go. Spike wasn't going to become a slave to the big cat.

Suddenly, the panther shifted, and in its place stood a giant of a man. His skin was ebony black. He was about ten feet tall and rippled with muscle. Hell, his muscles had muscles. His legs were tree trunks, and his cock was—enough to say that he'd put a horse to shame. He was hairless from the top of his head to his feet. Long talons curved from his toes and fingers. His jaw was slightly elongated. He smiled, revealing long fangs.

"You may breathe," he said.

Max shook her head. Had he dropped his shields to shift? Was he that stupid? There was no way to tell. A flicker of movement behind him warned her that someone was coming. She had to keep him from noticing. And pray to Mother Night that whoever was coming was one of hers.

She let out the breath she was holding. *Oh, this is so fucking stupid.* But if he was dead, his hold on her would die with it. Wouldn't it?

She drew a breath. "I'll never want you," she said, and a tingling sensation rushed through her. She smelled something like apricot, hot metal, and cardamom. It wrapped her senses and tangled her mind. Gentle hooks dug themselves into her essence, and her body and soul flooded with shuddering desire. She went dizzy, and suddenly, a rainbow aura flared around Pradaku. He looked amazing. She wanted him. She would do anything for just a single glance. Her mouth went dry, and she wanted to crawl on the ground to make him look at her, touch her, smile at her.

His widening smile told her that he knew exactly what she was experiencing. Inside, her Prime scrabbled and snapped at her to wake up. Pradaku gestured toward the ground. Her knees immediately started to buckle in response, but something in Max held her upright. He frowned and gestured harder.

She twitched, and her body shook as if she were having drug withdrawals, but she didn't fall. She couldn't. No, she *wouldn't*. Not to this bastard. But the truth was, she wouldn't be able to hold out for long. Already, her bones felt like water, and she ached for him to smile at her and caress her. In a few minutes, she'd probably be begging for him to use her like a blowup doll.

He stepped forward, his expression twisting. Magic streamed from his hands in long whips. He snapped them at her, and Max flew back, stripes of fire and blood seaming across her body. But the pain was a gift. It did more than anything to cut through the enchantment of his scent.

She climbed shakily to her feet, looked down at herself, and almost threw up. The flaying magic had cut deep into her, and she clutched her stomach to keep her guts from spilling out before her healing spells could fix the wound.

Pradaku laughed and lifted his arm again. Before he could move, something struck him in the back, and he pitched onto his face with a startled yowl. Instantly, he was back on his feet. He whirled around. Beyul faced him, the Grim's head low. Spike got into the action and rushed in to chomp his arm. Magic crawled over the Calopus, but it didn't let go, shaking its head and tearing out a chunk of Pradaku's flesh. He screamed and swung a massive fist at Spike.

Tyler's Grim slammed against the black giant's chest. The force carried them both to the ground. Beyul and

Spike leaped in to help. The panther-mage disappeared under a violent mass of furry bodies. The air filled with the sounds of snapping, biting, and growling. The mage screamed and struggled under the beasts, but it was no good. Suddenly, his shouts cut off, and he stiffened. As Max watched, his skin faded to gray, and he stopped moving.

Alexander and Thor got to Max at the same time. They put their arms around her.

"Are you all right?" Alexander demanded, his hand covering hers in an effort to help close the wound in her stomach.

"Been better," she said, gasping.

The tentacles of Pradaku's scent were sliding away, and she no longer felt like she would die without him.

She looked at Beyul and Spike, who had flopped down on top of the body. Tyler's Grim had run off. "I'm alive, though. Thanks to them. Guess they came to fight after all."

The words sounded bubbly in her throat, and the two men frowned at her. "We have to get you out of here," Alexander said. His eyes were hot with emotion, and his mouth was bracketed with white dents.

"No, we have to go finish this," Max said. "I'll be fine in a few minutes."

Before Alexander could protest, the spectral Giselle appeared, and her face went cold with rage at the sight of the blood-drenched Max. Instantly, she winked out and disappeared. The witch-bitch was on her way, Max had no doubt.

"Where's Asherah? And the dragon?" she asked.

"The dragon flew off. Heavily wounded," Oz said,

coming around the corner. He stopped when he saw Max, his nostrils flaring. "Thought we were going to do the guerrilla hit-and-run thing, not a full-on battle," he said.

"I didn't move fast enough," Max said. "Then I figured if I distracted him, one of you would take him down. But I accidentally pissed him off." She looked down at her wounds. They were closing.

"Where's Tyler?"

"Tracking them."

"Get going after him," she said, spitting blood onto the ground. "We need to finish this. I'll catch up. Asherah isn't going down easily."

Just then, Giselle and Ilanion dropped down out of the sky with powerful gusts of his wings. Giselle wordlessly strode to Max and grabbed her shoulders. Magic poured through her, bolstering her healing spells. Max tried to pull away, but Giselle's fingers were like claws.

"You're wasting energy," she told the witch.

"Shut up. I'm doing my fucking job," Giselle snapped. A minute later, she pulled away. "That should do it."

The wounds were entirely closed now, and the pain had mostly faded. Max twisted and cracked her back. "Feels better. How many did we get rid of?" she asked, returning to business.

Ilanion had knelt down beside Pradaku. Beyul and Spike made low growling sounds and moved away as he turned the dead man over. Beyul sat beside Alexander and leaned heavily into him. Spike shook before sitting down and nonchalantly licking its paws. Ilanion looked up at Max in awed disbelief. "How did you do it? He hardly looks hurt."

"You're the one who said the Grims had mysterious powers. Looks as if you were right."

"I never thought anybody could take Pradaku down so easily. You're . . ."

"Not as hopeless as you thought we'd be?" Max supplied when he seemed at a loss for words. "Thing is, I'm betting we've had more practice at killing than any of you have, and besides, it wasn't actually all that easy. I nearly got gutted."

She straightened, testing her body. It felt bruised like she'd been in a good bar fight, but she was ready to go.

"Let's get on with it," she said. "How many did we take out?"

"I counted eleven. Thirteen if you count the dragon and this guy," Oz said, nudging Pradaku with his foot.

"And us?"

"Horngate is accounted for. I don't know about the gargoyles or the earthworms."

"I sent them to finish off Kucedre if she still lives," Ilanion said. "The dragon," he clarified when the others looked confused.

"That means we're down to Asherah and six minions. Do who have a count on them?" Max asked.

"The four apes are still walking around. Those things are like tanks. Nothing seems to penetrate. Plus a couple of the ghouls," Alexander said. He had his hand on Max's hip as if he couldn't bear not to touch her.

She looked at Ilanion. "Go see if you can find her. Try not to be seen. And don't start a showdown until we get there," she added when his eyes shifted suddenly to pure gold. He wanted the chance at the other mage.

Fine by her, but if he lost, she wanted to be there to finish the job.

The eagle mage didn't answer. He simply leaped up into the air and skimmed away.

"Let's move," Max said. "I don't trust him to wait."

"Beyul has the trail," Alexander said, and they followed the Grim.

Drida's people met them two blocks away. The gargoyle looked pleased. Or as pleased as a statue can look. He and his team fell in behind without a word.

Asherah had taken time to set more traps. They were easy enough to avoid. Max was starting to wonder if the bitch had any plan whatsoever or if she just relied on brute force to get her way. It wouldn't be all that surprising. If you were the biggest bully in the schoolyard, why not just smash away the opposition? Why finesse anything? It would be a waste of time. And eventually, no one would challenge you anymore, and you'd let your fighting skills get rusty, if you ever had any to begin with.

They were warned that Asherah was near when they heard the explosions and saw a cloud of dust and debris rising into the air.

"Bastard didn't wait," Max said, breaking into a run.

They raced out into an open area and stopped. It was thick with choking dust and littered with a maze of rubble. Streaks of magic flashed through the cloud, and buildings exploded, sending stone and steel flying.

There was no way to tell where Asherah and Ilanion were. Nor was there any sign of the apes or the ghouls. Then a scuffle began among Drida's men. Max spun around. The apes had come out of nowhere and were tearing the gargoyles limb from limb and trampling them into the ground.

The Blades launched themselves into the fray. But Alexander was right. Nothing seemed to slow them down. They were impervious to everything.

Oz was knocked into the air. Tyler dropped down from a roof and wove in and out, punching and kicking until he was knocked in the head and fell in a heap. Thor, Max, and Alexander had about as much luck. Where the apes struck, bones broke. The gargoyles fared little better despite the rock strength of their bodies. The apes ground them to dust or used them as clubs.

Spike dove in, snapping and biting, but had little effect. The two Grims hung back. What they were waiting for, Max had no clue.

Giselle blasted the apes with magic, but the creatures shook it off and continued their assault.

Max dodged a massive fist. Thor was being crushed in a bear hug. Alexander was hammering at one ape with a length of pipe. Thor went limp, and the ape dropped him and snatched at Alexander. Before he could grab him, the ground opened beneath his feet. He fell into a hole and vanished. Seconds later, another did the same. Then the third and the fourth.

"What happened?" Giselle gasped as Alexander checked Thor. Tyler was helping Oz to his feet.

"The Zo'on," Drida said. He was swaying drunkenly, and one of his eyes was gone.

"Earthworms?" Oz said as he swayed, wiping blood from his chin. "Fucking fantastic. 'Bout time they got here."

"Are those apes dead? Or will they be digging out of their graves?" Alexander asked.

"The Zo'on will make sure they can't dig out," Drida said, and there was a sharp look of triumph on his face.

"That just leaves the last two ghouls and Asherah," Max said, turning her head to look for them.

"Easy as gettin' laid in a two-dollar whorehouse," Thor drawled sardonically.

"Do those even exist?" Giselle asked, startling the Blade.

He grinned. "I hear they do in heaven," he said.

"So you'll never know for sure," Tyler said. "Since you're going to hell in a handbasket."

"I was thinking I'd be going in a rocket, myself," Thor said. "Maybe real soon," he added as the ground shuddered and all around them the buildings creaked and shook ominously. "I'll save you a seat."

"Asherah still has her panties in a twist," Max said as she ran a hand through her hair. "Time to take her down. Everybody ready?" There were nods all around.

"What about Ilanion?" Alexander asked as the ground trembled again and dust whirled into the air.

"I told the fucker to wait," Max said. "He deserves what he gets." But she was already moving, prowling carefully through the dust fog toward the source of the magical concussions. She stopped and grabbed Giselle's arm. "Stick close," she told the witch. "Watch for the ghouls," she told the others. "This dust is perfect for them."

The others spread out in a skirmish line on either side, and she lost sight of them. Giselle curled her fingers into Max's waistband. Suddenly, the sounds of battle went silent. Max's skin prickled. She couldn't smell or see. Sounds seemed to come from everywhere and nowhere in the murky fog of dust. She felt like a sitting duck.

"There," Alexander said softly from the left, and then he bounded past with Beyul at his side.

Max's chest clenched as a screech tore through the air, followed by shouts and a long, eerie yowl that sent spider chills crawling down her spine.

The sound cut off suddenly. One ghoul down. She hoped.

"Everybody OK?" she called, then jumped as Spike nosed her leg. "Tyler? Thor? Oz? Alexander? What happened?"

There was a chorus of replies, and then Alexander stepped out of the fog and pressed a hard kiss to her lips. "One ghoul gone," he said with a wolfish grin as he dusted his hands together. "One to go." He whirled away before she could say anything else.

"He's actually hunting them," Max muttered, her intestines knotting with worry. "He's going to get himself killed."

"He won't. Not with you to come home to," Giselle said.

Max twisted to look at her. "What the hell do you know?"

The witch smiled thinly. "Not enough, apparently. But I'm learning. One thing I can say is that Alexander isn't going anywhere until you tell him to. And probably not then."

"Right. Because you're so good at relationships," Max said.

"Maybe not. But like I said, I've been learning. Alexander has been making a point of teaching me," Giselle said wryly.

What had been going on at Horngate while she was gone? Max wondered.

Another screech sounded and cut off as fast as it began. "And then there was one," Max murmured. "A hell of a big one."

"We'll get her," Giselle said.

"We'd better, and fast. Or Scooter is going to die. I'll be right behind. I promised I'd save him or die trying."

"You did *what*?" Giselle exclaimed, and magic sizzled through her fingers and jolted Max like she'd licked the end of a power line. "What were you thinking?"

"I was thinking—" Max broke off. She was thinking that she and he were a lot alike. What Giselle had done to Max the Korvad had done to Scooter. "He'd been tortured and mutilated. Everyone he'd trusted had betrayed him. He needed someone to fight in his corner, and I was the only one he had."

For once, her tone was neither bitter nor accusing. Scooter's experience mirrored her own all too closely, and Giselle knew it. But Max couldn't scrape up any anger at the moment. It was all old news, and the world was a different place now. There was no time left for old feuds.

Giselle sighed, her body wreathed in snaking black magic. "I don't want to lose you," she said quietly.

"Tell me something I don't know. I'm your favorite punching bag and pit bull," Max replied, scanning around her, trying to see *anything*.

"No. I fucked up our friendship thirty years ago, and I want a chance to—"

Max was shocked and not a little bit irritated that Giselle thought she might be able to fix the betrayal. "What? Make it up to me?"

"Maybe. Maybe I just want a chance to be friends again."

Max snorted but didn't tell the witch-bitch to go fuck herself. Maybe it was losing Niko. Maybe it was the fact that the world was a new and dangerous place. Or maybe it was looking down the barrel of her own mortality, but Giselle's comment didn't ignite the usual hatred inside Max. Instead, she let the idea settle inside her for later consideration and focused on the problem at hand.

She heard the beating of wings overhead. For a moment, her heart clutched, but Tutresiel and Xaphan were dead. She swallowed the tight ache in her throat. Ilanion was still alive.

There was a crunching of rocks and a rolling of rubble, and Tyler swore. "What's wrong?" she called in a low voice.

"Can't see a fucking thing in this soup," he said. "Where is Asherah?"

"I am here, little man," came the mage's voice. It was a ribbon of satiny promise circling them.

The building debris trembled and rattled. The air began to spin in a slow circle. It wouldn't stay slow for long, Max thought. Asherah liked to beat her opponents into the ground. Soon the spin would be a full-blown tornado. They were out of time.

"Alexander and Tyler, find her," Max ordered into the churning dust. With the Grims to help protect them, they stood a better chance of surviving if they tripped over her accidentally. "Everyone else, come to my voice. Ilanion, you, too!" she shouted.

A few minutes later, she was surrounded by Drida and his team, the two earthworms, Oz, Thor, Giselle, Spike, and last of all Ilanion. He glided down in a bubble of clear air. He was bloody and bruised, his armor dented and scratched. Blood coated his lips and chin.

"You OK?" Max asked.

"I'll be better when Asherah is dead," he said. His gaze flicked to Giselle and then to everyone else. "Glad you all made it."

"I thought I told you to wait for us before going after Asherah," Max said.

Ilanion grinned without remorse. "Did you? Must've forgot that."

The wind was speeding up, and Max was beginning to feel the pull. Her ears popped with the changing pressure. "We've got to take her down—and quick. Anybody have any ideas?"

"Best chance is to use the witch chain and cut her throat when she's unprotected," Oz said.

Max nodded. "First, we have to pinpoint her and then keep her distracted while we get close."

"Ilanion and I can do that," Giselle said. "We'll keep her too busy to notice what you're up to."

Max turned to Drida. "Can the earthworms—the Zo'on—come up underneath like they did with the ape critters? They shouldn't try to be too stealthy. If she thinks they are our ace in the hole, she'll be so proud of herself for fending them off that she won't look for us."

Drida spoke to the earthworms and turned back to Max. "They will."

"We'll need a signal to let them know when to strike. And I only want them to get noticed and then get the hell out before they get killed."

He spoke to them, and their stubby pink heads bobbled in what Max thought might be nods. Their voices were wet noises that sounded like mud gurgling.

"One of us will stay with you and stamp the ground," Drida said.

"They'll hear that?" Oz asked doubtfully.

Drida gave a little smile and slammed his foot into the ground. Max felt the shiver of the impact in her bones. "Good enough," she said.

"That leaves actually getting the chain on her and killing her. My unlocking ability might let me through her shields," Max said. "But we can't count on it. So the witch chain is our only leverage. We'll only have a split second before she protects herself again. It would help if she doesn't see us coming, so we can hit her fast before she realizes what the chain can do. Got any ideas on how to get close?"

"Set up an ambush and let her come to us," Thor suggested.

"We'd have to see to do it," Oz said doubtfully. "Otherwise, we won't be able to herd her where we need her to go."

"So we'll get Asherah to clear the air," Ilanion said. "Or do it for her." He looked at Giselle. "I've got some ideas about that." He pulled her aside, and they started talking together.

Max shrugged. "All right, suppose they can pull it off. How do we make it work?"

"Alexander and Tyler will have to use the Grims to

move her. She's not going to back down from anybody else."

"And us," Giselle said, rejoining the conversation. "Between Ilanion, me, and the Grims, we should be able to maneuver her."

"We can bait her. She likes to attack. Let her come after us," Thor said.

Max shook her head. "Not you and Oz. You'll be with me to kill her. Drida, tell your people to wait here, and once the air is clear, start shooting her with your arrows. All they're trying to do is piss her off. She won't care if they hurt her or not. She'll just be mad that they have the gall to attack at all." She looked around. "Anyone think of anything else?" When no one answered, she nodded. "Then all we need is Asherah and some room to see."

Just then, Tyler pushed through the whirling wind. It whined, flinging stinging bits of rock and debris through the air. Gritty blood made a spider-web pattern over his cheeks and forehead. A moment later, Alexander joined him. Like Tyler, he was caked with blood and dirt.

"Found her," Tyler said, coughing and spitting out the dust.

"She will not stay still for long. She is distinctly unhappy," Alexander said.

"That's all right. We don't plan to make her wait." Max laid the plan out tersely for them. "Now, Tyler and Alexander, it's up to you to figure out where the ambush should happen and then establish positions. After that, Giselle and Ilanion start clearing the air, and we get down to business. Timing is everything. One last thing:

if we don't kill her, fall back, and we'll figure out another plan. And try not to die."

She turned to follow Tyler and Alexander. The two Blades put their heads together for a few moments and then set off. Everyone stuck close, with Ilanion and Giselle sandwiched in the middle. The earthworms squirmed down into the dirt and vanished from sight, and the gargoyles hunkered down to wait for the air to clear.

The wind was growing stronger. Bigger pieces of debris were beginning to swirl in the murk. Something thumped against Max's shoulder, cutting deep. Spike pressed against her leg and miraculously didn't poke holes into her.

Their progress was slow. The wind pounded harder, the coil tightening the closer they came to Asherah. Max pulled the collar of her shirt up to cover her nose and mouth, squinting to keep the grit out of her eyes.

"Where are you, Ilanion? Are you afraid? I will crush you. I will eat your heart and drink your blood. I will hang your wings on my walls and feed your bones to my pets."

Asherah's voice spun around them like liquid gold. It was seductive and tempting, like a siren's song. Ilanion's body tensed against the summons, his wings clamping tight against his body.

They stopped, and Alexander disappeared into the murk. A few minutes later, he returned, putting a hand on Max's arm. He tugged. She followed, along with Drida, Thor, and Oz.

He led them over a tumbled mass of stone and twisted metal. Just beyond it was a long side of a building that was still intact. It was propped on the rubble and offered cover underneath. Before Alexander turned to leave, he splayed a hand on Max's hip and pulled her hard against him. As she had done, he had pulled his shirt up to cover his nose and mouth. He nuzzled close to her ear, his body hot and hard against hers.

"Make this quick," he told her. "And do not die. I have plans for you when we get back to Horngate. They will not be nearly as pleasant if you are a corpse." He pulled his shirt down and pulled hers down and gave her a hard kiss, his tongue sliding against hers in a caress that made her toes curl. He pulled back way too soon, waving as he faded into the maelstrom.

She grinned as she pulled her shirt over her mouth again. He was having fun. And even though Scooter's life and her own hung in the balance, a wild joy was fizzing through her veins.

"It's kissing time?" Thor asked. "Can I get me some sugar?"

"Sure," Max said. "You and Oz make a cute couple. Can I watch? It would be so hot."

She laughed when Thor blinked in surprise and then blushed. Oz slung an arm over the other man's shoulder and kissed his cheek, winking at Max. Thor turned and stared at Oz in slack-jawed shock. Max couldn't blame him. Oz didn't show his mischievous side very often.

"Does this mean you have plans for me, too?" Thor asked with a wicked look as he got into the game. He ran a suggestive hand down Oz's back to cup his ass.

"*Such* plans," Oz said dramatically as he pulled Thor against him and dipped him over his arm in classic romantic-movie style. "I shall woo you within an inch of your life."

"Woo?" Max repeated. "Is that another word for sex?" She shoved at the two men. "Take it under cover before Asherah gets an eyeful of you goofballs."

"Till later, then, my sweet candy-muffin gumdrop," Thor said while batting his eyelashes at Oz. "I don't know what I'll do if you are hurt. My heart will break into a thousand million pieces."

"My darling sugar-pudding custard pie, I will never let that happen. Let us cuddle together until the wicked witch crashes our party and we must gird ourselves for battle." Oz took Thor's hand and pulled him under the shelter of the fallen building.

Max rolled her eyes, smiling. *Idiots.*

Then memory intruded, and her smile faded, her humor souring. For just a minute, everything had felt normal and right. But it wasn't. Niko was gone, and so were the angels. She blinked as tears burned in her eyes. She bit her tongue, swallowing her grief back down. She couldn't afford the distraction right now. But she couldn't get rid of the ache in her chest that seemed to drill down into her soul.

She crawled under the wall slab and settled down beside the others to wait. Suddenly, she was in the mood to kill.

24

THE MINUTES STRETCHED. ONE. TWO. FIVE. TEN.

The wind continued to intensify, scouring the ground and picking up the rubble. Wood and rocks thundered against the fallen wall sheltering them. The wall lifted slightly and slid a few inches.

Then Max noticed that the air was starting to clear. The wind still spun hard, but the dirt was filtering out. Although she couldn't see Asherah yet, she was able to see more of their battleground.

"Thor and Oz, go dig down and cover yourself on the ground," she said, pointing to where she wanted them. "We want her to pass you on the way to me. I'll lasso her, and you kill her. I don't want her to see you coming."

The two men crawled out and dug shallow trenches, covering themselves with dirt and rock until they were practically invisible. Even if Asherah had a good sense of smell, she wouldn't be able to pinpoint them.

Now, for everything else to fall into place.

As the air cleared, Max scanned the battlefield. Asherah stood on a hill of crumbled masonry and dirt. She was surrounded by the remains of several buildings. It looked like half a dozen bombs had gone off. Ilanion and Giselle were off to the left and right, with Alexander and Tyler closer in, their Grims stalking at their sides.

Max glanced down, realizing that Spike had disappeared. Where had the Calopus gone? Max searched across the field of rubble, but there was no sign of the beast. Then Asherah took her attention.

"Who are your friends, Ilanion?" Asherah asked, casting a scathing look at Giselle and then at Alexander and Tyler. She didn't pay any attention to the Grims. "I thought you'd bring someone more worthy of my effort."

The eagle mage laughed. "You are alone, your minions dead. I wonder if *you* are worth *our* effort."

Asherah's face blotched greenish-purple, and her eyes bugged. She was pissed. Max's lips curved in a sharp smile. Angry witches made mistakes.

The wind died, and the silence was almost painful. At the same moment, a hail of arrows bounced down around her. Several more followed. With every wave, the witch twitched and fumed, her hands clenching and unclenching.

When the arrows stopped, she pointed at Ilanion. "I will destroy your little friends, and when I'm done, I will make you suffer. You will beg me for death. I will—"

She squawked as Alexander darted forward and slammed her shields with a metal pole he'd picked up out of the rubble. She staggered and whirled. One of her arms drove forward, and she let loose a bolt of orange magic. Alexander dodged the strike and gave her a small bow, designed to infuriate her more. Max grinned.

Asherah blasted at him again, all four arms lobbing

the fiery darts. Alexander gave a ringing laugh and danced aside. He was too fast for her to hit.

Magic flared around Asherah in a column of pink and orange flames. She tossed a ball of light high up into the air, and it spread out like a net. It fell down as if anchored by weights. Max sucked in a breath. Alexander couldn't get out from under it.

But then Beyul jumped up and grasped the net in his teeth. The Grim yanked it down and shook it fiercely before turning to growl at Asherah, his green eyes glowing brightly. Before she could react, Tyler leaped up behind her and smashed her shields with a length of wood. He leaped away, and Ilanion and Giselle each sent a slow wave of magic rolling across the ground at her. The black and yellow waves merged and washed up around Asherah's mound. They climbed higher. Their magic met Asherah's shields with an explosion. Rocks and wood flew through the air. Max dodged under the wall and peered out again.

Not giving Asherah time to react, Ilanion rose into the air and smashed at her shields with lances of magic, while Giselle sent burrowing threads to tear apart Asherah's mound. As her footing gave way, the witch staggered and fell. She screamed her fury. She sent a blast at Ilanion and struck him dead-on. Despite his shields, he slammed against a building and dropped to the ground in a heap.

Asherah leaped down off her mound, a few feet closer to where Max was hiding. Alexander and Tyler dashed at her again. She lashed out, but the Grims were there. They snarled and leaped at her. They knocked her down and Tyler's Grim snapped savagely at her face.

The four-armed witch rolled away, and the Grims let

her. Max winced. She was pretty sure the two beasts could take the bitch down all by themselves, but for whatever reason, they were holding back.

Asherah's roll had brought her a few feet closer. Max nodded to Drida, and he slammed his fist into the ground. Instantly, the dirt under the witch softened, and she sank. She struggled against the sudden quicksand, and magic enveloped her body in a sunset-colored cocoon. She floated up into the air, and both Alexander and Tyler smashed at her. She jolted forward like a tennis ball in Jell-O. Now she was between Oz and Thor.

Asherah dropped to her feet, and Max could feel her pulling power into herself. Her face had gone plum-colored, and her body was shaking with anger. *Uh-oh.* The bitch was going nuclear. Team Horngate was out of time.

Max crawled out from under the wall and stood, unwinding the chain from her waist just as sticky bolts of black magic struck Asherah's shields. Giselle's spell clung and spread across the sheath encasing the four-armed witch. Asherah screamed fury as the gummy black shroud enclosed her entirely. That was Max's cue.

She leaped forward. "Now!" she shouted, and whipped the chain around Asherah and yanked it tight. Instantly, the shields disappeared. Thor and Oz erupted from their trenches and slashed at her with their knives, Thor in the throat, Oz in the chest.

Too late.

The knives bounced away from newly formed shields. Asherah smiled, and power pulsed through her.

"No one touches me and lives," she said softly, her pointed white teeth gleaming between her pink lips.

Two arms closed around Max, holding her tightly in place, while the other two arms rose, the talons curving to rake the flesh from Max's bones.

Max tensed. This was going to hurt. But she felt something that Asherah didn't. She was *inside* the witch's shields. Maybe it was because of her ability to open any lock. Maybe Asherah was too arrogant or too careless. Pissed-off witches made mistakes, and this one was a doozy. Whatever it was, Max had one shot left to kill the bitch.

She was aware of Alexander, Thor, Tyler, and Oz hammering at Asherah with pipes and boards. Then Spike leaped in from nowhere, chomping on one of Asherah's upraised forearms. Blood spurted, and she shrieked, yanking her arm wildly. Spike growled ferociously and didn't let go.

The magic inside the witch pulsed and hit critical mass. Her skin went so hot Max's shirt burst into fire. Asherah's eyes flamed orange, and she snatched Max's throat in her one free hand. She clenched, her talons puncturing Max's trachea.

All of it happened in seconds. It was do or die. Just as Asherah's magic exploded in a nuclear blast, Max grabbed the witch's head and twisted. She heard the crack of bone and the pull of sinew. Then the witch's hand tore free, and Max was spinning into the air, choking as her throat filled with her own blood.

She bounced off a wall and fell flat on a mound of chunked stone. Momentary pain ripped through her, and then her head cracked on something, and everything went black.

* * *

She didn't know how long she'd been out before she woke. Dust clogged the air again, and everything was quiet. She tried to move, but she was wedged in some kind of crevice. She heard people calling her name.

"Here," she said, and choked. Her mouth was dry and full of dirt and blood. She coughed and spat and tried again. "Here!" she called more loudly. It wasn't much, but it was enough.

Footsteps crunched, and rocks spun and rolled.

"Hang on!" Tyler called, and she heard digging. Finally, he grabbed her arm and dragged her out from under a layer of dirt and gravel.

Tyler hugged her tightly. "You scared the shit out of me," he said hoarsely. His face was wet.

"Are you *crying*?"

"Yes. You'd better never make me do it again."

Before she could answer, Oz snatched her, and then Alexander did. They carried her down and set her on her feet. She sagged. Her body was broken, and her healing spells were slow. Pain netted her, but she was mostly numb to it. Spike nudged up against her with a whimper.

"Where's Asherah?"

"It's over," Ilanion said. He limped over, with his arm around Giselle. It was impossible to tell which one was supporting the other. Both were filthy. Ilanion bore burns and cuts over his exposed skin, and one of his wings hung in bloody ribbons. His face was white, and his helm was gone. Giselle was hashed with cuts, and her nails were torn and bleeding. There was a gash in her forehead and up into her scalp.

"Where is she?" Max asked.

They led her to where Asherah lay half buried. She looked startled. Max nudged her with a foot. "Told you I was going to kill you," she said. She looked at Ilanion. "So we're done? The challenge is over?"

"Yes. The bells rang. The judge has ruled. We won," he said.

"Then we should go get to work on Scooter."

They spoke little as they limped back to their starting point. The judge was gone, as was the pillar. Scooter, the box of silk, his horn, and his heart were all on the ground. The air barge waited nearby.

Max went to Scooter. He was still breathing, but just barely. She looked at Ilanion and Giselle. "Can you heal him?"

They both could hardly stand. Oz had taken over helping Giselle walk. She refused to be carried. Ilanion swayed.

"Of course," they said in unison.

"We should do it here and now. The coliseum will remain standing until we leave. No one will bother us here," Ilanion said. "He doesn't have much time left."

Max heard the words he didn't speak. *If he can handle the healing.*

"Do it," she said, and lowered herself to the ground. Spike came to lie beside her, propping its head in her lap. She was really going to have to figure out if the Calopus was a boy or a girl.

Alexander sat behind her and pulled her against him. She leaned back gratefully. Her belly hurt. Or, rather, it hurt more than everything else, but the numbness was wearing off and her body was turning into one big mass of agony.

Tyler and Oz came to sit, too. They laid Thor on the ground. He was healing, but it was going to be a while before he woke up. He needed food soon. A sugar IV would help him a lot. Max had brought a med kit with her, but it was back at Ilanion's compound. That would have to be soon enough.

They watched as Ilanion removed the bandages from Scooter's wasted body. The wounds were putrid, the edges black and green. The hole in his chest was the size of Max's fist. She couldn't believe he was still breathing.

Next, the eagle mage took the silk from the tiny box and shook it out. It glistened like diamonds and fire. He laid it over Scooter's body. Then he had Giselle hold the horn to Scooter's forehead. Last, Ilanion cracked open the box holding the heart and lifted it out. It was still encased inside the diamond. He inserted it through the hole in Scooter's chest and nodded to Giselle. She let go. The horn remained in place.

Ilanion splayed his hands on Scooter's stomach and chest. Giselle put her hands on top of his. They both began to chant. Black and gold ribbons of magic snaked around the dying Scooter.

Nothing happened. Minutes ticked past. Then an hour. Then two. Long before then, Max drifted to sleep, soothed by Alexander's warmth and the steady beating of his heart.

She didn't have any idea how much time had passed before he shook her gently awake.

"Max. It is done."

She blinked her dry eyes and stared. Scooter knelt in front of her. A tiny horn protruded from his forehead, and his silk traced a brilliant diamond pattern through his scales, which gleamed brightly. His hair was silky black once again, and his eyes were back to their blue-flecked obsidian.

"You're whole," she said, and rolled her eyes at herself. Talk about stating the obvious.

"Thanks to you. You didn't give up." He took her hand. His body resonated with life and magic. Healing energy poured through her, and her pain evaporated as strength and vigor returned.

"Oh, wow. I always forget how good it feels not to hurt," she said.

"I forget how good it is to be alive," Thor said. He was standing behind Scooter with Giselle and Ilanion, both of whom had also been healed.

"Ain't it grand?" Tyler said, and then fell silent.

Niko.

Max sighed and stood. It was time to go home. Now that she was healed, she just might be able to manage it.

"Will I see you again?" she asked Scooter, realizing suddenly that he had no reason to stay near Horngate or even on Earth any longer.

He smiled, and his expression was full of secrets. "You will," he said.

"Why does that sound vaguely like a threat?" she said with a rueful grin.

"You'll see me, too," Ilanion said. "Come visit anytime, and I want to come see this Horngate for myself." He pulled her close and kissed her cheek. "Thank you," he said softly. "I let the Korvad go on for too long. If not for you, I might never have fought them."

Max didn't get the chance to answer. Suddenly, they

were all in the abyss—including Spike. A moment later, she was back in Scooter's underground den, just him and her.

She raised her brows at him, her stomach tightening. "I thought I got to go back home now."

"In a moment," he said, and he chuckled as Spike wandered through the wall and sat beside Max.

"She is fond of you," Scooter observed. "There are few of her kind left. Have a care with her."

"I will," Max said, scratching the beast's ears. At least now she knew the animal was a female. "Why did you bring me here?"

"To say that I'm sorry about your loss. Niko was important to you."

Tears burned in Max's eyes, and she closed them, her throat tightening. "He was family. Losing him is like losing a piece of my soul."

"I know. But there is one more thing you should know," Scooter said slowly.

Max sniffed and swallowed. "What's that?"

"Each angel has a manner of dying peculiar to his nature and being. As you might imagine, they keep it a close secret. Even if one of your angels is truly dead, then the other is not. No two angels can be killed in the same manner. But I doubt that either is permanently dead."

Hope flooded Max. "Why do you think so?"

He shrugged. "Call it intuition. That doesn't mean they will wake on their own. They were deeply hurt. They will need help."

"What kind of help? What do I do?" she demanded. Maybe she didn't have to lose as much as she thought.

"I don't know."

"You have to know something. You've lived forever, and you've traveled across worlds. You have to have *some* idea."

"I wish I did. I will look. For you, I will do that."

He took her hand, turning it over and touching the scar on her palm. Inside was the feather Tutresiel had given her. "You are bound to them. Perhaps not with vows, but they are tangled in your heartstrings. They are yours. If anyone can, you will find a way to lead them home."

"You really are a master of cryptic horseshit, aren't you?" Max complained. "That doesn't tell me anything. Is that the best you can do?"

"You could always find another angel. Ask."

He smiled a taunting smile. Max's fingers curled into a fist. She wanted to hit him. Then she smiled, too. He was back to himself. She could hardly believe how stupidly happy that made her.

She opened her mouth to say more, but suddenly, she was back in the abyss, Spike hugging her leg. After a moment, she realized that Scooter wasn't going to take them the rest of the way. So she thought of Horngate. Of her family there. Of Tyler and Thor and Oz and Lise. Of Oak and Steel and Flint. Of Tris and Kyle and her parents. Of Giselle. And of Alexander. She smiled, and it tasted bittersweet.

A split second later, she went home.